D0411425

KEEPING SECRETS

Also by Andrew Rosenheim

Stillriver

Keeping Secrets

Andrew Rosenheim

HUTCHINSON
LONDON

Published by Hutchinson in 2006

1 3 5 7 9 10 8 6 4 2

Copyright © Andrew Rosenheim 2006

Andrew Rosenheim has asserted his right under the Copyright, Designs and
Patents Act, 1988 to be identified as the author of this work

Hutchinson
The Random House Group Limited
20 Vauxhall Bridge Road, London SW1V 2SA

Random House Australia (Pty) Limited
20 Alfred Street, Milsons Point, Sydney,
New South Wales 2061, Australia

Random House New Zealand Limited
18 Poland Road, Glenfield,
Auckland 10, New Zealand

Random House (Pty) Limited
Isle of Houghton, Corner of Boundary Road & Carse O'Gowrie,
Houghton 2198, South Africa

The Random House Group Limited Reg. No. 954009

www.randomhouse.co.uk

A CIP catalogue record for this book
is available from the British Library

Papers used by Random House
are natural, recyclable products made from wood grown in
sustainable forests. The manufacturing processes conform to
the environmental regulations of the country of origin

Typeset in Berkeley by Palimpsest Book Production Limited,
Polmont, Stirlingshire
Printed and bound in the United Kingdom by
Mackays of Chatham plc, Chatham, Kent

ISBN 0 09 180032 3 (hardback)
ISBN 9780091800321 (hardback – from Jan 2007)
ISBN 0 09 179679 2 (trade paperback)
ISBN 9780091796792 (trade paperback – from Jan 2007)

In memory of my father

Acknowledgements

The author would like to thank Alan Bell, Nigel Evans, Candia McWilliam and Jim Walter of Healdsburg for information and advice.

A Sonoma Afternoon

THE SCHOOL BUS braked and he said goodbye to his friend Ernie and to Sam the driver, then hopped down and waited as the bus drove away, throwing up a small shower of dust. He crossed the road to the track towards his uncle's house. It was hot, what his uncle working in the orchard would have called a 'fat day', where the air swelled around you like a warm bath. Here the forest was sparse and the sky was cloudless and the light was albino pure; the boy thought of what he would have to drink when he had walked the half-mile to the house, picturing the bottle of lemon-lime soda he'd find on the refrigerator's top shelf.

At Truebridge's shack of a house, the old Impala was parked just off the track, but Truebridge himself was in the hospital down in Petaluma – and Uncle Will said he'd probably never get out. The track curved and entered a mix of woods and brush. Here the sun moved in and out of the branches of the overhanging cottonwood trees, casting only intermittent rays of light through the few holes in the lattice-like arrangement of the leaves. A black-bird whistled sharply over to his right, and closer to the track something rustled in the fern beds – snake maybe, and he moved along quickly.

When he came to the final bend, he saw his uncle's pickup truck in front of the house, as well as an unfamiliar car, a maroon Camaro with black trim, parked awkwardly to block the back of the truck. The front door of the house was hooked open as usual, but where normally Ellie, the collie mix, would come out from under the acacia tree to greet him, now there was no sign of her.

As he came through the open door he called out, 'Hi, I'm home,' but no one replied. He went to the kitchen and got his drink out of the fridge and drank half of it at once, straight from the bottle, then went and stood in the big open room by the stone fireplace

3

while he finished the rest. The mail was on the dining room table and had been opened; there was a credit card bill lying on the table.

He walked through the kitchen again to the back door, at this time of year only a screen door, and stood on the new deck he'd helped his uncle build the spring before. He listened but heard nothing, so he figured his uncle must be in the Valley Orchard, probably showing his visitor around. Maybe it was the county agent, the boy thought, though that wasn't his car.

He came down the steps of the deck and took the path through the rhododendron and hydrangea bushes until it opened out in front of the frog pond. There was no one there or in the barn, where he stopped in the doorway and called out, so he walked through the small patch of pine and eucalyptus woods until he came to the start of the Valley Orchard – the bigger of the two sections of apples, it stretched for almost forty acres, first down then up, with views in the distance of the higher hills, almost mountains really, of the northern part of the county.

From the rise he could view the whole orchard, and his uncle wasn't there. He wondered whether he might be in the Back Orchard, which was a long slog away, but just then he heard Ellie bark, way back near the pond. And he thought *the greenhouse*. Of course; his uncle was in the greenhouse, showing off his latest Gravenstein grafts. But that didn't make any sense; the greenhouse was the last place his uncle would want visitors.

Now the boy tried to walk quietly as he moved back towards the greenhouse, straining to hear the dog again, but knowing that noise would be deadened here in the small section of dense woods and undergrowth. He left the path and took a shortcut through the woods until they gave way to grass on the far side of the pond, which ran on the left up to the greenhouse and the hill it backed against, and on the right back around towards the house. As he came out of the trees he saw the end of the greenhouse bathed in the honey-gold of the afternoon sun and he slowed down right away when he saw his uncle talking with two men right in front of the greenhouse door.

4

The other men were both tall, taller than his uncle, and one wore black cowboy boots and a showboat Stetson stuck on his head; the other was noticeably broad in the shoulders, with thick forearms sticking out of a short-sleeved shirt he wore which was bright canary yellow.

He had seen them twice before, most recently two weekends earlier when Maris had decided to take him shopping in Healdsburg for a new pair of sneakers. On their way out they passed another vehicle, which had pulled off the sandy road at Truebridge's and waited to let them by. 'Who's that?' he'd asked, and Maris had replied, shaking her head, 'Beats me. Must have come to see Will. Pickers maybe, looking for work.' The men had been driving a pickup truck instead of a Camaro, but he knew it was them because he recognised the Stetson.

Although Will was facing the boy, his attention seemed focused entirely on the two men. They all seemed to be talking and gesticulating so aggressively that the boy realised they were not so much talking but arguing. Ellie was sitting next to his uncle, panting a little as she always did in the heat. She must have caught the scent from the boy because she lifted her head up, wagging her tail furiously, and barked happily, then began to trot towards him. His uncle called to the dog, then looked the boy's way and saw him, just as the men turned around and saw him too.

And his uncle shouted, 'Run, Jack! Run!' And the man in the Stetson turned back to his uncle and suddenly lifted his arm and the boy saw that he held a gun in his hand. It looked like a shotgun and had twin barrels, but they had been cut down to virtually no barrels at all.

There was a flash of light, even in the brightness of the afternoon, and immediately after it came the noise of the gun firing. Then his uncle's chest exploded into a scarlet mess, as if half a gallon of paint had been thrown from close quarters right against it.

Suddenly the slow and humdrum passage of the day was gone, gone forever, though at first the boy almost laughed in his astonishment and part of him wanted to shout, *Hey! Let's see that again*, as if he could watch a video replay. And the boy stood for a moment, completely immobilised, as the man turned and said something to his friend, and both men then stared across the length of the pond directly at the boy, and their intense regard somehow penetrated the bubble of disbelief the boy was frantically inflating against the reality of what he had just witnessed and *there!* the bubble burst, and he at last broke out of his stunned inertia and began to run just as the man in the Stetson starting running towards him, carrying the amputated shotgun in his hand.

And as he raced down the trail towards the house the boy heard another shot, the same kind of boom he recognised as the cut-down shotgun, and he knew they couldn't hit him with buckshot at this distance – he must have had a hundred yards head start – so why were they firing at him? And then he realised that they must have shot Ellie, too, for he heard no barking now.

He headed for the house, thinking, *the phone the phone*, but there was no shortcut which only he would know, just the path all the way around the pond, then past the rhododendron bushes, and it was here that he realised from the noise behind him that the man in the Stetson was gaining on him, gaining fast. He'd fired both barrels but it wouldn't take him long to reload – unless he already had. The boy would still be dialling when the Stetson man caught up to him.

So as he came out of the bushes heading for the back door he was furiously thinking *gun*, one of his uncle's shotguns in the gun case next to the fireplace. As he leaped up onto the deck and scooted straight through the back door into the kitchen, he stopped and hooked the screen door shut just as the Stetson man came out of the rhododendron running full tilt towards him. Absurdly, his hat was still on, and the boy saw he had a moustache, a thin line, which looked slapped on above his tight lips, pursed now in a look of controlled and steely determination. And the boy turned and ran into the dining room, where he saw the remains of his uncle's lunch – he'd had a sandwich, the boy somehow managed to register – on a plate on the table, and he got to the gun case, a big mounted cabinet with a glass front, and pulled at its door. It was locked.

There was no sense of unreality now, but rather of a reality accelerating out of control, where his thoughts could not keep pace with the presented danger and his actions lagged accordingly. He heard the man shaking the back door, pulling at it, and panic suddenly came in one vast wave. He looked wildly around him for a weapon, but what good was an ashtray to him now, what would the poker by the fireplace say to a loaded gun? And when he looked out the front window he suddenly shivered and his right arm oddly, erratically started to shake, because the man in the yellow shirt had circled to the front and any minute was going to find the front door wide open and would come right in. The boy felt something warm and wet at the top of each thigh, and understood that he had pissed himself without even feeling his loss of control down there.

Panicked, he ran in some wild counterintuitive stroke back to the kitchen, only to see the man in the Stetson yanking with maniacal vigour at the back door. On the counter there was a cutting board with a fat cylinder of hard salami. Next to it lay a butcher's knife on its side with a streak of cold salami grease smeared on its wide moon blade. Just then the Stetson man finally managed to open the screen door, ripping it half off its hinges, holding the cut-off shotgun in one hand. As he came in and started to raise the gun, the boy grabbed the knife and, stepping forward, plunged it up deep and straight into the Stetson man's chest.

The boy saw the man's arm fall downwards and the gun point towards the floor, and he looked up at the man with apprehension and relief. The Stetson man's mouth opened in a large silent 'O' of surprise, and he fell straight backwards onto the floor. The gun crashing onto the floor made more noise than the man's body, for it was a body – the boy knew before the man hit the floor that he was dead. And before he could do anything other than register the fact, he heard noise in the dining room behind him and then a shout: 'Walt! Where are you?' and the boy stepped right over the dead man and the knife protruding from his chest and ran out through the open back door.

He was on the wrong side of the house, away from the road,

away from passing cars, away from help. He was running without thinking, praying that the man in the yellow shirt would stop for long enough to check on his friend and give the boy the head start he would have to have if he were going to survive. They'd killed his uncle and he knew – there was no reason to think otherwise – that they were going to kill him, too.

Running away from the house brought him to the pond and a choice of paths. He took the left side of the fork, which led to the orchard, but within twenty feet realised he had made a mistake. For the path went through a mixed stand of Douglas firs and oak but then suddenly opened out into the expanse of the Valley Orchard, where there was nowhere to hide for its mile of sloping – first gently downhill then more sharply uphill – apple trees. He'd be visible throughout the few minutes it would take the grown man to catch him.

He should have gone the other way, past the greenhouse and onto the rocky rise from which he'd always shied away – rattlesnakes were there in abundance. But by the greenhouse he would have had to run past the body of his uncle.

Instead he would have to hide somewhere right around him in the copse, and he left the path and ran towards the tree house in the middle of the wood. The brush was light here; if he tried to hide beneath the ferns he would get caught, since he'd leave a trail as obvious as the crushed beds of sleeping deer. He needed to get off the ground, he needed height.

The tree house had been built by his uncle, in the nexus of three large Monterey pines. The boy climbed up the biggest one, using the two board steps his uncle had nailed to its trunk. As he pulled himself up and stood on the pine planks that served as the tree house's bare floor, he paused to catch his breath, hanging on to one of the three walls his uncle had fashioned out of packing material, standing beneath the roof of two plywood slabs, pitched at an angle to meet and form a gable.

He stood still, listening for any noise from the man in the yellow shirt. But his heart was pounding so hard that his pulse thundered in his ears. Grabbing onto the outermost edge of this roof, the boy swung out and hoisted himself onto the roof itself. Without hesitation he stood and leaping up caught hold of a large bough that intruded from a neighbouring pepperwood tree; swinging his feet up, he lay with his back vertical against the big pine tree and extended his legs along the two contiguous branches of pine and bay. He knew he was invisible from the ground – even his uncle hadn't been able to spot him here. It was his hideout on those occasions when he wanted a solitude the house could not provide. Usually he came here out of nothing more serious than a desire for private play, but on the rare occasions when he was upset, this was his refuge. Yet now he did not feel safe at all.

He forced himself to breathe slowly and tried not to move his legs as he slowly shifted his arms and chest around so he could peek out – towards the perimeter of the woods, since anything closer was blocked from sight by the tree house roof below him. But as he slowly swivelled he heard a faint crackling in the part of the woods he had just come through, and he kept his head down now, and listened. Sure enough there was another crackle – like a bag of potato chips being crumpled – then silence. The birds had suddenly gone quiet and the boy was certain the man was in the woods below him. And then a voice fractured the unnatural hush.

'I know you're in there.' The voice was harsh but high-pitched, sounding strained. It chilled the boy, literally, as if a sharp cold breeze came suddenly out of sun to make him shiver.

The voice softened slightly. 'You might as well come out – there's nowhere to go.' It paused, then added, 'Nothing is going to happen to you if you come out now. I swear.'

Cross my heart and hope to die. For a brief moment the schoolboy familiarity of the words and the mellowing of the voice caught the boy off guard, since he was unprepared for cajolery. He almost lifted his head up until he appreciated this for the insanity it was, mentally kicked himself, and tucked his head even further into his shoulders.

'Listen,' the voice continued in its effort to charm. 'I know we can sort this out. But we can't do that until you come out, now can we?'

The voice was close now, no more than fifty feet away, judged the boy. *God, don't let him hear me*, he thought, conscious of the noise his beating heart was still making, feeling sick and terrified that inadvertently he might move, feeling so exposed that he found it hard to believe that he wasn't visible from the ground.

He heard the man slowly move through the bracken ferns beneath him and then onto the other side of the tree house. Somehow he had failed to spot the tree house; slowly the sound of his footsteps receded, and he guessed the man was working his way towards the back end of the wood, where the Valley Orchard began. But he'd be back, once he saw that the boy wasn't there. And the boy knew that if he climbed down to make a run for it, he would be heard. *An acre of trees*, that is what his uncle had said of this ancient planting between the pond and the Valley Orchard.

For the first time the boy moved mentally out of panic, long enough for some semblance of passing time to come to him. But he didn't wear a watch. He tried counting sixty twice in slow, metronomic fashion, then gave up – what did it matter how many minutes had passed? But it only seemed like for ever until he heard the faint thud of footsteps on the packed earth of the forest floor. Surprisingly it came again from the pond side of the tree house – the man in the yellow shirt must have doubled back to the place where he had entered the wood.

Then he heard the man say something, low and unintelligible; there was a pause, and then a whistle, like an appreciative wolf whistle without a short skirt at the other end. *Wheet-whoo*. 'Well, here we *are*,' the voice declared, sounding self-consciously cheerful, like an MC warming up an audience before the main act. 'And there I was, looking at my feet through all these trees when I get the big idea of looking *up*. And lo and behold, what do I see? I see me a hiding place.'

The voice was so close that the boy knew the man had found the tree house. He resisted the temptation to try and curl up even smaller in his little eyrie, knowing that anything he gained in terms of invisibility would be of no importance if he made even the smallest noise. He held his breath until he thought he would burst, then exhaled far more noisily than he intended, just – *thank God* – as he heard the man kick aside a stick as he came to stand below the tree house. The boy heard something bang against the tree trunk and thought, *It's the gun*, the funny cut-down gun, then heard the sliding clambering sound of the man's feet on the low step. There was a click, and the boy thought, *Trigger? No, safety*, and bit his bottom lip so as not to cry out with his sudden terror.

He felt the tree house shudder slightly and realised the man was standing just below it – his feet must have been balanced on the rough steps while his hands reached up to grip the tree house floorboards. 'Don't you dare fucking move,' the voice hissed from below, still high, but sibilant now and menacing. The boy froze and did exactly as he was told and waited for the next instructions. *Maybe he will let me go*, he told himself. Hadn't he said he would? After all, the boy hadn't done anything. Maybe he should believe the man.

Then he heard, curiously, '*Shit!*', the expletive sharp, all mellowness gone, and the boy understood at once that the man had only discovered the empty tree house. *He hasn't seen me at all*, the boy thought, and tried to keep his breathing shallow. He could almost feel the man's disappointment as he stood below him, not ten feet away, doubtless staring at the inside of the tree house – nothing but its rough floor of planks really, he and his uncle had never put so much as a chair inside – staring with disbelief, so confident had he sounded that the boy was there.

It was some time – ten seconds? A minute? – before the man clambered down again. Then he shouted, this time indiscriminately into the air around him, 'I know you're hiding somewhere. I'll find you, don't worry. *Goddamn it!*' This last said with a surprised kind of rage, so that the boy wondered for a minute if the man had hurt himself, pricking himself badly on stickerbush perhaps; or seen a snake, or thought he had. But no, it must have been just plain frustration, for the man continued, venting his rage. 'Come out,' he commanded.

He heard the man moving around the wood now, noisily, not

11

even bothering to disguise his progress – here and there, back and forth through the trees and the packed earth and soft beds of pine needles on the forest floor. The noises were of boots scuffing through the undergrowth, the occasional sharp crack of a stick being kicked, or moved, or stepped on, and the odd swish as the man walked through stands of ferns.

The noise would recede then return, and each time the boy found his steady, anxious fear flare into panic. He realised the light was starting to fade – at first it simply seemed as if the sunlight, filtered through the trees, was fainter, but then he realised there was no direct sunlight at all. What time must it be? Seven or eight o'clock, time for supper on any normal day. He wondered where Maris was, and pictured her in the kitchen, making supper. His uncle would return from the Valley Orchard, parking the tractor in the barn, ambling into the house, fetching the boy with a friendly shout for supper (no, that wasn't right; the boy would have already been inside, doing his homework at the long table in the big room) and whistling for Ellie, whom his uncle would feed in an aluminium bowl on the deck outside the kitchen door.

And then the scene blew apart, at the same time as the boy remembered that Maris was staying in town that night. The boy shivered again. He tried to shut out the image of his uncle blown up with blood, and struggled to block out the memory of the physical sensation as his knife had moved into the firm flesh of the other man, his astonished eyes, the resistance of muscle to the blade. Yet the image he could not suppress was an imagined one, of something he had not seen or felt: the shooting of Ellie. It came to him now again and again – her barking, the discharge of the gun, then nothing.

And maybe his uncle had survived, he tried to tell himself, floating the thought out in his mind like a balloon allowed provisional drift in the breeze. Until *snap*, and the owner yanked hard on the string – so now he found his wishful thinking aborted by the reality of what he had seen: the sheer impact of the blast which had knocked his uncle back against the wall of the greenhouse as he exploded with blood.

This time when the footsteps drew closer, the man spoke again, still in his whistling voice, but with an almost plaintive and appealing note to it now, more haunting than the barked version with its emphatic fruitless commands. 'Hey, it's getting dark now and you must be getting cold. There's no point going on like this. We're all square now; I've got nothing else to prove. So what do you say you come out now?'

The man was moving further away in the dusk but he continued to speak. The birds were still absent and there was no wind; the effect was of becalming silence in which the weirdly calm voice of the man in the yellow shirt rang clear. The boy's anxiety, inter-mittently joined by a jolting, draining panic, was fortified by the spooky timbre of the voice, and the way it was imploring him: 'Nothing is going to happen to you if you come out now. You've got to come out some time. Why not now?' The man must have realised how lame this sounded, for he changed tack. 'Listen, my beef was with Will. Now Will, well, he got hurt – yeah, fair enough, no denying that. But my friend Walt's not looking too hot either.'

The man was still talking as he walked slowly out of earshot. It was truly dark now with the moonless night shifting from grey to the colour of rich soil, the kind in which remaining light was scarce – the boy could not tell which of the shapes and shades he discerned in the distance were imagined, which real. Once he thought he saw a figure crouching on a high branch of a nearby spruce. He closed his eyes and when he opened them was alarmed to see the figure had moved. Had it? He peered into the dark, and decided it was the outline of two branches.

As he wondered what the man would do now to hunt for him, he heard a car start up in the distance – the whinnying of the ignition and the bass *vroom* as the engine caught and roared. He decided it must be the man's car – it was too thick and reverber-ating a noise to come from as far away as the road. Should he climb down? But what if he were wrong about the car? What if the man was still on foot, looking for him? He could head for the orchard end but if he was heard he'd be spotted making his way across the long slope of trees – even in the dark, it wouldn't be hard to see him in his light T-shirt. And the other way was daunting in the dark: he could not be sure of finding the path which led around the pond towards the house, and that is where the man would probably be watching out for him. The alternative to that, to go by the greenhouse, would require him to clamber among rocks, making noise, and then there were the sleeping rattlesnakes.

So he stayed put, and was soon relieved he had, since suddenly out of nowhere – there had been no warning sound – a wide and golden beam of light began moving through the wood. High at first, near the tops of some younger trees, then lower down. It was like an erratic light show, but there was method in its circling, and, peeking carefully, the boy could tell that the man in the yellow shirt was working his way with a high-powered flashlight systematically through the stand of trees. He would hold the beam for seconds at a time when he spied something of interest, and the beam held firm when it focused on the tree house. At last it moved away, but the boy's relief was short-lived: the beam returned and illuminated the thickest of the trunks which shielded him. *He must have seen me*, he thought, and cramp suddenly attacked his left leg in an agonising intermittent spasm. He forced himself not to touch it until the light moved away, and then the pain temporarily overrode his fear. As soon as he heard the man move through the brush on the orchard side of him he slowly bent his leg and kneaded his calf urgently but silently with his hand.

After this he knew he could not come down, but he found a new fear that he might fall asleep and fall from his perch, for despite his anxiety – or perhaps because of it – he was near complete exhaustion. He managed to wedge himself firmly enough in place but still did not trust himself to sleep, since he was scared of waking with a start that would alert the man in the yellow shirt to his position high in the branches.

At first he had welcomed the darkness, thinking the night might protect him, but now it worried him, since he feared the man's flashlight would somehow pierce the enveloping blackness and reveal him. Right then he could not see the flashlight's beam or hear the man, but he was certain he would be back. Without a watch he could only make rough stabs at time-keeping, counting again, then giving up in frustration at how small a dent his mental recital of numbers – *three hundred and two, three hundred and three* – made in the fabric of this endless night.

And yet he felt ambivalent about the passage of time, since daylight would bring fresh dangers – he felt, perhaps irrationally, that a new day would serve to expose him in his eyrie, that his ability to hide there would dissolve in a fresh kind of daylight. As his back began to ache from leaning against the tree trunk, he thought briefly of descending to the tree house, where he could lie down on solid floorboards without fear of falling off. But that would be the natural place for the man to double-check – if not now then in the middle of the night, and at first light, looking to see if the boy had taken shelter after all.

He heard a sudden rush through the brush, a scuffle that seemed to take place low on the ground, and a squeal followed by a crunch. *Fox*, he told himself, fox finding rabbit. He remembered the night when, in a show of ten-year-old independence, he had insisted on sleeping out here alone – until the unknown noises of the night had scared him so much that he had climbed down and started to run back to the house, encountering his uncle on the edge of the wood, who had come out to make sure he was all right. But it would not be his uncle whom he met now, and Maris was spending the night in town.

He tried hard not think about what he had seen, and for a while played a game in which he took inventory of the interior of his uncle's house, locating in his mind's eye as many items as he could remember. In this game, his uncle was somewhere in the background, in his office probably, and Maris was in the house as well, sitting in the recliner in the big room, reading one of her novels. But he paid no attention to either of them – in his mind's eye, that is – and focused on the safe objects of the house, recalling his uncle's very own mantra, *minimise, minimise*. The wooden standing lamp in the corner, and the central lamp suspended from

15

the high ceiling all the way down until it hovered over the long table, and the soapstone carvings of a whale and a seal his uncle had bought on their day trip to the coast, propped up on the stone ledge of the fireplace's mantelpiece, and a brass figurine – was that the word? – of a small bell which Maris liked, and then the gun cupboard, which he deftly avoided in this imaginary survey, heading for the kitchen instead, but no, there were knives there, so he turned around in his mind and on the long table he found the guide to wildflowers, thumbed and dog-eared, which his uncle and Maris took with them on their walks back behind the greenhouse or down to the bottom meadowland of the Valley Orchard, and there were the upright chairs on the kitchen side of the table, with high back posts you could hook a jacket on, and what was the colour of the cane matting of the seat? Dark brown, almost the colour of dried blood. And with the thought of blood he saw again the scarlet burst from his uncle's chest like rain.

He must have fallen asleep, for when his dream spoke the word 'blood' he jerked and hit his head against the pine's trunk. And it was then that the game collapsed, or at least its purpose did, which was to drive away his fear. And he felt such a sudden wave of panic, like a kind of manic flu racing through his bones, that for a split second he thought he might literally be so shaken by it that he would fall out of the tree.

And it simply wouldn't go away, not even as tears loosened in his eyes for the first time since he had seen his uncle murdered – what? five or six hours before? – and then seemed to flow in rivers down his cheeks, and then his chest seized up as he was racked with sobbing, which simply made the fear worse, since he was terrified the man would hear him crying. And yet from his sobbing he took a kernel of comfort, for it was an emotion he could embrace somehow and live through, whereas with the shocked fear he felt destabilised and there was nothing to embrace, for it was in control of him. He resisted the urge to cry out, and he held his breath expectantly instead, but there was nothing moving in the dark, nothing at all, not even an animal, and soon he started his inventory again, only this time he moved to the orchard and the Gravensteins, which he began to count, skipping the windfall dead, zeroing in and out only on the biggest fruit, filling them now in lugs he could miraculously lift all by himself and move back to the flatbed attached to the tractor. The lugs filled up like kitchen canisters when you poured in coffee beans or flour, and the flatbed sagged as if pregnant with the apples' weight, and the sun sparkled on the red stripes of the fruit, while the yellow patches of the skin matched the buttery richness of the sun. And in his dream – or was it a waking dream? – he was somehow awash in a hillside of apples, which rolled without bruising, and when he woke this time light was dispelling the black syrup of the night and he could make out the ground in the distance and then a neighbouring Douglas fir next to the pepperwood which leaned against the third of the Monterey pines. And the birds were beginning to sing, or twitter really, tentatively talking as if tuning their throats like an orchestra's instruments before the real playing begins, and he thought at once how pretty the blackbird's song was – Maris had taught him to recognise the call – and then its significance hit him with full force. *He's gone. The birds are making noise so he's not here.*

He lifted his head, and found his neck sore from the position he had fallen asleep in. Slowly he let his eyes cover the immediately adjacent area of woods, then as far as he could see, almost to the back edge of the trees. There was no sign of anyone, the bird calls had begun with intensity. His fear, lulled by falling asleep, now returned in full force. What should he do? The orchard was still as exposed as ever, but to go back towards the house seemed suicidal. The man in the yellow shirt could be hidden anywhere along the track, or in the rhododendrons of the pond's edge, or even in the house itself, waiting patiently with that strange short gun.

And what if the man had help now? The boy couldn't stay where he was; with more than one searcher, he would be found. There was only one way to go: he would have to work his way the long way around to the road. He sat up on the bough, then lowered himself until he was suspended just above the pitched roof of the tree house, his arms wrapped around the pine branch. He let go, landing awkwardly on one side of the gable, and as he slid down he reached up and grabbed the roof line to stop himself. Then he crouched on his heels on the incline and listened. There was no birdsong now, but suddenly he heard a shout from near the pond. Moving carefully down the side of the roof, he dropped as lightly as he could onto the tree house floor and listened. Still nothing nearby, and he now quickly climbed down to the base of the big pine and without pause moved through the woods towards the back end of the pond. He played the Indian game Maris had played with him, alternately walking on his toes and his heels to deaden the noise, avoiding sticks as best he could.

It was only a few hundred yards, but it seemed like miles – he had to keep from speeding up and making noise. There was poison oak here, which he would usually go to any lengths to avoid, but now it barely registered, and he concentrated only on taking a path which would be quietest. Short of the beginning of the Back Orchard he came to the edge of the wood, about a hundred yards past the end of the pond and the greenhouse. He crouched in the shelter of a large eucalyptus and waited. This was the one place where he would be totally exposed, crossing from these woods and climbing the rocky hill behind the greenhouse, from where he could run through the brush and woods out to the road.

He tried to still his breathing, hoped it would slow as he stood up ready to run. *One, two, three* and he was off, one sneaker slipping slightly on the early morning dewy grass. Finding his grip again, he charged head down, waiting for a warning shout – or worse. He moved with legs pumping and arms going up and down, just as they had taught him on the track at school, and when he reached the bottom of the hill behind the greenhouse he didn't stop but kept moving as fast as he could – it was the hill's slant which was slowing him down, as he fought his way up the sandy, rocky soil, using his hands to push off the larger rocks, something he would normally never do since his uncle had warned him from the beginning that the rattlesnakes liked this sun-soaked place. He thought he heard a shout again in the distance, a loud startled cry, and as he reached the top of the hill he didn't slow down at all, but merely straightened up and plunged into the woods, widening his eyes to adjust to the sudden darkness since the low morning sun was largely obscured here by the high growth of ferns – some as high as the boy – and the many trees, black and live oaks mixed with Douglas fir and the odd Madrone, gnarled in a desperate search for sun.

To his amazement he still felt energised, even after the scramble up the hill, and when after a hundred yards or so he came to a small spring-fed creek he jumped right over it, not even contemplating stopping to rest, though the sight of the creek made him realise how thirsty he was, how badly he wanted a drink. To his right there would be the old fire road, but he didn't want to go near it, since it would be the obvious route for strangers trying to follow him through the woods and, anyway, between the fire road and the boy there was a swamp marsh which Maris had warned him about – it was deceptively deep, she'd said, and parts of it were quicksand.

He swerved around a thicket of Himalayan blackberry, flush with fruit, and sprinted on, chanting to himself, *keep running, keep running, keep running*, but as he sensed he was nearing the road he tried to collect his thoughts. He reckoned he would come out about a quarter mile up from the turn-off to Truebridge's shack and his uncle's track, but he was doubtful anyone would drive by – there was no traffic to speak of at all on the road, since all the locals preferred the lower and better road that went around the base of this mountain.

And then as he stopped and listened to the light breeze tickling the poplar leaves, he as much felt as heard a low hum. Plane? No, it didn't have the vibrating shudder of the occasional jet which flew over this part of northern California – flights, according to his uncle, from San Francisco or Los Angeles heading north to Seattle or Vancouver. No, this was a vehicle on the road, and he felt hope followed by apprehension – could it not be the Camaro which had blocked his uncle's pickup truck the day before? It seemed more than a day, so much more – a world away in time, before what had happened. From the noise he could tell it was a pickup truck, not a car, and in his relief he ran helter skelter through the last bushes and high grass, and jumped the small ditch in front of the road. It was only as he landed that he saw the shadow moving in on him, only as his feet hit the gravel edge of the road that out of one eye he saw to his left an arm move in on him like a heavy falling branch. It grabbed him with incontestable force, seizing him around his right shoulder and upper arm like a cherry shaker latching onto a tree trunk. He was lifted suddenly into the air, and breathless and scared he wet his pants for the second time in twenty-four hours, and his last thought right then was to wonder if the man in the yellow shirt was going to kill him right away.

Meeting Kate

SHE CAME IN almost an hour late and he was already annoyed since he had bust up his morning by having to drive out to Cupertino to give this woman the standard visitors' tour which Eckerly, the head personnel honcho, would have conducted had he not been on his annual golf holiday. He planned to redeem the wasted time by having lunch at Nicky's over on the Bay waterfront, which was a small pleasure to be sure, but then his life seemed to consist of small pleasures, hard won and the more fiercely protected for that. But Ricky's would now be crowded by the time he arrived and he would also be starving it was so late, and his mounting irritation was not really allayed when a tall woman with short chestnut-coloured hair sailed in without even so much as a knock.

Sharply dressed, with white linen trousers covering legs that seemed to run up to her shoulders, she wore smart mocha-coloured leather shoes, and a blouse of deepest blue. Only a simple gold necklace for jewellery and a ring, also gold, that was not on the wedding finger. She carried a slim leather file case, so the effect was of smartness and energy and a confidence that only served to annoy him further since he was certain that she wouldn't care two hoots that she had kept him waiting.

'Renoir?' she asked with a fresh voice, slightly highly pitched. There was an accent there.

'That's me.'

'They said you're the tour guide.'

He realised she was English. 'That's not very flattering.'

'I'm not usually paid to flatter,' she said crisply.

'What is it you are paid to do?' he asked with a sharpness matching hers. 'I mean, other than keep me waiting?' he added, surprising himself – normally he might have thought this but would never have said it.

She looked at him more closely, then looked at her watch. 'I

23

see what you mean,' she said. He thought a smile began to open across her face. 'Perhaps I'm paid to take you to lunch? Or do I really have to have the tour?' And she looked up and grinned at him – grinned with white but slightly crooked teeth, but the naturalness of this disarmed him at once. And her face was otherwise immediately, strikingly pretty – by any standard. She had high strong cheekbones and soft, round blue eyes. And her mouth – well, the mouth unnerved him. There was nothing so obvious to it as a pouting Bardot pouch of bee-stung lips, for in fact her lips were thin and wide. But she had a pronounced pucker just above her lips – what was it called? Frenum? Such an ugly word for such a subtly lovely part – that worked to make lips and mouth and nose and jaw one wonderfully handsome whole. You wanted to kiss that mouth passionately, and that he realised was what made him nervous. It was bad enough insulting clients; kissing them would be fatal.

So he took the woman, whose name was Kate Palmer, to Nicky's, which was very crowded indeed, but they sat at the bar and each drank a glass of the Napa white and shared a bowl of large shrimp with mustard sauce and then sat down for a late lunch on the outside deck with the Bay view. It was hot for late April, almost touching eighty degrees, and he ate grilled tiny scallops with pilaf rice and thin string beans and she tucked into a monster piece of swordfish, using all her lemon and half of his, and he would remember the food forever because for some reason he didn't understand at all he found himself unaccountably nervous, to the point indeed where he almost didn't trust himself to speak. Not that Renoir was ever very talkative, but neither was he ever very nervous.

He managed to ask her questions, and she seemed happy enough to explain how she came to be there. She was a consultant for the oil industry, she explained, and her small outfit produced a newsletter that focused on exploration – which was where Renoir's company came in, since it adapted the expert system technology it had originally developed for the Pentagon into versions for private industry, oil and gas foremostly. So, in Santa Barbara to see offshore production units, she'd detoured north on her way home to make a visit. And, yes, she was English and yes she worked there and yes this was her first trip to the Bay Area, and what else did she say? He wasn't sure, he was too busy thinking what he should say next – or ask really, since he didn't want to have to put more than one sentence together at a time

'So was your morning okay?' he asked.

'Interesting, surprisingly interesting.' Then she blushed slightly for her rudeness, which he found appealing. 'Sorry,' she said, 'it's just that usually if you've seen one software company you've seen them all. But this time was different, though I'm sorry I missed your tour.'

'Who did you talk to then?' he asked, his interest piqued.

'The people in the Artificial Intelligence Unit. I wasn't supposed to be with them for long, but they had to come drag me away eventually. That's why I was so late.'

'They're quite a bunch,' he said in agreement. He liked them – the small cadre, perhaps seven or eight, working on the non-military uses of the company's expert system technology. 'Did you meet Ticky?' The leader of the group, a boyish and frighteningly young woman with a Ph.D. from Caltech.

She nodded. 'Is that her real name?'

'Of course not,' he said with a laugh. 'It's short for Ticonderoga.' Kate looked puzzled and he explained. 'Her father was a Revolutionary War buff – that was one of the bigger battles.'

Kate nodded. 'Like calling an English child Waterloo. Anyway, she was very nice. And clever. I've got a new client, a small company called Acer Oil, and its unique selling point is the use of expert systems. I've never really known how they work – even in my own kind of business. Frankly, I probably still don't, but for at least five glorious minutes this morning I thought I did. She explains things so clearly.'

'I know,' he said. Ticky's group was unusual, with almost as many women as men, a rarity among coders, and nothing similar about them at all, except for their intense intelligence and communally fierce style of debating . . . *anything*. Why sixty feet six inches was the perfect distance from the pitcher's rubber to home plate; why prime numbers for all their beauty and recent publicity were not important mathematical phenomena after all; why refried beans were a misnomer; and – this was a running gag *and* activity – where in the Bay Area you could find the finest German food. The conversations took place at the end of the day, in what for obscure AI reasons he didn't understand was nicknamed Prolog Alley, an assortment of desks and chairs and table tops and the odd television set in what had once been a meeting room. Here, when work formally ended, Ticky's group would gather and start to play, drinking beer in open defiance of the company's alcohol-free policy.

Slowly now at lunch, what with the wine and the food, he felt himself lose the anxious-making nervousness and so when the woman said, easy as pie, 'Enough of me talking about me, tell me what you think about me,' he could laugh with her and not get flustered when she added, 'So what did I miss by skipping the tour?'

He shrugged. 'I think you did best by sticking with Ticky's group. I don't usually give the tour – another reason to count your blessings for missing it today.'

'So I would have been getting a tour from The Great Man Himself,' she said, smiling but with the slightest *zing* to her tone, like the jab of a proficient fighter sparring lightly – not aggressive, but certainly letting you know it was there. 'I feel honoured, even if I didn't make it.'

'Don't. The Great Man Himself isn't me. It's Eckerly. And I work for him, not the other way round.'

'Doing the same sort of stuff?'

He shook his head. 'No, I'm not really a Human Resources person – I don't hire and fire, or motivate the troops, or deduct payroll taxes, or administer drug tests.'

'Your name came up with Ticky – it was probably on the copy of my schedule she had.'

'Probably,' he said, not that eager to know what had been said, since HR people were rarely popular among other parts of the company, and he liked Ticky and her bunch sufficiently not to have his own sense of their friendship (well, professional friendliness anyway) disabused.

'Ticky called you Renoir.'

'That's right.'

'Don't you have a Christian name?'

'That's no mystery – it's Jack. I don't know why, but Ticky just calls me Renoir.'

'She said you don't read thrillers.'

'What?'

She looked a little sheepish. 'We didn't talk business the *whole* time. She likes thrillers. You know, detective stories. So do I.'

'I never knew that about Ticky.'

'Why should you?' she said. 'Since you don't like them. She said the irony was that you were the only person in the company who could be out of the pages of one.'

'No,' he said firmly, though he felt uneasy. 'I like a quiet life.'

She shrugged to show it didn't matter to her one way or another, then said, 'She wasn't being critical. She called you a straight shooter. It sounded pretty complimentary to me.'

Embarrassed, he said, 'I thought you weren't paid to flatter.'

The waiter came and took their plates away. 'That was delicious,' Kate exclaimed, and Renoir liked the way she could say this without inhibition. He rarely ate dessert, but because he didn't want the lunch to end he ordered mango sorbet, then smiled when Kate ordered apple pie with vanilla ice-cream on top. 'When I travel,' she said with a little laugh, 'I eat and eat and eat. Anyway, what do you do for the company when you're not *not* giving tours?'

'I'm in charge of Security.' Her face was a beautiful blank he couldn't read. Did she think he was in charge of locking the doors? 'They should probably call it *In*security.'

'Why's that?'

'My job makes everyone uneasy. I vet all the new hires, or at least the ones who need security clearance. That's pretty much everyone, since most of our business is with the Defense Department.

They want level two clearance minimum on anyone working on their projects, and even the janitors get level one. I'm the guy who does the clearance.'

'Really?' she said, and he couldn't tell if she was merely being polite. But she added, 'Tell me, what exactly does that entail?' And she said this so crisply, her prompting seemed so sincere, that he found himself describing what he did in detail: the interviews with the recruits and the follow-up ones with people from their past; the occasional polygraph when it was needed to reconcile the differences between the two; in extreme cases, the technology or 'toys' for everything from wiretaps to satellite surveillance to hacking into private PCs.

Not of course that they didn't find things, it was just that it was never evidence of espionage. Secrets were unearthed by the dozen; of course they were – there wasn't a CV he'd seen in the last five years that didn't hide *something*. Not always illegal, not necessarily grounds for disqualification from employment, but just something the person in question wanted to hide.

Kate looked at him thoughtfully during this explanation, putting down her fork and propping her chin with one hand as he talked. When he paused she said coolly, 'I imagine the actual searching through people's lives gets pretty uninteresting after a while. It may give a little *frisson* when you catch your happily married programmer spending his down time in bed with a Chihuahua or whatever, but you've probably sat watching from a parked car for twelve hours in order to find that out. Aren't most secrets pretty dismal anyway? I mean, are you ever surprised by what you find out about people?'

She understands, he thought, *this woman understands*. For it *was* boring, almost mindless much of the time: the interviews were overwhelmingly routine; the technology, for all its whiz-bang innovation, was usually irrelevant and didn't get used; the secrets unearthed were the squalid ones of private lives with not the remotest relation to national security. Yet he had dated more than one woman whose initial attraction was founded on an unsettling fascination with his work; they'd act as if Renoir were

28

some latter-day Philip Marlowe, instead of a middle management buffer between the bureaucratic requirements of Federal
contract dispensers and the money-making ambitions of a
modern corporation.

'Not very often,' he said, at last remembering to answer her question. 'It's reached a point where I sometimes make a bet with myself
when a new recruit shows up about what their secret is going to
turn out to be. After all, how many secret vices are there? Booze?
There are fewer and fewer educated alcoholics these days, at least
among high-tech people. Drugs? More common, but usually people
have cleaned up before they try and work in the industry – we test
for drugs and so do almost all employers in the Valley. Sex? Well,
yes, it's the time-honoured favourite, and not about to go out of
fashion. But this is California after all, where pretty much anything
goes. Other than paedophilia I can't think of anything out of bounds
these days – I mean, that would disqualify you from employment.
Adultery, homosexuality, S&M, group sex—' he stopped, a little
embarrassed by the litany. 'Though once there was a FORTRAN
programmer who turned out to have two wives.'

She laughed, and, like her eating, her laugh was full of appetite,
natural. 'Surely that wasn't grounds for disqualification,' she said,
and he found her voice so beautiful – it was straight out of a PBS
import from the BBC – that he was tempted to ask her to say it
again.

She picked up her fork and examined it. 'So you've seen it all?
What's the part you like best?' she asked.

He shrugged, disconcerted by the implication that he was
somehow now above such things. 'There's always a surprise. I
don't get jaded, because the real thrill isn't finding out what's
being hidden – after a while, that always comes out. The real thrill
is matching it to what you predict it will be. When that correl-
ation gets to one to one, then I'll be *really* jaded. It will be time
to move on then.'

'You mean, when you don't even have to look any more?
Because your predictions will always be correct.' She said this with
great amusement.

'That's right,' he said, impressed, and they both laughed at the absurdity of this.

'So what's the worst part?'

He looked at her, feeling slightly abashed. 'Telling people what I've found out about them.' Her eyes stayed on him as he continued. 'That's the worst part; when they find out I know they've lied, and what they've lied about.' Sometimes they'd get angry, that he found comparatively easy to take. Usually, however, they broke down; men and women, young and old, collapsing as their fabrications were exposed. Realising they wouldn't be hired, the really desperate ones would even start to beg. He winced involuntarily at the memories.

'I'd say you're close to having done this job too long.' She dropped her eyes towards her plate as she said this, which he was glad for since he didn't know how to respond. What she said seemed at once disheartening and correct, but he didn't want to be cast as some kind of oddball – a 'character' to sit in this English woman's portfolio of unusual encounters. He realised how much he was drawn to her, though he couldn't put his finger on what in her exactly made him feel so attracted. Yes, she was refreshingly intelligent, but God knows he worked with plenty of smart people. Unlike most of Silicon Valley, however, she wasn't trying to act like Einstein. Her face was striking rather than beautiful, yet she was graceful in a lithe, unselfconscious way he found intensely sexy. There was something about her which suggested she was a class act and, he concluded, way out of his league.

She had mentioned someone named Emily but no other names, and he noticed that there was no wedding ring on her hand, nor had there been mention of any partner or suitor – no, suitors, since there must be many more than one of them. But though he was convinced he didn't stand a chance with this woman, he was still sufficiently enthralled that he was scared to spoil it – though what was *it*? He just knew he was in the presence of something he hadn't felt before, and he was daunted by whatever this feeling was. He had the sense that he needed to be the best he could with

30

her, as well as the intuition that it would be worth the effort. There was a sense of challenge about her, an attractive one – not daunting but simply . . . challenging.

Forget it, he suddenly told himself, reining in the fantasy. *It's just lunch!* Strictly speaking she shouldn't be sitting with him at all, but instead be with Eckerly having one of the healthy alcohol-free catered lunches visiting big shots were given in the board-room – a place where Renoir only appeared when he had to report on any especially tricky employee issue which might land the company in trouble.

'So,' she said lightly, 'do you always get your man?'

'Yes, ma'am,' he said, like John Wayne.

'Don't they ever get away?'

'Never,' he said with mock finality, then he admitted, 'though one almost did.'

'Tell me about it,' she said, and he was pleased she didn't seem in any hurry to go.

'There was a woman in marketing who suddenly left the company, without any warning. When we searched her computer at work we discovered she had hacked into a board member's PC to look at the quarterly results – before they'd been announced. She must have made a killing shorting the stock, because when she disappeared she took bearer bonds with her worth $600,000. But we couldn't trace the trade.'

'Why not?'

'Usually with insider trading, people either make the trade themselves or get a relative or friend to do it for them. Easy to trace – that's why they get caught. But this woman was too smart for that. She had opened an account with some old boy she'd met on vacation in La Jolla. Not long after, the old boy died. But she kept the account alive. That meant that when the Feds checked the particular trade in our shares they hit a brick wall. All they found was an account in a dead man's name. The money was long gone – she must have moved it offshore, and kept moving it until it was untraceable.'

'But how did you figure all this out?'

'I didn't,' he said a little sheepishly. 'The Florida police arrested her eighteen months later, using a fake ID to cash a cheque in a drugstore. They ran her prints through the missing persons database and discovered we were looking for her. She panicked and spilled the beans. If she'd kept her nerve we could never have proved a thing. In fact, if she hadn't run away in the first place, I don't see how she'd ever have been found out. It's only when she disappeared so suddenly that we got suspicious. Ticky and I call her scam the Dead Man's Hat.'

She laughed, and he looked at his watch and discovered they had been seated at the table for over two hours. It was almost four o'clock and very few people were left in the restaurant. *Have I bored her?* he suddenly wondered, and called for the check.

He paid and they went out into a sky-blue afternoon, where he had to resist the temptation to ask her if she'd like to drive to Monterey, or, closer, Santa Cruz, or maybe just Golden Gate Park – anywhere but back to the office, though behind the fantasised offer he had in mind the attractions of a $59 motel room of such spare decor that they would have no choice but to go to bed together right away. Why was he having this fantasy about a woman he had never met before and would never meet again? *That's why*, he thought, *and that's why you've talked so much about yourself. Because you'll never see her again. So you're safe.* 'Safe' – he even liked the sound of the word.

As he unlocked the driver's door to the ageing Saab he had bought off an old army buddy down on his luck, she asked, 'Do you live near here?'

He shook his head. 'I live in San Francisco. We have an office where I'm based about half the time. Though not when important guests come to town.'

She laughed. 'So what's there to do in the city at the weekend?'

He shrugged. 'Not a lot compared to London, I bet.' Until they broke up he'd spent weekends with his girlfriend, Jenny. She worked on Saturday mornings, in the antiques shop she owned off Russian Hill, and he would meet up with her in the afternoon, have dinner out – nothing fancy, Italian or a bar and grill – then together they would usually go back to his place. Lately nothing much had changed – well, except for no steady girlfriend. Sometimes he had a 'date', and sometimes Saturday night he didn't sleep alone. Now he remembered: 'Actually, this weekend I'm going away.'

She looked at him coolly then raised a mild eyebrow until he explained. 'I'm going out to the foothills of the Sierra, to a cabin of some friends of mine. Kaufman, the investigator, he and his wife are in New York for a couple of months so I said I'd open it up for them.'

'Nice country?'

'Beautiful, though it's a long drive to get there. There's a big lake and a long swelling hill – a kind of mini-mountain. It's halfway up it, in a big stand of virgin pine, so it's cool even this time of year.'

'It sounds heaven,' she said.

'It is,' he said, not thinking much about the way she was looking at him.

'Does your girlfriend like it?'

'She would,' he said slowly, watching her expression. It was hard to read. 'If I had one.'

She gave a small smile which looked involuntary; the muscles just below her eyes contracted momentarily. 'I'm not flying out until Monday. Can you recommend places for me to go?'

'You mean in the city?'

'I suppose so. I don't have a car.'

As he drove her back, he reeled off a list of sights: the Embarcadero, the boat trip to Alcatraz, a bus tour of Marin and the national park, Fisherman's Wharf, the trolley car in Union Square. Not his San Francisco, perhaps, but this covered the tourist beat and then some, though he couldn't tell as he talked whether she was listening carefully or not.

At his office she came up with him to phone for a taxi, and while she waited he took a call from the Pentagon, which he regretted when he couldn't get the man off the phone – Renoir suddenly realised that while he was discussing the ambiguous polygraph of a low-level coding applicant, she would be leaving. Then just as he finally got off, *her* cell phone rang and she picked it up, listened and said, 'Tell him I'll be right down.' She looked at Renoir. 'My cab's waiting for me,' she declared. She extended her hand. 'It's been nice meeting you. Thanks for your help.'

'It was a pleasure,' he said with a slight stumble to his voice, wishing there were some way to prolong the conversation. What had happened to their easy lunchtime talk? For a moment the silence hung between them like the thickening mist he'd grown up with in the Sunset District, rising to obscure a view which only moments before had been clear and beautiful. She turned and walked briskly out of the room, though he thought that as she neared the door she paused ever so briefly. Then she was gone. He wondered what to do as he listened to the noise of her heels clicking along the corridor floor, then heard the dual doors to the central stairs swing once, then twice, as she walked through them. And he stood feeling absolutely terrible, imagining her descending the stairs, then out through reception into the parking lot; seeing her in his mind's eye as she got in the cab and drove right out of his life.

Suddenly he was moving fast down the corridor, then faster down the stairs – two at a time – and as he powered out the front doors he was calling to her even though she hadn't made it to the cab, but he was taking no chances now, and as he sprinted she turned and looked at him with a small wry smile and he came to a halt before her, slightly out of breath, and lifted his head up as he inhaled and watched the inquisitive look in her eyes and the quizzical tilt to her head and he said in a breathless rush, 'Do you want to come too?'

And she immediately knew what he meant, for all she said, quietly now, was, 'I'd love to.' And then she laughed – the gutsy laugh he already liked to provoke, and he stopped feeling quite so foolish and laughed too.

*

He picked her up in downtown San Francisco at the Malmarlot Hotel, which was small, tasteful and expensive. It was an unusual choice for an oil consultant (he had expected the Hilton), but then so was opting for a weekend roughing it in the Sierra foothills. Did she have any idea what she was in for? He'd had several hours to think about this trip and worry that he hadn't warned her that it was really the most primitive of cabins in remote and rugged country, and that the nearest town was rough and ready rather than touristy or smart.

So he was relieved that she was dressed in jeans and a T-shirt; she carried a jacket and a small overnight bag which she threw in the back seat. He navigated through Union Square then joined the line for the Bay Bridge. Neither spoke and he turned the radio up, partly as cover for the awkward silence that sat between them, partly to listen for traffic jams. It was only as they moved onto the bridge that he turned it down.

'Were you always from San Francisco?' she said, stretching her legs and sitting up in her seat.

'Pretty much. Do you know Haight Ashbury?'

'Just by reputation. Hippies. Acid, Free Love.'

He nodded. 'That's where I was born.'

'You're joking.'

'Somebody had to live there. And my mom and I did.'

'Your father?'

'Never knew him. He was gone before I was two. The last my mother heard of him he was playing piano in a bar in Alaska. But that was over thirty years ago.'

'Didn't you ever want to find him?'

'Nope.' *I had a father figure*, he was tempted to say but didn't. Somehow it would have been a betrayal if he'd gone looking for the bum who'd given him his gene pool and nothing else.

'So it was just you and your mother.' *No*, he thought to himself, *it was just me*. 'Is she still alive?'

'No. She died last year.' He paused. 'She was in a home in Daly City – that's on the south side of San Francisco.'

'So you saw her a lot.'

'Not really. The last time I visited she didn't know who I was.'

'I'm sorry. Alzheimer's must be terrible.'

'If that's what it was. My mother was a drinker, high on the alcoholic Richter scale.' They were moving at speed, with the Bay on either side and the exit for the anomalous lump of Treasure Island fast approaching.

'What did she do for a living?'

'She was a singer. Backing, but a good one.' He smiled slightly. 'She backed Janis Joplin for a while, until my mother's drinking proved even too much for her.'

'Still, it must have been an interesting world to grow up in.'

He didn't say anything.

'Was it?' she insisted.

'Not really,' he said, thinking furiously, for he was worried she would ask what happened next. 'Anyway,' he said, softening his voice, 'it all got too much for her. So I went and lived with my grandmother. My mother was pretty much out of it from then on.'

Kate suddenly yawned, putting her hand to her mouth too late to suppress the exhalation.

'That sounds tired,' he said. 'When did you get into town anyway?'

'Yesterday.'

'From Santa Barbara, right? Were you somewhere else before that?'

She shook her head. 'No. I came straight from London.'

'You must be exhausted,' he said, though his familiarity with jet lag was strictly second hand, since he had never been east of an American time zone.

'I'm okay,' she said, but immediately had to put her hand to her mouth to stifle another yawn. She giggled lightly, dozily.

He reached behind him with one hand and felt on the back seat for his windbreaker, which he handed to her. 'Use that as a pillow,' he said. 'We've still got ourselves a way to go. You might as well take a nap.'

And ten minutes later he snuck a sideways look and saw from

the simple rhythms of her breathing, and the way her throat was relaxed as she lay with her head against the scrunched up jacket, that she was asleep. And though he had to concentrate on the road, since dusk was rapidly turning to dark, he couldn't contain himself entirely, and snuck glances at her face with a mix of shyness and appreciation.

Why did this woman have to flit across his horizon now – she'd be flying home Monday, wouldn't she? – just when he was most alone. It was only six months since he'd split up with Jenny, or rather she had split up with him, despairing over his reluctance to get married and his even greater reluctance to come out and admit it. He looked over now at the English woman again. She was breathing with her mouth slightly open, her lips puffed as if ready to be kissed. He felt a sudden tenderness for her, then told himself the feeling was ridiculous – she was virtually a stranger.

What had ended his feelings for Jenny, and kept him during these last six months from missing her? He supposed it was whatever had always limited his feelings for any woman other than his mother in the early years . . . and Maris. Women will leave you in the end, he had long ago decided, so what was the point in caring if they did? With men it never mattered, this kind of distancing, since a heterosexual could proceed with male friendships under an umbrella of camaraderie and shared experience – for Renoir the army, but for others school or sports or work.

No, the problems for him arose with women, where his relationships were a catalogue of failure, at least the long-term ones. For intimacy was expected in any long relationship – sometimes even in very short ones – and this he could not provide.

He had been a late starter with girls, thanks to natural shyness and a strict parental figure, his grandmother, who had kept him on a tight rein throughout high school. In the military he'd cut loose, making up for lost time perhaps. He was drawn to overtly sexy rather than demurely pretty women, naughty girls rather than proper young women his grandmother would have approved of. After the army he tried to grow up, but with someone like Jenny – a nice, nice girl (she even owned an antiques shop, for Christ's sake) – he found himself unable to compensate for the lack of sexual excitement with any other kind of intimacy. Once, during an argument, she told him he was a control freak – but not, she explained, in the usual sense of the term, for he never tried controlling her. 'No,' she went on, 'you're far too busy controlling yourself. You don't get mad, you don't get upset, I've never seen you cry. Nothing seems to move you.'

Which he knew was entirely true. He simply went along with what seemed safe, and steady, and secure. So he was a little sad but not surprised when, not long after this, Jenny announced she didn't want to see him any more, and three months later married a fellow dealer in antiques.

The English woman named Kate Palmer only woke on the very last stretch of the trip, after he left the highway, drove through Placerville, then along the shore of the lake until the road turned away uphill. He stopped and got out to open the cattle gate. It was a warm, windless night, and a pale full moon cast light on the lake, creating silver sparkles on the surface of its thick and inky black. When he came back to the car to drive through he found her sitting up and rubbing her eyes. 'Just five minutes more,' he said. He drove through and stopped, but before he could even open his door, she hopped out of the car without a word and closed the gate behind them. They drove slowly along the track which traversed the hillside, winding slowly back and forth against the face of its steep incline, almost immediately entering a stand of trees, planted carefully and regularly. Kate sniffed appreciatively. 'I smell balsam,' she said. 'And pine.'

A little higher up and the woods opened slightly to reveal the cabin, built to face the lake below. They climbed the half flight of stairs to the front deck, and while Renoir fumbled with the key to the stiff front door, Kate stood leaning against the deck's pine railing. Across the valley opposite were smaller foothills, their tops visible in the moonlight like ice-cream minarets.

Inside, he turned on the main light switch and was relieved that the power was on. To his eye, the Kaufman cabin was ideally simple: one large room with a small kitchen in the near corner, set apart by a curtain; in the back, a bathroom with a (leaky) shower. Set in a wall of the big room was a fireplace made of rough stone, with two armchairs drawn up close to it. In the middle of the room a table functioned as dining room, and at the back of the room, next to the bathroom door, were two bunk beds. They were fashioned out of cedar, and matched the colour of the walls; in the pale light of the shaded overhead bulb the wood glowed like burning oranges.

'It's kind of simple,' he said with a slight air of apology. What had he been thinking, inviting her out here? She had been staying in one of San Francisco's smartest boutique hotels. Here they would be lucky to have hot water.

'Simple?' she said. 'You've got electricity, haven't you? When you said "roughing it" I thought that meant kerosene lamps and no running water.'

'It's still pretty rustic. And cold,' he added, rubbing his hands together. He had changed but was wearing only a light windbreaker, too thin for the mountain nights even in May.

He brought in logs from the lean-to and found her kneeling in front of the grate, crumpling newspaper and using the hand axe to make kindling out of a large chunk of apple wood. She started the fire and when it caught added one of his smaller logs, then another, before sitting down in one of the easy chairs while he opened a bottle of red wine. He gave her a glass while he turned on the refrigerator and loosened the taps in the sink, then went back and ran the water in the bathroom. When he came back she'd left her chair and he found her standing in the dark on the deck, where he joined her with his own glass of wine.

'It's lovely here,' she said quietly, and he stared down the hillside towards the lake several hundred feet below, which spread out like a dark stain. Stars were out and the Milky Way was visible across the headland opposite. He pointed it out, and she nodded.

'I like the space here,' he said, putting his glass on the rail.

'Funny. San Francisco seems very spacious to me. I mean, for a city.'

'I guess so,' he said, thinking of his bachelor's apartment above the Korean grocery store on Lake Street. It was a nice neighbourhood, and in the middle of San Francisco, but he paid for it by having only enough room to swing a proverbial cat – small bedroom, small living room, small kitchen, a sun porch, and that was it. The garden downstairs in back belonged to the owners of the grocery store.

'Everything seems so *un*dense,' Kate said. 'I walked around Sea Cliff yesterday and couldn't believe how – I don't know the word, it's not rural, and it's not suburban. It's something like "floral", only more to do with vegetation. I just mean, things are *growing* everywhere. It doesn't feel city-like.'

He laughed. 'You pay for that. Houses start at two million dollars in that neighbourhood. Anyway, I thought you said you lived in the country.'

'Not really,' she said. 'It's the family home. I live in London.' She turned towards him and in the light from the living room he saw her smile. 'Let's go inside.'

They drank more wine and talked some more, mainly about *her* work this time, and the places it took her to, which seemed to include most of Scandinavia, which Renoir badly wanted to see himself, and all of the Middle East, which he didn't. She mentioned a trip with 'Emily', a name he recognised from her conversation at lunch, and he wondered whether this was a friend or a colleague.

Eventually, Renoir looked at his watch and saw it was half past one in the morning. 'I had no idea it was this late,' he said. 'Listen, about sleeping,' and he noticed her eyes widen slightly. 'Is a sleeping bag okay? I've brought two along. There are sheets in the cupboard in back, but this would be a lot easier if you don't mind.'

'That's fine,' she said. 'But I'm a little claustrophobic, so can I be on top?'

He tried not to laugh. 'Sure,' he said. 'Just don't roll off.'

He realised, as he said all this so matter-of-factly, that he wanted to sleep with this woman very badly. It was beyond the usual lust, engendered by her striking looks and those long, long legs. It was

40

a sudden, intense, unexpected and novel desire for *intimacy* with her. But equally he was afraid of spoiling things – how awkward the rest of the weekend would be if she turned him down. *The rest of the weekend? Don't you want to know her longer than that?* Yes, he did, in an entirely unpractical way, which he knew would never happen. She lived in England, after all, which for all its strangeness to Renoir might as well be the moon.

She used the bathroom first, but emerged still fully dressed, though when he came out of it several minutes later in a T-shirt and boxer shorts and saw her poking the fire, she was wearing a man's long shirt of pale pink cotton that came down almost to her knees. He noticed how slim but strong her legs looked, and that there was a large scar the size of a candy bar halfway down her right calf.

'Dog,' she said, moving the poker briskly among the embers.

'Pardon?'

'It was a dog what got me,' she said, sounding like Eliza Doolittle in *My Fair Lady*. 'My leg,' she said finally in explanation.

'Oh,' he said mildly, and got into his lower bunk bed. 'Take your time,' he said, 'but can you turn out the light when you come to bed?'

She didn't say anything, but put the poker down, walked across the room (he had a good look at the scar this time; it was impressively deep) and switched off the overhead light by the door. He could still see her clearly in the light cast by the dying fire, and the cedar walls of the room glowed with a burnished reflected light. As she walked across to the bed, his heart beat faster and he wondered what to say. He felt that she was absolutely in control; never had he felt more male or less masculine.

'Thank you for bringing me here,' she said quietly. She was by the bed now and to his immense surprise she leaned down. Before he could respond she pecked him once, twice, quickly and chastely on the cheek, and she must have been able to see his surprise, for she stepped away from the bed, and said with a light laugh, 'I don't bite.'

'You don't?' he said with the kind of mock-disappointment that wasn't altogether mock, since what he wished for more than anything was that she would come to him again so that he could kiss her back.

'No, you've got nothing to worry about,' she said determinedly, lifting a foot onto the end of the lower bunk and springing up onto the top bed. 'I like girls.'

He felt as if he had been slapped hard in the face. Was that why she kept talking about 'Emily', who must be her partner? That explained it. He knew he should say 'That's okay' in a light and carefree way. But he couldn't. It wasn't okay. He was expert at suppressing disappointment, but this was a big enough blow to sneak past his guard. A drag had been put on his spirits, which was going to last for at least the length of the weekend.

'Sorry,' she said lightly.

He tried not to wince.

'Sleep well,' he said, trying not to sound gruff.

'You too,' she said cheerfully.

In the morning he chopped the large logs of the lean-to into more manageable proportions, while Kate went exploring on the hillside above the cabin. She came back with a bouquet of wildflowers in her hand, and found a vase for them which she set in the middle of the table. 'Pretty,' he said admiringly, determined not to let the disappointment of the previous night ruin the day.

'Fritillaries and yarrow,' she said with knowing enthusiasm. 'And there's iris in the woods here which I didn't pick. Amazing.'

'How do you know the names?'

She shrugged. 'My mother taught me. She doesn't always remember her children's names but there isn't a flower or shrub she doesn't know.'

They went into town and ate breakfast in a diner which, like the town, seemed essentially unchanged since the '50s. They had two blue plate specials of fried eggs, bacon, toast and hash browns, and a waitress kept their coffee cups refilled. Renoir ate quickly, methodically and she pointed at his empty plate. 'Did you go to boarding school?'

'It's the army. "Keep your trap shut and your stomach full."'

'You don't strike me as a soldier.'

'I wasn't much of one. I was an MP. Then I managed to get into Intelligence for the last four years.'

'Was this National Service you were doing?'

'There was no draft in my time. I enlisted when I was seventeen – the first day I could. I was living with my grandmother in the Sunset. Nothing against her, but I felt stifled.' The Sunset – Jesus, how different from the popular conception of San Francisco. How to explain to this London sophisticate the working-class tedium of life there. No free love, no hippies strolling, or cable cars, or Chinese food, or seafood restaurants. Not even much of an elevation up and away from the cold and foggy shoreline of the city's western edge on the Pacific.

'Did you get sent overseas?'

'Nope. And that was the irony. I was eight months in San Diego, then I got transferred back to San Francisco, of all places. I had another seven years here, and then I got out.'

'Why didn't you go somewhere else then?'

Curiously, it was not a question he had ever answered before – to himself, as much as to anyone else. 'I don't know,' he said, 'it just didn't occur to me.' How lame it sounded.

'Well,' she said, 'if it made you happy who's to complain?'

This seemed slightly dismissive, and made him want to explain. But what could he say? That happiness had nothing to do with it, that in fact he was suspicious of happiness. Not that he looked for misery, but that in his experience conventional happiness always ended. By contrast, happiness for him meant something that couldn't be taken away. He said to her, 'It was the one thing I had to hold on to.'

'I can understand that,' she said quietly. 'You were virtually an orphan after your grandmother died – even if both your parents were alive.'

He thought of the piano player, somewhere up near Anchorage, playing the Billy Preston numbers which were all Renoir's mother could ever remember about his repertoire. 'I suppose he was alive

43

then. Maybe he still is. Not that it makes much difference now.'

'Or back then,' said Kate. 'The city was the only family you had left.'

She said this with such directness that he didn't know how to reply. As an adult, he didn't talk about himself this way – not to Jenny in the past, or Ticky, or anyone – so now embarrassment at his self-exposure replaced the urge to communicate. Kate may have sensed this, for she picked up a newspaper someone had left on the seat and, giving him a section, tactfully immersed herself in the local Gold Country news.

After breakfast they walked around town and bought groceries for dinner, then drove back to the lake. He parked next to the picnic area above a strip of sandy beach; it was a sunny morning, but still early enough for a residual nip in the air. The beach was deserted. He pointed to a boathouse at one end of the sandy strip. 'Kaufman keeps his boat and float in there; I promised to row the float out and moor it. Do you want to wait here or walk around?'

'I'll help you,' she said, as if mildly insulted, and as if she had been expecting to be put to work. And it was a good thing she had come along, he realised as they struggled to shift the float, turning it carefully in cartwheel fashion until they let it fall with a great flopping *whoosh* into the shallows. The rowboat was an old dinghy made from thin wood planks and he manhandled this alone while Kate collected the oars. Tying the float to the boat's rope ring, he clambered in first then held the boat steady while Kate climbed in and, pushing them off, sat down facing him in the stern. He rowed with long hard pulls and only made slow progress, while Kate looked over his shoulder at the hillside and into the air above them. 'Terns,' she declared, 'and a cormorant.'

'I wish I knew birds,' he said, wistfully recalling Maris's encyclopaedic knowledge of their names, even their calls. She had promised to teach him, but they had run out of time.

'Easy to learn,' she said. 'The guidebooks are good. Or go out with someone who knows.'

Go out? Did she mean take walks with or 'date'? His wondering about this was interrupted when Kate pointed towards his feet. 'I hate to tell you, but we're leaking. And fast.'

He looked down and saw she was right – water was beginning to gather in the well of the boat. He looked around for something to bail with, but there was nothing.

'I think we'll make it to the buoy,' he said, turning to look behind him. 'I can try and tip the water out there but I'm not sure we'll make it back without sinking. Can you swim?'

'Possibly,' she said sharply. It sounded very English. 'Can you?'

He nodded, and asked teasingly, 'What can't you do? You know how to make a fire, you can chop wood, you know the names of all the wildflowers and the trees. I'm half expecting you to wrestle a grizzly bear before the weekend's done.'

'Well, I can't fight very well. Roddy always won.'

'Roddy?' he said lightly, trying to disguise the intensity of his curiosity. For all the previous night's talk, she had told him virtually nothing about her personal life.

'My big brother. Only he's not very big – I'm taller than he is. But he was always able to beat me up.'

'Remind me to teach you how to fight dirty. If we get back to shore,' he said doubtfully. The tear in the canvas lining on the boat's bottom was widening and the water was welling up at an alarming rate. Soon it was sloshing around his shoes, so he perched them awkwardly on the gunwales while he rowed.

They reached the buoy and he untied the float from the stern and tied it tight to the ring. He clambered out onto its canvas-covered deck and stood for a moment, riding the lateral movement like a rodeo cowboy. He gave up and got down on all fours, holding onto the boat's sharp prow while Kate joined him on the float and he tied its painter to the same ring.

Kate was laughing. 'Is it you Americans who talk about up a creek without a paddle?'

Renoir looked thoughtfully at the boat, which now had a good twelve inches of water in it. 'We could try and tip it out, but it must weigh a ton. And even if we emptied it, we wouldn't get very far on the way back without its filling up again.'

'Can we leave the boat here and swim back?'

He shook his head. 'Kaufman wants it in the boathouse. If we leave it here it will fill up with water and then probably fall apart. Or kids will smash it up.' He shook his head, his mind made up. 'Tell you what. You get in, and I'll strip down and push you back to shore. The boat won't be weighed down so much with me out of it, so you shouldn't get wet.' He was looking at her trousers, smart white cotton ones, and a blue cable-knit sweater she'd put on when there had been a chill to the morning air.

'Don't be daft,' she said and started to unbutton her trousers. He looked around, suddenly circumspect; on the shore there was now a large grey SUV parked near his car, but no sign of its occupants. As he turned back to Kate she was sliding her trousers down her legs. He couldn't help noticing that she wore the briefest of panties; he stared briefly but frankly at her legs, which were fashionably pale, her thighs the colour of milk, her calves developed but not muscular. He realised she had caught him looking, for she said reproachfully, 'And don't get all excited.'

Before he could protest she added, 'I've got nothing on under this sweater, but I'll drown if I try to swim with it on.' And in one swift movement, she lifted it over her head, then shook her short hair, took a deep breath and jumped feet first into the lake.

'Hurry up,' she said, treading water next to the boat, as he struggled to take off his own clothes. He tied his jeans and shirt and her trousers and sweater into two neat bundles and placed them and their shoes on the middle bench of the boat. Then wearing only boxer shorts he slid into the water, which was icy, freezing cold

They each took a corner of the stern in their hands and started to kick the water-laden boat back towards shore. It was hard work, pushing with their extended arms, while kicking as hard as they could to make any progress at all. They stopped at one point halfway back, and Kate began to laugh. It was infectious, this laugh, wholly uncontrived and unselfconscious, and Renoir found himself joining in. 'Is that what you expected for the weekend?'

She shook her head. 'Nothing this romantic,' she said, and began to laugh again. Then she resumed pushing and Renoir joined her, bemused. *Romantic?* He wondered why she had chosen the word, regardless of the envelope of irony it came in.

They reached shore at last and, having pushed the boat up the sandy beach, stood a little shyly and caught their breath. Renoir tried not to stare at her breasts. The SUV was still parked next to his car, but there was no one on the beach. They struggled to tip the boat on its side to drain the water out, since it was colossally heavy – Renoir's protestations that he would do it alone soon gave way to welcoming her help. Together they managed to lift the corner of the stern high enough to let water slosh out of the far corner in irregular waves; as the burden lightened, they slowly flipped the entire boat over on its side, standing back as the water cascaded onto the beach around them.

'*Hurray!*' The shout came from up the beach, and Renoir saw a small group of kids – teenagers – standing outside the SUV. They waved at him and began applauding, and suddenly Renoir realised he had been concentrating so hard on the boat he had forgotten that Kate was naked from the waist up.

'God, I'm sorry, I didn't see anyone. Here,' he said, picking up Kate's sweater and handing it to her.

She seemed unfazed, taking the sweater with a wry smile. 'It's a little late for modesty, don't you think? If the little bastards hadn't seen a pair of tits before, they certainly have now. So I think they should pay for the privilege.' She draped the sweater awkwardly around both shoulders so it covered her front, more or less, and, advancing several steps towards the group of youths, beckoned them to come help. A little sheepishly, they did, and under Kate's supervision carried the rowboat to the boathouse. Inside they placed it on its rack, while Kate belatedly put on her sweater and the boys averted their eyes. 'Thanks,' she said, and they shyly went away.

Renoir and Kate drove back to the cabin, where they took turns standing under the dribbling shower. Once dressed in dry clothes, he made a fire and had Kate sit by it in one of the captain's chairs with a glass of wine while he cooked supper – baked potatoes wrapped in foil and placed in the now hot ash of the fire, stir-fried mangetouts and baby carrots, then two steaks he put in hand grills and propped over the largest burning apple log.

'Do you like cooking?' she asked as he put the food on their plates.

'I like to eat. I find one follows the other.'

'Not for me,' she said ruefully. 'I'm a hopeless cook. And London's single greatest subsidiser of restaurants.'

'San Francisco's not exactly short of restaurants. But it's expensive, and I get tired of eating alone with a paperback propped against my plate and everybody else thinking "who is that sad guy eating alone?"' She laughed at this, and he realised she probably never ate alone in a restaurant – there would be an endless stream of offers to take this woman out to dinner, gay or not.

They were drinking a bottle of Sonoma Zinfandel, and he opened another one. They sat in the two chairs facing the fire, each with a glass on a wide flat arm. 'This is my idea of heaven,' she said.

'I'm glad you like it.'

'If you could live anywhere,' she said, 'where would it be?'

'Some place like this.' An answer that surprised even himself, since this weekend was an exception – he was rarely outside San Francisco. His spare time was spent in bars or at ball games, or just reading in his apartment; when he'd been with Jenny it hadn't been all that different, except for dinner parties with her friends. Jenny didn't even like the country. Her idea of wilderness was walking in the Panhandle early enough in the morning that no one else was around.

Kate said to him, 'Not a lot of positive vetting out here.'

He shook his head. 'I wouldn't be in the same line of work.'

He paused, and asked, 'You meant a fantasy, right?'

'Sure. Go ahead.'

Almost reluctantly he said, 'I'd farm. I'd farm top fruit.'

'Top fruit?'

'Apples, pears. Not cherries – too difficult.'

She looked at him a little sceptically, and he realised how fanciful this must sound. 'How about you?' he asked to shift her attention.

'Oh, I'd like to live in the country too. I'd keep the day job – I'll leave the farming to you. Probably commute into London. But I travel so much anyway it wouldn't be much different. And we put out a newsletter which I can do from anywhere.'

'You wouldn't want to give up work then?'

'No.' Her voice was emphatic, almost harsh. He looked at her quizzically and she smiled in recognition of her sharpness. 'Sorry.'

They sat silently for a while, watching the fire burn down. 'You know,' she said, lifting her face to look at him with a generous smile, 'it must be strangely appealing to know that you can find out anybody's secrets. And maybe even guess them beforehand as well.'

'I'd never use it in my own life,' he said. He didn't mention 'tells', though certainly he was pleased that she kept stroking her hair, brushing it back over her ears, once even sweeping the whole front comma of it back onto her head, until he remembered that this could hardly be a sexual tell intended for him.

'Really?' Her tone was teasing, but interested. 'What about the women in your life? Do they mind what you do on the job?'

'They have done,' he admitted.

'But not any more?' She sounded playful.

'No. Not any more. I told you that already.'

Something in his tone must have sounded serious, possibly offended. 'I'm sorry. I didn't mean to pry . . .'

'Really?' he said, looking at her sceptically. 'I thought you were giving me a dose of my own medicine.' He smiled to lighten the edge in his voice.

She smiled back at him, yet said, 'But seriously, how can you keep it out of your life? Doesn't it make you distrust people?'

'If you spend your working life being paid not to trust anyone,' he said with emphasis, 'the one thing you want to do on your own time is give people the benefit of the doubt. It's a kind of rule I have.'

'Do you have many rules for life?'

He shook his head. 'Not other than don't have too many rules.'

'You don't really like to talk about yourself, do you?'

'Are you serious?' It seemed to him he had done little else throughout the weekend.

'Yes. This is unusual for you, isn't it? I've always been talkative. Not a chatterbox exactly, at least I hope not. But not a shrinking violet.' She got up and walked over to the fire, reached down for a log but looked at her watch and thought better of it. 'You know, it's late – maybe we should go to bed.'

They went round the cabin turning off the lights, and she was in bed with the light off when he came out and got into the lower bunk bed. He wanted to keep talking to her, so as he lay down he said, 'You haven't told me anything about yourself.' He added teasingly, 'Not even your secrets. And I can't guess them, whatever you think.'

'You'll learn them,' said Kate. 'Don't worry, you will. Sleep well.'

And this surprised him again, since he assumed that after this weekend he would never see this unusual woman again. *Why not?* he wondered, since he recognised how much he liked her and, until her admission, had been drawn in by – what? Sex? No, it wasn't just sex; it was, remarkably for him, more than that; it was *romantic*, to use the word she'd used at the lake. *And that's exactly why I won't be seeing her again*, he thought, deft at cushioning himself from disappointment. *What's the point?* he thought just before he fell asleep.

He hadn't had the nightmare for a long time, but it could have been yesterday for its familiar immediacy. It began, as it always did, with him standing by the pond looking towards the greenhouse, where a figure lay inert on the ground. There was a dark stain on its chest, and he realised it was a man, then consciously thought within the dream, *It's Uncle Will.* And though he knew Will was dead, he was unsurprised to hear him talking as he lay dead on the ground, saying, *Help me, help me.* And then, *Why did you run?*

And the boy was about to protest, *Because you told me to, Will; you told me to run*, but then he was in the kitchen and the man in the yellow shirt was coming through the back door with a gun in his hand which suddenly swelled, like an inflatable figure in a Disney parade, the barrels the length of a grown man and the trigger as big as a fat man's fist, and it was rising, as was his panic, and he felt without looking on the cheap Formica kitchen table for a knife. And the knife wasn't there. *It wasn't there.* And panic took hold of him like flu, and he wanted to shout but his throat was so completely constricted by fear that no sound would come out.

Somehow an arm was on him, and his first reaction was to duck under it, free himself, get away from the powerful constricting force. But it wasn't grabbing him; it was gentle, first stroking his shoulder, then his forehead, smoothly. He shuddered and quivered in fear, until a voice broke through his dreaming and like daylight woke him. 'It's okay, it's okay,' the voice said soothingly, low but female, resonant but calming.

And he opened his eyes and made out a figure leaning over him, and he realised first that he was in a bed, then remembered he was in the cabin, and then with an exhalation of relief knew it was this woman Kate next to him and he was out of the old familiar terror of the old familiar dream.

'Sorry,' he said weakly.

She got up from the bed and turned on a standing lamp. He noticed she was still wearing only the man's shirt. 'I wasn't sure what to do,' she said.

'You did fine,' he said, still shaken by the dream.

'You're shivering,' she said, looking at his arms, which were covered with goose bumps.

'It's cold in here,' he said.

'No it's not,' she said calmly and looked down at him. She took his forearm between both her hands and began rubbing it briskly. 'I'll make you a hot drink in a minute. What else can I do?'

And whether out of the slight shock created by the contrast between his terrifying nightmare and this calm reality, or because he thought, *What have I got to lose?*, he looked at her and said, 'What I'd really like right now, if you wouldn't mind – and I do appreciate what you told me last night – is a kiss.'

And she looked at him, he thought, incredulously, though not with any obvious hostility or disgust, and then her lips creased into a cupid's bow and she laughed. Her eyes, dark rather than sky blue, seemed intensely alive – even when her face was calm, they seemed to move, and now they danced so vividly that he did not realise for a second that the rest of her had moved too, and that she was sweeping back his bedclothes. 'Move over,' she said, with a cheerful bossiness.

She sat up on her knees next to him in the bed and slowly unbuttoned her shirt. In the lamplight her skin was the colour of light corn, and the short straight strands of her hair were lightly streaked. She leant back and shrugged the shirt off her shoulders, then moved over him until her knees were on either side of him while he lay on his back looking up at her. She leant down and kissed him lightly on the mouth, and she stroked his hair with her hand. The sensation was utterly soothing, and he felt about eight years old.

'I thought,' he began to murmur but she cut him off.

'Hush. Don't talk. And remember it was only a dream.' Her hands travelled down and began to lower his shorts. 'But this isn't,' she said.

She worked his shorts off then sat up slightly and he looked at her, then reached with one hand and slowly touched her breasts, which were round and full, the nipples now erect. She looked at him with a knowing smile. 'Don't you start applauding too,' she said, and then moved her face down towards his and kept it there. They kissed for a long time until he could feel both their bodies stirring, and she stretched her legs down, over his and almost as long, and they rolled over until he was on top, and when he reached down to stroke her she moved his hand away and touched him instead, saying, 'Now. Now, please.'

And as he moved very gently into her she gasped and drew his mouth down again onto hers and they moved together, gently at first, then with increasing vigour, and she broke her mouth away. 'Don't wait, don't wait,' she urged him, but he did, losing sense of himself in her, feeling the alternating softness and strength of her thighs gripping him as she encircled the backs of his legs with her own calves, and her arms held him tight, meeting in the middle of his back, and he watched her as her gaze left his and seemed to be searching high in the sky for something, though there was no sky, he told himself, and she was suddenly arching and then her whole body seemed to quiver from her spine and he was no longer waiting but felt overtaken by his own climax which came in an emptying rush and he held her even tighter and they rolled until facing each other sideways and looked intently into each other's eyes and she said softly, 'Usually it takes for ever,' and then she giggled happily.

'I thought you said you liked women.'

'Maybe I do,' she said, and she giggled again. 'Actually, it seemed a safe way to keep you out of my bunk. I wasn't sure if it was just a quick leg-over you were after. I wasn't having any of that.'

'"Leg-over"? I've never heard it called that before. What do you call what happened then?'

She giggled. 'I call it me calling the shots.'

'So the lesbian business was some kind of test then? To see if my intentions were honourable.'

'I didn't intend it that way, but I suppose that's how it turned out. I just thought that telling you I was gay would remove any tension about sex. I could see you weren't very pleased, but you did your best to hide it. A red-blooded American, in other words, but a gentleman too.'

'Pretty ingenious to say you were gay,' he said, not without acerbity. 'You get to know that you're desired without the awkwardness of saying no.'

'Yes,' she seemed to agree. 'So ingenious that I end up here.' She gestured at them both lying in bed, and he laughed, conceding the truth of this.

'Who is Emily then? You mention her so often I thought she must be your girlfriend.'

'Emily is exactly nine and a half.' She hesitated. 'She's my daughter.'

'You're married?' he asked bluntly. *Nice of her to let me know now.*

'Divorced.'

He was astonished by the turn events had taken. What had got into her so suddenly? The dream; of course, it was the dream. He'd had it many times with Jenny next to him in bed, but perhaps never quite so dramatically. He shuddered slightly at the thought of it, disturbed as he remembered his uncle's accusation: *Why did you run?* Then a hand pinched him lightly on the thigh. 'Hey,' said the voice, and it was Kate, her mouth not twelve inches from his. 'Don't go away.'

He forced himself to smile. 'Sorry.'

'Do you do that with all the girls?'

'What? Say I'm sorry?' he asked, intentionally misunderstanding her.

'No. Go away like that, like you just did. I wasn't with you any more.'

He exhaled slowly. 'There have been complaints,' he said quietly.

'Do you want to talk about it?'

'What, the complaints?'

'No, silly. The nightmare you were having. It sounded terrible.'

He shook his head.

'Okay,' she said in a way that discomfited him. He turned and now she was lying on her back, her eyes focused on the ceiling.

'Hey,' he said, 'why did you get irritated when I asked if you'd ever want to give up work? I wasn't chauvinist – most people's fantasy is to give up their job.'

'I know,' she said. 'But I've been through it once before with my ex-husband. He not only didn't want me to work, he thought it was up to him. Once Emily was born,' she looked away from him as she said this, 'he didn't even bother to use her as an argument. You know, a baby needs a full-time mother. He just thought he had made a decision and that was that.'

'What did you do?'

'I stuck it out for three years; I thought it was important for Emily to have a father. Then I decided it couldn't actually be any worse for a child to grow up in a single-parent household if the alternative was her mother going mad. I waited until Angus went stalking near Inverness, then took Emily and one big suitcase and caught the shuttle to London. I couldn't get my old job back at the *Economist*, and for a while it looked pretty bleak – Angus wouldn't give me a bean. He wouldn't even help me with Emily; I had to take him to court. Then I met Seymour Carlisle, the head of the consultancy, and he gave me a job. Things got better.'

This was put dispassionately, but he sensed a great well of emotion behind it. There was a sense of a long struggle, but of survival as well; of pride, but no triumph; a sense, too, of unhealed wounds. 'Didn't your parents help you?'

'My mother thought I should go back to Angus. My father seemed to understand.' Her voice faltered slightly. 'But then he died.'

'When was that?'

'Two years ago.'

'You were close?' He thought, *I sound like a psychotherapist.*

'Very. I *adored* him.'

She's not over it, he thought, and she seemed to read his thoughts because she said, 'I know it seems odd, that I still get upset about it. But I felt like I lost my only ally. And why do people always say you should "get over it" – he *is* gone after all, am I supposed to stop missing him?' He could sense her eyes on him, felt her breath slightly graze his chin on the exhale. 'Don't you miss the people you've lost?'

He paused before replying, saddened by the words he was about to say. 'I try not to let myself. I guess I thought once I started missing them I'd never be able to stop.'

They slept late, as sunshine flooded through the cabin, then made love again before Renoir brewed coffee and brought it back to bed in two tin mugs. When they got up at last, they went for a long walk up the mountain, packing ham sandwiches and a thermos of Sangria. It was warmer than the day before, and they both sweated freely as they emerged at last from the tree line onto the grassy slope beneath the summit. They stopped for their picnic, with a vista of the lake below. 'I love water,' said Kate. 'Even the most beautiful scenery isn't the same without it. And swimming in a lake.'

'Do you get much chance for that?' asked Renoir. He couldn't think of a single body of water in England except the Thames.

'At Belfield there's a lake.' Then she explained, 'That's where I grew up. My mother lives there now, and sometimes my brother.'

Was it their summer house? he wondered. He tried to imagine a beach house – no, it would be something classier, maybe an old Victorian pine house, like those he'd seen in photographs of Maine. The beach was probably rocky, too – somehow he couldn't associate England with sand. He pointed down at the lake in the valley below. 'They've managed to keep the developers out so far. But some day there'll be houses all around the shore. How about your lake? Is it very built up?'

'Oh no,' she said. 'It belongs to the house.' She looked embarrassed.

'Belfield?' he said with sudden understanding. She nodded. He resisted the impulse to tease her. She had money, that had been obvious from her first appearance in his office as a high flyer in her business. But now he understood that her family had money too. *Oh well*, he thought, another reason why he was unlikely to see her again.

'Sounds nice. Did you learn to swim there?'

'Yes. How about you?'

'I learned in a pond, actually.' And he remembered his uncle's patience as he struggled and kicked and struggled some more, until one day, just as even his uncle looked like he was about to give up hope, *presto* and he could swim. Soon you couldn't get him out of there; all those times when Maris would say, 'See if I care if your supper gets cold,' and stomp off back to the house.

'I thought everyone in California had swimming pools.'

'That's LA,' he said. 'We're hardier stock up here.'

'Speaking of stock, was your mother's family French too?'

He smiled and shook his head. 'My grandmother's name was Shaughnessy.'

'Oh, Irish. You probably don't like the English then.'

He shrugged. There was a large Irish community in San Francisco, with a long tradition of nationalist sympathy and, supposedly, a history of gun running for the IRA. But it hadn't been part of his upbringing, since for all her essential conservatism, and church-going habits, his grandmother had never been an ethnic 'type'. If anything, Renoir had always sensed she wanted to escape it – though with the name Shaughnessy and a house in the Sunset, she was never going to do that entirely. 'I don't think much of it one way or another,' he admitted. 'I've never been to England.' He looked at her out of the side of his eyes. 'Or Europe.'

Her own eyes widened. 'Gosh,' she said, and standing up began to brush the sandwich crumbs from her jeans, 'you'd better do something about that.'

As the time came to leave the cabin an awkwardness settled on them, at first lightly while they had chores to do before leaving, but then more heavily as they travelled west in the car. They were silent much of the time and it seemed impossible to make conversation: all the spontaneity of their earlier talking had gone, and he found himself feeling the edgy anxiety of their first lunch, just forty-eight hours before, even though at the beginning of the day, when they had made love for a second time, he felt he had known her for months. Had he done something? Not that he could think of; perhaps this was just her way of establishing distance, making it clear that yes, it had been fun, thank you very much, but now we had better forget about it.

Which troubled him more than he wanted to admit, and in turn made for an internal sense of annoyance which translated into coolness. They slowly edged their way in traffic over the Bay Bridge and into the city, just as the sun was setting on the west side of the peninsula, its final strands of light the colour of pink grapefruit, reflecting off the skyscrapers of the financial district.

Once off the bridge, he drove quickly to her hotel and parked with a small screech of brakes in front.

'How vibrant,' she said, with mock respect, and he grimaced, which he realised must seem to say that that was that, thank you very much, so he almost jumped with the coincidence when she said, 'So is that that then?' And in his surprise he lifted his eyebrows, which must have conveyed some measure of – what? disdain? contempt? in any case nothing very pleasant, for with an impulsiveness which seemed to match his own, she grabbed for the door handle and made to get out, and her face was thunder.

'I hope not,' he said out of nowhere, instinctively really, and the door was halfway open before she seemed to take this in, but then her foot, which was reaching out for the street, hovered in air and came back into the car and Kate closed the door. Without looking directly at him, she said, 'Well, that's nice to hear. I couldn't really tell. You're not the easiest man in the world to read.'

'Likewise,' he managed to say. And recovering he added, 'You still haven't seen the city, you know.'

She looked down at her lap. 'Is that an invitation?'

'I think even Americans call it that.'

She turned to him, looking happier, but then her lips set and her face grew serious. 'I'd like to, Renoir.' This sounded so strange that it took him a moment to realise that it was the first time she had called him by name. 'But . . .' she said.

His disappointment was immediate, and in his usual effort to suppress it he said hastily, 'I know, I know, you've got to get home. Don't worry, it was just an idea,' and he doubtless would have continued to babble in this vein had she not reached out with her hand and placed it on his.

'Sh-sh-sh,' she said, only slightly louder than her whisper in bed when he'd come out of his dream. 'It's not because of work and, yes, I would like to. But it wouldn't be fair to Emily to stay any longer. It's half-term and she shouldn't spend her holiday with school friends. I really have to fly.'

It was so sincerely put that he admired her diplomatic way of saying no. She looked searchingly at him. 'You think I'm just being polite, don't you?'

He didn't know what to say and she continued to stare at him. 'Renoir,' she said for the second time, instead of 'Jack', and he knew that if he did ever see this woman again this was going to be what she called him. 'Don't be an idiot.' The tone was instructional but affectionate. 'Planes that go to London have been known to come back from London. I may fly out of here, but I can fly back again, you know.' And she smiled at him so disarmingly – her eyes alive, the upper lip slightly curled, that he suddenly felt that she would.

She came for three days, on her way back from a pipeline visit in Alaska, where she claimed to have seen more bears than women, bringing with her a soapstone Eskimo carving he put on the mantelpiece of the fireplace that didn't work in his Lake Street apartment. She stayed with him there, which surprised and initially alarmed him – he took a day off work to spring clean and iron the fresh sheets for his big double bed. He had tried to warn her off when she phoned from Anchorage, but she'd refused to take the hint.

Fortunately, she seemed to like his place, which he'd always kept simple: sanding down the floors to show off the maple boards, which he waxed once a year and kept to a warm shine; painting the walls white, so the feeling was of a light and breezy summer house, rather than the small and thin apartment it really was. He had photographs on the walls, mainly of the woods in the Presidio, which he'd taken during a short-lived photography phase when he'd first come out of the army, and a few simple watercolours, usually of ocean vistas, which he had found in his weekly visits with Jenny to antiques stores.

Kate made friends at once with the Korean family in the grocery shop downstairs, and appreciated the park across the street where early in the morning from his front windows you could sometimes spot a buzzard in the high eucalyptus trees. They did some tourist things – walked the Embarcadero, took a cable car up and down

Russian Hill, and ate one night in a ritzy place south of Market. The Giants were in town, and he thought of taking her to the ball park, with tickets from work, where his boss Eckerly sat on the board of directors and thus had access to the company box. But he found he didn't want to share the limited time he had with her with anybody else – much less 40,000 fellow spectators. So the company they kept on this visit was their own, and what he liked was how the almost premature intimacy of their weekend at the cabin was easily resumed.

There was such a strong sexual attraction between them that they spent a lot of time in bed, where they each liked taking care and being taken care of in roughly equal measure; Renoir found that as often as he felt eight years old again so equally often he was the one in charge. To his slight surprise, she seemed sexually experienced, indeed a little more adventurous than him, without the act becoming depersonalised – he never felt he was just the latest in a list.

But even in bed they talked, continuing the conversation they had begun on a walk through the Presidio, then carried on in the living room with the fan going full blast until the exceptional heat for spring in San Francisco drove them into the bedroom, putatively because it was air-conditioned but also because they couldn't keep their hands off each other. Yet even the intensity of sex took second place to talking – 'I can't remember,' said Kate during one afternoon's story of a trip to the desert in Qatar when her driver got lost, 'whether we've made love yet.' He touched the soft inner pad of her thigh under the covers and she said with her eyes closed, 'I remember now.'

She got up and used his grandfather's brush from the top of the chest of drawers to try and smooth her hair, which was naturally straight but now tangled from humidity and an hour of rolling around his brass bed. She winced as she pulled out strands of hair.

'Ouch,' he said sympathetically.

'*Il faut souffrir pour être belle.*'

'What does that mean?'

'Don't you know any French, Renoir?' She said his name again with Parisian zeal. 'Monsieur Renoir.'

'Not a *mot*. I told you, my papa skedaddled when I was rising three. So tell me, what's it mean?'

' "One must suffer to be beautiful." My mother used to say it when we complained that nanny brushed our hair too hard.' She put the brush back on the chest of drawers and added, a little wistfully, 'I always thought it was her way of letting us know that she was beautiful, which she still is, or that we weren't.'

'Or just that you didn't like to suffer?' Renoir offered. He was always amazed how women carried their problems with their mothers deep into adulthood. With fathers they were either adoring daddy's girls or contemptuous of the male pig who brought them up; with mothers it always seemed so complicated. Even when there'd been a nanny.

She laughed. 'Golly, there's no self-pity allowed around you, is there?'

'None. This is a zero tolerance zone for self-pity.' Lying on the bed, he gave her an appraising look, as she stood at the end of his bed wearing a pair of white panties and nothing else. She had a lovely figure by any standard – those legs for one thing – but he liked the unusual traits even more: the slightly prominent rib cage, as if she'd trained as a dancer (she hadn't), or the dime-sized mole on her upper chest, about four inches up from her heart.

She didn't seem to mind this scrutiny and put her hands on her hips as she looked back at him, stretched out on the bed. 'Is that your grandmother's influence?'

'I guess so.'

'She must have been tough.'

'She was in some ways. My grandfather died early – drank himself to death before he was fifty. Then she got to watch her daughter follow in his footsteps.' He was shaking his head.

Kate said, 'Did she have any other children?'

'One. My uncle.'

'Was he a drunk?'

'No,' he said. Despite himself, he knew his voice had gone

61

quieter; he tried to lift its pitch but couldn't. 'He was an apple farmer.' *And a few other things besides.*

'Ah, "top fruit",' she said knowingly. 'Where does he live now?'

'He doesn't. He's been dead for almost thirty years.'

Kate's eyes widened. 'I am clumsy, Renoir. Were you close to him?'

He shrugged as nonchalantly as possible. 'I didn't know him for that long.'

She looked at him curiously, started to say something but thought better of it. She kept brushing her hair with hard, short strokes, then asked, 'Did he die suddenly?' she asked.

Does three seconds – that was about the time it took – count as 'suddenly'? He said in a flat voice, 'It was an accident.'

They were both silent for a long time. At last Kate remarked, 'It sounds as if your grandmother had a hard life. No wonder she was tough.'

'But she wasn't grim,' he protested. 'She could be fun. I mean, considering that in her sixties she got stuck with a ten-year-old boy to raise, she did pretty well. She liked to play cards.'

He said this as if card playing were an infallible indicator of high spirits, and Kate looked unpersuaded. 'Was she very old when she died?'

'No, she had just taken retirement. She was thinking of moving to Florida. "Somewhere sunny", she said, after a lifetime of fog. The Sunset District gets the morning mist, you see. But before she could do that she had a heart attack and died.'

'Were you there?'

He shook his head. 'I was still stationed in San Diego.'

'It must have been a shock.'

'I don't know. She smoked a pack of Pall Malls a day. "Smoke the Red, you're dead" – that's what they used to say in the service. She always had a terrible cough. And wheezing. If she hadn't had a coronary I'm sure she'd have developed emphysema.'

'She doesn't sound very Californian.'

He laughed at the bluntness of this. 'She wasn't. Or if she was it wasn't the cliché. She was decent Irish working class, though she didn't conform to that stereotype either.'

'Why?' Kate sat back on the bed and tucked her legs under her.

And he wondered, *why are you so interested?* 'She was Catholic, of course, and she went to Mass on Sunday. But she never forced me to go.' He remembered his obstinacy when he had first come back to live with her, still shell-shocked, how he'd shook his head when she had proposed his joining her that first Sunday morning. *What kind of God would have done that?* he'd thought; his grandmother must have understood what he was thinking, for she accepted his initial no and never asked again. Miss Lily, the old black lady next door (there couldn't have been more than half a dozen black people in the entire district) looked after him on Sundays while his grandmother went to Mass, though by the time he reached the age of fourteen he realised he was keeping Miss Lily company rather than being looked after.

'And look how well you've turned out,' Kate teased. 'Come on, get up. I bet your grandmother wouldn't let you lie in bed when the sun was shining and there was hard work to be done.'

'What work?'

'I need feeding,' she declared. 'It's your job to put the bread on the table.'

The visit must have been a success because she came again, three times in fact over the next three months, and Renoir found himself looking forward to her visits so much that during the weeks in between he stopped seeing any of the other women he had been dating before, finding he preferred being on his own, missing Kate, to taking solace in secondary consolation elsewhere.

He and Kate continued to spend almost all their time together alone, and he kept her a pretty fair distance from his drinking buddies, many of them ex-Service, who had a tendency to act like the bar crowd in *Cheers* – friendly but relentlessly male. And the friends he'd had with Jenny, a circle really of other couples, had dropped away on her side of the post-relationship divide.

The exception to this unsociable behaviour was Ticky, who to Renoir's surprise telephoned his apartment after he let slip that Kate was coming for a visit. He had never seen Ticky outside the

confines of the company, and in general didn't carry work friendships into non-work arenas, but he needn't have worried since it
was Kate she wanted to talk to, not him. 'You're jealous, aren't
you?' Kate said mockingly when she arranged to meet for lunch
with the AI head, and he admitted he was – he didn't really want
to share Kate with anyone. Though on Kate's next visit Ticky took
her on an all-day expedition to Sonoma County, which Renoir
was happy enough to miss.

For these visits Kate had no excuse about being in the neighbourhood, since she was in New York on each occasion, talking
with Mobil. She flew out Friday afternoon, before returning to
London either late on Sunday or – if she could swing it – on
Monday night. She was coming a long way just to see him, and
perhaps that instilled a note of pressure in their time together that
had not been there before. But he found there was so much he
liked about her, and so little he didn't. She was funny, sharpish
at times, but never towards him; she was objective, too, which
meant she was unusually generous about even those people she
didn't like or approve of.

Her education, so much more extensive than Renoir's, didn't
sit like a divider between them, but was instead something which
gradually, tactfully, she was able to share, without impugning his
pride. He knew perfectly well he wasn't stupid, but knew too just
how many fundamental items of a sophisticated liberal arts education – who was Dante? What were Keynesian economics? – he
did not possess.

She was also pretty, increasingly so the more he knew her; that
her face was so expressive that some days she could look down-
right plain meant he treasured her usual prettiness all the more.

For all their talk, they did things, too, for she insisted they get
out of his apartment however much he wanted to make love and
eat Chinese takeaway for the duration of her stays, which seemed
achingly short. He was usually quite sedentary, rarely straying
from a semi-commuting path between his apartment and either
the office near Union Square or the office in Cupertino; all that
distinguished them was that one was a two-mile commute, the

other twenty-five. He was not insensitive to the natural beauty of his surroundings: the placement of the city on the ocean and Bay, and its own extraordinary, vertical topography; or the varied landscapes within fifty miles on any side except the west, where the Pacific provided its own diversity. He was not insensitive perhaps, but hardly took full advantage. His exposure to the wildlife and countryside which he professed (even to himself) to love was confined chiefly to the paths and walks of the Presidio, the vast park and military complex where he had spent so many of his army years. There, a remarkable habitat for flora and fauna and birds lay within the confines of a major American city, but was inevitably limited and in no sense real country.

Kate took him out of this, forced him out of the city in a series of short trips, south down the peninsula, north over the Bridge (he could cope with Marin, which was south of Sonoma, and was happy to do the wine tours of Napa). Yet the activities didn't seem forced, and she was never keen to stay away overnight – in fact she liked nothing better than an early night in, when they could pretend to watch a DVD and read their books, her thrillers and his outdoors writing by Jim Harrison or Thomas McGuane.

She surprised him almost continuously, by the energy she seemed to have for everything (jet lag never seemed to slow her down), by her willingness to think and think hard about almost everything. She seemed endlessly fascinated by his native city, and perhaps she had a sense of her own tutelage by him as he gradually unfolded the city's rich tapestry of neighbourhoods for her – from the Italian bakery in now trendy North Beach to the discount clothes emporium South of Market. He realised how much he'd fallen into a rut, and how near-reclusive he had become. He had seen people – that wasn't the issue – but he had not engaged with them.

Yet if he found himself awakening, he often wondered just what was in it for her. He was flattered that she was willing to come so far and so often to see him, but he was puzzled, too. For he didn't know what this very classy lady could possibly see in him. He wasn't really a hard guy, that clichéd object of desire. Though he was sufficiently familiar with the stereotype to know that it was often true. She seemed too old, moreover, to be acting out some kind of adolescent rebellion – picking someone 'unsuitable' as an act of defiance against both her parents and upbringing. If that had been the agenda, surely she would have acted it out already with her first husband – who was in fact, Renoir gathered, a wealthy Scottish landowner.

And from her own words, Kate didn't seem to be hung up on class issues.

'Renoir, if you were in the army so long, why don't you have any tattoos?'

'I may not be well educated, but I'm not entirely stupid.'

'But these days everybody has tattoos.' This was true: even middle-aged and middle-class ladies were contemplating the addition of, say, a small green anchor on their left haunch.

'Revolting,' he said.

She laughed. 'Renoir, one of the many things I love about you is that you're such a mix. Your grandmother was solid working class, decency and all, your mother was a hippy, you're now an executive—'

'Hardly.'

'Yes you are. Ticky said you even have shares.'

'Everybody has shares.'

'Don't interrupt my flow, and the end result is that you're absolutely classless. And that means you don't have a chip.'

'A chip?'

'A chip on your shoulder. About class. You're not "chippy".'

'No, I'm American. We don't believe in that garbage.'

'Balls. Lots of Americans do. Just not you. But why is that?'

Wanting to shrug this off, he found himself thinking about it instead. He said, 'I don't mean this to sound arrogant. But if you have taken a fine-tooth comb through as many private lives as I have, what you find is, however grand the veneer, underneath the bad smells are all the same. Secrets don't discriminate.'

'So why aren't you more cynical about people? You seem to like everybody unless they give you a really good reason not to.

How can you have such a high opinion of human nature when you know what you do.'

'Who said the opinion was high? I just said it was equal across the board.'

'What about the people close to you? You know, people not at work.'

There isn't anyone close to me, he thought, but was embarrassed to admit. *Except you*, which he didn't dare say in case it frightened her off.

'Put it this way,' she said in amendment. 'What is the one thing you couldn't stand? I mean, in a person you knew really well. Like a girlfriend,' she added, letting the obvious implication stand unmodified.

'Lies, I'm not good with lies. I see too many at work to be able to live with them at home.'

'Can you always tell when a person is lying?'

She said this lightly enough, but he sensed that something hung on his answer. Yet he wasn't sure what to say. In some respects, he was about as close to a polygraph as a human being could be – his career was built on the ability to detect lying. And he had a nose for it, like the hero of the Lovejoy novels Kate read, an antiques dealer who could spot a fake piece instantly. But, despite this, he said emphatically to Kate, 'No,' adding for good measure, 'I'm no better at it than you are.' And though this was a lie he hoped paradoxically that just this once it was also true.

'That's a relief,' she said, and he could tell she meant it.

'So what's the one thing you can't stand?' he asked.

She nodded slightly, as if acknowledging that it was indeed her turn. 'You'll laugh, considering your job, but I can't stand being spied on. Or jealousy. Angus did both,' she said. 'He hired a private detective to follow me. He couldn't believe I was simply unhappy; there had to be another man.'

'How did you discover you were being followed?'

She snickered cynically. 'Because Angus was too mean to hire a good detective. The chap stuck out like a sore thumb: once in Pitlochry I retraced my steps and actually caught him changing hats. He looked so embarrassed that I pretended not to notice him.'

'I don't understand why you married Angus to begin with.'

'Neither do I,' she said wistfully. 'Perhaps it was because he was rich,' she added, with an insouciance he saw through right away.

'That won't wash with me. Belfield doesn't sound exactly like a tenement to me – you and your own family lake. Was he very intelligent?'

'Who, Angus?' She hooted at the thought. 'No. And not educated either.'

'Oh, like me,' said Renoir; it was his turn for phoney nonchalance.

'But you're clever, Renoir. I don't care what you say, you run rings around people when you want to. I know you didn't go to Harvard but believe me you're in a different league from Angus.'

He was flattered by this – as he imagined he was intended to be. But she hadn't really answered his question, and he still couldn't make sense of her marriage; she seemed far too level headed to have married that dolt. Had she been so different ten years before? He doubted it, but didn't want to push things; perhaps in time he would learn enough about the circumstances of the marriage to make sense of it. Maybe it was a class thing – not in the American sense of 'classy', denoting gracefulness, but something more rigid, a hierarchy he didn't understand but which Kate occasionally alluded to in conversation. There was money in her 'class', whatever she said, but there was something subtler about it, apparently, though he didn't know what this subtlety was.

He said, 'You'd never have found out if I had been following you.'

She groaned, and said, 'I know, I know.'

He reached out to touch her arm, and said gently, 'That's why I'd never do it.'

'Promise?' she said lightly.

'Promise,' he said, more heavily and from what he thought was the heart.

*

He was curious how she'd got into the oil business, which he saw as overwhelmingly male, and she explained that she had studied geography as an undergraduate ('It's supposed to be for dimwits, but I liked it, and I was good at it') then took an MA in economics in London. 'The two converge into petroleum pretty easily,' she explained. 'It's in the ground and it makes money if you take it out.'

It was clear that the newsletter she and the senior partner, Seymour Carlisle, produced was very successful and much respected in the field. But it alone did not account for her professional prosperity – 'To be honest,' she said, 'the newsletter could support Seymour alone in some style, but not an office in Berkeley Square, my services (not to mention a secretary) and two half-time researchers.'

Consultancy was the real money-spinner. The focus of the newsletter was on exploration – part report, part prediction of where petroleum reserves would come from in future; the consultancy, if he understood it correctly, provided specific advice to specific clients about their individual exploration strategies. It was not so much, 'How do you find the 75 million barrels worth of retrievable oil under a Finnish pocket of tundra?' but rather was the price of extracting it worth it? And what were the odds that the putative 75 million barrels were actually 12 million? Sometimes they had to tell their clients what they didn't want to hear. Increasingly, Kate said, she and Carlisle were becoming suspicious of the levels of reserves being claimed by the major producers, especially when the projections were hypotheticals arrived at with the help of state of the art expert systems.

She made good money – very good money by Renoir's standards, as far as he could tell, which was not the result of snooping around her cheque book but just the inferences drawn from a lifestyle she seemed to take for granted: her flat in central London was at least three bedrooms from her casual descriptions; she dressed expensively and stylishly, if without a trace of show-off glitz; her tastes in food and wine were, though not pretentious, high quality and expensive. For the moment he could keep up – he was making $110K and had no dependents. He was a saver, not a spender, and had always been careful to have some reserves. But he was aware of the earning differential between them, though it helped from the start that they effortlessly shared the expense of restaurants and movies and even – at her insistence – gasoline for his car on their excursions out of town. But Kate was by nature generous, and she liked to give him presents, bringing duty-free smoked salmon and CDs of the music she was learning he liked, and once a cashmere sweater so soft to the touch that he was reluctant to wear it.

It was more the perspective on money than money itself that revealed the difference for Renoir, for sometimes Kate unwittingly tripped over it, as if hitting a relationship landmine. She asked him why if he liked the High Sierra foothills so much he didn't buy a cabin like the Kaufmans'. 'Money,' he said simply. 'I pay a lot of rent,' he added, pointing to the rooms around them, 'despite the unfancy nature of this place. I want to live in the city, and it's so expensive that I just couldn't swing both.' It sounded almost pathetic. What else could he tell this rich girl? 'I'm just a middle manager, ma'am,' he said.

'Sure,' she said, 'but let's not overdo the modest bit. I think you are what you want to be.' *Oh God*, he thought, *San Francisco's got to her with shrink gobbledygook at last*. But she seemed intrigued by Renoir's comparative lack of ambition. 'Someone told me,' she said later that night, while he steamed rice and grilled tuna in the apartment's bachelor kitchen, 'that when the old head of HR at your company left, the senior management asked you to apply but you wouldn't. Is that true?'

He looked at her sceptically. 'You've been talking to Ticky.'

She reddened slightly; he liked it, since it was such a girly contrast to her usual crisp confidence. 'She wasn't being critical,' said Kate. 'I think she admired it.'

'What, my lack of ambition? You don't.'

'Yes, I do.' She seemed keen to persuade him. 'I have never admired ambition for the sake of ambition. But I do think,' and she looked at him in a meaningful way he didn't really understand, 'that when you do know what you want to do you should be ambitious. It's wrong to be anything else.'

He would have been suspicious if there were no downside to her, no aspects he disliked, yet even those he found intrigued him. There was a whiff of snobbery he didn't like at all, for though he wasn't especially politically correct, he had, thanks to his grandmother, none of the prejudices so common in his childhood neighbourhood. It was not that Kate was racist, far from it; it was a subtler prejudice which came out as words he did not at first fully understand – rough-acting people were 'common', drunks were 'yobs', there was even a word called 'oik' which Renoir suspected could be applied to most of his drinking buddies. And there was a tacit assumption too that 'one's friends' were of a certain type with certain holdings. Holdings? Yes, *land*, or houses seemed a key part of it, particularly for the country people, mainly family friends, who were neighbours of Belfield.

'You know,' he said once, 'you act sniffy about people who grew up in houses with numbers instead of names.'

'I do not,' she protested, but she blushed.

'So what I want to know is, what are you doing with me? Where I grew up, it wasn't just my house that had a number – the street had a number, too.'

'Ah,' she said, and her voice grew plummier, as if to say *I'm not backing down one inch*, 'but wasn't there a cross street?'

'Yes. Quintara.'

'That's prettier. If I were you, I'd say that was the street where you grew up.' And he could only laugh, unable in the face of such defiant elitism to pursue the argument.

She was five years younger than he was, but the combination of her professional standing, her extensive travelling around the world, and the dual experience of marriage and motherhood meant he thought of her as his contemporary. Not that this made her any easier to understand, for she was utterly different from any woman he had known.

71

Which he liked, and he loved to have her talk about the simplest things: how often she took a cab to work (shockingly often); where she ate lunch (usually at her desk, though sometimes with clients in ridiculously fancy restaurants); where her friends lived (mainly Notting Hill, it seemed, which thanks to the movie he had heard of); where she took Emily on holidays (to France or Belfield for happy ones; to Kate's ex-husband in Scotland for dutiful ones). In its complete unfamiliarity, all this information intrigued him.

Only once did a difference emerge that he didn't like. She had come in early on a Friday afternoon flight from Calgary and he came home to Lake Street early, hoping to surprise her. When he entered the apartment she was sitting in the back room next to an open window, smoking a joint. She looked at him guiltily.

'I didn't know you did that,' he said, trying to sound completely neutral about it.

'Sometimes,' she said. She pointed to the open window. 'Sorry, I wasn't sure if you'd mind.'

'Where did you buy it?' he asked. She'd seen Ticky on her last visit, maybe she'd got it from her. He hoped so; he didn't want Kate buying it off the street.

'I brought it with me,' she said.

'What do you mean? From *Canada*?' When she nodded, his voice began to rise. 'You mean you brought it through Customs? You idiot.' He stopped momentarily, shocked at himself, since he'd never been abusive to her in any way. She was looking down at her feet, so he couldn't tell how she was reacting. But he didn't care. 'Do you realise how stupid you've been?'

'They don't throw you in jail any more. I asked a friend about it. They barely check the Canadian passengers anyway.'

'It's not jail I'm worried about, Kate,' he said, his voice rising again. 'Don't you understand? If you get caught they won't let you in the country again. Honest, they almost threw John Lennon out, and he had a Green card. Maybe you wouldn't care – maybe that's the point – but how am I supposed to feel when I don't get to see you any more because you've brought in some shitty grass from Calgary? Christ, it's not as if it's better than what you'd get here. How could you be so dumb?'

He went and took a shower to cool off. Had he overreacted? No, he decided, not really; he knew how dim a view the government took of even the mildest drug offence by foreigners. But he also knew his explosive reaction was not to do solely with the law. Marijuana did not mean for him DRUGS, as in the first step to heroin hell, impotence, loss of memory and untreatable schizophrenia. It was more personal than that, personal history.

When he came out of the shower Kate was just getting off the phone. As he dressed she came into the bedroom. 'Why didn't you tell me you played golf?'

'What's to tell?'

'Are you an ace?'

Renoir was proficient enough to be called a golfer, but not enough to be called a good one. 'That's a sore point. But why are you talking about golf? Who was on the phone just now?'

'Someone named Hank.'

His golfing partner at Presidio. 'What did he want?'

'He said he had a tee time for tomorrow at nine fifteen and could you please let him know if you weren't going to show up so he could get somebody else. I said I didn't know; I was telling the truth, since I'm not altogether sure what a tee time is. Then he said and I quote: "You must be some babe to make Renoir miss his golf."'

'I'm sorry. He's an old army pal and one of my more unreconstructed friends.'

'Oh, I didn't mind. It's quite flattering. Pale English women like me don't often get called "babes".' She giggled. 'I was just worried you were giving up something you love to do.'

'I was. Or I am. Or I will be. Take your pick.'

'But—'

'I wouldn't if I didn't want to. End of story. Okay?'

The marijuana episode was as angry as he ever got with her, but Kate was far more volatile, though the two of them didn't really argue – when Kate got cross Renoir would go quiet until the microburst of temper passed over. His refusal to respond in kind annoyed her, he could tell, and once she actually complained: 'Why don't you ever row?'

'Is that what the English call bickering? I can't stand couples who do that all the time. Why be together if you don't like each other's company? Anyway, I guess I don't know how to "row" because I never learned.'

'Saint Renoir,' she said sarcastically, and he assumed an expression of such piety that her mood improved immediately.

But he worried about her bad temper, which when mixed with what he saw as her ignorance (possibly fear) of 'common people' could be a potentially explosive combination. For she was not the suppressing type, and her temper would flare indiscriminately and without any sense of caution. When people other than Renoir angered her, she was not so easily appeased, as he saw for himself in a gas station, of all places, in the Twin Peaks neighbourhood where they stopped to fill up on the way back from a day trip south to Santa Cruz. It had been such a lovely day that he couldn't understand, as he finished filling the car and she went to pay, why she grew so furious when a teenager, black and dressed in gangsta duds, cut in on her in the line. 'Excuse me,' she said sharply, and he could hear her from outside, 'I think you should be behind me.'

'That's cool,' said the kid and started humming.

Renoir was fast approaching, and he could see Kate's jaw clench and her eyes widen as she tapped the boy on the shoulder, not gently either, more like a poke one *two* with her extended index finger, and her voice lowered almost to a growl as she said, 'If that's cool, why don't you just do it?'

And the kid turned around, at once outraged and surprised, just as Renoir arrived, and as the kid started to expostulate, more fiercely even now that a white man had joined the discussion, Renoir said in a loud and friendly voice – loud, so as to publicise the dialogue before it could escalate through words unmediated by a larger audience; friendly, so as immediately to deflate

74

the tension starting to swell up in this encounter like a balloon – 'No problem.' He gave his broadest smile, then pointed at the counter where the teller waited, looking anxious. 'Go ahead. All yours.'

The kid looked at him for a moment, said 'That's cool' with amusement and walked slowly to the counter. Kate was fuming, and started to say, 'But he was jumping the queue,' until Renoir put an expansive arm around her, squeezed her shoulder tight and kissed her with a big smack on her cheek, whispering, 'I will jump *your* queue if you say another word.' And fortunately, before she could carry on arguing, another counter space opened up and he shuffled her there, his arm still around her shoulder, vice-like, and paid cash from his pocket to speed the transaction before hustling Kate out to the car before she could as much as squawk.

'Why did you give in like that?' she demanded. 'Did that little pipsqueak scare you?'

'Sure,' he said. 'He looked just the kind of jerk-off who's happy to kill someone because he's decided he's been "dissed". And nobody else there was about to intervene if he did.'

'You were absolutely hopeless,' she declared, and then said, only half joking. 'It's not even as if he were bigger than you. My knight in shining armour.'

'I never said I was brave; I'm *careful*. In this country it's not really intelligent to pick fights with strangers – not when about eighty per cent of this local population likes to carry a concealed weapon.'

'Didn't they teach you how to defend yourself in the army?'

He shrugged and she continued. 'Didn't you say you were an instructor? Well, what exactly did you teach?'

She's going to love this, he thought. He said with the faintest of grins, 'Unarmed combat.' He remembered the rigours of Hand-to-Hand Fighting – An Introduction. He'd had the skills for it, but not the disposition. He remembered how he had only been interested in its practical, unaesthetic aspects – the shortcuts to getting people to leave you alone. That was the point, he had felt – not to excel at it, as if it were some sort of physical art form;

not to develop an unhealthy interest in actively hurting other people; but simply being able, ruthlessly, efficiently and with no fuss (an expression he had already picked up from Kate) to deal with people trying to hurt you.

'How long did you teach it for?'

'Six days,' he said defiantly, as if the figure were twelve years.

Kate laughed. 'So what happened after six days?'

'I told you, I joined Army Intelligence.'

'I forgot. I'd had you pegged as the muscle. Someone who kills men with his bare hands.'

'Not in the army,' he said without thinking, then found Kate staring at him. He tried to concentrate on his driving, and since it was not a neighbourhood he knew well, he had plenty of reason not to glance over at Kate.

'Renoir, did something bad happen to you when you were little?'

He pretended to think about this. 'Well, I told you it got a little hairy with my mom before Gram took me away. But it wasn't that bad – I mean, she never really hurt me.' *Except towards the end when she lost it a couple of times a week.*

'I don't mean that. I mean something awful.' She was eying him in her unique forensic way. 'Something you've never told me.'

He turned his head to look her straight in the eye, trying not to speak either too deliberately or too slowly. 'No,' he said calmly. 'What makes you think it did?'

She shrugged one shoulder. 'You had another nightmare the other night. You talked a lot; most of it was babble, but you sounded very scared. What was it about?'

'How would I know? First I've heard about it was right now. You know,' he said, adopting as light a tone as he could and ostentatiously looking around as they drove to the end of a cul-de-sac, 'I haven't the faintest idea where we are.'

In late summer she came twice in four weeks. He had missed her so much that the shortness of the time they would have together cast a pall on her stay before she had even landed. They had been in almost daily contact, through phone or email or – how teenage it made him feel – text messaging, and he almost preferred the distant communication, since there was no reason for it to end, whereas with her visit he could only think of when she would be flying out.

They were growing intimate with no prospect of that intimacy sticking. Years before, when he was first transferred back to San Francisco, he managed to retain a San Diego girlfriend for all of six weeks and two tiring weekend visits there (she had refused to visit him, the accommodation of the base at Presidio proving untempting). So when he thought about it, he couldn't see sustaining a transatlantic relationship more effectively, which was why he tried not to think about it.

Kate seemed to share this sense of fleeting time, as he discovered when he woke in the middle of the night to find the bed empty. She was in the living room, lying on the sofa, reading the *New Yorker*, or pretending to, since, as he pointed out to her, she was holding that week's issue upside down. She didn't laugh, and managed only half a smile.

He looked at her face closely. 'Sweetheart, have you been crying?'

She shook her head so vigorously that it made it clear she had been, since two tears promptly popped out of her eyes. He sat down and put a hand on her shoulder. 'Come on, what is it?'

'I don't know,' she said and her voice broke. She spoke again but in a cracked teary-sounding voice. 'It's just been so nice being here with you.'

'Why does that make you cry?'

'Because I hate going away from you, Renoir, I hate it. But it's so hard buying time to come here. Seymour's trying to be understanding, but he's not young any more, and then there's Emily.'

'Have you thought at all about coming here for longer?' He was a little startled to find himself saying this.

'What do you mean? I was just saying how hard it was to come here as much as I have.'

He figured he might as well keep going. 'I don't know, like coming to live here?' He hesitated. 'For a while anyway.'

She wiped her cheeks dry and sniffled. 'Oh Renoir, I'd love to. But how can I? Emily means everything to me.'

'Bring Emily. Not all the schools here are as bad as mine was.'

'I can't.'

'Why not?'

'Angus would never have it. It's part of the settlement, Renoir. He didn't contest custody provided I promised to keep Emily in the country. Not that I ever thought I'd want to live anywhere else.' She looked at him dry eyed. 'Until I met you.'

She had never talked that much about the past, though over the weeks then months of their relationship he could fill in most of the bigger blanks to her life history, as he presumed she could fill in his – well, most of his. But the emphasis was on the immediate – *Ticky wants to meet up at the farmers' market; Renoir, I bought crabs at the Wharf, so I hope you know how to cook them* – or on the future, that long-term dream landscape she had first set out for them in the cabin. One night as they walked home from pizza at a local Italian place, she said, 'Renoir, if you had your druthers . . .'

And he said, 'Druthers?'

She blushed and said, 'Isn't that the word? I heard it in Alaska. But you know – the fantasy game we played at the cabin. Could you imagine living somewhere else?'

'Who knows? I'm here because I never managed to leave. Not that I don't like it – everybody likes their home town, at least they do if they're still there when they're forty.'

'You didn't answer my question. Could you easily, happily, live somewhere else?'

'I don't know. I'm pretty settled in my ways.' He looked hard at her at this point. She was wearing a white cotton short-sleeved shirt, and trousers that stopped halfway down her calves. Stylish but not affected. He added, trying to take his eyes off her, 'I'd like to live in the country, as you know. But it's not very realistic.'

*

78

She may have shared his fatalism, but she did not show it. On her next visit she brought a small watercolour painting of trees on the slopes rising from a smallish valley. It looked like early spring; the painter had stippled in small green buds and a light tinge to the grass beneath the trees. 'It's so green,' he said. 'It must be England. Who's the artist?'

'My sister,' she said.

'Really? It's very good.'

'Runs in the family,' said Kate, 'though I had an artistic bypass. That's the view from the lake by the way. They call it Treefall Down. Most of the trees you see were planted after a great storm in the nineteenth century.'

'It's beautiful,' he said, and he felt it, but it seemed so strange to see this painting of Kate's family place. She had never shown him any photographs.

'You'd like it there,' she said, and he nodded politely. 'I mean, living there,' she continued, and he was startled. Their relationship lay so much in California that he had trouble envisaging himself being with her anywhere else. Live at Belfield? Or in London? That seemed no more real now to Renoir than had his fantasy of farming.

Yet the possibility of his upping sticks wouldn't go away, because Kate wouldn't let it. And the night before she was due to fly out to London, as they lay in bed, she stopped him when he tried to kiss her. 'I want to talk to you.'

Her voice was firm but also friendly, but he sensed what was coming and was irritated that she wouldn't leave it alone, even on her last night. He said tersely, 'It wouldn't work.'

She did not pretend there were any grounds for misunderstanding, saying, 'Why not?'

'I just wouldn't fit in. I'm totally American – you know that, you're always telling me so. And besides, what would I do?'

'Farm.'

'Kate,' he said, 'let's be serious. I don't have the money to start farming, not to mention the knowledge or the experience. And anyway, land costs three or four thousand dollars an acre.'

'That's in California.'

'No, that's in the South of England.'

'How do you know?' she asked.

'I looked it up with Google.'

She was happily surprised. 'Ah, you were thinking of it. But don't you see, we already have the land. Belfield's eight hundred acres; there's an orchard there already, and the Gatehouse.'

'It's not mine, it's yours.'

'No,' she said firmly, 'it's not. It's Roddy's, and I'm sure he'd sell us what we need – the Gatehouse, the Old Orchard (most of the trees are caput, I admit) and Burdick's Field – Burdick always said apples would grow well there.'

She was growing excited, thought Renoir. 'What's the Gatehouse?' he asked in spite of himself. The idea was insane, but it was their last night; *humour her*, he decided.

'What it sounds like. A gatehouse from the old days when the estate was a lot bigger. In Queen Victoria's time it was over three thousand acres. No one's been living in it, so there's no sitting tenant to evict, and we could fix it up how we liked. It's listed, but it's only the outside we couldn't touch. It's almost a mile from the Hall. You'd never have to see the family if you didn't want to.'

'I'm sure your family's fine, Kate,' he added, though from what she'd told him he wasn't sure at all. 'But I'd be living off you. And I couldn't do that, sweetheart.'

'I'm not asking you to. But why can't I help? At least to start with.'

'I'd just feel funny about it.'

She stood up, gesticulating with her hands. 'You'd rather stay in a job you can't stand any more – don't pretend, it's obvious – than do what you've always wanted to do because of *pride*? Necessity I could understand, but it's not that – it's stupid, silly, ridiculous *pride*.'

He looked at her, and his sense of vulnerability during her outburst gave way to the impersonal feeling of detachment he had felt throughout his adult life. He didn't like it any more, but it was there, the same ice that had made him so unaffected by Jenny's declaration of departure; the same steel that had made his visits to his brain-addled mother entirely a bore, incapable of eliciting the smallest sense of sadness, the tiniest tear.

'That's not all,' he said shortly. 'Say I do go over there, okay? Say I cash in my pension and withdraw all my savings, say goodbye to the Golden Gate and come over. And three months later, while I'm struggling trying to figure out if apples pay – shit, I don't even know if you've got the right soil in your place – *you get tired of me*. All the simple unaffected habits of your regular Joe named Jack Renoir suddenly seem . . . simple. The accent's not so cute when you have to hear it day after day and the fact he doesn't really like the opera starts to tell. Your daughter thinks he's a jerk, your mother's not impressed by the vulgar cut to his jib, and your friends make it clear they think you're crazy.

'So then what? You're okay, with a well-paying job and a daughter and family behind you, not to mention the private lake. And me? I've given up the security I've worked my ass for – let's face it, I wasn't exactly born into bluegrass, blueblood breeding country. I'll be six thousand miles from home without a helping hand in sight, much less a job, and a rapidly declining bank balance that was never too robust to begin with.'

And after this outburst of his own, Kate began to cry, and the iciness within him melted at once. He suddenly couldn't bear her distress – it made him feel the way he did looking at war photographs where children had been hurt. He would have done anything to stop Kate crying, and to stop her pain, but when he went to comfort her she shook him off, almost extravagantly, with anger, and what she said surprised him with its ferocious clearness. 'I was about to say,' she said, shaking off her tears as vehemently as she had rejected his comforting arm, 'that I know our differences, thank you very much, I've known them since the day I missed your tour.' She had stopped sniffling by now and was looking at him with rapidly clearing eyes and transparent anger. 'But they didn't matter – not to me, and I thought not to you either. And I was sure we could do this crazy thing knowing that we simply couldn't fail because we were mad about each other. That was what counted; that was what mattered. But that's where I was wrong.' And she got up out of the bed and walked into the living room, and he thought it best if he didn't even try to follow her. *Let her calm down*, he thought, *wait until she comes back to bed*. But she didn't come back, and after giving it forty-five minutes he went out to check and found her fast asleep on the sofa.

And though she was due to come out two weeks after this, Renoir was not surprised when at the last minute she cancelled – and not even personally, as the secretary from Carlisle's rang him to say Kate had gone to Indonesia but would be in touch. *I don't care if she has to go to the moon, she could tell me herself*. Her mobile phone stayed resolutely switched off; his text messages – he felt like a kid, jabbing away with his thumb – went unanswered. His hurt was soon displaced by worry when after five days he still had no word of any kind from her, but when he called London the secretary assured him she had called in that very morning and was absolutely fine. So his worry was then displaced by anger, and inevitably in Renoir that led to a shutdown altogether. *Minimise*.

He told himself that he should never have got involved with this woman in the first place. Too much geography, too many differences – of money and education and status and nationality. Given time, Renoir knew he would find more reasons, but these would do for now.

Yet the hatches, once opened, proved hard to batten down again. Renoir started to find his work life very dull and repetitive. It sounded clichéd, but he found little there that stretched him, and even the interest in simple human variety no longer sustained him through what was so predominantly predictable. The dreams of farming, which had always been pleasant but remote – like a dream of becoming a world-famous opera singer – now nagged at him.

He couldn't understand either why Kate figured so much in his thoughts. He'd gone out with Jenny for three years but had managed to get over her in a matter of days. Days? Hours – he'd lined up a date with a receptionist at the Marriott within forty-eight hours of their final not-so-fraught exchange. But with Kate gone he didn't want to pick up the phone to call another woman. He'd never understood the phrase 'meaningless sex' – not when sex had been a staple of fun for him for so many years – but now he recognised that to sleep with other women would only fill him with greater regret than that already swelling inside him.

For he could see, however dimly, that he had done this to himself. *Why did I let her go?* he asked himself. But he knew why. The only way ahead for them meant he would have to move – not just physically to a new place, a new culture, a new life, but shift emotionally and metaphorically out of the cocooned life he had so successfully created for himself. It scared him, scared him greatly, but as the days and then the weeks passed, the simple fact of missing Kate Palmer began to compete with his fear, started to vie with it in an increasingly fraught race which, one night deep in his cups, Renoir reckoned was a race for his soul.

And he didn't know what to do, as the mobile phone back in England stayed on voicemail, and he stopped trying to reach the number. Until one day he walked out of work near Union Square – he didn't want the company in on this in any way – and bought a box of stationery from a boutique store on Maiden Lane. He checked the postage at the post office and carefully wrote out the London address, W8 code and all, and his letter had no salutation and no farewell and consisted of four words. *I miss you so.*

And seven days later the ticket came via Federal Express, with a note that read, *Renoir, you said you had holiday in November so I hope I got the date right. And no, you can't pay me back – I got these through air miles and the only payment acceptable to me is a red-blooded American one. I think you'll like it over here. Trust me. K*

Belfield

THE CARD WAS postmarked London but featured a photograph of the Golden Gate Bridge, luminously orange, with the Pacific Ocean a rich aquamarine. The overall effect was '50s retro, as if the postcard had been bought in a store specialising in kitsch. The message was written in a swirl of copperplate italics: *Renoir, Don't You Think It's Time to Head Home?*

Its arrival was the only reason he was glad Kate was away, since its message – breezily anonymous – would have upset her. As it was, he took it in his stride, though he would have admitted that the postcard did not exactly improve his mood, which had been bad even before he'd picked up the post.

For a start, he didn't like fact that Kate was in Dubai, at a producers meeting which the head of the consultancy hadn't wanted to attend; he didn't like going to stay with Kate's family; and he dreaded the prospect of Friday traffic leaving town. What Renoir really wanted instead was to stay home in the London flat with a bottle of whisky for company. But someone had to check that the builders weren't using winter as an excuse – they had promised to be done rebuilding the Gatehouse by now but they weren't.

He set the burglar alarm, picked up his overnight bag and left the flat, giving the brass cage lift a miss and walking down the two flights of stairs to the ground floor. It was an old-fashioned mansion block, five storeys of red brick solidly constructed in the 1930s. He liked its old-fashioned feel: the heavy mahogany banister of the stairs, the thick if faded carpet soft beneath his feet, the burnished brass bowl of dried roses in the alcove on the landing.

He passed the flat of the poet's widow and came down the last short flight to the long hall. Unusually for the neighbourhood, the residents were almost entirely English – most very old, all older than Renoir or Kate, who felt a little like teenagers when they encountered their seniors on the stairs or in the foyer.

Outside, he walked past the blue plaque proclaiming that the famous poet had lived in the building for twenty-seven years. Winter had pushed autumn out of the way two months before, but there was still not the faintest hint of a lift to the envelope of grey he had come to recognise as England post-Christmas. Back in San Francisco, he would by now have been watching the early flowering of japonica and western redbud.

Even in mid-afternoon, the traffic on Kensington Gore was stuck, and he worked his way around opposing taxis and crossed into Kensington Gardens where suddenly he felt the homey cosiness of the mansion block desert him and England became a strange country again. He always felt this way when Kate travelled, as if only her presence drew him into the Englishness of a city that otherwise struck him as entirely *international*. Like the Venetians, so keen to hide their lives from the tourist circus around them, the English in London were starting to seem submerged in a polyglot stew of other nationalities. And their society was penetrable only to outsiders who, like Renoir through Kate, had a proper introduction. Remove the link, Renoir had discovered, and you were an outsider again.

As he walked past Kensington Palace, its ornamental grace subdued in the unwelcoming gloom of the winter light, he thought again of the postcard he'd received. He had been threatened many times in his professional life, more than once quite seriously, but for some reason the mild unpleasantness of the postcard made it more rather than less disturbing. He didn't have any particular enemies that he knew of in this country, not that he had that many friends. 'That many'? Who was his friend? Of his new English acquaintances there were a few he liked, but there wasn't enough shared experience for them to become friends. For the English this seemed the prerequisite for adult friendships: shared experience of school, or the army, or university. Which kept Renoir outside the loop and without intimates. Except for Kate, the only certainty he needed and the only certainty he had.

Or did he?

There wasn't any real reason to think anything was wrong. But it – that trivial 'it' – nagged at him nonetheless.

That Thursday she had rung to say she'd be late – Carlisle needed her help on a conference call with Venezuelan producers and a Santa Barbara investor. When she'd got home a little after eight Renoir cooked rump steak and chips to fuel her late-night session attacking the proofs of the next issue of the newsletter she and Seymour Carlisle produced twice a month. She seemed preoccupied as he made small talk – reporting on the progress of the gatehouse they were renovating, telling her about a deal he could get on the T-Tape which he would use to water the eight thousand trees he hoped to plant in Burdick's Field. Then, feeling he'd gone on too much, he'd asked how her conference call had gone.

Almost imperceptibly, she was startled; he half expected her to say *what conference call?* Then he watched as memory clicked, and she nodded slowly, smiled broadly and said, 'It was fine, absolutely fine, thank you.' And twenty years' experience kicked in automatically. Bells rung, hard as he tried to still them. Tells – famous now, thanks to poker's popularity, but long known to Renoir, since so much of his career had been spent spotting them. Tics and verbal patterns, hand against the nose, undue formality of speech and laboured explanations – all indicators of mendacity.

And the smile. How liars liked to smile. Not understanding that there was a physiological difference between the posed grin of the phoney and the spontaneous flash of the sincere. The false smile used only the muscles below the mouth; the authentic one involved an involuntary creasing of the lines beneath the eyes. A distinction that might sound like hogwash to the outside observer, but one which in twenty years of spotting liars Renoir found virtually infallible. So that evening, when Kate seemed to catch herself, speaking very slowly in reply to his innocuous question, and though her jaw moved and her lips spread in a smile, the telltale muscles higher up in her cheeks stayed absolutely still, Renoir thought instinctively, *She's lying.*

89

Which he had tried to ignore, losing himself in television and two more than usual glasses of wine while Kate worked in her study on the proofs. It must be harmless, he told himself, or maybe he was wrong – after all, he was out of practice, it had been over a year since he'd left his job and moved to London. And Renoir was in any case determined not to bring home his former working skills. He would be a fruit grower now, concerned with aphids and hectare yields, the cost of irrigating new trees and the best way to prune a Bramley in wintertime. Not a digger into people's secrets.

It would all be fine, he had told himself not for the first time, when the land sale finally went through, the Gatehouse was finished and their new life began. He had taken such a gamble that he simply wasn't prepared to contemplate the possibility that what he had done might be going wrong.

That night, Kate crept into bed in the early hours of the morning, proofs finished, still keyed up rather than exhausted by her all night work. She moved over underneath the sheets and nudged him once, twice until he turned and slowly worked off the old army shorts he sometimes wore in bed, and he found she herself had nothing on, and they made slow love until the sky outside turned a slightly lighter shade of dark as the winter day broke, and as they finished she whispered *love you love you* and he pushed the unprecedented sliver of doubt like a fistful of pennies into the back of his mind.

And let it stay there, he told himself now, eight days later, as he left the park on its Bayswater side and moved west into Notting Hill. There, in a side street, he came to the underground garage, and the manager came out of the subterranean office to greet him while someone fetched the car. The manager was Greek, and they made small talk about how nice it would be in the islands (though Renoir had never been there), certainly when contrasted with this wintry grey of London. When the car pulled up sharply beside them Renoir took the keys from the attendant and tipped him. He found the car a little embarrassing, but Kate had taken such pleasure from giving it to him that he had never said a negative word about it. An Audi cabriolet, the darkest blue with vanilla leather inside. Powerful and easy to drive, it looked as if it belonged to a Hollywood divorce lawyer. Conspicuous wasn't his style, so, in every kind of weather, he kept the top up.

Now the manager himself looked a little embarrassed, hesitated, then spoke. 'When you get a chance, could you ask the missus about something for me please?'

'What's that?' asked Renoir, mystified.

'We haven't had this quarter's rental payment.' He added hastily, 'It's not a problem. It's just she's usually like clockwork. I thought maybe it's gone astray in the post.'

'I'll check it out,' he promised, surprised.

'Thanks. Drive carefully, Mr Palmer.' Which wasn't his name. It was Kate's name and Kate they knew best, for it was Kate who paid the garage rent. Only not recently it seemed, which was unusual – Kate was beady about money, and paid her bills promptly. Though he tried to keep his distance from her dough.

In his rearview mirror he could see as he drove off both manager and Nigerian minion look at him with the mix of admiration and smirk that, after over a year of living with Kate, he was almost getting used to. What had Gram liked to say? *It's just as easy to marry a rich woman as a poor one*. In his case, she'd have been right – if he'd let it happen.

But he hadn't married Kate Palmer for her money because he hadn't married her at all. Too easy; it would be like a cat who got the cream by living with the owner of the dairy. Call it pride, or some residual machismo hang-up, but he found it easier to be a kept man if he were not legally a husband as well. He knew Kate wanted children with him, and, in the vaguest way, he did too – but not yet. Did other people wonder why they hadn't married? Probably, though in this age of 'partners' it would only be an older generation who really cared. And they probably thought it was Kate who resisted, seeing the disparity in money and class between Kate Palmer and her American. *Nice enough bloke*, then a knowing laugh, *but you wouldn't want your daughter to marry one*.

What was he supposed to do? Pretend he was rich in his own right? At least by the comparatively low standards of his upbringing, he had some money of his own: he could pay for groceries, settle a hotel bill, purchase (though not impulsively) a long-distance airplane ticket in economy class. He wasn't dependent on anyone, even after he'd resigned his job and come here. He'd converted his pension, cashed in his company shares and taken out all his savings from his army years, bringing half in cash over with him to the UK. He paid his own way, or at least the fees for his 'mature student' courses in horticulture; he would pay for the eight thousand little apple trees. Yet there was no denying the financial disparity between them, and he could imagine pretty well what was said behind his back. But should he leave the woman he loved rather than suffer embarrassment? Or force her to live differently from what she was used to? For the sake of what? His pride? What would be the point of that?

Usually a zippy driver, Renoir had slowed down since coming to England, more worried by the prospect of driving on the left-hand side of the road than by any actual difficulty in doing so, though sometimes he found roundabouts confusing and on motorways he had to remind himself which was the fast lane. What he couldn't do at all was combine the system: the summer before in France, driving this right-hand drive car on left-hand roads, his adopted side coping with his native one, he grew so confused that Kate had to take over.

Now he fought his way down to the Hammersmith roundabout, then got onto the A4 out of town, sat in the middle lane, and relaxed. He turned on the CD player, finding Fleetwood Mac already ensconced there. A favourite of Kate's. She loved the folky rock of the West Coast – the Eagles – which he, the Californian, should have liked. But he liked singers pure and simple instead, wanting character in a voice, which meant he liked as many 'impure' singers as not – Bonnie Raitt, Joe Cocker. Better them than smoothy metro crooners, though he liked the retro velvet of Dean Martin, and even rated Barry Manilow – which led Kate to declare, 'I am continually amazed and admiring that you are willing to admit you like his music.'

He put on Joss Stone, latest white aspirant to the Aretha crown, and drove quickly out through the pleasant western suburbs. He would happily move from Kensington to the soft comforts of, say, Richmond and its deer park any time, but Kate loathed the suburbs. Class again, thought Renoir, wondering if he was being drawn into the unilluminating English obsession – spoken and unspoken – which he had never given any thought to in the United States. *You're just an ordinary Joe*, he reminded himself, then thought again of the creepy postcard he had received that morning, telling him to go home. Somebody out there didn't think him unexceptional; somebody out there didn't like him much at all. Proving Kate's own point, he supposed, which she had made only a week or so before. He forgot the catalyst but remembered her words very clearly: 'You always think everybody's going to like you, don't you? You're just an easygoing guy.' Then she added in a parody of his own American voice, '"I'm just an ordinary Joe, whom everybody loves."'

'That's not fair,' he said. 'It's just that most of the time people dislike other people because they don't know them.' He was thinking of the reflexive anti-Americanism he sometimes encountered, which he never thought had much to do with him, Renoir the person. It was about his nationality, something that seemed to Renoir as far away from his character as, say, the kind of socks a man wore.

Kate scoffed gently. 'Oh, so you think if people get to know you they'll automatically like you?'

'I didn't say that.'

She ignored his reply. 'Because the point is, maybe some people don't *want* to get to know you. Perhaps some people are perfectly happy to dislike you on the basis of entirely superficial acquaintance. *That* doesn't lessen the fact of the animus.'

Further out of town, the urban sprawl grew less attractive, and he thought, with a slight ache, of how dramatic the exit had been from San Francisco, crossing the Golden Gate north and plunging immediately into a national park in west Marin, where there were deer, bobcats, even the odd mountain lion. Or east, quickly passing Berkeley, with Mount Diablo looming. Here, as soon as country-side seemed to appear, Heathrow intervened, followed by the septic reservoirs of Slough.

But comparisons no longer seemed so inevitable, or constant. And in any case the San Francisco of celebrity – of hazy sunshine and pastel houses, gorgeous food, scenic hills, friendly and attract-ive people – was not his town, that city where most people's alter-native had become the norm: middle class, Democrats, radical feminists, lesbians and gays, website designers. Sometimes Renoir felt he had been raised in San Francisco's true alternative culture – working-class Irish, the Sunset District of morning fog, after-noon rain, which left him with a view of the city as emotionally overcast, enclosed and cool. It was the greyness of England – all that rain, the almost soot-like darkness of the winter months – that felt most familiar.

So he didn't romanticise the reality of where he now was. Far from it. Anglophiles always boasted about England's greenery, how a country the size of Minnesota had assiduously preserved its countryside, throwing green belts around even small conur-bations to check urban sprawl. But Renoir didn't see much sign of that; if anything, he noted the propensity for American-like growth of exurban constellations of shopping malls and service industry parks, forcing people into their cars, putting pavement and asphalt down willy-nilly when space should have been at a premium.

He saw that the GPS light was on and switched it off im-patiently. The world viewed by satellite. While television or radio or computers or mobile phones facilitated global communica-tion, GPS's goal seemed to be *exposure*, down to a frighteningly precise level: it could pick out a lamppost in a minor village lane, or tell a mountain climber to the exact yard how far he was from a summit four miles high. All this through a pene-trating satellite eye that to Renoir seemed the ultimate Orwellian overseer, reducing the physical complexity of the planet to the simple status of a surveillance target. GPS was inescapable, all-seeing.

But Kate loved gizmos, gadgets, executive toys – duty-free was never safe from her, on the prowl for the latest anything which took a plug or battery. He had teased her about the GPS system, how expensive a precaution it was – *It won't stop them from stealing the car, you know*. And she retorted, *But it will help me get it back*. She rented space in the Notting Hill garage nonetheless.

An hour later he got off the M4 at the Newbury exit and headed north on the A34, exiting from the highway as it climbed to the top of the Downs, while he drove at their feet, moving west until he came to Wantage, an old market town he liked for its failure to come up much in the world, despite its situation among the affluence of the Thames Valley. He parked just short of the old central square, which had largely local shops. A few were smart ones (ladies' lovely leather shoes; an Indian interiors shop full of teak), but most were mildly dilapidated. In the market itself cheap clothes and produce predominated, with 'bargains' that went unappreciated when brought home, like the rugs from a Moroccan honeymoon when the couple returned to England. In a side street there was a mixed garden tools and hardware shop which Renoir favoured enough to pay over the top for a pair of lopping shears he needed. He meant to pay with his own debit card – that was the arrangement he had insisted upon with Kate – but discovered he'd left it on the chest of drawers in the London flat. Supplying the card for their joint household account instead, he was surprised (and embarrassed – there were two women queuing behind him) when the card was rejected by the processing machine and he had to pay cash.

What's going on? he wondered as he drove out of town, since despite the distance he tried to maintain between his money and Kate's he did know that her salary, bonus and profit share from Seymour Carlisle's business the year before was a little over £317,000.

Driving south, rising into the Downs, he was soon in stud

country, with long rolling hills, richly grassed and neatly fenced. Few houses, and the villages mainly hamlets, without post offices or shops. He drove in the dark through the soft carving of the mild escarpment, small stands of second growth woods interspersed amidst the prevailing sweep of the grass slopes, pocked white in their thinner rooted parts by the underlying chalk of the Downs. Past Uffington, then climbing high into a small pocket of the Downs towards the land of Kate's family's estate.

Not a holding; not a farm; not even a *large* farm, as it would have been in Northern California. Here it was an estate.

He stopped two villages short at a pub, since he didn't want supper with the family – there would be meals enough with them this weekend. It was called the Fisherman's Arms, though there were no rivers nearby and no fishermen, but the walls were dotted with photographs of famous trout streams and framed mounts holding ancient fly patterns. In their very early days, he and Kate would come here like furtive lovers, happy to find a hideaway of their own so close to Belfield.

It had one large public room, and a small snug where the local farm workers sat, monopolising the fire. There was no garden to speak of, though outside the front door the tiny village green began, and Renoir managed to persuade the landlady Annie to serve them supper in an alcove under the overhanging roof of the pub's one bedroom, so that from May to October he and Kate ate outside, under the shade of a large horse chestnut tree, next to the green. The food was simple but fresh and good. Local, without the faddism that touted pig hearts as Britain's chief culinary virtue.

This evening he stood at the bar and ate a large ham sandwich on rough stone bread with mustard and a handful of cherry tomatoes for salad, and drank two pints of best bitter. It was only as he was ready to go that Annie came over to him from behind the bar. 'So where's Kate then?'

'She's away on a business trip.'

'So you're down to keep the rest of them in order?'

He laughed. Annie was always cheerfully impertinent, unlike

many of the other locals who simulated an old-fashioned defer-
ence to the local land-owning families. He said, 'You think they'd
listen to the likes of me?'

Annie shrugged. 'You Yanks rule the rest of the world, don't
you? Why not here? Though I'm not sure her brother will listen
to anyone.' She leaned forward on the bar. 'He's been in once or
twice lately.'

'What, here?' Renoir was surprised and displeased. He thought
of the pub as private property, and Roddy's arrival somehow
spoiled it a little for him.

'He says he likes the food,' said Annie, drying a glass with a
tea towel and holding it up for inspection against the light. 'Though
it seems to me it's more a liquid lunch he likes to have.'

'Was he on his own?'

'Once on his own; once with another man. Big bloke with a
moustache.' She looked at Renoir. 'I wouldn't have mentioned it,
only both times he was driving. I saw him as he left. He wants
to be careful or he'll get done.' And after this unprecedented chat-
tiness, Annie moved on along the bar.

He drove carefully in the dark, conscious after Annie's words of
what he had drunk, for the five miles through fields of wheat and
several gallops (this was racing country) until he came to the front
gate. He remembered the trepidation of his first visit with Kate –
Why didn't she tell me? he'd thought as they'd turned into the
grand sweep of the drive. You couldn't have much to do with
Silicon Valley without encountering some very wealthy people, but
he had not slept with any of them, or moved six thousand miles
to be with them.

He went down the avenue of limes, with light forest – second
or even third growth – set off on either side, until he emerged
from woodland to find the house set on its own, fronted by a
circular turnaround of bone-white gravel at the end of the drive.
It was such a lovely house, and on first seeing it he'd said so.

Kate said, 'I wasn't sure you'd like it, but I'm glad you do. It's
a bit of a small jewel, I think.'

Small? he thought. Later he learned there were ten bedrooms. 'How old is it?'

'It's Queen Anne,' she'd said

'What's Queen Anne?' he'd asked and she looked so startled that he laughed. 'Why should I know about Queen Anne? Can you tell me within fifty years when Thomas Jefferson died?'

'1670.'

'I win,' he said, though he had admired the confidence of her immediate reply.

As he got out of his car tonight the security lights went on and their false luminescence gave the bricks of the Queen Anne walls an orange and garish hue; the effect was slightly surreal, like that of being on a film set designed to mimic nightfall. He crunched on the gravel around to the back, where a light was on in the kitchen.

Inside he found Kate's mother, Beatrice, waiting for the kettle on the Aga. *You mean it's on all the time?* he'd asked incredulously when Kate first explained this fundament of the country house kitchen.

Beatrice wore a faded silk dressing gown and looked ready for bed. She remained beautiful in her seventies, though why beauty was meant to be the province of youth alone always mystified Renoir. Her manner towards everyone was graceful, but also simple and direct. Renoir admired this, though he was slightly wary of her. *She likes Americans*, Kate told him, which was oddly unreassuring, since it was said in the same tone as *She's very fond of dogs*. He never found her very warm or easy, though neither did her children, except Roddy, whom she doted on. She and her son shared a preoccupation with the place – Belfield – which Jack found unhealthy, even though sometimes it seemed Kate shared it too.

'Jack,' she said now, 'you made it at last. Can I get you something to eat? Mrs Hills has gone but I'm sure I can find something.'

'I've eaten, thanks,' he said.

'You'll stay for Sunday lunch, won't you? I don't think we'll get much chance for a chat tomorrow, do you?'

'No. Are there many staying?'

'Enough,' she said with a hint of tiredness. 'Somehow when you get to my age the last thing you feel like on Saturday night after a long day's shooting is having people stay the night.' She suddenly looked embarrassed. 'I am *not* including you in that remark.'

When he left the kitchen, he paused in the hall, staring at one of the ancestor's drawings – a pen and ink sketch of the Vale of the White Horse – while he decided whether to go upstairs with his bag or join the others for a drink.

You have to remember, Kate had explained, *they were all taught to draw back then. And play the piano. And know the names of plants and birds. That's what their education consisted of.* She'd said this without respect, but it seemed admirable to Renoir, who couldn't draw a lick; even his uncle, who had liked drawing – simple pen and ink sketches of wild flowers and trees – wasn't in the same league as these genteel amateurs of the past.

He decided he wanted a drink after all, and he opened the drawing-room door, hoping the rest were still at the dining-room table.

'Renoir!' It was Kate's sister, Sarah, sounding pleased. She was sitting on the sofa next to her husband, Alastair, wearing a linen dress the colour of cranberries and a choker of pearls. In her hand she held a weak whisky and water – her husband's looked much stronger.

'Hello,' said Renoir, smiling, since this was the part of Kate's family he liked. 'I thought I'd cadge a nightcap if I could. Can I give either of you a refill?' They both shook their heads, and he noticed that Alastair was still wearing a suit from work – he would have come down in a rush from the City, picking up Sarah from their house in Holland Park.

'There's probably ice in the kitchen if you want some.' Sarah was younger than Kate but looked and acted older. A brunette, she had her hair tied back, framing her high cheekbones and the small sharp nose she had inherited, along with her height, from her father, who, from the photographs Renoir had seen, had been a big man with a small face.

'That's all right.' He walked over to the corner, where an array of bottles stood on top of a Pembroke table. On the wall above it hung a Seago landscape Renoir liked – it was of a church in Italy, the building itself receding behind dark trees that verged on the abstract. He found the whisky in a decanter, and poured two inches into a large tumbler, then added water from the Toby jug. He didn't mind it without ice, had got used to it in fact; it was iceless gin and tonic he found unbearable.

'Are you shooting tomorrow?' Sarah asked.

Renoir shook his head. 'I've only come down to check the Gatehouse,' he explained. He took his drink and was about to join them when the door to the dining room opened and Roddy came in.

He was a small man, dapper, and good-looking in a boyish kind of way – like the Duke of Windsor, according to Kate, who had added spikily, 'and with the same strength of character'. He had gone to school at Harrow, which he enjoyed, and university at Oxford, which he had not. He had the slightly bogus affability of the 'well bred', though not when he drank, which meant Annie's warning in the pub now put Renoir on his guard.

He was also unemployed, having lost his City job two years before, though he seemed little inconvenienced by the absence of a pay cheque: there were always deals in the offing, the 'offing' proving their recurring characteristic. Most recently, he had become involved in various start-ups in Latvia, which he talked about in a fashion which Kate caustically said aped that of his colonial pre-decessors a century before – with a mixture of awe, racialist distaste and capitalist evangelism. Unlike Cecil Rhodes, however, none of Roddy's faraway ships had come in, though he had managed to hang onto his small flat in Belgravia, despite his divorce from a French wife, who had taken most of his redundancy money and their young son back with her to live in the Languedoc. Rarely visiting there, Roddy could be found most weekends at Belfield, where his chief recreational pursuit, shooting, took place.

Unlike Alastair, Roddy had changed, and was dressed for the country: a tweed jacket, Viyella shirt and red wool tie, corduroy trousers and brown brogues. He nodded at Renoir, who nodded back with his own false look of amity, which Kate had once described as 'your American *"hi pal how's it going?"* kind of look.' Bland and seemingly unruffleable, it could annoy people who were already disposed to find Americans fatuously easygoing. Renoir saw no point trying to disabuse them.

Roddy peered sourly at him, and walked over and sat down exactly where Renoir had planned to sit. 'Excuse us if you will, Jack,' said Roddy with the tone he used when talking to Mrs Hills, the cook. The words, though perfectly polite if tran-scribed, were delivered with an air of benign indulgence, as if allowances were being made for the fact that the listener was a fool. Roddy was clearly tight, for it was then he adopted an exaggerated air of precision. 'But we need to talk about some family business.'

'Roddy,' said Sarah sharply, who had little patience with her brother's high gentleman mode. Renoir felt himself begin to blush, the inevitable accompaniment to anger he knew he shouldn't display. He tried to look friendlier still. 'It's fine,' he said in Sarah's direction, 'I'm tired anyway.' He lifted up the glass. 'I'll take this upstairs and see you in the morning.'

As he went out into the hall, he heard Roddy's voice, saying something about apple juice, then laughing at his own wit. Sarah said, 'Oh do stop it, won't you?'

At the top of the main staircase he turned left, away from the main body of the house where the others would be sleeping. Even as a girl Kate had preferred the distance of the wing, and as he walked down the darkened corridor he reflected on the mix of dependence and independence she showed towards her family. Not for the first time, he wished he had met her father, Thomas Palmer, who had brought to his own marital union money made in manu-facturing industries when there was money still to be made there. And with it he had managed to save this estate of his wife's family from forced sale.

Not, it turned out, that Thomas had been self-made. If super-ficially Lady Palmer supplied the class and her husband the cash, it was in fact his grandfather – Kate's great-grandfather – who in Kate's words had made 'iron widgets, or whatever Victorian manufacturing fortunes came from. The ones made here, I mean – the export ones always seemed based on guano. But the point is, my father was two generations removed from the grosser aspects of new money. Yet Roddy always talks about Papa as if he were a miner's son.' This was true; listening to Roddy, Thomas had been an insignificant figure, a peripheral blip who'd had his uses, but not ones requiring acknowledgement.

Kate had said, 'I suppose that in one sense he was an *arriviste* in a way my mother never could be.'

'So regardless of what he did for your mother's family, he was less classy.'

'"Less grand" is a better way of putting it. And only in the subtlest kind of way.'

Renoir nodded. 'Not behaviour then, right?'

'Behaviour?' She looked at him with a fond incomprehension.

'I mean, there was nothing different in the way they acted that would show the difference.'

'Good God no,' said Kate. 'My father had beautiful manners.'

This was not something that would ever be said of Renoir, however politely he conducted himself. 'Well,' he said, starting to see the conversation as a slightly unreal tutorial, 'how could you tell the difference between the old bluebloods and the upstarts? I mean, if there was no difference in behaviour, how could a stranger tell?'

'It's difficult,' she said, and Renoir resisted the temptation to say, *You bet it is*. It was bad enough trying to learn the basic mores of the English, adapt to a country which, though superficially familiar, was deeply different from his own. But to be faced with even finer distinctions – the intricate byways of the thinnest upper slice of the English class system – made the task incalculably harder. It meant a second code had to be deciphered, and though he never had the slightest inclination to join in the traffic, like any cryptanalyst he wanted to understand it.

'As well as being ridiculous,' Kate added. 'It's little, subtle things. And nothing to do with money – that's the key point. It's to do with taste.'

'Really?' Renoir asked sceptically.

Kate shrugged. 'Taste becomes a euphemism for anything which lets people think they're superior. For instance, they'd always rather live in a grand old property they can't afford to maintain than some place *un*grand, even if the latter gave them far more money to live on. They'd rather serve four pound plonk in a Regency decanter than twenty pound Bordeaux poured into nouveau goblets. Take pictures – my father's family bought pictures. But they wouldn't have all those sketches and water-colours done by Mummy's lady ancestors in the nineteenth century. *San Gimignano in Sunlight – 1847* by my great-great-grandmother. That sort of thing. And books – the Palmers would have bought the best library money and aspirations could find, but none of those ancestors *wrote* any. They were too busy making money.'

In the corridor he stopped at the bookcase outside the bedroom to look for something to read among the faded spines of its shelves. Most of the books belonged to Beatrice or came from her family. Reading books, Beatrice called them; *As opposed to what?* Renoir wondered as he passed his eyes over the dusty sets of Kipling and Stevenson. Most meant nothing to him: he had vaguely heard of *The Green Hat*, but not Sassoon's *The Weald of Youth* or Diana Holman Hunt's *My Grandmothers and I* or *Good Behaviour* by Harold Nicolson. He picked up the latter, chose a page at random, and read the following:

> *Froissart has left a not unattractive picture of the house-hold life, or 'Menie' of Gaston de Foix with whom he lived for three months and whom he much admired in that 'he loved that which ought to be loved and hated that which ought to be hated'.*

That was enough for Renoir, who put the book back on the shelf, then opened the door to Kate's bedroom and turned on the light. It remained a young girl's room, for Kate was completely unselfconscious about its decoration – the white wallpaper dotted with pink roses, the schoolgirl watercolours from vacations in Scotland (the Tay above Pitlochry, Blair Atholl out of proportion), ribbons and badges pinned up from horse shows, two mounted photographs of her school hockey team.

He always liked this room, felt a simultaneous comfort and curiosity from the evidence around him of Kate's past. What had she been like as a girl? Frisky, strong-willed, an outdoors girl one notch too pretty to convince as a tomboy, a Daddy's girl, someone sometimes completely English.

Emptying his trouser pockets of keys and change, Renoir put them down on Kate's dressing table and looked at the small collection of books on the windowsill: *The Wind in the Willows*, *A Child's Treasury of Verse*, *To Kill a Mockingbird*, *Gardens of Provence*, and a blend of other bedside children's reading, assigned O-level texts and adult reference. He sat on the four-poster bed, leaving the curtains half open since at this dark time of year it would only be light well after he was up. He had slept here alone before, since Kate was so often away on business, but for the first time he felt ill at ease in the room, as if perhaps the books and pictures and *bibelots* around him belonged to someone he didn't know as well as he imagined.

He double checked his mobile phone, but Kate hadn't called, and he placed it on the rickety fruitwood bedside table, leaving it on in hope. She had warned him that she would have a late dinner with the chairman of one of the local subsidiaries, and his circle of assistants and cronies. The world of petrochemicals was male, old-fashioned, not unlike the computer hardware business, and Kate was an oddity as a woman in it. She was odder still for being young and attractive, but by now her opinions mattered to that world more than her looks. The scandal of Shell Oil might never have broken if the general press had not picked up the story from the Carlisle newsletter, where Kate first voiced suspicions about the corporate behemoth's declared reserves.

He got into bed, unrolling the folded tartan blanket against the cold, since the central heating went off early at Belfield; indeed, when Beatrice was alone in the house it rarely even went on. She was almost comically frugal, always saving used wrapping paper for reuse at the next Christmas, soaking unfranked stamps off letters to put on her own correspondence. And a fanatic for retaining leftover food.

Renoir lay back and tried to relax and let his mind wander into sleep. Instead, he found himself wondering at the strangeness of the day: the weird unpleasant postcard, the rejected cash card, Roddy's unconcealed hostility. They were discomfiting rather than alarming, and none of them would have mattered at all if Kate had been there. He conjured up the image of Kate – she was in the flat alternately talking and laughing, and then she smiled. But with a start that brought him back to full wakefulness, he recognised the constricted, artificial smile of the week before. The smile that told him she was lying.

He tried to ignore the image, but it was slow to leave his head. He wished Kate had telephoned – he was sure it would have reassured him, even the lie about her conference call would not have mattered once he heard her voice. But then for the first time since leaving California he allowed himself to wonder just what she saw in him, and to wonder if, whatever it was, there wouldn't come a day when she didn't see it any more.

Apples just don't pay. His uncle Will had said more than once.

Renoir skipped breakfast and had a quick coffee in the kitchen before the visiting guns arrived for the shoot. On his way out he saw the beaters gathering around Hal, the keeper, by the stables, where soon Roddy and his guests would meet for the ritual invocation of the minimal rules – no shooting ground game (i.e. foxes), no shooting after the horn had sounded at the end of each drive – before driving off in assorted Land Rovers and four-wheel drive vehicles to the winter wheat fields on the northeast corner of the estate where the shoot's first drive traditionally took place.

Part of him wished he were shooting too, even if Roddy was

among the guns. Kate loathed it, which was curious considering her attachment to Belfield, where shooting was such a major part of life. There was no swimming pool at Belfield, and the tennis court built by Kate's father had long ago crumbled (wild roses sprouted where one service line had been). No fish worth catching lurked in the lake, and none of the local hunts made foray into the Belfield acreage. But Kate was scathing in her aversion: 'What is the point?' she would say. 'It contributes nothing to the countryside and it's completely artificial. When the birds are too cheap it's not even worth selling them. In Norfolk one year they were burying them. Why can't they just shoot clay pigeons and be done with it?'

Renoir himself had been taught to shoot by his uncle, with clay pigeons thrown with a hand spring. The farm was not game-rich, and when out for birds, his uncle usually only fired his gun once or twice in an afternoon; the bag limit was a brace in any case. Renoir was therefore staggered when he first saw the Belfield game wagon, loaded with three hundred birds, and watched a guest switch guns because his barrels had grown too hot from firing so many shells. The conventions of an English shoot (plus-twos, those heavy green coats, sloe gin after the second drive) seemed a palaver to Renoir, as he supposed they would have to most Englishmen. But he soon grew to understand that to the extraordinarily small slice of English society who did shoot, it was a way of life.

When first asked, reluctantly by Roddy, he had not imagined the shooting itself would be especially difficult – after all, were not the birds virtually driven onto the point of your gun? But he had been wrong – it was very difficult, for the birds moved at fantastic speed, diving and swooping in the wind, often flying impossibly high.

Now Renoir walked down through the formal gardens behind the house, then around the west side of the lake and up the track – wide enough to take the farm tractor to the Old Orchard and Burdick's Field – that climbed through the firs and Corsican pines of Treefall Down. There were pockets of snowdrops in these woods, and yellow aconites and early primroses. These and the imminent crocuses seemed to deny the winter he had expected in England. The climate was surprisingly mild, much like San Francisco, and on the one occasion it snowed the winter before, it was gone by nightfall.

He walked through the Old Orchard, part of the fifty acres Kate was acquiring. Thirty of them surrounded the gatehouse they were renovating and extending, including the large garden they had planned around it, the sweeping chunk of hillside that ran below it called Burdick's Field, the site planned for his eight thousand trees. The remainder was mainly woods, situated on this flat plateau, a hardwood mix of beech, oak and ash, though in its centre, effectively hidden and a surprise to anyone coming upon it unawares, were two acres, shaped in a long rectangle, of old untended apple trees he was now trying his best to revive. It was a labour of love.

He entered the woods on the far end of the Old Orchard, thinking of how the legal process of extricating their holding from the larger estate was almost mindlessly involved. He stayed aloof from it, since he both gauged it none of his business and knew he would find its complications exasperating. *Trust me,* Kate had said, as he began to plan his tree orders. *Of course I trust you,* he'd answered. *I meant trust him,* she elaborated, meaning her brother. In the resulting silence lay his unspoken refusal.

As he emerged, the Gatehouse was before him. It sat on the crest of the hill just clear of the woods; beneath it ran the gentle slope of Burdick's Field. He had initially resisted their move into the Gatehouse and its expensive renovation; it would cost over £200,000 when all was said and done. It was not that he wanted to remain in the Hall, but that he would have preferred a place of their own, outside Berkshire, away from Kate's mother and brother. But Kate was adamant, arguing that the land and house were ideal for them, that they could never afford such a large house with such a beautiful setting anywhere else. Behind these arguments lay a visceral attachment to Belfield; sometimes it seemed as if she thought that without the estate the family would fall apart, which made Renoir wonder just what – considering Kate's ambivalence towards her mother, the problems of Roddy – Kate thought was being preserved. Only with her sister did she enjoy unequivocal closeness, and Sarah and Alastair had their own place and their own distance from Belfield. But then perhaps it was not the family which lay behind Kate's insistence that he and she live there, but some idea of the estate itself as inviolable. If it were whole, the implication seemed, Kate would be whole too.

He entered the Gatehouse by the back door, where the ground floor had been extended to hold what Kate called a tack room, though she didn't ride any longer, and a small spare bedroom room for visitors. Behind these was a large kitchen, with windows facing down the hill. He was pleased to see the large refectory table had arrived and the hardwood cabinets they had bought in Wantage were now installed. The large gas cooker sat against the wall; Kate had been happy to share his doubts about an Aga. They had kept the old larder, which was a thin, long window-less room with the solid walls of the original building; its thick oak door locked from the kitchen side with an enormous iron key. Kate had pointed out light-heartedly that it could double as a jail cell if he misbehaved.

He walked down a corridor and opened another door, stepping into the entrance hall, where a new oak staircase led to the rooms upstairs – three good-sized bedrooms and a study for Kate. Crossing this hall he went into the sitting room, the largest room of the house, over thirty feet long and almost as deep, created by taking down an interior wall that had sat between two rooms before. At the far end a door led to a small office intended for him, which also had windows facing the field in front. Panes had not been puttied into the sitting-room windows yet, and the late January wind made the room especially cold, so as he walked into his study he closed the door behind him and turned on a small space heater next to the desk.

He sat down in a director's chair with a frayed canvas back, looking at a pad of paper and a pen – all the instruments he needed to feed his dream. He looked out the window, down the hill at the field where his fantasy would be played out. There was something unnerving about this view of his future source of livelihood, though Kate had plans for a small meadow to front the house. She had already strewn the ground, dug up by the contractors, with wildflower seeds, and they should see the first results that spring.

He worked for most of the morning, trying to put the projections of his ambitions on paper. He forecast earn-out in five years, with positive cash flow in three; ten years down and . . . *I'll be rich*, he thought, and laughed at his self-delusion. He was determined to make it work, yet he was pursuing a small, individual and counterintuitive route. Not the intensive farming of post-1990s Britain, which saw yields of ten to fifteen tons of fruit an acre from two thousand ballerina trees planted per acre, none more than a yard apart. The orchard as assembly line.

He would instead take the dramatic step of farming entirely organically, with fewer trees spaced far more expansively, so that at most he'd have four hundred on each acre. He planned a mix of standard and half-standard trees using M9 rootstock, spacing them ten feet apart both sideways and up and down the hill, which meant he could run the tractor with its three three-foot cutting blades, leaving just a little circle of grass around the tree to stop evaporation from the soil.

He had hesitated before opting to go organic, deterred by a vision of sandals and vegetarians, bad folk music and hash brownies, roll-up cigarettes and too much cinnamon in apple pies – just the sort of things he *didn't* miss about San Francisco. But the independence and the premium on offer overcame these prejudices, which he could not seriously defend, even to himself. There was growing demand for any organic produce, the price paid was more than double what he would receive for pesticide-sprayed crops, and he would not be in thrall to the supermarkets.

Of course his prospects were improved by having the land

already: he would have been looking at paying almost £4000 an acre for organic land, at least half that for conventional. And he was blessed too by the fact that his fortunes would be based, quite literally, on 'green sand', the geologists' label for the richest of soils, named for its green components, which were sometimes so plentiful as to give a green hue to the black earth. Green sand came in belts, long thin bands crossing England, the longest running all the way from the Wash to Southampton, and on its way running through a large portion of Belfield.

There was a noise next door and he sat still, listening. Burglars? He dismissed the thought; there wasn't really anything to steal. Though burglary did seem to be the national disease. Belfield couldn't be left unoccupied, for example, when Beatrice went on holiday, and he supposed he and Kate would need an alarm here when they finally moved in. Kate, whose view of crime in the United States derived entirely from cop shows on TV, didn't believe him when he explained how uncommon burglary was in rural America, and indeed how even in the Irish neighborhood where he grew up burglars didn't try it on – too many off-duty cops living there, too many households with guns.

The noise from next door continued, and he got up more out of curiosity than trepidation and opened the door. A man was standing on a wooden chair in the middle of the room, screwing a light bulb into one of the holes made for the recessed spotlights Kate wanted installed across the ceiling of the room. 'Need some help?' asked Renoir in a low voice that seemed to come out of nowhere in the vast blank space of the room. The other man was so startled that he swayed on the top of the step ladder, brought both hands down from inside the hole, and fell off. He managed to put a foot out to soften his landing, but then crumpled on the floor.

Renoir advanced on him, then relaxed. 'Stacey,' he said. 'What are you doing here?'

The man sat up and then slowly got to his feet. 'You scared me, Mr Renoir,' he said. Stacey was very young – not much more than twenty – but built like an Afrikaans farmer. Pleasant but slightly incompetent, he was a handyman on the estate and general assistant to Hal, the head keeper. 'I didn't think anybody was here. I just wanted to finish the lighting here.'

'Where is everybody?'

'Well, Hal's got the shoot today.'

'I know that. But the others?'

Stacey shrugged. 'You better ask Hal. I know some of them are beating – two of the regulars couldn't make it and he persuaded a couple of these blokes to help him out.'

Renoir cursed silently. The schedule was already tight enough without Hal poaching workmen to help out with Roddy's shoot.

Stacey came off his ladder and wiped his hands on his jeans. 'It's awfully busy now that Mr Palmer's renting out the shooting.'

'I didn't know he was.'

'It's only a few days. But it's got to be right.'

It certainly did. At a charge of £25 per bird downed, you could not afford a dud day. You would need to guarantee two hundred birds as well, though the keeper kept a tally of shots fired with a clicker, so if the paying guests were hopeless there would be no refunds. Two hundred was comparatively small, compared to other paying shoots in the county, but the birds here were high and the scenery exquisite.

'I'm sure Hal can manage it just fine,' said Renoir dryly. 'I only hope you all stay busy over here, too.'

Stacey nodded, and Renoir realised there was no point complaining to him. He was too junior, and probably scared of Hal, who was famously bad tempered – he had once knocked down a beater who questioned his orders.

'It's okay,' said Stacey and changed the subject. 'You know Burdick's has been sold?'

'I heard.' Burdick had two sons, one into drugs and the other simply feckless, so after the old man's death a sale of the farm had been inevitable. Renoir missed the old man; Burdick had encouraged his own fruit-growing aspirations, and helped him turn a fantasy into a plan. He asked, 'Who's bought it?'

Stacey shook his head. 'Someone from London. Lots of money.

They've started fixing the house in a big way – Hal says they'll spend more renovating than if they tore it down and started again.'

City bonus money, probably – an extra million one year, though it would have taken more like two to buy Burdick's, rundown house and all. He said as much to Stacey, who replied with a laugh, 'Or else he's got a rich wife.'

Suddenly, Stacey blushed – it looked like he'd spilled plum juice all over his face. *Poor Stacey*, Renoir thought, not even slightly annoyed. He didn't look at the younger man, to spare him further embarrassment.

At lunch-time he left the house, noting that Stacey had managed not to finish installing the recessed lights, and walked back to Belfield. In the stable yard the beaters were gathered around a fire in a disused oil drum, eating sandwiches and drinking squash from plastic bottles. Renoir didn't want to join the shooting lunch in the house so drove to the pub again, where he ate fishcakes with caper mayonnaise and a side bowl of rocket salad with lemon dressing. He politely ignored Annie's suggestion that he try some local wine and drank a large glass of French Sauvignon instead. Resisting the temptation to drink another he had a large espresso and drove directly back to the Gatehouse, coming up through Burdick's Field below it. It had a year before been in terrible shape, clumpy and filled with ragwort that had taken him days to remove through a mixture of spraying and backbreaking pulling out by hand. He had hired a JCB for five days and a man to run it for one; by the end of the first day he had learned enough to use it himself, and by the end of day five his swept mounds were almost as smooth as the hired man's. He had 'demogulised' the field as best he could, so although the trees would be planted on the moderate downhill slant of the field he could cut the grass around them easily with a tractor and an attached six foot cutting blade, which was not for decorative purposes but so the trees didn't have to share water and nutrients with the competitive rough rye cut.

And most important he had dug the vast sloping hole that had filled up from the descent of water from the natural spring – two springs really – which came up next to the small stand of hardwood he had just walked through between the Old Orchard and the Gatehouse. And from the pond he would be able to water the entire orchard. Most organic farmers would not water, seeing it as needless waste of aquifers, but since he had carved out the pond, fed by two natural springs, he had no compunction about using water that would otherwise simply drain away. Recently, through assiduous reading, he had discovered T-Tape, an Israeli invention designed for watering in the Negev Desert, in which every metre of plastic pipe contained a tiny valve that dripped water in a slow and constant economical way. He would try that out in the Old Orchard if the coming summer proved dry.

Inside, he worked some more, chiefly trying to calculate (or predict really) likely yields to see what kind of cold storage he would need to lease in the coming years, and watched the rugby on television with the desultory eye of an only semi-interested foreigner. He was thinking of stopping before dark when he heard a car behind the house. When he went to the back door he found Alastair in the tack room, dressed for the shoot in standard green wool jacket and plus-twos, holding a shotgun broken over one forearm. 'Hello, Jack,' he said with a grin. 'We're about to have the final drive. I thought I'd alert you. Better still, I thought you might like to join us. Abeling had to leave early – he hates driving after dark.'

'Thanks, Alastair, but I haven't got a gun.' Renoir gestured at his clothes, old khakis and a flannel hunter's shirt, and said, 'I'm not exactly dressed right either.'

'Doesn't matter,' said Alastair. 'What's the point of a family shoot if you have to stand on ceremony? Come on, I've got a gun in the car.'

'Roddy will have a fit. Best leave it.'

'Bollocks,' said Alastair sharply. 'Roddy won't say a bloody word. Not if he knows what's good for him.'

And so against his better judgement Renoir closed up the Gatehouse and joined him. As they drove the few hundred yards down the hill to the pegs spaced neatly in a line a stone's throw in from the road, Renoir remembered what Kate had said about the financial underpinnings of the shoot: 'The shoot is half Alastair's, actually. He pays half the costs, but he lets Roddy pretend it's all his. That's the way Alastair is. Unfortunately, that's the way my brother is as well.'

They parked by two other four-wheel drive vehicles, and when they got out Renoir saw that the other guns were already on their pegs between the last half-acre of field, where he'd staked wire lines for the raspberry canes, and the hedge just inside the road. He recognised several of them, unsurprising since in looking through the game books of Belfield he had seen how year in and year out the same people were guests. One man he noticed particularly looked only vaguely familiar. Like the others he wore the standard issue shooting coat, but with the dandyish addition of a fur ruff of silver fox around the neck.

The light was beginning to go, but in the distance Renoir saw Roddy pointing to their left, and he followed Alastair to the west edge of the field where it was adjoined by a scraggly plantation of scrub oak, young ash and gorse. Alastair took the last peg in the field by the alder wind break and directed Renoir into this mix. The beaters would come from over the hill, driving the pheasants from the Old Orchard down past the Gatehouse. Those that swerved wide of the new plantings would come over Renoir's head.

He waited, uninsulated in his Barbour. Gloveless, he blew on his hands and stamped his feet and tried not to think about the nerves he always felt whenever he took part in a shoot. He remembered something old Burdick had said when Renoir asked him if he liked shooting. *I like it on my own land. Everywhere else I'm too worried about making a fool of myself to enjoy it.*

In the lowering sun the temperature had dropped and already he could feel the ground had hardened, crust-like. Alastair wandered over within talking distance. 'How's the Gatehouse?'

114

'They're behind, goddammit. Too busy helping Hal over here. By the way, who else is shooting?'

Alastair gave some names, some of them known to Renoir, and explained that one of them was a young colleague down from London. 'You'll meet him at dinner; his wife's here as well. Oh, and Conrad Benedict.' He paused, and his voice assumed the slightest tinge of anxiety. 'Have you met him before?'

'No,' he said, falsely easy. 'Wasn't he an old boyfriend of Kate's?'

'Years ago,' said Alastair emphatically. 'He's chummy with Roddy. Actually, he used to be a client of mine.' His voice rose a little. 'Here they come, I think,' and he walked back towards his peg.

Renoir stamped his feet again to keep warm and waited, hearing the whistling and clucking of the beaters, and the clackety-clack of their sticks as they beat the brush and trees at the crest of the rise along from the Gatehouse. *Conrad Benedict.* Not American – not in the slightest – but with the East Coast kind of name where either could be surname. *Ogden Forbes; Oakley Honeywell.* That kind of name, though at least the English eschewed the preposterous numerals after the name – *William McKinley Nobody IV.*

Fifteen years passage of time and her ill-fated marriage meant Renoir could hardly feel jealous about any of her former *beaux*, most of whom were the subject of funny accounts by Kate. Such as 'Flip', the aspiring politician (he had never won a seat) with whom the young pugnacious Kate had constantly argued – thrown out of their cheap Venice hotel one night for rowing too loudly they had gone to a hostel in Giudecca, only to be thrown out for the second night running when their tempers flared again. Or Karl, the Czech political philosopher she had brought home to a sceptical family when, aged twenty, Kate had declared Englishmen too boring. He had been labelled 'Mars' by Kate's little sister Sarah because of a Bohemian abstractedness, most clearly revealed one Sunday morning when, leaving Kate's bedroom for his own, he had wandered instead, half-naked, into the boudoir of the senior Palmers.

But there had been no funny stories about Benedict, and Renoir had only first heard his name mentioned by Roddy. 'I learned about another of your old suitors,' he said to Kate as they had gone to bed that night.

'Which one?' she'd said with a light laugh. 'I had so many.'

'Conrad Benedict,' he said.

'*Oh*,' she said, with a sudden exhalation, as if he had hit her in the solar plexus.

He looked at her. 'You're blushing,' he declared teasingly. 'Your cheeks are the colour of Gravenstein apples.'

She gave a manic double shake of her head, and grimaced as if she had bitten into a lemon by mistake. He laughed. 'Was he "the one who got away"?'

She made a deprecatory cluck with her tongue, but she wasn't looking at him, and the flush stayed full in her face. 'Some other time,' she said, forcing a smile. 'Don't tell me you haven't got a few floozies up your sleeve you don't like to talk about.'

And he had been distracted then by the slight shame he could manage to feel about escapades in his own life – Dilys the drunk dancer who'd stolen all his Jim Harrison novels, and mad Susie Rendall, who'd almost got his brains beat out in a Tenderloin bar. So he had forgotten all about Conrad Benedict and the response his name had provoked in Kate. Until now, when quite by chance he found himself in the man's company.

Suddenly in the fading light a cock pheasant sounded his guttural chukka-chuk and beat his wings with a noise like sheets being flapped out to dry and undulating once, then twice, swooped down the hill, seeming to gather speed as it straightened out its line of flight and then *bang* and the bird fell down just short of the road, where a solitary woman in a knee-length green Barbour and a headscarf stood with a black Labrador which had all of six steps to take to pick up the dead bird.

Renoir's eyes shifted back up the orchard and three more birds were crossing diagonally, and he waited impatiently, and two of them cut back towards the middle of the line and he heard one bang then two, no three more, but the third bird continued and cut right across the line of Alastair's gun next to him, which went *bang bang* in rapid succession, but the bird kept flying and Renoir fired before even realising he had pulled the trigger. He was too far ahead and he fired again and then watched as the bird skewed suddenly, pitching awkwardly and then low until he heard it hit heavily somewhere behind him on the road on the other side of the hedge. 'Got him,' waved another woman there and Renoir turned back and two more birds came in almost exact duplication of the cross-field traversing of the earlier bird, and this time Alastair took the right one with his first shot and Renoir swung beautifully at the second bird, feeling altogether confident in his timing, and missed the bird completely.

He felt at once exhilarated and flustered now, eager for more birds to come his way. It was becoming very hard to see; the Gatehouse at the top of the hill now merged with the trees behind it to form an undetailed bulk of dark. One bird flew straight down the middle of the field, then veered in the direction away from Renoir, and when he heard the gun of the peg at the other end of the line he could not see if the bird had been hit or not. He looked behind at one point, and saw that the woman in the road was no longer there, so he would have to look for his own birds, an incentive to hit them plug.

Birds were coming in ones and twos, but well down the line to his right. One strayed after a central gun missed and headed his way, but Alastair despatched it with his second barrel just before Renoir fired. He felt the usual agitation towards the end of a drive, worried lest the horn signalling its end go off before he had another shot at a bird. He was warm now and found the Barbour stifling; he moved a few feet over and carefully leaned his gun against the trunk of an ash tree, took off his coat and hung it from a branch. He remained under the tree, waiting in the hope of a last bird. Several flew across the line further down, drawing volleys of shots, and then Alastair called, urgently, 'Bird left,' and Renoir swung his gun up, tense and expectant, straining to see the pheasant in what was the later stage of dusk. And then he

117

spied the bird, lifting suddenly from its low position well in front of Alastair – too far in front for him to fire, but moving very much Renoir's way – and Renoir started to swing as the bird ascended high above the slope behind it, up higher even than the Gatehouse perched distantly at the top of the rise, and he could see it clearly against the background of ash-coloured sky and slid the safety off with his thumb and his barrel rose and then the horn blew.

He relaxed the gun at once and without question, despite his disappointment. He was about to open the breech of his gun and extract its shells when another gun fired, very close behind him, and its noise seemed especially startling because it was so unexpected. Then he felt a sharp sting against his neck and a double tap against his back, and he realised he had been hit by someone else's shot. He put a hand up to his neck, and when he looked at it there was a smear of blood on his palm.

He almost dropped his gun; turning he saw no one between himself and the hedge in front of the road, some twenty-five yards away. Then he heard footsteps and realised someone was running on the road.

He went and got his coat, and walked over to join Alastair by his Land Rover. As he reached him Roddy detached himself from the group of gathering guns and stormed over, looking absolutely furious. 'Didn't you hear the horn?' he demanded.

Renoir nodded but didn't say anything. This seemed to infuriate Roddy even more. 'Never fire after the horn. Even you know that.'

Renoir started to explain that he hadn't fired, but Roddy interrupted, scoffing, 'Who else could it have been? You were the last peg.'

You tell me, he wanted to say, but it seemed pointless. Even Alastair would think he was fibbing. Then out of the growing darkness a figure loomed and joined them. It was Hal, a massive hulk of a man, with a black beard and wet ringlets of dark hair. He was holding a shotgun, broken, and handed it over to Roddy. 'Mr Abeling's other gun, sir. He left it in the Range Rover when we finished at Treefall Down. He was in a bit of a hurry and said he'd collect it from you tomorrow.'

'Thank you, Hal,' said Roddy, distractedly, but the interruption had served to stop the flow of his anger.

Alastair raised an eyebrow at Renoir, and asked quietly, 'Do you want a lift back up the hill?' Roddy stalked off to join the other guns.

'No, I'll be fine.' Alastair could go with the others on the road back to the Hall, where the game wagon would be unloaded by the stables, the visiting guns each given a brace, and Hal the keeper tipped. 'By the way, where was Hal during the drive?'

'Behind the beaters. He's always the last one down. Why?'

'No reason. Anyway, Let me give you some money for him.'

'Forget it,' said Alastair. 'Abeling gave me more than enough. Thirty quid. I'm tempted to keep ten of it for myself. Or give it to Roddy, miserable bugger. See you back at the Hall.'

He had a long soak in a hot bath, feeling shaken by the last drive. He could live with his 'disgrace' in Roddy's eyes, since he had done nothing wrong, but he was puzzled and a little alarmed by the fact he'd been hit, however glancing. Such accidents had been known to happen. Shooting in the woods, pellets fired far away would often come down through the leaves like rain sprinkling a tin roof. He was more mystified than frightened, though having worked since childhood to contain it, he found it strange to feel fear starting to curl around him again. And he especially disliked any sense of threat when its source was unknown to him.

At work there had been the odd bad moment, inevitable in a job that required him to poke around the darker side of people's private lives. He'd had his tyres slashed once, right outside the apartment on Lake Street. And there had been Makito, a Japanese-American employee whose five-yearly check threw up some financial oddities, explained by Renoir's discovery of the man's weekly visits to an expensive escort off Telegraph Hill. Makito's wife had shown up at the Cupertino reception and insisted on seeing Renoir. Because he'd emerged cautiously, his guard up, he

119

managed to avoid the thermos of boiling water she'd tried to throw in his face.

No one was doing anything so overt now. But it was the fact that there was 'no one' that troubled him – he would have suspected Hal at once, but he had been behind the beaters throughout. There had been a woman picking up when he'd first taken his position in the scrappy woods. What had happened to her? He shook his head and tried not to think about it.

He was slightly late coming down to dinner, but there was still time for a drink. Everyone had changed, though the women were better dressed than the men, for they wore dresses and jewellery, whereas none of the men except Alastair had bothered with neck-ties. There was a younger couple staying, he the junior colleague whom Alastair had mentioned, his wife young and nervous-looking; also a local couple who trained racehorses near West Ilsley; and the Benedicts, though Renoir wasn't sure which woman was Benedict's wife.

He made himself a weak Scotch and talked to Alastair and his young colleague. Then he had a second whisky, even weaker this time, and was beckoned by Beatrice to join her and Sarah and the colleague's wife by the fireplace. They were listening to Benedict, who was standing against the mantelpiece. He was dressed in a tweed jacket of chocolate brown with a blue silk handkerchief that flowed out of his jacket's breast pocket like an iris in bloom. The effect, as with his shooting jacket and its fur ruff, was cocky, almost floppish.

As Beatrice introduced him to Renoir, Benedict gave a cool, knowing nod. Renoir was quite unprepared for the handshake which followed, bone-crushing in its strength. Benedict was an inch or two taller than Renoir, and quite a bit wider, and was one of the few grown men Renoir had encountered who acted as if this made a difference.

'Don't let me interrupt,' said Renoir, as he withdrew his hand. Benedict was talking about his time as a soldier in Northern Ireland. While he spoke, Renoir inspected him carefully. He had

120

a heavy jaw and a small straight nose beneath cold grey eyes, with short hair which was greying at the temples. Renoir was only half listening as Benedict described a patrol he'd led in Belfast, how they had been harassed by a sniper, who then stopped to light a cigarette, which gave away his position with fatal consequences. Benedict joked, 'Saved by the Paddy factor again.' Renoir tried not to react.

'Did anyone like being posted to Northern Ireland?' asked the wife of Alastair's colleague. She looked to be in her late twenties, her youth emphasised by the contrastingly old-fashioned black velvet dress she wore, and a necklace that looked as if it must have come down from her grandmother.

Benedict chuckled. 'Some of the men did – it takes all sorts to make an army. Still, it keeps lads out of trouble who would other- wise get locked up back home. Didn't you find that?' he asked suddenly, turning towards Renoir.

'How do you mean?'

'You were in the army, weren't you?' Renoir nodded. 'Didn't you find your men included a few who anywhere else would have been dangerous?'

For a moment Renoir didn't understand this, and then it clicked. He said simply, 'I didn't have "men". I wasn't an officer.'

'Ah, I see,' said Benedict with a false politeness, although he looked as if Renoir had broken wind, a *faux pas* which he, Benedict, would be gentleman enough to ignore. The two men locked eyes, no love lost.

The wife of Alastair's colleague stirred with mild embarrass- ment, and Beatrice declared, rather than enquired, 'Why don't we go through to dinner?'

Renoir was more accustomed in his California existence to barbecues or picnics, or occasional assemblies of friends in restaur- ants. Occasionally a director would invite him to a gathering at home, but they were kept deliberately low key, since in the meri- tocratic world of Silicon Valley there were plenty of employees who, however gifted (some to the point of genius), didn't know a soup spoon from a butter knife. And Renoir's own entertaining had, in the days with Jenny, rarely extended beyond supper thrown together in his tiny kitchen for another couple after seeing a movie, or latterly, with Kate, to feeding Ticky large plates of pasta when she was looking unduly boyish and thin.

But over a year's experience of Belfield evenings had schooled him in most of the niceties, and he found he could glide along quietly enough without disgracing himself, watching the proceedings around him all the while. Kate had spotted this early on: 'Honestly, you survey people the way Mummy eyeballs paintings. You like watching best. You should just sit back and take it all in.'

Yet he could by now take part in the usual Belfield table conversation without much effort, affecting an interest in gun dog pedigrees, the myriad and, if closely inspected, contradictory effects of global warming, salmon fishing in Iceland, the name of the shop selling lavender bread in Hungerford and the presence of nightingales on the Kenmarty estate ten miles away. And when interest proved impossible to feign, it was never difficult to draw other people out, since England, like America, had plenty of inhabitants who liked nothing better than to talk about themselves.

Tonight in the dining room the extenders were out on the pale oak table, and the silver feather-edge forks were laid. The room was impressive – there were family portraits on the wall, in one corner stood a beautiful four-fold leather screen with tooled scenes of country life. But this was formality that didn't require staff, and food was put on the sideboard, not served.

The first course was already on the table, a cold game terrine with baskets of almost equally cold toast. Beatrice sat at one end, and directed him to a seat, where he found himself between an older, dark-complexioned woman (Mediterranean he thought – Turkish maybe) and Julie, the young wife of Alastair's colleague. On Julie's far side, at the end of the table, sat Roddy, presiding in what had always been his father's place.

Renoir sat down to find Roddy in full conversational flow with Julie, and Mrs Benedict was taken up by Alastair on the other side of her. So he sat in silence and ate his terrine, staring across at the two Roberts pictures of the Holy Land, one a water-colour, the other a – what was it Kate had said? Aquatint? Mezzotint? He didn't know the difference, but he loved its graceful lightly etched beauty, the innocence conveyed from a time when Petra saw only travellers and explorers – tourists had yet to be invented. But then the English were a nation of travellers and explorers, even now when there was nothing novel left to explore.

And how this vagabonding passion had persisted, with so many Englishmen still intent on 'exploration'. Not for them the mental journeys of Pascal which Ticky had once told him about, all conducted from an armchair. Since in exploring terms almost everything *had* been done, they were driven to the most outlandish acts: ballooning around the world with their shirt off, walking 120 miles a day on their hands, swimming across the Channel with one arm tied behind their back, crawling backwards on all fours to the North Pole.

What funny people, he thought, although the patronising view of the English as quaint folk, mild in their ways, utterly harmless, was receding fast for Renoir. He thought with a slight chill of the unpleasant postcard of the Golden Gate Bridge, and the pellets which had sprinkled his neck and Barbour. What was the line in *Goldfinger* about coincidence? Once is happenstance; twice is coincidence; three times is enemy action. He wasn't in action yet, but he wasn't popular with someone, that seemed clear.

Steady, he told himself, *do not go there*. For here in England – here with Kate – he had changed. And he did not want to revert. Time was, being paranoid was a necessary tool of his trade; it made him better prepared. But in a normal life – the life he'd made here in England with Kate – the tension was pointless; it made life unnecessarily exhausting. There were no real threats; enemies didn't lurk; precautions were utterly un-necessary. *Turn off the alarm bells.*

'Renoir, my boy, come and have some food,' a voice said gently, and he came out of this reverie to find Alastair smiling down at him and everyone getting up. He went and stood with the other men while the women served themselves from the sideboard, underneath the portrait of Wilberforce, of whom, as she was always happy to explain, Beatrice was a direct descendant. He helped himself to lamb cutlets with mint sauce and redcurrant jelly, peas, mashed potato, gravy. It wasn't terrible food at all, even if it reminded him of eating in the Presidio canteen during his army days.

As he sat down again, Roddy was still talking with Julie, who was saying with a certain strain to her voice, 'Surely we've got to choose one or the other. Either stand by Europe or stick with America. Nobody thinks we should go it alone.'

'I don't see why not. If that makes me unfashionably right wing then there we are.'

'But even Oswald Mosley was pro-Europe.'

'Ah, but that was fifty years ago. He saw the battle – rightly in my view – as against communism. The war was just a diversion. And in that kind of fight you have to have allies. Not America; if push came to shove they'd have sold us down the river.'

'Like they did in the war?' Renoir interjected mildly.

Roddy shrugged. 'If Pearl Harbor hadn't happened, Europe would be Nazi today.' He said Nazi with a long drawling 'z'. 'The Soviet Union would have fallen apart long before it actually did.' He turned back to the woman named Julie. 'But the point is, we don't need Europe any more as a bulwark. Russia's no threat. If any country is, it's the US of A, though it's our culture they want to destroy. So the argument is overwhelming for staying strictly on our own. Not part of Europe, and not attached like an imploring, dependent limpet on the fat rear of America.'

Julie seemed a little embarrassed by the vehemence of this. She said to Renoir, 'I take it you're American. What brings you over here?'

Roddy interrupted. 'Money!' he exclaimed, waving a hand over his wine glass. 'That's what brings him over here. It's like the Gold Rush in reverse.'

Renoir forced himself to grin, since failing to rise to the bait wouldn't please Roddy at all.

Sarah leaned across the table towards Julie; Renoir hadn't realised she was listening. 'Jack lives with my sister Kate. He's her partner.'

'Terrible word "partner",' said Roddy after a pause.

'You would prefer "husband"?' asked Renoir, and Roddy winced dramatically.

'So what do you do?' asked Julie. She was struggling to ignore Roddy now, though once started, Roddy didn't like to stop.

'I'm hoping to farm,' said Renoir.

'Crops?' she said, with a citified air, as if she were describing a wild animal.

'Fruit.'

'Don't look surprised,' Roddy piped up. 'He's from San Francisco, so he knows all about fruits.'

Sarah looked at Renoir from across the table and rolled her eyes in sympathy.

'What did you used to do?' asked Julie.

'I worked for a high-tech company in Silicon Valley.'

'I better leave it at that then,' she said with a self-deprecating laugh. 'It wouldn't mean a thing to me.'

'We all think he was a spy,' said Roddy. 'A master of industrial espionage.'

'How exciting,' said Julie, though her eyes betrayed this, since they were darting around nervously. 'So you live here then?'

'No, in London,' he said, not about to explain his imminent move to the Gatehouse and draw yet more fire from Roddy.

'Oh,' she said, obviously puzzled. But her face brightened at the chance to change subjects. 'So are you going to the Cézanne exhibition?'

But Roddy couldn't resist. 'Of course he is,' he almost shouted. 'He'll probably claim he's descended from him as well.'

When Julie looked baffled, Renoir explained. 'My surname's Renoir, one of Roddy's little jokes.'

'But are you French?' The poor woman was working hard.

'A little French Canadian on my father's side. But no relation to the painter. None at all.' Which was true as far as he knew, despite Kate's half-hopeful suggestion that there must be *some* link.

Roddy poured himself more claret. Renoir was intentionally drinking very little, sensing it would merely aggravate the irritation he was starting to feel, for with Roddy he felt handcuffed. The men he'd known all his life – at school, in the army, the workplace, socially – didn't act like this. If they did, they were confronted – in the playground and in the army, confronted physically – or avoided. But Renoir could not, alas, avoid Roddy altogether, and he couldn't confront him either. For Kate's sake, he ate crow, and doubtless, however putatively separate their lives would be in the Gatehouse, would in future get to eat lots more.

Now Roddy moved onto farming, with a long speech about the mistreatment of landowners by what he called 'this Metropolitan government'. When he paused to drink from his glass, Julie asked, 'Can't anyone live off the land any more?'

Roddy shook his head. 'Not without thousands of acres. Of course, we once had that here,' he said, as if this had been twenty rather than a hundred years before. He called down the table to Benedict, who broke off from his conversation with Alastair's colleague. 'Conrad, I was just saying it's impossible to make a living farming. As a new landowner, would you agree?'

'I'm happy to own the land,' said Benedict dryly, 'so long as I'm not expected to make money owning it.'

'At some point something's going to have to give,' declared Roddy. 'There are too few houses in this country and too much unprofitable farm land. A genius is not required to see the solution.'

To his left, Renoir found that Benedict's wife – she was called Helena – had turned his way. Close up she looked older than her husband, who like Renoir seemed forty-ish; she was quite darkly tanned and heavily made up, and wore an elegant dress of grey wool. She had on a Mediterranean amount of jewellery – heavy earrings, a gold necklace, a bracelet and on her hand both a thick gold wedding band and an engagement ring of diamond clusters. She looked him over, a little glassy eyed. 'So you are Miss Palmer's man then?'

It was the accent of international London – not English, but impossible to trace. The product of years of English at school and some intensive one-on-one tutorials in Istanbul or wherever, followed by X years of an English husband.

'Something like that,' he said with a smile, and refilled both their glasses. Judging from the decanter, she had already put away several glasses.

'I know my husband was very eager to meet you.'

'Really?'

She nodded awkwardly while she drank from her glass. 'Of course. Old habits die hard,' she said and smiled knowingly.

He shrugged, not sure how to respond. The woman was drunk. 'Where are you from?'

'Belgravia,' she said provocatively, and laughed. 'Don't look so serious,' she said, putting her hand on his arm. 'I am from Athens. Have you been there?'

'No.' He and Kate had been to France and Italy in the summers, but never to Greece, though he wanted to go to the islands some day. He said as much and she nodded approvingly. 'They are lovely,' she said, 'especially for children. You should take yours.'

'Not mine,' he said. 'Kate has a daughter. Do you have children?'

'No,' she said, slightly louder than necessary. The glassy-eyed look had returned and he realised he shouldn't have refilled her glass. Renoir saw Benedict glance at her, not in a warning way, but simply taking note. 'I can't have them,' she said. 'Sadly.'

He was a little startled by this – not *we* can't have children, but *I*, as if accustomed to blaming herself. Her bluntness seemed more English than European, something he had needed getting used to. Some of this apparent candour was due to different diction, but some of it was also an unwillingness to coat life in romantic froth: more than once Renoir had been startled to hear English parents declare of their own child, 'Of course Ivo' – or Simon or Lucretia or Georgia – 'isn't really very clever,' or good-looking or coordinated, or whatever quality would have American parents reflexively praising their offspring to the sky, however inaccurately.

In the face of this confession what could he possibly say? *Relax, I haven't got kids either. Anyway, kids are overrated. Just think – you never have to participate in those endless dinner party arguments about private education versus state.* 'I'm sorry,' he said.

'Burdick's would be a perfect place for kids to grow up,' she said wistfully.

Why Burdick's? He looked at her quizzically and she saw his puzzlement. 'Do you know it? It's not very far from here.'

He nodded. 'I liked Mr Burdick.'

'We never met him. He had died, of course, when we bought the estate.'

He was listening carefully now. 'What estate?' It came out a little rudely, but he didn't care – he needed to know.

'Why his, of course. Didn't you know?' She pointed towards her husband, who happened at that moment to stare directly at Renoir. 'We bought it before Christmas. We still have London, of course, but this is our new home.'

He stayed for lunch the next day, since he had promised Kate to begin moving some of her things from her Belfield room to the Gatehouse – with any luck, on their next visit they would be sleeping there. Beatrice served roast beef and they drank two bottles of very good claret brought down from London by Alastair.

After lunch he walked around the garden with Beatrice and Julie. 'It will be very strange when you move into the Gatehouse,' Beatrice said. 'Kate's always been such a part of Belfield. Even when she was in Scotland, we'd keep her room ready.'

Julie asked, 'Did your daughter live in Scotland for long?'

'Several years,' said Beatrice, her mouth making a small moue.

'She was married to a Scotsman,' said Renoir, and Beatrice's lips turned down into a frown.

They walked in silence along the rhododendron walk which opened suddenly to reveal the lake. It was no more than a hundred yards across, with a small island (tiny actually, no more than ten feet across) near the Hall end where the Palmer children and now Emily would swing from a rope on the branch of a solitary willow to land with a splash out in the water. There was a circular walk around the lake and Beatrice struck out along it now, still vigorous in her seventies. On the far side she stopped and they all stood, looking away from the house, down the thin cut which ran between two hills. On the right the rise was gradual and the slope itself was grass with a thin line of trees at the top. This was the drive called Harvest Walk, and the beaters would come across the wheat fields on the top plateau, driving stray pheasants before them until they reached the thin line of oaks and ash, where they would stand and watch the guns fire as the birds flew down towards the lake.

On the left the hillside was steeper, higher and more wooded, the edge populated by Corsican pines and high firs, prone to high-wind damage and lightning strikes: Treefall Down. Further in, a mix of conifer and oak stretched back until it opened around the Old Orchard of apple trees. Driven from there towards the cliff, the birds would then explode out of cover and fly at terrifically high speed across and above the cut where the guns waited. They would swirl in the wind, twisting and diving, and were famously difficult to shoot.

'I love this view,' said Beatrice. She turned around and looked back at the house across the lake. Renoir was struck by the simple progression towards rusticity – house, garden, lake, country. Beatrice said as much: 'From the house you have the same view, but with the things people have made in the foreground – the lake and the gardens.'

'If houses were built,' said Julie, 'presumably they'd be out of view.'

From the pained look on Beatrice's face, Julie must have realised how gauche her intervention had been. 'Sorry. It was just that Roddy was saying permission might be given to build new houses.'

Beatrice shook her head. 'Not while the land's farmable. And the woods themselves are listed. Did you know you can have a preservation order put on trees? My husband did it not long before he died.' She frowned. 'Honestly, sometimes you'd think my son had been trained as a builder. Well, It won't happen in my lifetime. *I'll* never see new houses at Belfield.' She smiled with oozing benevolence at Renoir. 'Except for the Gatehouse.'

Julie had moved out of earshot to look at the rose beds. Beatrice turned towards him, as if to wrap them both in privacy. 'Any news of Emily?'

He shook his head. 'We were going to take her out for exeat this weekend, but then Kate had to go away. She's gone to a friend in London instead.'

'I had a letter from her last week. She said she didn't want to go to Glen Ferban at Easter. She said she hoped she'd spend it here. I was rather taken aback.'

Renoir shrugged. 'She's almost a teenager now,' he said.

Beatrice nodded, more out of politeness he thought than assent. 'She's never got on terribly well with her father.' This was true, but Renoir decided to say nothing. After a moment Beatrice said, 'Not that I ever did, either. But she's very fond of you, you know.'

To his relief Julie was coming back to them, but Beatrice said quickly, almost under her breath, 'Though it might help if you regularised your arrangements with her mother.'

What? he thought, fighting to stifle his outrage. *First they decide I want to marry Kate for her money, then they get huffy when I don't marry her.*

He found some empty boxes in the stables and filled them with Kate's books from her bedroom. She had already started and he loaded these cartons as well into the car. One was especially heavy, and as he put it into the car it started to buckle under its weight. He broke its tape seal to lighten the load, and found it loaded with books with a tin box on top. It was the colour of gun metal, old and knocked about, long and light with a locked lid.

He finished unloading in the dark, then locked up the Gatehouse and drove towards London. Ninety minutes later as he sat immobilised in traffic on the A4 near the Hogarth roundabout, a faint whiff of hops in the air from the brewery up the road, he looked forward to the time when this Sunday evening drive would no longer be a regular part of his life. He thought, too, of his weekend, and the unwelcome news that Kate's old heart-throb and his peculiar wife would be living at Burdick's Farm.

He hadn't known Burdick very long, since the old man died within six months of Renoir's arrival in the UK, but they'd once had a walk, after a big Belfield lunch, through this very part of the estate. It was Burdick who pointed out the acreage right beneath the Gatehouse itself, and told Renoir about the green sand and its amazing fertility. 'But there's something even more valuable here, and that's water.' He gestured to the top corner of the field. 'There are little springs over there. I know, because I found two of them, when I used to lease the Old Orchard. If you dug out a pond on the hillside, those springs would fill it up.'

But Burdick's Farm belonged to Benedict, only now it had apparently been transformed into an estate, at least according to Mrs Benedict. Renoir thought there had been something infinitely sad about her; the failure to have children, yes that was part of it, but some other note of melancholy in her tone, resigned and knowing at the same time.

What a contrast her husband had been. Renoir hadn't liked the man, though he admitted to himself that this was one ex-boyfriend he would not have liked regardless. Still, Benedict projected such an air of insouciant arrogance; he seemed almost a caricature hate object from a left-wing polemic against the upper class. It didn't take a class warrior to see that Benedict thought he was simply *better* than other people. Better looking, taller, stronger, healthier, braver, even more reasonable (as opposed to more clever;

131

cleverness would not be a virtue in Benedict's eyes) than run of the mill folk. What had Fitzgerald said, mocked later by his ex-friend Hemingway? *The rich are different from you and me.* Yes, thought, Renoir, they have more *confidence.*

And part of Renoir envied this, since any social confidence he possessed had been laboriously acquired; there was nothing natural about it. People like Benedict made him feel foreign, even at Belfield – perhaps especially at Belfield, which seemed so quintessentially English. Although Renoir was determined to remain grounded in his very Americanness, it was tiring to feel it always constituted a distinguishing mark, and he enjoyed the days when he was allowed to forget about it. Which he could do with Kate, since to Renoir Kate was no longer English, Kate was simply Kate.

When he parked the car in the Notting Hill garage, the GPS light flashed and the display read *History*, then listed on its small screen the trips registered over the last few months. Unlike most of these gizmos, this model was designed primarily for tracking purposes rather than as a navigational aid. Companies employed them to check their sales reps' mileage, parents used them to make sure their little Annabel really was spending the night at a girl-friend's, private detectives installed them surreptitiously to follow people they were being paid to follow, and rich people (*like Kate*, thought Renoir) put them in to find their cars when they got stolen.

He left the garage and walked along Notting Hill Gate, then, since the park would be closed, strolled down Kensington Church Street, past the locked-up antique shops and down the hill to Kensington High Street. He realised something was niggling at the back of his mind, but he couldn't figure out what it was. Was it something to do with the stray pellets that had hit him? No; that would be enough to unsettle anyone, but this was some-thing else, something waiting to be discovered but obstinately refusing to reveal itself. It seemed tantalisingly close, poised like a name on the tip of one's tongue that stubbornly refuses to materialise.

He crossed the High Street and moved down Kensington Court, the atmosphere changing almost at once from bustle to the quiet of any neighbourhood on Sunday evening. He liked the quietness, as he liked the steady residential comfort of the building where he and Kate lived, but he wished there were more of what he liked to describe to Kate as 'normal people' living in the streets around them. As in much of San Francisco, the middle class had been driven out long before from so many parts of London, especially this one; it was the international rich who now seemed to populate most of Kensington. They had introduced grander cars in the parking bays of the side streets, with special parking allocated to the diplomats, security bars and grilles on the house windows and astronomical inflation in both rents and freehold prices for the houses themselves.

He came through the foyer of his building and was about to start up the stairs when he heard a cough above him in the stairwell, then a slight shuffle of feet. He stopped, and tried to slow his breathing. He put down his overnight bag gently onto the stairs, feeling at once ridiculous and apprehensive, and moved slowly up the staircase, gripping the iron banister. Before he reached the first floor he stopped to listen. Again there was a shuffling of feet, another floor up, so he moved stealthily up to the first floor and turned the corner. Here he waited again, listening for more movements. It was cold in the hallway; the radiators on the landings were losing their competition with the cold air brought in each time someone entered the building. He heard nothing at first, then, improbably, a loud sigh – weary yet youthful sounding.

He tried to still his growing tension, and went past the poet's widow's door, which was firmly shut, then passed the landing's burnished bowl of roses before he stopped again, held his breath and listened as someone sighed again above him. Was it female? Almost certainly. He relaxed involuntarily – something he wouldn't have done in the past, not after Mrs Makito – and moved quickly up the last section of carpeted stairs.

As his eyes came up to the level of the landing, what he saw first were the soles of a pair of pointed leather boots, then a pair of legs, enveloped snugly in tight designer jeans. Then the rest of a girl's figure, wearing a blue down parka. Sitting with her back against the wall of his flat, her face hidden behind a teenage girl's magazine she was reading.

'Emily,' he said incredulously, suddenly extricated from the paranoid world he had re-entered, 'what are you doing here?'

The girl scrambled to her feet, looking nervous but happy. 'Renoir,' she said softly, and stood there hesitantly with the same sweet shy half-smile of the little girl he had come to care so much about. The puppy fat was gone, and there was a gawkiness to her, caught in the territory between little girl and adolescent. Yet if extraordinary looks came, paradoxically, from standard features, Emily was going to be a stunner. Not yet as striking as her mother, she was already more conventionally beautiful, with a classic symmetry of cheeks and eyes, a small and perfect nose, and a mouth which teenage boys would absolutely die to kiss.

Meeting her, men would say, 'She's going to break a lot of hearts.' Perhaps, but Renoir thought she would never do it on purpose, never show the callousness of the self-absorbed. True, she was slightly spoiled, in a material sense, thanks to her father the laird's insistence that she live 'to a certain standard'. But she had an enormous capacity for love, and there was an insecurity to her (Renoir knew that unlike her grandmother she would never believe in her own beauty), a very deep softness and fragility which worried Renoir, worried him a lot.

'Why aren't you with the Faradays?' he demanded. He spoke more sharply than he meant to, and Emily suddenly looked to be on the verge of tears. Her chin wobbled, she blinked several times, and he could see the little girl in her take over again.

'Never mind,' he said, and reaching down picked up her bag in one hand while he extracted his keys and opened the door to the flat. Inside, she took off her coat and hung it up in the hall closet.

'Renoir, I'm desperate for the loo. Absolutely bursting.' And she ran down the corridor towards her own bedroom and bathroom while Renoir retrieved his bag from the stairs. When he came back he went into the sitting room and drew the curtains, and when Emily returned she had taken off her coat. She was wearing a soft beige jumper with a rollneck, and looked grown up – until she sat down with a pre-adolescent slump on the long soft sofa where Kate liked to stretch in the evenings after work. He remembered the ten-year-old of his first acquaintance and smiled a little. 'What's funny, Renoir?' she asked, sounding insecure.

'I was just thinking you're lucky your mom's not here. She'd be furious. What happened with the Faradays? I thought they were taking you back to school.'

She shook her head. 'They were meant to, but I said there'd been a change of plan.'

'And they believed you?'

She nodded. 'I told them Mummy had rung me on my mobile. Mr Faraday wouldn't let me take the Tube. He put me in a taxi.'

'You know your mother's not back until tomorrow. What would you have done if I hadn't shown up?'

'Oh, I would have gone down to Valerie's. She's the one who let me into the building.'

'Valerie?'

'You know,' she said pointing to the floor. 'The lady downstairs.'

'You called her *Valerie?*' he said and began to laugh. Even in her absence, neither he nor Kate would dream of calling the poet's widow by her first name.

'She told me to call her that. I wouldn't have done it otherwise,' she said defensively, as if he had ticked her off.

He shook his head in amazement. 'Okay, well it's nice to see you,' he said, starting, a little perplexed to find her there. 'Let me get you something to eat, and then I'd better run you back to school.'

She didn't reply, and looking at her he saw that she was again on the edge of tears. 'What is it Em?' he said, sitting down across from her and lowering his head so it was at eye level.

'Please, Renoir, just this once. I promise I'll go back in the morning. Just not yet. *Please.*'

He decided to relent. 'All right,' he declared. 'But you have to tell me what's wrong. I thought you liked school.'

'I don't like it at all. But please, Renoir, don't tell Mummy I said that.'

'Why not?'

'She'll just worry. But nothing will change. She travels too much to have me here. Please promise you won't say anything.'

'I promise. Now I'd better phone the school.'

Emily's house mistress was named Miss Dalrymple. When he explained that Emily was with him – and who he was, using the dread 'partner' word – her immediate reaction was relief. But it was followed by annoyance when he said he would bring her back in the morning. 'Not tonight? She was due here by six.'

'I know,' he said, adding pointedly, 'that's why I'm calling. She's exhausted, so I'd rather bring her back in the morning.'

'It will be very disruptive that way.' There was no concession in the voice.

'All right, let's say *I'm* exhausted. I would still like to bring her back in the morning.'

He rang off and returned to the sitting room where Emily looked at him anxiously. 'Is it all right?'

'Fine,' he said. 'No problem. They were just worried about where you were. I said I'd bring you back first thing.' He looked at his watch. 'Which means, young lady, that you'd better get to bed. I have to have you there before school starts.'

'Are you still going to take me to California?'

'Yes, but I don't know when. There's a lot to do at Belfield. The Gatehouse is almost finished. I think you'll like it. You might not even have to sleep on the floor.'

'Will you come up to Glen Ferban at Easter?' she asked. 'Please. Say you will. *Please.*'

'We'll see,' he said.

'That means you won't come. It *always* means that, Renoir.'

He laughed at her perceptiveness and sent her to bed while he listened for messages on the answering machine and checked the fridge for milk and eggs. When he went back to her room she'd brushed her teeth and put on a pair of blue pyjamas. As she got into bed he said, 'Lights out now. We've got an early start.'

'Please can I keep this on?' she asked about her bedside lamp. She was in so many ways still a little girl, much younger than her contemporaries, Renoir supposed, perhaps on account of that softness. He nodded and came over and leaned down to kiss her goodnight. As he stood up she said, 'And, Renoir, please will you tell me one of your stories?'

'Come on, Emily, it's late.' He didn't want to say she was too old for story-telling, though he thought it.

'Please,' she said, her voice regressing to little girl talk. An enchanting little girl when she wanted to be. But also wilful.

'You're too old for a story.'

She said nothing but looked hurt, and Renoir wished he hadn't said it – *Why would you want her to grow up any* faster?

'I'm too tired for a story,' Renoir said, though the truth of the matter was that he was not confident he could remember the ones he had previously made up and told her. Billy the Bear, George the Gorilla – a cast of minor characters from the animal kingdom, almost certainly fixed in her memory but utterly absent from his.

'I don't want one of those stories. I know I'm too old.'

'What then?'

'Tell me again about the California farm. Our secret, remember?'

'I remember.'

'Well go on then. Start in the orchard.'

He paused, and a voice collected inside him. 'Every day that summer it was hot, hotter than hot ever is over here. Here you *say* hot, but in California that would just be warm. It was true that a breeze could reach that high, on the hillside of the farm, though on the hottest of the summer days the farmer there felt that the breeze itself was just so much more hot air streaming in all over him.

'And it didn't rain, and it didn't rain. The farmer didn't know quite what to do, because he was an apple farmer and his trees needed water very badly. He was scared his trees were going to die if rain didn't come soon.

'But just as things were getting really desperate, the farmer had to go to town for provisions. And it so happened that on that very day in town they were having a festival. And at the festival someone had brought along some native Americans (we used to call them Indians) to show off their rituals and dances. And one of these dances was a rain dance, performed by the oldest Indian there, an old, old man who couldn't speak English and who went barefoot.

'Now when this man began to dance it wasn't very pretty to watch – he was an old man, after all, and a little shaky on his pins. Most of the people watching him felt sorry for the old man, though a few – I am sorry to say – just laughed at him. But the farmer didn't. He watched very carefully and then he got back in his truck and drove back to his farm, which was way up in the hills.

'And when he got home he went behind his house and stood there on the parched grass, which was almost white from the dryness, and he took his clothes off.'

Emily giggled drowsily, then Renoir continued. 'Which didn't matter because there was no one else around to see him. And then, slowly at first, he began to dance, with the same jerky steps he had seen the old Indian perform down in the town, and pretty quickly he got the hang of it and he began to dance faster. And he danced faster and faster until he ran plumb out of breath and had to stop.

'Now at first nothing happened. The sun shone bright as ever, and the grass in the fields stayed almost white in its dryness, and the sky stayed empty of clouds, and the heat seemed to be sucking the life right out of the trees. But then one day the farmer woke up and when he looked outside for the first time in weeks he saw a cloud in the sky. At first, there was just one, but soon the sky was positively dotted with them, and some of them were even dark. And the wind had picked up, and it was cooler now, and then, lo and behold, there was a drop on the farmer's arm when he went outside. And at first he thought it had to be a drop of sweat – that was all the wet he'd seen for ages – but no, there was another drop on his arm, and then another and another.'

Renoir paused here, before the deluge, and listened to Emily's breathing, which was regular and soft and sounded full of sleep.

In the kitchen he poured himself a large glass of Chianti, then walked into the living room, put on a Van Morrison CD and stood by the window, looking out across the rooftops in the direction of the park. He thought of the girl in her bed, so much more grown up than when they'd first met. She'd been boarding since the age of seven. At a pinch Renoir could understand why after her divorce Kate had needed to send Emily away to school, what with her own busy travelling career, which took off rapidly once she was at it full time. But why now? It continued to baffle him. Because he had not been brought up by his own parents, Renoir could not understand why any child should be brought up by non-parents when they didn't have to be. He didn't believe in it – not at Emily's age. Not when her mother had a 'partner' now (how he hated the word, one argument for getting married) who was willing and able to act as a parent, especially when the mother was away. And who wanted to act as a parent; who cared enough now to do so.

Though it had certainly taken time to reach that point. Initially, when he had first visited, Emily hadn't said much at all, and he'd found her hard to read. But when he'd actually come back and stayed, when he'd moved in, the hostility bloomed like hothouse flowers. When Renoir was in the room, she ostentatiously left it; when Renoir said anything, she sniffed in disdain. With Kate she picked fights, talked back and sulked like a precocious drama queen. One particularly bad day she also left the freezer door open for twelve hours, leading Kate to remark as she and Renoir threw out a freezer's worth of food, 'Well, at least it can't get any worse than this.' When Emily promptly let her bath overflow, Kate lost her temper completely. Hearing the commotion, Renoir appeared in the bathroom door to find Kate shouting at Emily and Emily crying. As they both calmed down a little, Emily exclaimed, 'But you said it couldn't get any worse.' Renoir had laughed out loud, and to his great relief Emily had too.

After that it slowly got better, though he was not her father. He could worry about her marks or her friendships or her weight (too thin for a time) without having any stake in the rather larger issue of where she went to school and where home was. The natural father, Angus the Laird, seemed remarkably uninvolved, or maybe just plain uninterested, focusing his attention and expending his energies on the children he had with his second wife. Emily could certainly use a father, but Renoir didn't see how he could play that role, not when no one seemed to want him to, not even Kate. It saddened him now, and then the melancholy he felt staring out the window, as Van Morrison sang 'Someone Like You', was joined by a slight unease, until he realised he had been accumulating a series of small uneases since the postcard of two days before.

And it was made far worse when he suddenly knew what had been nagging at him since returning that evening to London. Among the trips listed by the GPS were two to Berkshire, which Kate had made alone. Each within the last month, and at first glance visits to Belfield. How had she explained them? *I thought I'd see how the Gatehouse is getting along and look in on my mother. Two birds with one stone.* And the second trip? *I forgot to pick up some things when I went down last week.*

But the readings of the GPS were precise. And though the first trip had been 78.8 miles, the exact distance to Belfield, the second read only 74.2 miles. If it had been *more* than the first 78.8 miles it wouldn't have meant a thing – maybe Kate had taken the longer and prettier way, maybe she'd gone via the shop in the neighbouring village. But the fact that the mileage was *less* than 78.8 miles meant a good deal; it meant she hadn't travelled as far as Belfield. She had certainly gone to Berkshire: he'd seen on the tiny screen of the GPS in almost nauseating detail the details of her journey – M4, then A34, exiting at Chieveley. But she had driven only as far as a point four miles short and east of Belfield. Which could only be one place, well known to Renoir – Burdick's Farm.

And that would have been fine, thought Renoir, as he visualised how Kate would have pulled into the farmyard there in the Audi and could imagine her light and lovely voice as she gossiped with the old boy, whom she had adored and often visited, especially in the years after the death of her own father.

But there was one thing wrong with this touching mental picture: when Kate had gone to Burdick's Farm just before New Year's, old man Burdick had been dead for a little over six months. His farm had been sold. '*Oh*,' she said when he'd first mentioned the new owner's name to her, and he remembered how she'd blushed. What had that meant? Why hadn't he pressed her on it? *Oh*. Did she still have feelings for Conrad Benedict? Was that why she had visited him? And was that why she kept it a secret from Renoir?

Four days before Renoir had felt a rough perfection to his life that now seemed to be crumbling. Was it all about to disappear? he wondered, as he tried to rationalise away Kate's trip to Burdick's Farm, tried not to link it in any case to the bogus smile he had seen through.

'Renoir.' It was Emily calling from her bedroom. *Damn*, he thought, *she should be asleep by now. She'll be exhausted tomorrow*.

'Coming.' He walked down the corridor to her door, which he had left slightly ajar. 'What's the matter?'

'Renoir,' she said urgently.

'Yes,' he whispered back, trying to keep her calm and close to sleep.

'Why didn't you call the farmer by his name?'

'I didn't think we knew his name.'

'Yes we did. It was Will.'

'Oh,' he said, surprised. *Did I tell her that?*

'Was that short for William?'

'Yes,' he said. 'Though he was always "Will" to me. Sleep tight.'

'Was Will married?'

141

He sighed. 'Honey, you really have to go to sleep. You've got school tomorrow.'

'I know, but was he?'

'No. He wasn't married.'

'But did he have a partner then? You know, like you and Mummy.'

Renoir hesitated. 'Yes, he had a partner. Back then she was called a girlfriend.'

'What was her name?'

'Maris. Now come on—'

'Was she pretty?'

'Kind of. Now that's enough.'

'Please, Renoir, just one more. Was she nice?'

'Most of the time. Though she got irritated if you asked her too many questions.'

'Oh.' This seemed to sink in.

'Goodnight now,' he commanded.

'Renoir?'

'*Yes*,' he said with ill-concealed annoyance.

There was a slight pause. 'I love you.'

She had never said that before, and he felt dismayed to find emotion suddenly overtaking him. 'That's nice,' he managed to say.

As he started to go he heard Emily sit up in bed. '*Renoir*,' she said, and there was no question in her voice, only a child's demand.

He held the door still for a moment, then finally said, 'I love you too, Emily. Now go to sleep before I change my mind.'

Will and Maris

ON THE THIRD morning that he had to get his own breakfast, he started to worry. There were not enough Cheerios for a full helping, but he poured what was left from the box into a bowl, then managed to pour the milk from the bottle without spilling very much of it. He drank a little orange juice straight from the carton, though it tasted very acid. On the refrigerator was a pad of paper held to the door by a large magnet shaped like a frog. Lately his mother hadn't been writing anything down at all, so in large letters he now wrote CEREAL, then MILK, and finally, on a third line, OJ.

He looked in at his mother from her bedroom door, which was ajar. She lay sprawled on her back, half covered by a sheet, her mouth open as she lay in a deep sleep on the big brass bed she had bought at a junk sale in Daly City. It had cost more to have the man deliver it than to buy it in the first place.

At least she was alone. The week before there had been a man in bed next to her. He had worn boxer shorts but nothing else, though there was a tattoo of a dragon on his left arm. When the dragon suddenly started moving the boy realised the man was waking up, and he had beat a swift retreat down the hall to collect his book bag and shoot out the door to school. On an earlier occasion there had been another man, who'd jumped out of bed when he'd seen the boy, and moved buck naked for his clothes, exclaiming, 'You never said you had a kid!'

When he got to school he tried to forget his hunger during the morning, and fortunately he had a week's worth of tickets for the cafeteria lunch. Mrs Dielecki, his homeroom teacher, walked by him in the afternoon as they all trooped to the auditorium for some geography film, and she seemed to make a special point of asking if he was all right. He nodded but kept his eyes down, though usually he liked to look at her – she had a big freckly smile, and a head of blond curls he was always tempted to reach out and touch.

When he walked home that afternoon he wondered if his mother would have been shopping. But there were no new groceries – and no mother. He was not worried at first, since she would stay after her shift and socialise with the other waitresses, but when supper-time came and went he began to wonder where she was. He had watched his mother cook often enough, and there were dried beans and rice and pasta in jars stored in the cabinet next to the fridge. But he was scared to turn on the stove, which was gas, and usually needed a match for a burner to catch – which it would do with a great *whoosh* that made him nervous, even though it was his mother doing it, standing right there beside him. So now he went out to the corner store and used the thirty-five cents he'd found to buy two candy bars, leaving a note for his mother in case she came back. But when he returned she hadn't come back, and he ate the candy and finished the rest of the milk, which he drank fast as it was beginning to sour. He was both worried and still hungry, so even watching television way past his bed time did not entirely distract him. He wasn't sure if there was something he should do.

Eventually, for all his waiting vigil, he must have got drowsy, for he woke up to find the sun streaming like a billowing golden sheet into the living room and the *Today* show playing on the TV. Outside he could hear the early morning traffic on Oak Street down the block, but when he went to check his mother's bed had not been slept in.

On the way to school he used his remaining change to buy one last candy bar, which he ate as slowly as he could. This time Mrs Dielecki spoke to him in the morning, catching onto him at recess before he could get away to the playground. She made him sit down on a chair and started to ask him questions which he did his best not to answer. But this evasion made tears well up in his eyes, enough for them to be visible and make him wipe them away with his clenched fist. Fortunately, some other teacher came back to the classroom to ask Mrs Dielecki a question, and the boy took the opportunity to sneak away to the playground. By the time recess was over and they had trooped back in for math class, Mrs Dielecki seemed to have forgotten all about it.

So when the school day ended and he gathered his notebooks together he was surprised to find his grandmother standing at the classroom door. She must have come directly from work, for she was dressed for her job at City Hall, where she was a clerical administrator, whatever that was, and wore what she wore now – a white blouse and a mid-length skirt, and a cloth overcoat against the chill of the early fall morning as she took the bus to work.

Now she spoke a few words with Mrs Dielecki, who smiled over each time they turned to look at him. Then his grandmother beckoned him and when he walked over she took his hand, holding her purse in the other. As they left the school together he asked, 'Where are we going, Gram?'

'To get your things,' she said. Otherwise they walked in silence, and she seemed oblivious to the colour and characters of pavement life as they moved into Haight Ashbury. She ignored the sax player who held out his hat for her change, and nodded politely but uninterestedly at Louis the Juggler, who today had stripes painted all over his face and made a special show of three balls in the air as they walked by.

Four black men were standing on the far corner and one whom the boy recognised shouted out across the street, 'Hey, my man, my little man! Who's that fox you're walking with?' The boy couldn't tell if his grandmother heard this or not, for she looked straight ahead, keeping a firm grip on his hand.

They turned off Haight when they came to his street, a quiet one of Victorian wooden frame houses, painted in light pastels and all with high and sharply angled gables, but differentiated from each other by idiosyncratic additions of *château*-like turrets or screened side porches or even a boxed-in widow's walk at the top. Once single-family residences, most had been broken up into units – like the boy's house, which was the third one down and separated into three apartments, one on each floor, with an external uncovered staircase at one side of the building. The boy and his grandmother climbed these stairs to the second-floor landing, where he took off the house key which he wore on a string around his neck, and handed it to his grandmother. She opened the door and they both stepped into the kitchen. When he looked through to the living room he saw his mother.

She was sober, he knew at once, because she was vacuuming the living room. When she was drinking she never cleaned up at all. As she looked up at them he couldn't read her expression. She didn't seem surprised to see his grandmother there, didn't look embarrassed, or guilty, or give any indication that she had left her nine-year-old son unchaperoned, unsupervised and utterly alone overnight.

His grandmother touched him lightly on the shoulder. 'Why don't you go play,' she said. It was not a question. He went past his mother and down the hall to his little room, next to the bathroom. He left the door ajar, so he could hear their voices as he tried to read *The Fireside Book of Baseball*, an anthology he had picked up for twenty-five cents at a school book sale one weekend. Though he didn't want to know what they were talking about, he was still about to go out and interrupt them to say he was hungry when he heard his mother's voice rise. 'Don't lecture me, Mother,' she said. 'Just don't lecture me.'

'The boy is nine years old, Maggie.'

The boy – he hated being called that. It reminded him of how his mother would talk in company when she'd been drinking, mentioning him sometimes as if he weren't even in the same apartment. So he closed his door and turned on his radio. Now he could hear the noise of the voices without hearing the words themselves. After a few minutes the door to the apartment slammed shut, which meant his grandmother had left, though it would have been his mother who slammed the door.

He emerged only later, cautiously, wary of his mother's mood. Lately she had seemed a different person from the mother she had been when he was very little. Lately she seemed as interested in hitting him as in kissing or hugging him, maybe more in fact since the scale was turning almost two to one in favour of the hitting by his most recent reckoning. And the number of times was well past counting on his fingers, even if he used both hands.

But she was whistling now – interestingly, for a singer, she never sang to herself – and said nothing to him until, after he'd watched a late-afternoon cartoon in the living room, she called out from the kitchen that supper was ready. While he ate – it was fried hamburger, with a baked potato and tomato salad and a large glass of milk – she moved around the kitchen wiping surfaces and adjusting the position of things. He wanted to talk to her – wanted to ask where she'd been, wanted to explain that *he* hadn't turned her in, *he* hadn't asked his grandmother to intervene – but he didn't know how to begin, and she didn't give him much of an opportunity, moving around the room as she was, whistling still and sometimes humming to herself, with the wash cloth from the sink in her hand. When he finished he put his plate and knife and fork and the glass in the sink and mumbled thanks and went back to his room.

And the next two days were normal – his mother went shopping and gave him his cereal in the morning and she was home when he returned from school. On Saturday she left early to work breakfast, and she wasn't back after lunch. She didn't call, either, to say she was working a double shift. There was food to eat this time, and he managed not to fall asleep that night in front of the television, but early Sunday morning when he went down the hall he found her bedroom empty.

He waited all morning, then went at lunch to the restaurant where she waitressed. It was a long walk, and he stood by the kitchen door in back of the brick single-storey building off Market Street, and waited while one of the kitchen boys fetched the manager, an unsmiling Eurasian who wore a tight grey suit. No, his mother wasn't working that day, the man said, then hesitated and the boy got worried that the man would ask *him* questions, so he said thank you very quickly and left, walking west along Haight, feeling a mixture of puzzlement and fear.

He thought of going to his grandmother's house, out in the Sunset, but he had only ever been there with his mother, and he was uncertain which bus to take, or where precisely he should get off. He knew it wasn't that far away, probably only three or four miles, but the way his mother spoke of it – *so foggy and wet* – made it sound like a different country. He knew how to use the telephone, and his mother's address book was in the hall, where he was pretty sure he could find his grandmother's number – though her last name was not the same; it was Shaughnessy, and he knew how to spell it – but something held him back, some hope that he had perhaps misheard his mother or misunderstood her, or that she had been detained unavoidably, or that she had in fact telephoned while he was just now out, or rung the night before only he had been asleep or the television had been on too loud for him to hear the phone.

And he continued with this rationalisation through the rest of the day, through the evening when he ate cereal for what now seemed the thousandth time, and into the night and the late movie until he fell asleep, again, on the sofa. In the morning he was about to go to school when the front door suddenly opened and his mother came in. Her hair was a mess and one of her stockings was torn and when he started to ask where she'd been she snapped at him – 'Don't ask' – and when he tried again, she suddenly took two steps and hit him very hard across the face, with a closed fist, so hard it half closed one of his eyes. When she had hit him before, as recently she had done a lot, she had only slapped him, which stung but didn't do much damage. And didn't show.

And he ran from the apartment, fast down the steps, crying and feeling frightened and alone, and when he got to school it took Mrs Dielecki no time at all to see that something was wrong, for she stared hard at his eye and asked if he was all right, and when he nodded his chin wobbled and again tears welled up, though curiously only in the eye that hadn't been hit, and he did not trust himself to speak.

This time his grandmother came to the school within an hour, and this time there was a policeman with her.

It was raining when he crossed the bridge, sitting in the front row of the bus. His grandmother had spoken to the driver as the boy took his seat, but he was nervous anyway, worried that the driver would forget about him and not him when they'd reached his destination. *I'll probably end up in Oregon*, he thought, for though he wasn't very sure about where he was heading, he knew it was in that direction. He could not really see the Pacific out the left side of the bus, but turning right he made out Alcatraz, where his mother had often promised to take him but he'd never been.

He had been across the Bridge before: a school trip to Muir Woods, walking through the towering redwoods there; a jaunt with his mother to friends on the coast near Stinson Beach back in the days when they still had an automobile. The friends had owned a dog he'd played with almost all day long, a little boot-brush of a terrier mutt, and the boy had cried when he wasn't allowed to take him home.

And there had been a trip for a family reunion in Sausalito, lunch at a harbour-side restaurant, outdoors on a big deck, with cousins who had subsequently moved to – where? What had his grandmother said? Buffalo? That was it. A funny kind of name for a town. And his uncle had been there, he knew that, because his grandmother had explained just two nights before today that the man he was going to be staying with – *while your mother gets better* – was someone the boy had met before. He wasn't an entire stranger after all; he was not just a blood relative (his mother's brother) but also someone he had seen with his own eyes.

The problem was, the boy couldn't locate any clear visual memory for the man, only the vague impression of someone big and dark. Had he been dark-skinned with a shadowy hint of

151

beard? Or did he have an actual beard? The boy wasn't sure, though he thought he could remember someone designated as his uncle coming up and hugging his grandmother as they had entered the restaurant. Hugging her hard enough, actually, for her to squeak when she laughingly protested, the air escaping from her like toothpaste squeezed from a tube. Then his uncle had kissed the boy's mother, his sister, but without the hug. The boy remembered that. And knew, too, from mentions by his mother (not that there were many) that his uncle had been a soldier. Served in Vietnam.

The Bay was now behind him and out of sight, and the hills on either side of the road looked impossibly lush and green. They came down slowly through the rain into a flatland stretch of highway where water lay in long slick puddles on the road. Now there was a town again – he saw the sign *San Rafael*, and wondered how you pronounced that. On either side there were sloping hills of green woodland, with the occasional new office carved out in low buildings of brick. Soon they were back in country again, and here he saw several herds of cows, black and white, poking along in grasslands dotted by the odd scrub oak.

You'll like it there. It's the country, his grandmother had said, after explaining to him where he was going. He had been too surprised to form objections in his mind, much less express them. His grandmother was always so *determined* – he remembered that day in Sausalito when she had driven them there, in her ancient automobile, both hands gripping the steering wheel, face taut and concentrated as they had driven slowly across the bridge.

So was this 'the country'? he wondered. His spirits sank at the prospect of his unknown destination, this strange uncle of his he couldn't for the life of him really remember at all. *It can't be for too long*, he told himself, but why hadn't his grandmother said how many days he'd be away? Why, for that matter, couldn't he have stayed with her, just until his mother got back on her feet and he could go home to Cole Street and their apartment again? Though in fact part of him didn't want to go back to Cole Street, didn't ever want to see the apartment again, didn't actually want to see his mother for a good long while.

'Where *is* Mom?' he'd asked, just before his grandmother told him he'd be going to stay with his uncle.

She looked at him with a mild detachment, as if to think before speaking. 'She's in the hospital.'

'Will she be okay?'

'Yes,' his grandmother said firmly. 'But she has to stay there for a while. Your mother's not well.'

Your mother's not well – not *your mom*, or even *Maggie*, since that after all was his mother's name and what Gram called her as a daughter, rather than as his mom. That was on the second evening of his stay with her, in the small pink stone house in the Sunset, just blocks up from the Pacific Highway and the ocean itself. He stayed in the spare bedroom, which he helped Gram clear of boxes and wrapping paper and spare blankets she stored on the floor and on the bed.

'Can we go see her?' he asked, curious as much as concerned, and indeed he was partly relieved that his grandmother shook her head at once. 'Not for a while,' she said, and he'd thought, *What's 'a while' mean?*

The bus came to a large town – there were houses stretching as far as he could see to his left, though on the right in the distance he saw hills. When the bus stopped at the terminal he looked anxiously at the driver. 'Petaluma,' the driver barked, and stood up. He looked at the boy and seemed to sense his anxiety. 'Not yet,' he said. 'I'll let you know.' When he came back a few minutes later he chucked a Snickers bar at him, which the boy caught.

Now the country grew less populated, and the hills seemed higher on the right side as they travelled north. There were orchards instead of cattle here, and a few fields with long lines of wire stretched between stakes, and leafy plants which swarmed all over them. In one field people with baskets were moving through rows of wires, but he couldn't see what they were picking through the filtered glass of the bus.

He realised as they came off the highway and into a town that the rain had stopped, but it was still a surprise, when the bus halted in a little square and the driver said, 'Here you go, son,' to come down into startling, white sunshine. He stood blinking as the driver retrieved his suitcase out of the luggage compartment, then said, 'So long,' and hopped back onto the bus. As it moved away the boy looked around the sidewalk for his uncle. A fat woman with short black hair cut like one of the early Beatles his mother liked so much was hugging a teenage girl who'd got off the bus behind him. Behind them stood a young man, his back to the wall of the drug store, who wore khaki-coloured pants and a blue T-shirt, with sunglasses pushed back over his head. He seemed to be smiling faintly as if he found something funny. He looked friendly, which made the boy hope that the same would be true of the large, dark-bearded figure he was looking for.

He turned to face the square and looked out hopefully. Two men sat side by side talking on a bench in the small park, but both were too old to be his uncle, and there was nobody else in the square. He remembered the mix of bewilderment and fear he felt as he'd walked home from his fruitless search for his mother at the restaurant, and recognised the combination starting to take hold again. Anxiously, he began to inspect the cars that were parked around the square, peering at each one for occupants. Was that a man sitting in the fancy black car? No, only the headrest of the front seat.

There was a restaurant on the far side of the square, next to what looked like a newsstand. Maybe he should walk over there and ask. But ask what? He was starting to feel more frightened than nervous, and tried to consider what to do calmly. In his pocket he had a piece of paper with a phone number on it, but his uncle was supposed to be here, waiting for him, and he didn't begin to know where to make a phone call. Maybe in the restaurant over there, but what if his uncle arrived while he was inside trying to phone him? What if no one answered the phone, or the number he had wasn't right? What if his grandmother had written it down wrong?

'Would you happen to be Jack?' said a voice behind him, and turning he found himself looking up at the smiling man in khaki-coloured trousers. In Haight Ashbury the boy would talk to anyone – Louis the Juggler, the affable drunks drinking beer out of paper sacks, Emilio who some days tended an ice-cream van, other days a hot dog stand. But here on strange turf he felt on his guard. He didn't know what to say to this stranger who somehow knew his name, other than not to say anything, though he did give a small reluctant nod.

'Thought so,' said the man, looking amused. 'Even if you don't look much like your mom.' He held out his hand. 'I'm your Uncle Will.'

And suddenly filled with relief, Jack exhaled and shook his uncle's hand.

'You hungry?' asked the man, taking a Marlboro from a pack he had tucked into the rolled-up short sleeve of his T-shirt. Jack shook his head. 'Sure?' asked the man, as he inhaled and shook out the match. 'We got us a bit of a drive.'

'I'm okay,' said Jack a little squeakily, for he hadn't spoken once since leaving San Francisco and he realised he hadn't even thanked the bus driver for the candy bar, which he regretted since the man had been nice.

'Let's go then. I'm parked over here,' his uncle said, pointing to a pickup truck they now walked to. He carried Jack's suitcase, then lifted it with one light swing of his arm into the back of the truck, where a wheelbarrow sat, pristine and gleaming in the sun. 'There was a sale at the hardware store,' his uncle said as they got into the cab.

They pulled away and drove halfway around the square, then shot out in the opposite direction from which the bus had entered. The town seemed neat and tidy to the boy, with wooden houses, many smaller than those in San Francisco, but with nice lawns and large back yards. It was not a big town, and soon they reached the outskirts, then went under the highway. The land here was rolling, though in the distance there were higher hills and his uncle pointed towards them. 'We're going thataway. You must have brought the good weather with you. We've had nothing but rain for a week. See that,' he said and pointed at the ditch by the side of the road, where Jack could see a long line of moving water on its bottom. 'This road's called Dry Creek Road – and it's wet.' He laughed at this, and Jack smiled with him, relaxing slightly. 'So do you like the country?'

Startled, Jack stared out the windscreen at the broken white dividing line of the road, watching as each section his eyes focused on neared, then disappeared underneath the truck. He didn't know what to say. The man added gently, 'Maybe you never spent much time in it.' When the boy didn't react he went on. 'I didn't when I was a kid. When your mom and I were growing up we always lived right in San Francisco. But you must know that.' And Jack nodded, relaxing just a little more at the mention of his mother. 'Anyway, we're in the country now. Hope you like it. Something tells me that you probably will.'

Slowly they began climbing, but the twisting road was sided by abundant bushes and high grass which obscured the view. When they levelled off, Jack could see the hilly landscape for the first time; there were small valleys in the distance, lushly green, like the landscape of Vietnam he had seen in a movie on television. Thinking of Vietnam, he cast a shy glance at his uncle, who seemed impossibly young and normal to have been a soldier.

'That's Swiss Cheese Road,' said his uncle, pointing to a turn. 'We'll give it a miss. It's not its real name, actually; I don't want you getting confused from the beginning.'

Jack decided to volunteer a question. 'Why's it called that then?'

'Because it's full of holes.' He laughed. 'Every year or so the county fills the potholes and twelve months later they've got to fill them again. After last winter they must have forgot, and with this rain it would be a pretty bumpy ride.'

Soon they turned off the paved road onto a smaller one of hard-packed sand, so smooth they only slowed down marginally, though they were also climbing again. Again, there was no view, both sides of the road were lined with dense vegetation and trees with thick branches which towered above them. It felt as if the road was there against the odds, and that with any inattention it would slip back into natural habitat, overwhelmed by greenery.

After a few minutes of ascent, Will turned sharply left onto another smaller track, with a grassy hummock in its middle. About fifty yards in there was a log cabin off to the right, neatly constructed but old: the logs were dark with age and the window frames badly needed painting. 'That's old man Truebridge's place. He's been there about as long as forever. He acts grumpy, and if I'm here another fifty years he'll still think of me as a newcomer.' He looked over at the boy and grinned. 'But he'll help if you need it. We don't usually get snow up here, but the first winter there was a storm that just dumped it down, and then it froze over for almost a week. I didn't have this truck then, and I couldn't get my car out. Truebridge gave me a ride to town to get supplies.'

The track was becoming increasingly bumpy, but Will failed to slow down, so Jack found himself almost thrown into the air as the truck bucked up and down. Just as he started to feel sick, and was gathering courage to ask Will to stop for a minute, the woods suddenly gave way and they came into a flat clearing, where the track ended in a turnaround.

Behind sat a house, presumably his uncle's. It was two storeys and made of wood, with long horizontal boards stained a smoky grey. It was a wide house, though the second storey was not as wide as the ground floor, and had slanted overhangs so rainwater would run down and not gather on the flat roofs of the ground floor at each end.

An acacia tree stood in front of the house on the left side, taller than the house. Nearer the front door, which was just slightly to the right side of the house, was a magnolia, shaped like a fat wine-glass, which the boy recognised from one in a neighbour's yard in Haight Ashbury. A dog came out of the shade, a big collie mongrel, and Jack stiffened. The only dogs he knew were other people's – city dogs, often unpredictable, sometimes growling. But Will went towards this dog without hesitation. Kneeling, he cuffed it lightly round the ears and scratched its chin. 'This is Ellie,' he said. 'The world's worst watchdog. Wouldn't hurt a flea.'

They went into the house by the front door, and Jack stood still for a minute to allow his eyes to adjust to the comparative darkness of the room before him and then to the sudden drama of its space. It was a vast open room, the height of both storeys, and it stretched across the entire width of the house. Up above, a gallery ran the width of the room as well, with a thin balustrade of polished pine

In this downstairs space there was a sitting area at the far end, with a long low sofa, full of red and green cushions, and two big armchairs, grouped in front of a stone fireplace. On the wall hung a gun cabinet, and next to it two mounted heads of deer. Nearer Jack a long pine table was covered at one end in stacks of papers, with several wooden chairs stationed around it.

On this ground floor a pine wall, halfway back, separated the rear of the house from this immense open room. It was punctuated by several doors, and Jack followed his uncle diagonally across the room to one of them, which was open. Peering in, Jack saw a kitchen, and standing by the table in the middle of it was a young woman, roughly the age of his uncle.

'This is Maris,' his uncle said, nodding towards the woman, who wore jeans and Indian moccasins, and a soft flannel work shirt of faded blue. She was about his mother's height, which was slightly above average, but where his mother had run to fat (*Irish bones*, she had liked to say, in what was half complaint, half explanation) this woman looked firmer, trim. Her hair was long, light brown and ran down her back in a long pigtail studded halfway down by a mahogany-dark leather slide.

She looked at Jack with an expression that was serious, almost stern, but her face seemed warm, with soft eyes of silvery blue and a hint of colour in her high, round cheeks. Her face was not exactly pretty, for she had an awkward-looking overbite, as if her two front teeth were too big for her mouth, but it looked the kind of face which its owner has long ago accepted. She nodded at him and shook his hand, gravely at first, but then with a slight, toothy smile which made him feel more welcome.

'Are you hungry?' she asked and his eyes widened, for other

than the driver's candy bar he hadn't eaten anything since his grandmother's poached eggs at breakfast. But he still felt too shy to say yes, and feeling nervous in the close confines of the kitchen started to say no when his uncle cut in. 'Well I am. Why don't I show you where you'll be sleeping and then we can eat.'

Jack followed Will out into the big room again, then trailed him as he opened another door, revealing a corridor running towards the rear of the house, with a room on either side. 'The laundry room,' Will said, pointing to a washer and drier, 'and there's a shower in there you might want to use. It would be all yours.' Then he turned and crossed the passage. In this other room was a desk with an accountant's calculating machine on it and a stack of ledger books. 'This is the office. My office,' he said a little wistfully, 'though it's Maris in here most of the time.'

They went out and climbed the staircase, his uncle carrying the tin suitcase. At the top Jack stopped for a moment, and looked down over the railing at the vast sitting room below them. Behind him another short hallway led back to a large bedroom and a bathroom next to it. 'That's my bedroom,' his uncle said, then led him down the gallery until they came to a room at the end – well, it would have been a room except that it lacked a dividing wall and a door to separate it from the gallery. But it did hold a single bed, which was neatly made with a patchwork quilt, and there was a big pine chest of drawers in one corner, and a stuffed armchair the colour of burned vanilla in the other. The outer side wall consisted of a glass sliding door, and through it Jack could see a deck, with two director's chairs pulled up close to the outer railing on the perimeter of the house.

'It's not exactly private,' his uncle said apologetically, 'but at least there's lots of room.' He looked at Jack. 'Will this be okay?'

Jack was so surprised to be asked that it took a moment for him to nod, even though he thought it was more than okay. For it was about three times the size of his San Francisco bedroom, and the bed itself was twice the size of the small camp bed he was used to. And there was a skylight in the roof. *Maybe I will see the stars*, he thought.

Will put his suitcase on the floor next to the bed. 'You might want to rest for a minute. You can use the bathroom up here if you like. I'll come get you in a bit.'

He heard his uncle walk along the gallery and go down the stairs. The boy sat down heavily on his bed. Suddenly, and for the first time that day, he felt absolutely alone. He knew this man Will meant well – he could tell already – and maybe the lady downstairs would turn out to be nice. But he didn't know them, and sitting in this strange and unusual kind of bedroom (*It doesn't even have a door*, he thought, not resentfully but as a small expression of how odd he found everything just then), he thought of how far he was from home.

Home? What was home now? His mother was lying in a hospital somewhere, and even if she weren't in the hospital he would feel funny seeing her right now – what with his eye which was still sore, and the memory of her socking him, and a feeling that his grandmother's intervention (however necessary) would be seen by his mother as somehow his fault.

So there was nowhere to go back to right now: if Gram had wanted him there why had she put him on the bus? He had better make the best of it right where he was, with these strange people and in this strange place. And that very strangeness scared him, so much so that he didn't even feel teary or like crying, but just hoped something would happen soon to take his mind off this emptiness, and aloneness, and fear. Actually, some company would do the trick – that was what he wanted just then, more than anything, even the company of these strangers. But he didn't feel he could go downstairs yet, however much he wanted to. He should unpack, he knew, but in his anxiety his thoughts raced and his arms twitched – once, twice, then a repeated small throb right in his forearm and he had again this new and really not nice sensation of feeling shaky.

And whether his uncle realised this the boy never knew, but blessedly he decided not to leave the boy alone after all, for Jack heard steps on the stairs again, then the *click-clack* of boots on the gallery's wooden floor and he looked up and his uncle was in the doorway, and the smile was shy and understanding as much as warm, and his uncle said, very matter of factly and casually, 'Maybe we should eat right now. What do you think?'

And the boy nodded, and eagerly moved to the door and as he passed his uncle he felt the man's hand ruffle quickly through his hair and Jack recognised it at once for the affectionate gesture it was, and looking down from the gallery he saw Maris putting plates on the table, and when she looked up and met his gaze she smiled.

They sat down together at the big pine table in the large open room, where food was laid out on plates, and Maris served stew from a large casserole into earth-coloured bowls, and passed a plate with slices of rye bread, and there was a large salad bowl with lettuce which she seemed to be holding back for later. The stew came as a shock, for the meat in it was gamy and hard to chew, and the sauce – a rich mocha-maroon – was too peppery for him. He did his best but wondered how he was going to get through it all. He coughed and Maris quickly poured him a glass of water from the clear pitcher she'd brought out. He drank, swallowed, then coughed some more.

'Venison,' his uncle said apologetically, and Maris went out to the kitchen. When she came back it was with a plate of ham slices. 'Try this,' she said, putting a large slice between two pieces of bread. 'Deer meat's an acquired taste.'

Deer meat? He looked over at the mounted head nearest them in wonderment, and Maris seeing him do this laughed. 'It's not that deer,' she said.

'Oh,' said the boy. He looked at his uncle. 'Did you shoot it?'

'Nope,' Will said, chewing a large piece of stew meat. He took a drink from his glass of water, swallowed and said, 'Maris did.'

The boy looked at her with astonishment, and she nodded matter-of-factly. 'Just down in the Valley Orchard,' she said. 'Not half a mile from here.'

'He ate good too,' said Will.

Maris pretended to grimace. '*Well*,' she announced. 'He ate well.'

161

'Did you shoot the other one?' he asked his uncle hopefully, nodding towards the other head.

This time when his uncle shook his head he looked positively mournful. Maris said, 'He bought that one in a junk shop in Healdsburg.' And when the two adults laughed, the boy joined them. And he looked at the end of the room at the gun cabinet, through its glass front at the guns lying horizontally in racks.

'You're going to have to go to school,' his uncle said, looking at the boy carefully. 'What grade were you down there?'

'Fourth grade.'

'You've just scraped by.' He laughed and pointed at Maris. 'Lucky for you, she only teaches third grade.' Maris frowned, but again Jack could tell she was only pretending. His mom had used to kid him; it was nice to hear it again.

His uncle said, 'The school doesn't even know you're here yet, so we thought maybe you wouldn't start this week. That way you can get used to this place, see how things work around here. Maybe you can help me out with the apples, too. Most of the work's done, and the pickers have moved on. But there's the near end of the Back Valley to do, and I could use the help. And the company. What do you say?'

The boy was full of questions – what was the 'back valley'? who were the 'pickers'? – but understood the gist, which was that he needn't go right away to school. He nodded.

'Good,' said his uncle and Maris smiled at Jack, who felt sufficiently emboldened to ask his uncle, 'Don't you have to go to work?'

Maris giggled and Will looked momentarily nonplussed. 'That *is* my work.' He scratched his chin while he tried to word an explanation. 'That's what I do here. Grow apples. I'm a farmer. Didn't your grandmother tell you?'

Jack shook his head. 'She just said you lived in the country.' And he sensed for the first time that if his uncle seemed a distant figure to him, he probably seemed that way to his grandmother as well. And though there seemed no hostility in it, the boy also felt comforted by the thought that somebody else wasn't that close to his own mother either.

After supper Maris came upstairs with him and showed him the empty drawers in his dresser. 'You can put your clothes in there,' she said shortly. Pointing to a painted bookshelf on the far side of the bed, she added, 'I don't know if you're much of a reader but I got some books out of the library. The television's downstairs if you want to watch it.'

She left him alone and he put the few clothes he'd brought all into one drawer. He felt shy about going downstairs right away, so he sat on the bed and looked at the titles of the books. None of them was familiar but he discovered that Gram had put *My Story* by Henry Aaron in the bottom of his suitcase and he started to read it. He lay down for a minute, just to stretch out while he read.

The next thing he knew the light had gone from the windows and his room – well, it was not a room, since it had no dividing wall or door – was dark. For a brief second he felt panic as he wondered where he was, trying to find the familiarity of first the room on Cole Street, then the spare room at Gram's. Nothing fit and then he heard a noise from downstairs and he remembered where he was. He got up to use the bathroom down the hall, and stopped when he heard voices downstairs. 'Leave some ice cream for your nephew,' Maris scolded.

'Don't worry about him. I checked a minute ago and he was out for the count.'

'He must be exhausted.'

'He sure doesn't show much, does he?'

'It'll come out. Just give it time. He seems a little sweetheart to me.'

'Well I hope you're right,' his uncle said. 'He's had a rough time of it. I think my sister must have been a nightmare and he never knew his father. There are plenty of better ways to start life. But you were the one worried about having him here.'

'I just don't want you getting sucked into something you can't get out of. If things don't work out here he's always got your mom, remember?' Maris's voice was uncompromising, but softened to a tease as she said, 'You may think she's an old hag, but she didn't do that bad a job with you.'

'I wouldn't wish her on anyone, much less my nephew.'

'You may not have to. If it works out here.'

'We'll see,' said his uncle, and Jack tiptoed down the hall to the bathroom, where the light had been left on. He was as uncertain as his uncle seemed to be as to how long he would be staying. Part of him was still nervous, part of him still scared. Maris in particular didn't seem that happy to have him there, but he comforted himself with what she called him – *sweetheart* – which was something his mother hadn't called him for a long time.

When he woke up the next day and came downstairs, his uncle was in the office. 'Maris left early,' he explained. 'She's got her own place in town, and most week nights she stays there. But don't worry,' he added, mistaking his nephew's look of curiosity for concern. 'I can cook breakfast okay. Just not anything else.'

And he could – instead of his usual cereal, Jack found himself eating pancakes and bacon and fresh orange juice and even two inches of coffee heavily diluted by milk and liberally dosed with dark brown sugar.

When he'd finished, his uncle said, 'That should hold you,' then looked at Jack's sneakers. 'You bring any boots?'

Jack shook his head.

Will nodded. 'You're going to need some for winter. We don't get much snow here, but it's wetter than hell from November until March. I'll take you into town later and get you some gear. Maris said you didn't bring that many clothes.'

They went outside through the back door in the kitchen and stood on the low deck looking at a line of high trees that faced the back of the house in a sweeping semicircle. The stand was a mix of eucalyptus and firs, well spaced to give an airy feel of forest rather than of dense wood.

To their left was a well-worn path across a short section of lawn that continued into the trees. 'Come on, I'll show you around,' said his uncle, and they walked this way, with Ellie the collie suddenly appearing to pad along behind them, coming through the trees into a clearing with a long oval-shaped pond, about the length of a tennis court. The surface was studded by water lilies at the far end, which was framed by a bank of rhododendrons, in bloom with pink and purple flowers. Behind them sat a long greenhouse, its side a series of diamond-shaped panes of glass. At their end of the pond, a rough diving board had been fashioned out of a long plank balanced precariously on a line of three fat tree stumps.

'Is it deep?' the boy asked cautiously, staring at the dark reflective water.

'Deep enough to dive. Can you swim?'

Jack shook his head.

'Well then, this is a pretty good place to learn.' Will pointed to the far side of the pond. 'It's shallow there. And after a day in the orchard there's nothing can beat a swim. It's the *best*.' He said this with an enthusiasm the boy was unused to.

They walked around the pond and came to the greenhouse. It was backed against a sharp rise in the land, so that it was sheltered from wind, nestled against the hill. As he followed his uncle through its door he felt as if he'd stepped into a sauna, like the one the parents of his school friend Mickey, back in San Francisco, had in their basement on the other side of the Panhandle. The air was thick and moist; after only a moment Jack could sense sweat gathering on his neck.

In the greenhouse there were two long trestle tables on which sat small terracotta pots, each containing a plant. His uncle gestured at the pots. 'Strawberries. And a few tomatoes. Maris is crazy about tomatoes,' he added appreciatively.

Further down on several tables were small bundles of what looked like sticks, wrapped together with electrical tape.

'These are the scions for the grafts,' said his uncle. 'The rootstock's in the orchard already – I bring these out later on in spring and put the two together. Bet you've never seen a graft before.'

The boy shook his head. He hadn't understood a word Will had said. The greenhouse seemed surprisingly shallow, but it was

165

wide, almost fifty feet long he'd have guessed. There weren't that many plants, but it seemed crowded nonetheless, with the imminent, burgeoning growth and the moist air somehow dense with expectation.

'Nothing much else to see in here,' his uncle declared, and led him outside. They walked back past the pond in the general direction of the house. For the first time Jack saw that near the house, across from the turnaround, there was a wooden barn, once clearly painted red but now, except for a few off-scarlet flakes, the silvery grainy grey of the ageing boards. Inside Jack could see a tractor with a flatbed behind it, stacked with empty lugs. Against the far inner wall of the barn there were more lugs stacked neatly in high piles, and a vast assembly of tools hanging from pegs pounded into the cross beams.

Will took a long, funny-looking saw off the wall, then clambered onto the tractor. He looked down at the boy. 'Hop on,' he said, 'unless you want to walk.' He had Jack stand behind him, and the boy gripped the back of the seat with both hands as Will slowly reversed the tractor out of the barn. Then he shifted gears and the tractor jerked forward; they moved unsteadily away from the house, on a worn path of ash-coloured dirt, with Ellie trotting behind.

The path went through a mix of flowering bushes and brush which swept against the side of the tractor's front tank, and, his forward view blocked by his uncle's wide shoulders, Jack could only see the greenery on each side. Gradually, it grew lighter, and he sensed that they had emerged from the jungle of growth and were moving ever so slightly downhill. His uncle braked and the engine coughed, then stopped. As his uncle stood up and stretched, the boy loosened his hold on the back of the seat, and using the tyre as a step awkwardly hopped down to the ground. 'This is the Valley Orchard,' his uncle announced. Blinking from the light of the high sun overhead, the boy felt dizzy for a second, and only lifted his gaze when his slight vertigo dissolved. Then he looked ahead.

They were at the top end of a soft and grassy slope which

gradually declined for several hundred yards, then bottomed out briefly before ascending in the distance, until it levelled off at about the same height as the ground where he and his uncle stood. The two slopes thus formed a gradual valley, which had an air of having an unsupervised life of its own – like a secret garden spreading over dozens of acres. There was a picturesque vista of much higher hills in the distance, but they were so far away that they seemed not to intrude at all on this valley, but only served to provide a kind of remote frame to the picture in front of him.

Throughout the valley were rows and rows of trees – apple trees, the boy concluded, of a high and standard sort, reaching into the air with full extended arms of greenery. The trees were well spaced and well rounded, and every single one seemed to be absolutely loaded with fruit, which hung on the branches of the trees like the ballooned bulbs of his grandmother's Christmas ornaments. There were here a million dots of vermilion, pink and gold, the orchard a contrasting neat sea of tree greenery and colourful fruit. The apples shimmered in the warm sun, as if the humid temperature somehow moistened the light itself.

He had never seen anything remotely like it in his life.

'What's the matter?' asked his uncle.

This time Jack spoke at once, too wonderstruck for shyness. 'Nothing's the matter,' he said. 'It's *amazing*,' he said, of the magic in front of him.

His uncle laughed. 'They're called Gravensteins,' he said. 'Late ones, too.'

'Oh?' said the boy with disappointment. 'I thought they were apples.'

He was forever grateful to his uncle for not laughing at him.

The magic did not wear off, even as the week progressed and the boy helped his uncle pick the latest and Gravenstein part of the harvest. He had never actually *worked* before – the chores he had done around the apartment, especially when his mother was drinking, weren't really work, and had the advantage of being

167

short-lived. It was not easy, but the exhausting aspects of picking apple after apple did not diminish the sense of wonder that this transplanted city boy felt. The inevitable realities – the apples bruised by wind or branches, the ones half eaten by worms – were not debasing ones. Even when his uncle pointed out a rattlesnake, curled up and sleeping against some bricks outside the barn warmed up by the sun, this could not bring him entirely down to earth.

At first he picked the juice apples, including the windfalls on the ground if they weren't too bruised. He wore one of the old-fashioned aprons Will tied up double so it wouldn't sag, yet when empty its large front pocket still swept in a billowing fold down to his knees. Every half a dozen trees there was a large wooden box on the ground, and he would unclasp the three hooks on the apron's pocket from its clasp just below his throat and let the fruit tumble like lucky dice into the bins.

His uncle picked the table fruit, slowly moving through a tree from the lowest branch up, shifting onto a ladder for the older part of the orchard, at the near end of the valley, where the trees had grown as high as twenty feet. He showed Jack how to pick for the table. 'Never pull,' he commanded from ten feet up on a ladder rung, while Jack peered upwards from below. Will turned and moved his hand towards a large apple on an inside leader. 'They say *lift and twist*. But actually, the best way to do it is to kind of *push* the apple. Away from you, towards the trunk of the tree. There,' he said, turning with the apple held delicately in his hand.

And by the end of the week Jack was picking top fruit for the table too, and, with Will on board, steering the tractor when they drove the flatbed stacked with full crates back to the barn. There Will used an ageing fork-lift to unload and stack the crates. Jack would have to wait until he was a lot older, Will explained, to use the fork-lift. At lunch-time they ate sandwiches and drank frozen Kool-Aid slush from lunch boxes Maris packed the night before; at the weekend she made fancy lunch, as Will called it, and they ate inside. And in the late afternoon when they knocked off work, they stopped on their way back to the house at the pond and stripped off. Jack was shy, since he couldn't really swim, and waded in slowly from the shallow end on the greenhouse side. Will did a large cannonball from the diving board, then swam across to Jack, who had yet to get wet above the waist. 'Take your time,' he said gently, and the next day he brought a lifebelt he'd gone and bought in town. 'Once you get used to the water, I'll teach you how to swim. Correction: I'll try to teach you how to swim.'

Despite his uncle's friendliness, it took several days before Jack felt comfortable enough to volunteer conversation, or questions. But once comfortable, he found himself asking questions almost non-stop. If this tried his uncle's patience he didn't show it.

'Uncle Will, why did you come and live here?'

'It was when I was over there.' He pointed vaguely over his shoulder, and it took the boy a moment to realise his uncle meant Vietnam. 'We'd sleep at the base, then every morning get helicoptered out to the countryside. It wasn't for sightseeing purposes, and between you and me, when they say "Join the army and see the world", they mean see the asshole end of the world. But in spite of that, every morning I would look around at the countryside we landed in and I'd think to myself "This is beautiful". And you know, if you took away the guns and the VC and people like me, it would have been beautiful too. It may sound weird, but the countryside there wasn't a million miles different from the one we got here.' He pointed out over the Valley Orchard, and Jack was struck that his uncle, who had actually been in Vietnam, also saw a resemblance.

'Were there apple trees over there?'

His uncle smiled. 'Nope. Too hot. But that's okay. I wouldn't want too close a resemblance.'

And as his uncle also became comfortable with the presence of another person, he began volunteering information. 'I don't actually *own* this place,' he said one afternoon. 'I rent it from a cousin of Maris's. That's how we met – she wanted to see what kind of fool would pay good money for this kind of land.'

'What's wrong with the land?' asked Jack, already feeling proprietary about the acreage.

'You can't farm it really. Top fruit's about all you can grow – it's too hilly, too many trees, and the topsoil's thin up here. Apples are okay – but not many people grow them in this part of Sonoma. To be honest with you, people think the best apples are over towards Sebastopol.'

'What's wrong with these?' demanded Jack.

Will smiled at the boy's fierceness. 'Nothing's wrong with these. Nothing at all. Finest apples between Cloverdale and Healdsburg.' He laughed. 'Pretty much the only apples too.'

The boy was nervous about going to school – it had been the only sour note of the week, hanging like a black cloud when he thought about it – and on the first day his uncle drove him in, though thereafter he would usually take the school bus. But school didn't prove difficult at all. It was easier for one thing – the math he had done the year before, and his spelling and composition were 'excellent' they told him when he was tested first day, in a small room all by himself. There were three other new kids in his very year, and though they had been attending class for the four weeks since school began, they were not such old hands by now not to feel some charity towards the newcomer. He soon made friends with Ernie Weiskranz, who rode the school bus every day and lived down the mountain from him in a house on the edge of the nearest town (a 'townlet' really, according to Will), called Haley's Ford, which had a gas station, a few houses and a lot of dust.

There was one kid who was unfriendly: Jerry Simonson, who right away seemed to know where Jack lived and was snotty about it, given to sarcastic remarks, acting as if Jack were living in a trailer parked out in the wilderness. Yet the teachers seemed extra nice, as nice as Mrs Dielecki, as if somehow they knew his situation, though he was careful not to explain himself in full to anyone: he was staying with his uncle, went his account, while his parents travelled round the world, 'on business' – that was the phrase he fetched from some recess in his memory. It seemed to work with his classmates, and the teacher Mrs Kite nodded sagely when he explained the present touring condition of his mom and dad.

Soon he found himself settled into a routine which was only occasionally varied. Some days Maris gave him a ride home and when she stayed over took him with her in the morning, stopping by her neat small house on the Russian River side of town, where he waited in the car while she changed for school, put her hair up in a more feminine bun and collected her mail. Mostly, though, he took the school bus, which dropped an older girl on Hill Road a mile down from his uncle's place, so Sam the driver seemed happy to collect and deposit him at the end of the track by Truebridge's cabin. Early on, he had the choice of staying on after school for Little League, but he was eager to get back to the farm, where there was always something to do with his uncle, or sometimes with Maris when she came in – always later – from her own day at school.

When the harvest was over, there was still work to be done in the orchards, at first collecting the final windfalls, then helping Will with the old cider press he'd installed in the barn, feeding it for hours at a time – virtually all of one weekend too – then carefully filling with its cloudy pulpy juice all the plastic containers Will had collected since the previous autumn. The weather only gradually cooled, and while the late-afternoon light remained Will started to teach him to swim.

He wore the lifebelt, which took away his fear of the water, even in the deep parts, but swimming was harder than he'd thought, and though Will said he was making good progress he found it frustrating that he could only manage a stroke or two of crawl before everything seemed to collapse and he went literally nowhere, buoyant only because of the belt.

Usually Maris was out of the way when he and Will were outside together; she was either in the house doing homework or cooking supper, or, while the light remained, tending her garden plot she'd carved out on the west side of the house, the end where Jack slept. But occasionally she came round to the pond and watched the progress of his lessons, and it was she who questioned the use of the lifebelt, telling Will right in front of Jack in her blunt straight-up way that it might tempt Jack to go into the pond alone and unsupervised. He was surprised when Will brought him into the argument right there and then, as they stood on the bank dripping water, to ask him to promise not to do any such thing. He was flattered by this inclusion in the grown-up discussion of worries about him, and happy to promise this anyway, since he didn't want to let Uncle Will down and wanted Maris to understand that he was grown up, and not just a little kid.

He was learning fast that with Maris he had to be careful, since unlike Will she could be moody. Will himself just had two gears, it seemed – easygoing and enthusiastic. His eruptions of high spirits at first unnerved the boy, who was accustomed to the emotional volatility of his mother and distrusted it accordingly. But as far as he could tell, Will's deviations were only on the good side of the emotional spectrum, and seemed entirely authentic, if boyish and younger than his years at times. The boy had to remind himself sometimes that Will was actually his uncle.

Maris was never so enthusiastic, and though friendly enough kept a slight distance from Jack; he recognised this and out of self-protection tried to match her coolness. But aloofness did not come naturally to him, since he liked affection and was by nature affectionate himself, and as the weeks passed he found that although most of his time in this new home was spent with Will, it was Maris's companionship he especially savoured.

She seemed to know everything about the countryside around them, and had abilities Jack had never before thought possible in a girl. She could shoot, using the same rifle from the cabinet she had shot the deer with; one day she waited patiently for half an hour until two jack rabbits appeared in her vegetable garden, then calmly plonked them both. She skinned them herself, then cooked them in a Mexican chocolate sauce that night, which both Jack and Will thought was wonderful but she declared disgusting. She could drive the tractor, a lot better than Will in fact, and she was surprisingly strong – Jack found her one Saturday cutting high grass by the barn with a long old-fashioned Dutch scythe. And she was handy. When Will built a birdhouse whose two sides didn't meet right at the top, she took a power sander and smoothed them down until they matched almost seamlessly where they met. But though Jack was a little confused at first by the presence in her of so many masculine attributes, there were occasional indicators that, however brusque her manner, she could be completely feminine too – like the time he over-heard her singing unabashedly to a Joni Mitchell record in a clear soprano voice.

Like any student of an inspiring teacher, he found he wanted her approval, though he would not have been able to put this desire into words. The sneaking sense that he might not get it made him unwilling to put it to the test, and on the rare occa-sions when he elicited her praise he glowed the more for its being unprompted. There was the day in early November when the cold was starting to set in earnest and swimming should have ended, but somehow he managed to get Will to go with him into the pond. As if sensing that he was running out of time, some-thing intervened to reward him for the work he'd done; suddenly, when he usually would run out of steam or coordination, a confi-dence pushed him through that barrier and he was swimming, swimming for real, awkwardly maybe, and with a kind of fragility to the motion of his arms, but swimming *chug chug chug* until, unbelievably, he was at the far bank, having swum across the pond. And there was a shout from Will of triumph and he raised his own hand with the modest acknowledgement of a magnanimous conqueror, and then there was clapping – *applause* he thought, wondering where on earth it came from, and he looked past his uncle and there was Maris with her hands smacking together. Though as soon as he began to wave to her she turned and went back into the house, as if embarrassed by her own display.

It was, he sensed himself, a happy time, though he wondered occasionally as he sank into the curious household of the farm –

not depressingly, but like a tired child sinks into its bed with insensitive contentment – just how long it could possibly last. He thought sometimes about his mother, despite trying not to, and though he didn't ask Will about her at all he listened carefully each time the phone rang, and he inspected the mail surreptitiously each day as it lay half opened and half digested on the big pine table in the downstairs open room. But as far as he could tell there was no communication from her, and nothing even from Gram.

There was so much to explore, moreover, in this new world that whenever he felt sadness or anxiety start to move inside him like worms, he would go and stand on the deck outside his bedroom. From there he could look out over most of the variety of the farm, and he would pretend to be a great landowner, maybe of a vast plantation like the ones he'd read about at school, thinking, *I Am The Master of All I Survey*, which was a phrase from something or other, saying this to himself while he turned one hundred and eighty degrees in almost synchronised slowness as he regarded his empire: from the barn next to the turnaround with the tractor sticking halfway out; then over the bushes and Maris's vegetable garden plot by the side of the house; the entrance to the path through the woods to the Valley Orchard; through the rhododendrons until he could just make out the diving board, partly obscured by the bushes; finally, the hill which the greenhouse backed against, with the far tip of the Back Orchard visible in the distance behind it. When he was on the ground outside, seeing these places at their own level, he would remember how they figured on the mental map he collated while standing up on the deck, and so, even in the lush abundance of the land and woods around the house, he never felt lost.

There were not rules *per se* in the household. He helped Maris when she let him, and he always assisted with the dishes, and he would take the garbage out when asked, and feed Ellie on the deck when Will forgot to or was too busy, and he made his bed each morning and tried to keep his dirty clothes in the wicker hamper Maris had placed in the corner of his room. But he didn't really have to be told to do any of these things, and other than bedtime – which Will would let him bend a bit when Maris wasn't there and he was watching television – there weren't really any guideposts.

Except outside, where in addition to Maris's concern about the pond, Will had early on been unusually specific and strict. 'I don't mind you going anywhere you want on the property except for two places. One is the greenhouse. I've got it temperature controlled for both the grafts and the strawberry plants, and I just can't have the door opening and closing all the time. If you want to go in there, wait until I do – or ask me special. Understood? The other place is the sandy bank behind there and the woods on top. I can't believe you're fond of rattlesnakes, and there are *tons* of them there – there must have been a nest back there sometime. So you stay out of there, okay?'

Jack was happy to nod assent to both, though he was a little surprised by the proscription of the greenhouse, since Will himself seemed to be in and out of it twenty times a day. But nothing much else seemed forbidden, or even strange, though there was one night when he couldn't sleep and had slid out ever so slowly, to stand in the gallery a few feet back from the rail, where Will and Maris, sitting downstairs by the fireplace, couldn't see him – not unless they actually stood up and looked up and back. And he heard their quiet talking and then Will laughed and Maris coughed, hesitantly at first, then in a full fit, and out of curiosity and concern, Jack edged forward and looked down to see her doubled up. He couldn't understand why Will was laughing, and then he saw Maris hand him the cigarette that had made her cough so much.

And the next afternoon as he walked with Will to the Back Orchard to check for stray crates in case they'd left one or two under a tree, he said, 'I didn't know Maris smoked.'

Will gave him a look and said curtly, 'She doesn't.' Then he seemed to catch himself, and hesitated, then said, 'Well, maybe once in a while. Why, did you see her smoking?' Jack nodded and his uncle looked at him curiously. 'Don't let on that you saw her, okay? She wouldn't want you to know.'

By mid-November he'd been there two months, and one night Will knocked and came into his bedroom while he was reading before bed. 'I was thinking maybe we'd go some place for Thanksgiving.'

'Oh,' he said, wondering where. The ocean? Will was always saying they should take a trip up north along the coast. He felt a little disappointed – in San Francisco they always had dinner at Gram's. Occasionally cousins joined them, some nice people on his father's side who lived in Daly City, but otherwise it was just Gram and his mother. So he had been looking forward to a Sonoma version, to helping Maris cook, then watching football on TV with Will. 'Where do you want to go?' he asked his uncle.

'We thought maybe San Francisco,' said Will. He looked awkward standing at the edge of the gallery. He paused. 'At your gram's house.'

It was Jack's turn to be surprised. Will had never been there for Thanksgiving that he could remember. He thought for a moment, and asked, 'Is Maris coming?'

'I hope so. Gram's never met her. Do you mind if she does?'

'Of course not.' How could his uncle think such a thing? 'Who else will be there?'

Will sighed and came into the room, then sat down on the kitchen chair Maris had installed next to the glass sliding doors to the deck. Will rubbed his hands together and spoke as if he were being especially careful. 'Your mom's supposed to be there.'

Jack looked at Will with a smile that began tentatively, then despite itself widened into a face-splitting grin. 'She's better then?' he asked, ducking his head a little, for it momentarily seemed too good to be true.

Will nodded. 'That's what Gram says. She's out of the place where she was and back in the apartment. She's working too, in a steakhouse downtown.'

'Why can't we go there then? You know, to my—' he hesitated, was it home any more? He compromised. 'At the apartment?'

'Slow down, Jacko. Let's take it one step at a time. Okay?'

Take what one step at a time? 'Does she know we're coming?'

'Sure she does.' Will stood up to go, then added as if an afterthought. 'She can't wait to see you.'

They left mid-morning on Thanksgiving Day, taking Maris's Chevy instead of the pickup truck since it was more comfortable and also, as Jack said, more of a town car. Will drove with Maris up front next to him, and they seemed more subdued than usual, though in his excitement it took Jack some while to notice this. Now that he was going to see her again he realised how much he had missed his mother but had not allowed himself to feel.

Still he felt oddly disoriented as they paid the toll and barely noticed when he watched Will reach over and hold Maris's hand as they started over the Golden Gate Bridge. Jack tried to look out over the Bay towards the Pacific and found only a vast bowl of fog, yellowed at the corners by the sun. He knew he was going to his home town, but he already felt so settled at the farm that the prospect of a city unsettled him. When he remembered the bus ride he had taken going in the opposite direction it didn't seem ten weeks ago but ten years.

Outside Gram's he felt the stinging west wind off the ocean, five blocks away, and its salt smell mingled with the light rain that had started. He ran towards the door and pressed the bell. Gram answered in an apron, and he hugged her but was already looking behind her. 'Is she here? Is Mom here?'

Gram only gradually let go of him, calling out as he rushed towards the living room. 'She's not here yet Jack, you're early.'

So they all sat down in the living room, the grown-ups with grown-up drinks and a Coke for Jack, which surprised him since his grandmother had never let him have Coke, and they made polite conversation while Jack waited impatiently for the doorbell to ring.

'So how are things up there?' Gram asked.

'Good,' said Will, nodding his head. 'We had a good year.'

Maris explained. 'He's got apple orchards. It was a good harvest.'

His grandmother just looked at Will, with the set expression Jack was familiar with. It betrayed nothing; it wasn't sceptical, it wasn't disbelieving – it wasn't really anything. Except if you were lying it seemed uncannily to catch you out.

'What's the matter, Mom?' asked Will. 'Mom' sounded funny to Jack coming out of his uncle's mouth. 'You think I can't farm?'

'I am sure you can do anything you set your mind to, William,' she said dryly. She turned to Maris. 'Are you farming too?'

'No ma'am,' Maris said politely. 'I'm a schoolteacher.' This seemed to meet with Gram's approval, and Jack drained his glass of Coke while the two women went at it, all about teaching reading versus teaching maths, and how parents these days didn't rule the roost at home, and an awful lot of other chitchat about education systems that seemed to go on forever while Jack sat there wondering when his mother would come. He could smell the turkey in the oven, and from time to time Gram would go out into the kitchen to check on the bird and whatever else she was cooking, and Maris got up the second time as well, and Will winked at Jack and said in a whisper, 'They're getting along just fine.'

And Jack said, 'Who?' with genuine curiosity, and Will pointed towards the kitchen, and Jack realised that Will must have been nervous about Maris meeting Gram for the first time. Then he wondered again where his mother was. 'What time is it now, Will?' he asked.

Will shook his head. 'I better be getting you a watch, you keep asking me the time. It's three thirty now.'

And at exactly four thirty, by which time Gram had given him permission to watch football on the TV in the corner of the living room, as long as he kept the volume down while she and Maris yapped some more and Will had another whisky and ginger ale ('No thank you,' Maris had said, with an inauthentic primness when Will had offered to refill her drink), Gram announced that they should eat or the food would be ruined. And at the announcement Jack looked with mild outrage at Will, who just shrugged. 'I'm sure she's coming, Jacko, but we can't hold dinner for ever.'

And they sat down in the small dining room, and Jack had Gram on one side and his mother's empty place on the other. And he felt so upset that they were actually sitting down to eat, because somehow it seemed to confirm his mother's absence, but he struggled not to show it as Will carved and heaped his plate with dark meat, which he preferred. Gram served him as if he were a little kid, spooning out mashed potato, and candied yams, and green beans and carrot rounds, and pecan stuffing from out of the bird, and a dinner roll, and the only thing he got to do himself was pour the gravy from her only-on-special-occasions silver tureen. And he looked down at the plate brimming with food and thought he would gladly go hungry for even just five minutes of his mother's company. And he tried to eat, but the food stuck in his throat – *honest*, he thought, *it tastes like sand* – and Gram said, 'Eat your food, Jack,' in a low quiet voice to him twice, not meanly but as if calling his attention to the meal. And then she started to say something else, only the phone rang in the kitchen as she did. 'I'll get it,' said Will in a hurry, and he was up and out of the room before Gram could even acknowledge or protest his answering the phone in her own house.

They all sat in silence, straining to hear, but it was impossible, and when Will came back he stared at Gram and gave an almost imperceptible shake of his head, and Jack knew he was trying to hide the news but what was the point? 'She's not coming, is she, Will?' he asked as his uncle sat down. And Gram had reached over and put her hand on Jack's arm, he didn't know whether to hush him or comfort him, but he didn't care which it was because he was intent on Will's reply, and Will fiddled with sitting down and then unfolded his napkin and took a sip out of his water glass and picked up his fork as if to start eating again but then finally, maybe sensing the intensity of Jack's stare, he looked up and shook his head. 'I'm sorry, Jacko,' he said.

'What happened?' Gram asked, and there was reasonableness to her voice, as if she felt there must have been some unavoidable cause for her daughter's no-show, as if perhaps another grandchild she knew nothing about had fallen ill with flu (temperature 105 and rising) or a small kitchen fire meant her daughter had to stay home to help the firemen.

And Will shrugged, as if he did not want to be drawn on this, and said, 'She got real caught up.'

And Gram nodded, which puzzled Jack since his uncle hadn't answered in any satisfactory way at all. And he wasn't going to take that: no, if the cat was out of the bag – *she's not coming* – he wanted to know why not. 'Where is she?' he demanded, since if she were at home then he didn't care if an earthquake was in progress, she could still come over. Get in a cab – Gram could pay; hell, he'd even pay her back when he got back to Sonoma and his piggybank of spending money – and come over right away.

Will looked at Jack with exasperation and propped both elbows on the table, and normally Maris would have corrected this, jokingly whacking him with a spoon the way she did at home in Sonoma, but she was being awful quiet herself, not saying a word, and Will rubbed his eye with his hand, and then he looked again at Jack with his right eye bleary and said, 'She's in Las Vegas.'

'*What?*' said Gram and Jack simultaneously.

And Will held both hands out like an Italian in a television ad, with that sort of helpless 'what can I tell you?' gesture of palms opened imploringly towards their audience, and he said, 'She says she's working there now. And she missed her flight. She hopes you'll all understand.'

'You'll all understand'. *Does that mean me?* thought Jack with disbelief. And Will said, almost as if trying to make excuses for his sister, 'I have to say she didn't sound real well.' And he looked meaningfully at Maris, and then at Gram. Gram nodded quietly, as if trying to take this in. 'Eat your dinner, Jack,' she said, almost mechanically.

He tried but he couldn't, and when dessert came and Gram put ice cream on top of his pumpkin pie, even that did not stir his appetite, and though he tried to make the motions to be polite to Gram, he found the disappointment again was like a blockage in his throat. He didn't want to look at Will, and once he found Maris's eyes on him and he ducked his own eyes down, not trusting himself not to cry, and Gram said in a tone full of old age common sense and false cheer (he could tell; he wasn't fooled), 'Well, Jack, you can be excused if you like, and maybe you'll be hungry later. Why don't you look at the football in my room?'

And he was grateful for her tact, as he wanted more than anything not to be in their company right now, while he tried to make sense of what had happened and why conceivably his mother hadn't come, unless as he knew in his heart it was because *she didn't care.* As he sat in the stuffed armchair in the corner of Gram's bedroom, he tried with a kind of sour desperation to think of another reason she hadn't come. He looked, as if for the first time, at Gram's bedroom with its prim single bed and the old-fashioned mahogany headboard, a low dresser with a lace doily along the top, holding hairbrushes and a set of framed photos – of his grandfather as a young man, fresh-faced and serious, Will in his army uniform, his mom graduating from high school, and one of himself as a toddler. The walls were painted a dull light green, and the carpet was brown and threadbare. It *depressed* him, this room, he realised with almost adult insight into its effect, and he wondered whether it was Gram – with her humourless steady moral progress through life – who had put off his mother. Yes, maybe it was Gram's fault. If only they had insisted on having Thanksgiving at the farm. How he wished he were there, up on the mountain, where he could have gone outside if he'd felt this upset; he could have parked himself on the diving board of tree stumps and listened to the frogs croak and the wind moaning through the shimmering eucalyptus leaves. Mom would have liked it there; she would have come if they'd had Thanksgiving there; he was sure of that.

But of course he wasn't, and when he thought of the simple fact of her being in Las Vegas, which no one in her immediate family had even known, his heart sank with another certainty: that if they had held Thanksgiving in Candlestick Park, with a line of trumpeters to greet his mother and Janis Joplin come to life again to sing back-up for *her*, she still would have missed that flight. *I bet she's drinking*, he thought, and for a moment he thought he couldn't bear it, then slid into a kind of wounded passivity.

He watched dumbly as the 49ers fought back from 21–13 down to 21–19 after two field goals. In the last thirty seconds of play they attempted a final field goal which would have won the game. It was blocked, and he reacted for the first time by laughing bitterly out loud. *Fuck them*, he thought, taking a small hard pleasure from the words which he had never said before. Will didn't talk that way, nor Maris, or his Gram. It was his mother who used that word, he remembered, so *fuck her too*. And he was still laughing about the field goal when Will came into the room and took one look at him and said, 'Okay, Jacko, I think it's time we went home.'

And he struggled to thank Gram, who just kissed his cheek and made him do up his coat, even though the car was virtually right outside, and as they drove off he forced a wave since he could not bring himself to resent his grandmother, not really. But he didn't want to talk, and when they went over the Bridge and the fog had lifted and Will said, 'Look at that,' pointing to the lights of Alcatraz Island, Jack didn't say anything. Later in Marin his uncle asked him a question but he didn't reply because there was a lump the size of a lead baseball in his stomach, and Maris must have said something because his uncle pulled over, and there on the edge of the highway Maris got out and waited for a gap in the traffic and then came and got into the back seat.

As they rejoined the highway she scooted over and put an arm around Jack. And he didn't react at first, but then in a minute or two he found his head was lying against her side, cupped between her breast and the sharper edge of her ribs, and he started to cry, then cried for what seemed to him forever. His whole body shuddered as he sobbed, and Maris's arm tightened its grip around him as he continued his crying and in a high clear voice she began to sing:

> *Long ago but gentle now,*
> *Let me hold you, Darling.*
>
> *Far away but gentle now,*
> *Let me show you how to love.*

And as she sang his head slid down into her lap and his shuddering stopped and gradually his sobs subsided and he slept.

He woke up in the dark to find himself upside down, with blood rushing to his head, then suddenly he was turned sideways and put down like a sack of potatoes into bed and under the covers. When he next opened his eyes the sun was flooding the deck outside and from his bedside clock he saw it was the middle of the morning. *I'm late for school*, he thought with a start, then remembered it was a holiday, and then he remembered the events of the day before.

He heard steps and Will came in, looking thoughtful. 'Morning,' he said vaguely, and sat down on the chair.

Jack sat up against the pillows and looked at his uncle, whose face was unusually solemn.

'I'm sorry about yesterday,' said Will. 'If I'd known that was going to happen, we wouldn't have gone.'

'It's not your fault,' Jack said, and at the thought of his mother's failure to show, his chin wobbled and he felt teary. Embarrassed he shook his head, trying to drive away his upset.

'But I need to talk to you about something else,' Will said, and his air of determination made Jack feel even shakier. Will was looking at his hands as he spoke, slipping and unslipping the fingers together almost ritualistically. 'You're going to need to decide something.'

'What's that?' he asked warily. He didn't want to decide anything.

'About where you want to live. For now anyway.' He kept his eyes looking down. 'You can stay here with us, just like it's been. Or, you can go and live at Gram's.'

'What about Mom's? Can I go there?' he asked, as if the day before had just been a mistake, an accident really, and Mom would get on an airplane and be home soon.

Will looked up from his hands right at him. His expression was not unfriendly, but it was steady and fixed. 'No,' he said. 'You can't.'

Jack realised he had known the answer as soon as he had posed the question, and Will didn't need to explain anything more. *She doesn't want me*, thought Jack. *She can't even come to Thanksgiving so I shouldn't be surprised.* And he blinked through embryonic tears and looked back at Will, expecting the worst. He asked, 'What do you want me to do?'

And Will didn't give his characteristic aw shucks shrug, but continued to look at him with atypical seriousness, saying, 'I want you to do what you want to do.'

And the boy hated this imposition. Why couldn't they just go along as they had been – wasn't that easiest? Why did he have to decide? Unless Will wanted him to say he wanted a change. 'What does Gram want?'

'Gram would be happy to have you.' And the slightly oblique slant of this reply actually reassured the boy – not because he was gratified that he could go there, but because he was worried he was supposed to feel *obliged* to go there. But it didn't really close the matter at all. He waited a second and when he spoke his voice sounded even to himself half strangled. 'Do *you* want me here?'

'It's what you want, Jack. That's what I'm asking you.' The boy nodded, trying to mask the disappointment he felt crawling inside himself. But he wanted to have one more try, just to confirm that he wasn't really wanted here either – it wasn't just his mother then – so he spoke again, and his voice was still weak, almost

184

cracking with the tremulous urgency of his question. 'But do you want me here or not?'

Here it comes, he thought and tried to distance himself as his uncle's stare did not waver and his mouth opened with what Jack knew already would be disappointing words. 'You bet I do.'

Jack almost said '*What?*' such was his surprise. As relief flooded in he was tempted just to nod, but there was still something missing: when he'd said, 'Do you want me here?' he'd meant Will *and* Maris, so Will's 'I' in reply left a question unanswered. And for Jack it was equally important. So he said with a slightly firmer voice now, bolstered by his uncle's unequivocal reply, 'What about Maris?'

'What about Maris?' his uncle said tersely.

'Does she mind if I stay?'

'Well,' said Will, and he seemed to be suppressing a smile, 'you know Maris. She thinks you're a pretty major pain in the ass.' And as the boy's face started to fall he continued. 'Almost as big a pain in the ass as me. But she did tell me that she's got used to having kitchen help around here. So you'd be doing me a favour if you stayed, Jacko. I ate cold food too many years in the army, and I sure don't want to face it all over again.'

Maris, who had gone to town, came back in the afternoon, and she put three peeled potatoes down on the kitchen table where Jack was sitting and handed him a knife. 'Cut these small,' she said, 'I'm making corned beef hash.' And when he smiled at her without restraint she clucked her tongue. 'Quit sitting there with a grin on your face like some dimwit.' Adding with such gruffness that even Jack could see through it, 'Now how about getting to work.' And he figured that this was as much answer to the question he had put to Will as Maris was ever going to offer him. *It'll do*, he thought to himself. *It'll have to.*

Will explained that for Christmas Gram had decided to visit friends in Sarasota, so Jack would be spending it in Sonoma. Jack wondered if after the Thanksgiving fiasco his mother would even be mentioned, but Will tackled the matter head on. 'I guess you know your mom's not well again.'

'Yeah,' said Jack, thinking, *Is that what they call it?*

'She's been working in Vegas all right, but she's in the hospital.'

Jack shrugged, determined to show that he didn't care.

Will looked about as keen to have this conversation as Jack, but he struggled on dutifully. 'What it means, Jack, is that if you don't hear from her it's because she's sick. It's not that she doesn't care.'

On Christmas Day there was the three of them, since Maris decided not go to her family up near the Oregon border as she usually did. And even though he had long ceased to believe in Santa Claus, Jack was happy when he woke up to find stockings hanging from the fireplace downstairs. Maris and Will had coffee while he extracted the candy and toothbrush and Heath bar and packet of cashews and superball and comb ('Not that you'll use that,' said Maris) and pencils and pack of Pez which Maris had stuffed in an old wool stocking she used for hiking, and then they ate an enormous breakfast of waffles and sausage and Maris had him and Will fetch firewood from the barn and light a fire in the big room even though it was over fifty degrees outside and the sun had come out.

Finally they got to open presents and he gave Maris a large bottle of toilet water which Will had him buy in Healdsburg, though he couldn't believe that was what it was really called (the water, not Healdsburg), and he gave Will new work gloves since Maris had told him he needed them. Both seemed pleased enough so the duty part of Christmas was over and he found a very handsome sweater from Gram which he might wear twice a year if he ever went to church. Then Will gave him a diving mask and flippers so he could explore the bottom of the pond and Maris gave him a set of hand gardening tools – trowel and secateurs and clippers and a sharp pruning knife. He'd never had practical presents before, and they made him feel grown up. There was an envelope, too, and when he opened it there was a note from Will which simply said, *This is one present you will have to wait for until spring.* And he laughed at the quirkiness of a present that was only promised on a piece of paper, and Will wouldn't tell him what it was no matter how much he tried to pump him so finally he gave up.

After Christmas the weather turned colder, as the wind shifted around to the north and east, and it seemed to rain for weeks. This part of Sonoma got fifty inches of rain a year, according to Will, 'and forty-eight of them come in winter.' He felt stuck inside, which was made worse when his grades came. There were four levels in each subject – Unsatisfactory, Satisfactory, Very Good and Excellent. Will took the envelope Jack brought home and looked at the slips carefully at the big room dining table while Maris stood in the kitchen door watching. 'Satisfactory,' Will announced, 'every single one. That's not bad, Jacko. Now is it?' he asked rhetorically of Maris.

But Maris frowned and went back into the kitchen. Later on, before supper was ready, she called up to Jack in his bedroom, and when he came downstairs she was sitting at the dining table, with a book and a pad and two pencils. He knew better than to argue, and thereafter every afternoon ended, no matter what he had been doing, with tutoring from Maris. She concentrated mainly on his writing – not his handwriting, which was adequate, but forming sentences that, according to Maris, 'actually say what you're trying to say'.

But that wasn't all. He found his television time after supper was cut by half an hour, which Maris insisted be spent reading, and in the big room with her there so he couldn't cheat. He tried protesting to Will – he was his relative, after all, not hers – but got precisely nowhere, Will throwing his hands up and retreating to his office. But Jack didn't resent it very much, since he liked sitting in the big room with Maris – he just wished it wasn't schoolwork bringing them together. She justified the strict regimen by saying, 'The average boy reads for pleasure fewer than eight minutes a day.'

'If that's so,' Jack said, sensing an opening, 'why are you making me read for half an hour?'

'Because you're not an average boy.' She looked at him

187

triumphantly. '"Satisfactory" is just not good enough for the likes of you.'

He saw another side to her through their sessions together, one which was less moody and more giving. She seemed to like going through the exercises she set him, and took more satisfaction from his progress than he did, since for the life of him he couldn't really see that he was making progress at all. Fortunately when they sat down to work Maris was usually cooking something, so there were pretty constant distractions. Once a week she made chilli, and he loved the smell as she browned the meat and added onions and cayenne pepper. 'If you liked to read as much as you liked to eat,' said Maris, 'you'd get Excellents in everything.'

And it was true that he loved food, though he didn't want to explain to Maris that her cooking in the kitchen reminded him of the early years with his mother, before cold cereal and sandwiches became the staple meals she made. Maris loved hot food, even more than Will, and sometimes the chilli was just too spicy for Jack to eat. 'I forgot to tone it down,' she'd say. 'Sorry, Jack.'

Will himself seemed preoccupied. One of his apple contracts had not been renewed, and he heard Will discuss something called 'bitter pit' with Maris. 'I should never have sprayed with nitrogen,' he said, 'not when the crop was so light and the fruit so big. I won't do it again, but try telling Jorgensen's that.' And the boy understood that Jorgensen's, whatever that might be, was what had refused to renew their contract.

Unwittingly, Jack seemed to contribute to his uncle's worries. They were having supper one Friday night – it was barbecue with Maris's spicy sauce that she toned down for Jack and early corn from the Central Valley – when Jack piped up, asking, 'Will, what is sinsemilla?'

Maris exhaled loudly and said, 'Lordy.'

Will wiped his mouth with about his twentieth paper napkin and pursed his lips like he always did when he wanted to buy time before replying. 'It's to do with marijuana. You know what that is?'

'Of course I do,' Jack said irritably. When would they understand he wasn't three years old? Sometimes they acted just like
his friends' parents.

'Well sinsemilla is sort of like the essence of marijuana.'

'You mean it's a smell?' Jack had heard of essence before; it
was perfume.

'Not exactly,' said Will, entering what Jack always thought of
as his 'mature' mode. It was usually unconvincing. 'It's a little
more than that. But where did you hear the word?'

'At school. Jerry Simonson was talking.' There was no point
saying 'some kid at school', since it might not mean much to Will
but Maris knew the name of every one of them.

'Did he have some?' Will asked, his eyes swinging back and
forth between the two of them, but Maris was fingering her spoon
and wouldn't meet his look.

'No,' Jack said. 'He was just talking.' He didn't want Will to
think they had been doing anything so he explained further. 'He
said his father claimed you can't make a living out of apple
growing—'

'Who can't?' Will was starting to look concerned.

'You, Will. He was talking about you.'

'Jerry Simonson's father was talking about me?' He looked at
Maris with an expression that was both appalled and disbelieving,
but she still kept her eyes on her spoon. 'He sells real estate,' Will
protested. 'What's he got to do with me?'

'Beats me, Will. I'm just telling you what Jerry said. His dad
said nobody in their right mind would grow apples in this part
of Sonoma. He says you'd only grow them for cover. Then Jerry
pretended to be smoking – you know,' Jack said, putting up his
hand and pinching his thumb and forefinger together, then mock-
inhaling. 'And that's when he said "sinsemilla".'

Maris was shaking her head now and Will looked flushed and
unhappy. 'What did you say?'

'I told him to shut up,' Jack said, which wasn't true since he
had been puzzled more than angered by what Jerry Simonson said.
And he was a little scared of him, though now he added with

boyish bravado, 'I told him if he said it again I'd punch his lights out.'

But Will didn't look impressed by this at all. 'Jesus Christ, don't hit him, whatever you do. That's the last thing we need – a visit here from the school. Or his father.'

'Or the police,' said Maris flatly. She stood up and began collecting the plates. 'Jack, you can help me do the dishes. Your uncle can sit out here by himself and sweat.'

He was not always stuck inside, and leaped at the chance to help when Will began the annual pruning cycle of the orchards late in January. While his uncle stood on the rungs of a metal ladder propped against the old standard Gravensteins in the Valley Orchard, Jack raked up the thin sticks of new growth and collected them in a large pile beside each tree. He could stay well ahead of Will's pruning, so he would make neat bundles out of the dropped twigs, and hold them together with thin rubber bands for storage in the barn – a year later they would make the most perfect kindling. And he still had time to cut the water spouts, or 'suckers' as he thought of them, which popped out like unwanted children from the base of the tree trunks.

There was limited time to help after the school bus deposited him at Truebridge's in the afternoon, though already by February he could gauge the light lengthening in almost visible daily incre-ments. And helping Will never got him out of his tutoring with Maris, though at least she gave him a pre-supper snack before sitting him down in the late afternoon. Weekends there was no one-on-one with her, though he almost wished there were since he had so many more hours free to help Will with the long slog. Usually Will worked in silence, though sometimes he brought a transistor radio along; occasionally he'd tell Jack about what he was doing, describing the methods for pruning: with some old neglected trees in the Back Orchard, he cut extravagantly, reducing the leader and removing the tangles of interior branches that sucked up the light and air. With healthier trees he mainly headed back, shortening branches, thinning out the new growth. With the youngest, still to fruit, he trained rather than cut their branches, sometimes even tying the thin branches to the leader.

All this he'd demonstrate to Jack as he worked, until it became ingrained in the boy like a tree's rings of growth. But much as he loved the orchards, Jack would try and change the subject sometimes, eager to hear his uncle talk about himself. He rarely succeeded, until one day, trying a different tack, he asked, 'Uncle Will, who taught you so much about apple trees? Was it your daddy?'

'God no. I don't think he'd have known an apple tree from a rhododendron. I had to teach myself. I don't think your granddad even liked the country.'

'Didn't he ever take you out of San Francisco?'

'Not very often. He worked pretty long hours and when he wasn't working he liked to relax at home. Drink a few beers and watch baseball on TV.' Will finished tying back an elusive leader and looked down at Jack. 'Nothing wrong with that of course.'

Jack thought for a minute. 'Did you know *my* daddy?'

Will came down the ladder and picked a grass blade. Sometimes he would split them with his fingernail and whistle through them. 'Uh-huh,' he said. 'A little bit.'

'What was he like?'

'Oh that's kind of hard to say. I only saw him a few times.'

'Did you like him?'

'I'm sure he was fine,' Will said, and tried to whistle through the grass blade. It didn't work.

'Yes but did you like him?'

Will pursed his lips and looked up the slope of the Valley Orchard in the direction of the house. 'Not a lot,' he said finally. 'Understand, I'm not trying to hurt your feelings. But I figure if you're troubling to ask me then you probably want the truth.'

Jack was silent for a moment. It was strange, but he had no particular view of his father, not even a fantasised image. His father was a big hole in his mind. Sometimes it seemed to Jack that as far as his mother was concerned his father had been an accident. Which Jack supposed made him one too. The man had played piano and run off to Alaska – that was the extent of what Jack knew.

'What was wrong with him, Will?' he asked. For if Will didn't like the man something must have been the matter with him, since Will liked everybody, except his old commanding officers.

'There was nothing really wrong with him – he was a good piano player; I heard him once in a club near Union Square – except he drank too much. And like a lot of people, when he was drinking he got nasty. He was just a little guy – I mean, your mom was bigger than he was – but he sure got mean when he drank. That was the problem.'

'But Mom drinks too,' Jack said, not revealing what had entered his mind – *and she didn't run off to Alaska*. But now she might as well have, for all the good it did Jack.

'Yes, she does. Yes sirree,' said Will, almost in wonder at the thought of his sister and her drinking. 'And that didn't help very much, I'm telling you. I'm sure you must have realised they didn't get along too great.' Jack nodded shyly. 'Anyway,' said Will, his voice lightening a little, 'what's with the questions? Have you been thinking about your dad lately?'

Jack shook his head.

'Well I think your dad's probably still alive, if that's what you're wondering. Why? Would you like to know where he is?'

Jack looked at his uncle with surprise; he had always known his father was in Alaska. Miles away. A different world. *Nothing to do with me*, Jack thought, not for the first time.

'Do you want to see him?' Will asked, surprising Jack even more.

'Hell no!' he said instantaneously, almost angrily.

'Just asking,' said Will, putting his hands up in mock surrender. 'We'll leave him be then.' He picked up another blade of grass, and this time managed a thin, weak whistle.

They didn't always stay on the farm, and sometimes they took day trips, once to the coast. It was ostensibly for Jack's benefit, though in fact Jack would have been happy to stay at the farm all the time. He had moved around so much with his mother (the last apartment had been 'home' only for four months) that he wanted to put roots down as much as possible, and roots meant not moving from a place.

He still thought quite often about his mother, but the pain of his separation from her was being dulled by time and the settled domestic routine of his new household. And Maris for all her moodiness and distance did lots of things his mother had stopped doing – like towelling his hair dry each night after he'd showered so he wouldn't go to bed with it still damp, then reading him a story when he was in bed, something which old as he was he still enjoyed; like nursing him when he was sick, bringing him hot drinks and sports magazines and comics she bought for him in town. And though she had her house in town, more and more it seemed she spent the night with Will, even referring to 'our bedroom' once when she asked Jack to fetch her handbag. As a family unit they were bound neither by blood nor marriage, but they cohered – getting along, doing things together, and this was something Jack had never had.

They went one Saturday almost directly west to the ocean, to the state park at Salt Point. It was a grey, gusty day, and they all wore rain gear as they walked along the wild grassed cliffs above the waves crashing against the shore. Jack could barely believe that it was the same ocean as the one which thudded onto the monotonous flat beach just five blocks from his grandmother, only a hundred miles south from where they now stood.

The park seemed virtually deserted to Jack, but Maris complained about the number of visitors. 'It used to be in winter you could spend all day here and barely see a soul,' she said as they got in the car to leave. 'It's all getting too built up. This county's going to be a suburb soon of the whole Bay Area. Mark my words.'

'Not near us,' said Jack.

'You'll see,' she said. 'They just won't be able to leave it alone. All these millionaires in Palo Alto I keep reading about are going to start looking for property.'

'That's awful far away,' said Will. 'They'll buy land down there.'

'You'll see,' said Maris again, and Jack wondered why she sounded so gloomy.

But what Jack really wanted to hear was something his uncle only rarely talked about, for, despite the boy's intense curiosity, Will never described his time in Vietnam, except for that first account of the beauty of its countryside. Once when Jack expressed his fear of rattlesnakes, his uncle said, 'Be thankful that's all we've got. Now, coral snakes,' he said, 'they're something to watch for. But we haven't got any here.' And he told how at Officers' Candidate School in Georgia men were forced to crawl under a line of live ammunition fire. One aspiring second lieutenant came across a coral snake and in his panic stood up, only to be killed instantly by a live round.

'I didn't know you were an officer, Will.'

'I wasn't. Though it was a close call,' Will said, and when Jack looked at him questioningly he added derisively, 'Goddamn dumbest thing I ever almost did.'

'What do you mean?'

'After Basic I just kept my head down, but I must have tested pretty high, because after about six months my sergeant came along and he said, "Son, I know and you know you're a sorry-assed excuse for an infantryman, but the powers that be think otherwise. For reasons I won't explain – and to be honest *cannot* explain either – it has been decided that you are potential officer material."'

Will laughed at the memory. '"Golly," I thought to myself, "think of that, little old me, with bars on his shoulders and men under his command. Won't Mom be proud?" And I came within all of twenty minutes of signing the form and heading off for Fort Benning Georgia, which has to be the asshole end of an asshole state.'

'Is that where you become an officer?'

'Yes sirree,' said Will, 'but fortunately that same sergeant, a southerner by the name of Lamar T. Firestone, believe it or not, he had the goodness in his heart to call me over for a little talk. He said, "Shaughnessy, I can see you are flattered by the exciting prospect of becoming an officer, something superior in rank even to yours truly, who has chewed your ass and made your life a misery. But can I point out one thing?" "Sure," I said, but I was thinking *he's just jealous*. And then he said, "There is a thing called the Vietnam War in progress, and despite the belief that airpower conquers all, there is plenty to do for old-fashioned grunts like you and me. Only we have to be led, don't we, as we walk along in the jungles of Vietnam looking for our country's enemies? So before you get too excited, ask yourself where second lieutenants – which is what you would become, if you're stupid enough to get on the airplane east – are likely to go with their brand-new shiny commissions. Leading patrols in the jungles of southeast Asia, that's where."'

'And fortunately I listened to the counsel of Lamar T. Firestone. Thanks be to God, I swallowed my pride and told them to go stick their OCS right up where the sun don't shine.'

'But you went to Vietnam anyway.'

'I did indeed, and it sure weren't no picnic. But when I was there, my own platoon lost three second lieutenants, two of them before my very eyes. While, as you can see, I'm still standing and breathing God's free air. Corporal was high as I got, and happy with it too. The moral of the story is always remember when you get offered things to ask yourself one question – "What's in it for them?" Don't think: "Gosh, they must think I'm the bee's knees to offer me this"; don't think "How can I turn them down and what will my relatives say?"; don't ever think, "Who am I to say no?" Just ask yourself whether you're really going to benefit from it, or whether the people praising you to the skies are the ones who make out the most.'

'But what was Vietnam like?'

'I told you before, just like here but without the apples.'

'Why won't you ever talk about it?' he complained.

His uncle looked at him with a mix of seriousness and tolerance. 'Jack, do you know what "minimise" means?'

Jack shook his head.

'It means to make small. Small as possible. That's what I learned to do, thanks to Lamar T. Firestone. Keep your ass away from the fire at all times. And when something bad happens, which it's bound to sooner or later, then in my experience the best way to handle it is to figure out first if you're okay, then try and make sure it doesn't happen again, and then *make it as goddamned small as you can*. Minimise. Know what I mean?"'

He wasn't sure if he did, though he understood the bit about making it small – you ducked your head, and if you got hit anyway then you tried to take the bad memory of the experience and tuck it away, so far away inside you that you didn't even know it was there. He thought: *Minimise. That's what I'm trying to do with Mom.*

At last, towards the end of February, the pruning was done and it was then that the prospect of his mysteriously delayed Christmas present materialised. Maris was in the kitchen when Jack ran in, unable to contain his excitement. 'Will says he's going to build me a tree house.'

'He did, did he?'

He sensed she was not impressed. 'It's real nice of him, Maris,' he said, wanting her to know that he was grateful. 'Has he got the time to do it, do you think?'

Maris snorted. 'Don't worry about that. He'll make time. Your uncle always does.' Later as he did his homework at the table in the big room, he heard her in the kitchen, talking on the wall phone with her friend Loraine. 'Honestly, sometimes I think he's just a big kid. And now that there's a real child here, he's got an excuse to act like one, too.' She didn't sound angry, but she didn't sound enthusiastic, either.

At first, Will wanted to build the tree house visible from the house, but there were no suitable trees – the eucalyptus weren't that close together. Jack felt in any case that building there would defeat half the purpose of a tree house, if it was right under the eyes of his . . . what would he call Will and Maris? Guardians? He certainly knew what that meant. But no, they were more than that – Will because he was his uncle, and Maris because Jack wanted her to be.

So he and Will went looking for a site in the acre or so of woods between the pond and the beginning of the Valley Orchard, a mix of firs and pines and oaks behind the bordering ring of eucalyptus on the pond side. About halfway into this stand they found three Monterey pines close together which would be perfect. They had thick branches, and the wide crutches of the trees were about eight feet off the ground, providing a perfect platform for a tree house floor. There was spare lumber in the barn, but Will wanted to do it properly, so they measured it out carefully; his uncle boosted Jack up onto a big limb and had him measure the rough floor area formed by the convergence of the trees. Will even insisted on sides to the house and a roof. They drove into Cloverdale on Saturday afternoon to the lumber yard, and started first thing Sunday morning. All day they worked, though Jack knew he was mainly just watching Will and fetching him drinks, and by four o'clock the plank floor was down, the packing cases were the sides, and even the two slanted sides of the roof were up and nailed together.

And it would have been hard to get Jack out of there ever again, such was his happiness with this private place, had there not been so much else to do. Both Maris and Will were tactful about his time in the tree house, never coming out there except when Jack invited them. The most his uncle did was come to the edge of this patch of wood and call out: *Jack, supper's ready*; or, when the boy was feeling low but had spent long enough time to recover his spirits, *Best come in now, Jack, it'll be dark soon*; or, *Maris wants you* and, if that failed, *Maris has been baking*.

Spring came stop-start, stop-start, with warm days in the high sixties, followed by windy cold rain which was twenty degrees lower, and then back to warm again. School remained a largely painless, slightly dull way of passing time until the school bus opened its cranky door and he jumped out and walked down the track to the farm where, as the days lengthened, life was increasingly conducted out of doors. There was simply so much to do.

197

He helped Maris plant lettuce and carrots and beets and sprouting broccoli, but though he appreciated the function of these – Maris claimed there was nothing more satisfying than eating what you yourself had planted – what he enjoyed most were the flowers they planted, using seeds Maris had collected, partly by her own harvesting efforts, some from a friend in town, some by mail order catalogues she looked through during the dark winter nights. Some Maris had him sow in the bed between the ground-floor deck outside the kitchen and her vegetable garden – iris and rose bushes she bought in Healdsburg and tulips, all protected now by a wide rectangle of rabbit-proof fencing which he and Will were made to lay one Sunday afternoon. But her special love was for wildflowers, and they would go for walks together, sometimes to go see Will when he was out in the orchards, sometimes just to have a walk. They were careful in the woods because of poison oak, and Maris would lead the way and stop to point out blue dicks (he would have laughed had they not been so beautiful) and mountain iris and wood strawberries which he ate, green and hard as they were. Near the Back Orchard there was California lilac trying to bud, and a little patch of sticky monkey flower, ridiculously named but structured like a complicated pagoda, and all over there was huckleberry.

This time when his grades came he had a handful of Very Good, only two Satisfactory (he was never going to be any good at math, he told Maris) and one Excellent. Even Maris allowed as how this wasn't too bad at all.

As the weather warmed for good, he was allowed to swim in the pond again, and usually Will joined him, hot from his work in the greenhouse, where he was busy readying the scion sticks for grafting. Even supper usually got eaten outside, on the back deck, where Will barbecued chicken or hamburgers, and they ate salads with lettuce and tomatoes from the garden, and the most incredible kinds of fruit from the market in Healdsburg. Strawberries from Watsonville (though Maris's were almost ready in the greenhouse), peaches and apricots from even further south.

There was the occasional shadow. Maybe apples did better than Simonson the realtor realised, but sometimes it was hard to see how, and late at night he heard tense conversations going on between Will and Maris, with words and phrases, none of them sounding happily spoken, like 'mortgage' and 'price per pound' and once even 'bales', though he thought Will had already pre-sold all the hay to a farmer on the other side of Geyserville.

Then one afternoon Maris planted wild onion plants on the sandy bank behind the greenhouse. Jack was nervous about it – 'I thought there were rattlers around here.'

Maris looked at him. 'Jack, there're rattlers almost everywhere in this entire county. But when was the last time you saw one?'

He had to think for a moment. 'There was a dead one last autumn up on the road near Truebridge's.'

'See what I mean? There are plenty of snakes around, and I've always told you to be careful about picking up big rocks or stepping where you can't see. But they're a lot more scared of us than we are of them.' She stopped and looked at Jack, smiling as she added, 'Well, maybe not. But they're shy enough to get out of your way. They'd have heard us coming over here and made themselves scarce. Okay?'

And it was, except that it didn't answer the question now forming in Jack's head, which was why Will had told him to stay away from this very bank precisely because of snakes. And why never to explore the area up at the top of the bank. And it was these unanswered questions, and the sense he had from time to time of a shadow coming over all of them – for reasons he couldn't specify; the tensions of the apple business didn't help, but that didn't seem to account for all of it – which prompted him to try and figure out just what was going on.

For something was. He knew that, and he found himself unwilling to respect the no-go areas Will had set out.

First, the tangled acres above the sandy bank behind the greenhouse where his uncle said he must never play. He *was* scared of rattlesnakes, of which there were more than a few around, but since talking to Maris he was confident it wasn't true about the bank. And thus he went and saw for himself, taking a big stick along just in case he saw a rattler, and not fifty yards from the top of the bank he found, in the middle of dense under-growth, an area of cleared ground, shaded by the overhanging branches of a circle of eucalyptus trees. In this space there were three now-raggedy rows of plants, green stalks with small abun-dant leaves the colour of bright, light emeralds, almost lumi-nescently coloured. They had a skunky smell as well, though he could not be sure if this didn't come from the swamp which began behind them. And he wondered, *Is this sinsemilla?*

If it was, he figured out as he lay in bed that night, then it didn't seem much of a crop, and pretty obviously it hadn't been harvested the year before. In which case what was the point of having it at all?

He found the answer by accident, when he violated the second no-go prohibition. Will was in the Valley Orchard, cutting early grass with the tractor, and Maris was grading a math test imposed by the state authorities, sitting at the table in the big room in front of a stack of multiple-choice answers. He told her he was going to the pond, but kept on going around it to the greenhouse.

Inside it seemed unfamiliar. The strawberry plants had been moved out and planted along the edges of Maris's vegetable plot, and most of the scion bud packs were now grafted onto the root stock of older trees in the Valley Orchard. He walked around the wooden trestle tables, largely empty, trying to think what could have been happening to explain his uncle's sternness about his unaccompanied presence here. He happened to look back and then, intrigued, looked again. There was a faint shape, the trace of an outline, against the back wall of the greenhouse. A door? How could this be, since the greenhouse abutted the hillside, which formed its back wall? He brushed aside the leaves of a ficus plant barring his way, stepped around several large tins of paint, then moved an old wooden stool. With these obstacles out of the way, he could clearly see that the outline on the wall was indubitably the frame of a door, but mysteriously there was no doorknob. Closer inspection revealed an indentation in the outline, just above the floor, and when he crouched down he saw a brass-coloured slide of metal. Reaching with his hand, he pulled on it, and it turned at right angles, extending outwards, so that by gripping it he could pull. He did, and the door moved, opening smoothly, silently towards him.

Beyond the door it was pitch black, but as he stepped forward he sensed a cavernous space, like a cellar carved out of the side of the hill. A hidden room, which excited his curiosity even more than it did his apprehension. He stood just inside it, slightly spooked, trying fruitlessly to adjust his eyes to the dark so he could gain some sense of the volume of the space before him. He put a hand tentatively forward, then felt around the sides of the inner side of the door. He found a switch and flicked it. Nothing at first, then after several seconds came the wavering, shaky onset of strange square lights, across the low ceiling of the room, set in two rows of horizontal strip.

But the lights only briefly held his attention. For beneath them in individual black plastic pots, sitting on planks covering a rough earth floor, were plants, four or five feet high, each with a long thin green central stalk, off which hung small green leaves. He stepped forward to look at them more closely.

'What are you doing?'

It was Will in the doorway behind him, holding a claw hammer which he now put down on a shelf.

'I'm sorry, Uncle Will,' Jack said, swallowing rapidly.

'Didn't I tell you not to come in here without me?'

Jack started towards the door with his head down, planning to walk past his uncle. It was as he passed him that he suddenly felt his head rocked, detonated by a terrific slap across the cheek. At first he simply didn't know what had happened – had something fallen from a shelf? – but looking at Will as his ears literally rang and the pain grew, he saw Will was furious.

He hit me, and all Jack could think of next was his mother, and how when she used to slap him she would follow up the first big hit with a series of supplementary smacks, some of them just as hard, and though Will looked a little astonished now too,

Jack wasn't going to wait around and watch whatever internal debate his uncle might conduct about what to do next. So he charged out the door and into the 'normal' greenhouse, then through its outer door. Once outside, he didn't stop, but ran around the far side of the pond and into the copse, heading for the tree house, his sanctuary. He came to the Monterey pine and climbed quickly, then regretted his choice, since it would be the first place his uncle would go to look for him. And indeed as he climbed down and stood on the forest floor of soft needles again, he heard his uncle coming through the ferns, calling out, 'Jack! Where are you, Jack?' He didn't sound angry any more, but Jack didn't want to know.

He turned around to climb back up, and this time on impulse he didn't stop when he reached the plank floor of the tree house but kept climbing, up the packing crate slats of its side walls, pulling himself up onto the pitched roof, where the flat plywood panels bowed under his weight but did not give way.

He stood up carefully on the slanted pitch of the roof, and moved cautiously up to the gable line, where he teetered on both feet; from here he reached up and grabbed a large knotted limb of the big Monterey pine. He pulled himself up and found that where the thick branch joined the trunk of the tree, another branch, from a neighbouring Douglas fir, slanted across and ran next to the arm of the pine. The two of them lay side by side, and formed a kind of platform, a floor of limbs that was wide enough for the boy to swing both legs up and lie on, fully extended. He rested with his legs out this way, and his back leaning against the pine trunk. He was not uncomfortable, and when he leaned over to look down all he could see was the roof of the tree house several feet below him. The ground below on either side of the tree house was blocked from view by the thick and shaggy arms of the Monterey; the other trees of the wood obscured any sight of him from further away. He was invisible from the ground.

Within seconds he heard his uncle arrive, fifteen feet below. 'Jack,' he called, and the boy assumed he had been spotted. But then his uncle called again. 'Jack, are you up there?'

He said nothing. After a moment, he heard his uncle swing a leg up onto the boards hammered to the tree trunk, which served as steps for climbing into the tree house. Then his uncle's boots rang from the tree house planks. 'Shit,' his uncle exclaimed, and the boy heard him sit down heavily, not much more than eight feet below him.

He thought about making his unseen presence known, maybe even trying to scare his uncle at first – he could snap a twig off and drop it onto the roof of the tree house, say, or make a clicking noise, rolling his tongue under the soft inner side of his mouth, a pale imitation of a rattlesnake which lately he was practising, to Maris's distraction. His uncle didn't sound angry any more, and he would probably laugh, but then Jack felt the stinging on his cheek and thought, *Hell no, let him wait.*

And then he heard Maris calling out, and his uncle called back, and after a moment she too came through the chain ferns, stopping at the base of the big pine. 'What are you doing up there?'

'I was looking for Jack.'

'I thought he was swimming in the pond.'

'He was supposed to be. I found him in the greenhouse. Looking at things he shouldn't be looking at. I kind of lost my temper when I found him there.' He added in a low voice, 'I smacked him one.'

'Oh Lordy,' she said. 'Is he okay?'

'I didn't *hit* him, Maris,' Will said, managing to sound both aggrieved and guilty. 'I slapped him. And yes, I know I shouldn't have. But it's his pride that's hurt, more than anything else.'

'That depends how hard you slapped him. Come on: let's go find him.'

After they left, Jack waited almost twenty minutes before he made his way down. He was still a little stunned, but he was relieved that his uncle was contrite and pleased that Maris wasn't indifferent about it. He knew now that Jerry Simonson was right, and that his uncle was growing sinsemilla or marijuana or whatever the right term was in a secret room with special lights in the greenhouse.

He took his time going back to the house, where both Will and Maris gave him relieved hugs and asked him where he'd been. Walking in the Valley Orchard, he replied, and did not let on about the niche he'd found above the tree house. He liked the idea of having a hiding place entirely to himself.

At supper there was an air of tension between Maris and Will. Jack excused himself early and went upstairs, since there was nothing good on television. He read an old-fashioned baseball story by John Tunis until he was half asleep, and had just managed to get undressed and put his pyjamas on when Maris came in to say goodnight, then heard her tell Will not to bother since he was probably already asleep.

And he was soon asleep, but the tense earnestness of the talk below must have wakened him. He wanted some water, and in his fatigue had forgotten to fill his night side glass, but when he moved towards the gallery he slowed down and stood on tiptoe. It was not the volume – for all her sharpness, Maris never shouted and Will, even when stressed, spoke in mild and folksy tones – but the tenor of the conversation, which sounded unprecedentedly stressed, and made him stop and hide his presence up above them, within earshot.

Maris was saying, 'You know I don't like this business. I wish you would stop. You know I do.'

'Sure I can stop. And then what do we live on? Apple juice?'

'My salary's not *that* bad. We'd get by.'

'We might have before, but now we've got another mouth to feed.'

'It's not like he costs very much. And he helps out with the orchards.'

'Sure he does. But it's not *now* I'm thinking about. What happens in a few years when he wants to go to college? What do we do then if I don't have two nickels to rub together.'

'This situation may not last forever.'

'Why not? Who else is going to raise him? My sister? Pigs might fly and I might win a trip to Hawaii. And he's better off here than with Gram. At least *I* think he is.'

'Of course he is. And don't act like I don't want him here. All I mean is that I'd rather be poor as church mice than have money in the bank and you in a Federal penitentiary. Or worse. I bet Jack would feel the same way.'

'Hey!' His uncle must have stood up while they were talking, because he was standing on the front side of the big room and turning back had an excellent view of Jack eavesdropping in his pyjamas. 'Have you been listening in?' his uncle said, but his tone was only slightly accusatory.

He doesn't want to think I heard him, thought Jack, and he shook his head. 'I couldn't sleep. I was just going to the bathroom to get some water.'

'Go ahead. But then get on back to bed.'

The rest of their conversation downstairs was conducted in whispers, and the next day when Jack came home from school he found Will inside, upstairs on the gallery. He was surrounded by tools and had a band saw set up; he'd built a wall frame to make a separate room out of Jack's bedroom space and was busy nailing in stud partition board. 'I thought it was time you had some privacy,' was all he said to Jack.

But that was not the end of it.

He caught a cold the next week, which at first he endured while going to school. It seemed ridiculous to have a cold when the temperature was seventy degrees and the sun shone all day long and he should be enjoying the hours outside the classroom, but instead he just felt miserable in his head and blew his nose about every forty seconds. He was worse when he woke up the next morning, and Will had already gone to see a man about insurance first thing down in Santa Rosa, and Maris was about to take him to school with her when she looked at him and declared that he was staying home. 'You stay here today, and don't you dare watch television downstairs. I want you in bed where you belong. Will should be back at lunch-time to look after you. If there's any problem, phone the school and they'll find me.'

And in truth he felt so rotten that he did stay in bed. Even reading tired him out and he slept on and off all morning. He heard Will come back and park his truck, and then come into the house, and he was about to shout down to him when he heard Will go out the front door again, its screen door swinging shut with its usual *whack*, and then he heard another truck come into the turnaround. There were voices, and he could make out Will's, but then they trailed off slightly, and out of curiosity Jack got up, feeling slightly dizzy, and opened the sliding glass door and stepped out onto the deck.

He saw Will and a taller man wearing a sharp-brimmed cowboy hat, walking towards the barn, while a third man backed his pickup truck towards the barn. He was going to shout out hello, but it occurred to him that Will did not know he was home, and as he watched, leaning out around the edge of the deck's railing, he felt there was something stealthy in the visit of these other men. It was the same feeling he'd had once when, as he sat downstairs, Maris came out of Will's bedroom naked. She must have thought Jack was outside, and he watched as she went along the gallery to the bathroom, and by the time he thought to cough or say something it was too late, for if he did that she would know he had been watching her.

Now too he froze, as he watched one of the men lift a bale wrapped in black plastic and throw it into the back of the truck, where the driver climbed up and covered it and another bale Will brought out with a tarpaulin.

It was far too late to make his presence known; caution overcame his curiosity, and Jack moved fast and silently back into his room and into bed. And he pretended to be asleep when some time later, which seemed an hour but he knew was probably only minutes, he heard the truck drive off. Will came into the house and must have seen Jack's school books on the kitchen table, because he came upstairs at once.

'I didn't know you were home. Something wrong?'

Jack simulated a lengthy yawn. 'Maris told me to stay home because my cold is a lot worse.'

Will nodded and Jack thought he had carried it off. But then

Will pointed at the sliding door. 'Why's that open?'

Jack looked at the sliding door and cursed his haste in leaving the deck. He tried to shrug, as if to say *who knows?* but couldn't seem to manage it, and he knew his face was starting to flush. He wouldn't look at Will.

'Did you see my visitors?' Jack hesitated, and Will made a cluck with his tongue and went out onto the deck. He stood where Jack had been just five minutes before. 'A bird's eye view,' his uncle announced loudly and shook his head. When he came back in he closed the sliding door behind him and looked down at Jack. 'Did you know what all that was about?'

And very slowly Jack nodded, though in truth he didn't know for sure. He was frightened now that Will would get angry again, but instead his uncle's face softened and he said, 'I'm not wild about the business myself. But you see, apples just don't pay. At least, not enough they don't. Mine anyway. Still, I'm sorry you were here. The last thing I want is to drag you into my business.' He paused and looked at Jack. Now his tone was even softer, almost imploring. 'I'd like to ask you a favour, okay?'

Jack waited, but when Will did not go on he nodded his assent. Will said, 'Could you not tell Maris about those guys coming here today?' He gestured with his head in the direction of the barn. 'Do that for me please. There's no good going to come from her knowing about it. It will just upset her.'

Jack realised that Will must be even more anxious than he seemed, that this was something he – Jack – could do to help him. So he said, 'Okay, Will,' dropping the 'uncle' because for just a moment, a fleeting split second, he felt they were equals.

Yet when they ate the supper that night which Maris cooked, fish wrapped in foil over coals with local corn, French bread and a tomato salad, Jack felt deeply uncomfortable. He had never had any secrets from Maris or Will, except for the times when he felt intermittent sadness about his mom. This was different, keeping a secret with one of them from the other. It would have been easier the other way round – conspiring with Maris to keep Will in the dark. He didn't know why, but it was true. This he didn't like at all.

School was out at last, and they went for a weekend camping in the upper part of the state, almost four hours' drive, to the northernmost redwood park called Jedediah Smith State Park. Here they pitched a tent at a campsite, and grilled steaks on a brick barbecue. Jack had a kayak lesson in the Smith River, and Will fished with no luck for king salmon from the bank. There were plenty of other people camping there, but Maris seemed far happier than she'd been at Salt Point, though she went off in the afternoon of their second day there, saying she had some errands to run.

'See what you want?' asked Will when she returned just before suppertime.

'There're a lot of nice places and a lot cheaper than Sonoma. I'd say land is about two-thirds the price, and the houses can't be half as much.'

'What are you talking about?' asked Jack.

'Maris was looking at real estate.'

'Why?' he asked, feeling as if a sensor had set off an internal alarm.

'In case we wanted to move. Who knows? It might be nice to have a change.'

Maris was watching him carefully, Jack could see that, but he couldn't help his reaction. Change was the last thing he wanted. In his experience change was bad – it was precisely the recent lack of change in his life that had made him happy.

'Jack, we wouldn't go anywhere you didn't like,' she said soothingly.

'But I like the farm,' he protested.

'I know you do,' said Maris, and she went off to get groceries she'd bought out of the car.

'She's talking dreams, Jack,' said Will in a quick whisper. 'That's all.'

*

208

But it was real, as became clear on their return to Sonoma the next afternoon. After supper, Maris brought out a list of properties she'd gathered on her side trip. There was one place in particular she liked, an old wood farmhouse with forty acres of mixed top and soft fruit. It didn't have a pond, but it bordered the Smith River, the same one which ran through the state park and was, said Maris, the cleanest large river in the state. The house was older than theirs, set back from the nearest road with shutters on the windows, and a lawn in back that ran down into meadow and the edge of the river. On a hill, just visible in the particulars, were the soft fruit plantings, stretched like grape vines across the slope, with the orchard above it.

Even Jack could see it was pretty, but he was determined not to say so. He kept quiet while Maris made a pitch for the place, talking money numbers he couldn't follow, except their drift – which was that their current bad situation could be reversed if they moved.

Will listened patiently until Maris finished. Then he said, 'Well, it's a hell of a big decision. Maybe we should have a vote on it. I've got one vote, you've got one, and it's only fair that Jack here's got a little bit of a vote. You want to go there; I want to stay here, at least until next autumn. Jack, what do you think?'

He felt shy, especially when Maris didn't make it any easier by staring at him. He looked down at his knees as he said, 'I'd like to have this school year here,' thinking that maybe in a year Maris would change her mind.

'That swings it,' Will declared. He looked at Maris, whose face was stony now. 'Don't be a sore loser, darling. Fair's fair.'

'All right,' she said, and it seemed worse to Jack that her voice was so level and subdued. 'You win. But when we do move your crop selection's got to change.'

'It will,' said Will, trying to be accommodating.

'You're not going to grow prunes instead of apples are you?' demanded Jack, but the two were looking directly at each other now. He might as well have not even been there for all the attention they were paying him.

Maris said, 'I wish you'd forget this year while we're at it.'

'Darling,' Will said, 'you don't want to throw all that money away. That's the whole point of staying.'

'It's not going to be much use to us if you land yourself in—' and she looked at Jack as she broke off. Shaking her head she walked away, and a moment later they could hear the kitchen screen door slam and her footsteps sound on the outside deck.

'Thanks, Jack,' his uncle whispered. 'Thanks for the support.' And Jack basked in this only briefly, since part of him knew that his vote of confidence in Will had also let Maris down.

Through two days of coolness she let him know it too, and she was still acting frosty when she called to him one Saturday afternoon while he was catching and releasing frogs at the near and algae-coated end of the pond. 'Jack, hurry up and come to town with me. I forgot all about your shoes for school.'

He came up to the back deck where Maris was cleaning out the ash from the barbecue. 'Why can't I wear these?' he said, pointing to his sneakers.

'Because they've got holes in both toes is why. Now come on.'

So they got into Maris's car, and she rolled down the window as she turned around, shouting to Will in the barn that they'd be back before supper and that he should shuck the corn, and then they moved along the track. Jack sensed Maris was still annoyed with him, so he didn't say a word, until as they approached Truebridge's shack he saw another car up ahead, heading their way, which pulled over. As they approached them, Jack said, 'Who are they, Maris?'

She shrugged. 'Pickers maybe, looking for work. They're not local, I know that,' and she barely slowed down, saying, 'I've got to get you to the store before it closes. I'm not having you go to school looking like Oliver Twist.'

And that would have been that, except as they passed the car, waiting off to the side of the track, the man who wasn't driving suddenly raised his arm and put a hat on his head, and it was a Stetson, and Jack saw with a thump of recognition that it was the same man he'd seen hoisting bales out of the barn with Will not two weeks before.

Why are they back here? he thought to himself, and he decided he just had to tell Maris about them, and the fact that he had seen them before and seen what they had been doing. But he didn't know how to say all this, since telling her straight out would seem such a betrayal of Will – though not telling seemed suddenly an even greater betrayal of Maris. And he considered how he could best inform her, without seeming a snitch. And he thought of their prospective move to the northernmost part of California, and he wondered what good would that do. Why would it change anything? Why would Will not just repeat this shady business of adding to his apple income by growing the sinsemilla there?

So since Maris now seemed at least willing to talk a bit, he said tentatively, 'Maris, if we do go up north . . .' He hesitated, trying how best to get to the point, which was to let her in on the secret he so unhappily carried.

'Yes,' she said, sounding wary but not altogether hostile.

'I mean, what actually would change? If Will's no good at growing apples . . .'

'What do you mean?' she asked, and the wariness was gone altogether, replaced by anger. And she pulled over on the mountain road, not that there was space to, but it didn't matter since there was hardly ever any traffic on the road, and as she slowed Jack noticed the most enormous redbud growing on the side of the road, which normally he would have commented on, but not now because he sensed he had said something terribly wrong, and sure enough Maris shouted, as the car came to a stop, 'How dare you, you little . . . *bastard*! How dare you criticise your uncle, after all he's done for you?' She was furious.

He felt so crushed – tart as she could be, Maris had never called him that before – that he gave up right then, abandoned his subtle plan to divulge the earlier visit of the bale-packing marijuana-dealing crooks (they must be crooks, he figured; it was illegal wasn't it?). And he put his hands in his lap and looked down at them and muttered, 'Sorry.'

And he felt Maris's angry gaze on him as she said, in school-teacher mode, recovering herself, 'I should hope so too.' And then she pulled out again, quite sharply, and they drove to Healdsburg in silence to buy him new shoes before the store closed.

He was going to stay after school and watch the varsity football team scrimmage, then go home with Maris. But when the bell went he found Maris waiting discreetly outside class. 'Jack, would you mind taking the bus home today? I've got a teachers' meeting this evening and a lot of stuff to do before then, so I haven't really got time to go out to Will's. Do you mind?'

She must have seen the disappointment in his face about missing the football practice, because she said, 'If it's a problem you can always stay with me in town tonight if you like. I'll call Will and let him know.'

He shook his head. For some reason, the prospect of staying in town alone with Maris – something he had never done before – made him feel awkward. 'That's okay, Maris. I've got a lot of homework anyway.'

'So what are you going to cook Will for supper then?' Maris asked.

'Pot luck,' he said, expecting Maris to laugh.

But she didn't, saying only, 'See you tomorrow.'

So he caught the bus, sitting right behind Sam the driver, and he talked with his friend Ernie Weiskranz as the bus left town and went east along the Russian River, before eventually swinging north and climbing, then descending west into the valley of the local wine country. The bus stopped every few minutes to let other kids off, and after one of the kids from junior high got out at Dry Creek Road, the bus began to climb up to his uncle's place. There was only Ernie and two other kids left, and by now Jack and his friend had pretty much run out of anything to talk about and both were tired, as was Sam, who drove the morning shift as well. Sam didn't like to talk while he was driving, but he did mutter to himself, and today he was saying *hot, whew it's hot* repeatedly, and it was true that even with all the windows open the temperature was unpleasantly high, and though the air circulated this did not serve to cool things off. So Jack was glad when the bus stopped at last, and as he got up and said goodbye to Ernie and got ready to say goodbye to Sam, he thought how nice it would be to be in the dark cool house and have a long cold drink and how maybe he would go swimming in the frog pond, especially if Will went swimming with him, and then he stepped down into the heat and dusty gravel of the roadside.

A Private Affair

'I SHOULD THINK HE weighed almost thirty stone,' said Kate, able to find comedy in even the driest of oil producers' confabs. 'He was *so* large!' she added unnecessarily, beginning to laugh again, hard enough that in a minute Renoir wouldn't be able to understand what she was saying. 'And he got into the lift and said . . .' She stopped to giggle at the memory of it. '"I like Helsinki. Though the food's a little thin on the ground."'

He laughed too, as much from happiness at seeing her so relaxed as at anything she said. They were sitting in the sitting room of the flat, he in the rocking chair, she lying down on the sofa with her work shoes off and her suit jacket – Donna Something? He could never remember the designer names – folded on the coffee table. Each of them held a large drink in hand, bourbon and ice for Renoir, gin and tonic for Kate. It was like old times, he thought, then smiled inside at the thought of 'old times' in a relationship less than two years old.

It was that point in early spring, towards the end of March, when the days were long enough that they could sit like this after work with daylight from the window and no lamps turned on. And everything else seemed to be lengthening as well – the leaves on the trees, the shrubs, flowers, the grass in Hyde Park. It was the time of year when everything was still to play for.

He liked the fact that though their talk was always easily come by they didn't ever feel the need to fill the silence, and now they listened to the early spring sounds of school kids back for bed from playing in the park, and couples returning from restaurant meals, and the cars and cabs moving faster now in the distance on High Street Kensington and down Queen's Gate.

They would sit like this most weekdays, over a drink, comparing notes on what had happened to each of them since the morning. Kate's accounts were full of meetings and people, but Renoir's was

217

also rarely empty. For 'what to do today' was never a problem for him; he woke each morning with the day before him like a painter's palette. He had the most open-ended of routines, but he was never bored. He ran errands and bought the groceries, since Kate was so busy at work and, besides, she shopped like a bachelor banker; she'd buy a six-pound chicken, then wonder why dinner took two hours to cook. In the afternoon, he read books and listened to music and cooked supper.

And he liked to walk. Knowing San Francisco so well from a lifetime there he was initially frustrated by moving to a city he didn't know at all; the solution was to walk it daily, and he'd done so with the vigour of an apprentice cabbie learning the Knowledge. He was learning London like a language; after more than a year he was starting to feel almost fluent.

Six weeks before, when Kate returned from Dubai, he did not say anything about the GPS reading. But within a week he felt forced to do *something*, not because of anything Kate had said or done but because of his own need to know. *Know what?* Know that she still loved him, or, and he swallowed hard contemplating this, know that she didn't any more.

Such was the company of the thoughts he had kept, running like wallpaper on a PC screen, and he could tell that if he did nothing about them they would soon poison his life with Kate. Black-and-white Renoir had come back with a vengeance. Try as he did, he could not help but examine everything she said, each gesture she made, for signs of a change she was hiding from him. The mundane became forged with meaning, which in a relationship was an unbearable state of affairs. Clarity became a necessity.

Fortunately it was not difficult to engineer. One afternoon he went to the garage and downloaded the data from the car recorder, then printed it out at home. He left it with a Soil Society pamphlet on organic orchards in the flat's front hall, in the big blue china bowl which sat on the Regency chest of drawers.

'What's this?' asked Kate. She had just come in from work that evening and it was still just light outside, which now marked for Renoir the true beginning of spring. She was looking through the post.

'Oh, when I took the car out to go to Belfield, the GPS was going on and off. I thought I'd make sure it was working in case anything happened.'

She came into the living room, studying the printout. 'We don't use the car much, do we?'

'No, we don't. Just Belfield, pretty much.'

'Not even Belfield, I see,' she said with a laugh. 'And we certainly don't need the GPS any more, do we? Not if we've got the garage.'

'You're right,' he said. 'Should I get it taken out?'

He waited as she continued to inspect the paper. 'I see it logged my visit to Burdick's Farm. I stopped there when I went down after Christmas. The Benedicts were just moving in and I dropped by to say hello.'

Why? he thought, and this must have been apparent in his eyes when she looked at him, for she said, 'Have to be polite, you know. Neighbours and all that.'

He nodded grudgingly and she continued. 'Helena Benedict wanted to see the Gatehouse so she drove me over.' She held up the printout. 'That's why I never got as far as Belfield.'

He could feel her eyes on him but he kept his glued to the page of the *Evening Standard*. 'I didn't know you knew his wife,' he said as casually as he could.

'Who, Conrad's? I barely do. But when she asked to see the Gatehouse, I couldn't really say no.'

'I saw him at Belfield, you know. He was shooting with Roddy.'

She looked at him, giving nothing away. He went on, 'He came to dinner with Helena. He's not at all what I would have expected.'

'How's that?'

'He's not very tactful, is he? He started banging on about the Irish and his time in Northern Ireland when he was in the army. It made you realise why there was so much trouble there.' Kate shrugged. 'He didn't know I was Irish, I guess, or he probably wouldn't have been so candid.'

219

Kate laughed, slightly shrilly. 'He wouldn't have cared even if he had known,' she said. 'That's the way he is.'

'I sat next to his wife at dinner. She was a little unusual too.'

'A nightmare,' said Kate, then changed the subject. She must have sensed that he'd noticed she hadn't gone to Belfield; perhaps she'd sensed his unease about it too.

Now, six weeks later, the Gatehouse was still not entirely finished, but was sufficiently complete for them to move books into the bedroom and fill the rooms with cast-off furniture from the vast attics of Belfield. The actual purchase of the Gatehouse and its surrounding fifty acres was still incomplete, remaining in the hands of the solicitors (each side described themselves as the family's firm). Unhappy with this loose end, Renoir was nonetheless reluctant to nag Kate about it, especially when all seemed right again with their world. This weekend they were in London, staying in town, since Kate had only got back late Friday from a four-day trek through the natural gas fields of Scandinavia. She slept in Saturday morning, and they spent the afternoon touring antiques shops.

This night he cooked while Kate sat at the kitchen table, reading out the interesting bits from the papers. He grilled wild salmon fillets, marinated in lemon and dill, and cooked a mix of wild and long grain rice, with steamed green beans topped by almonds. Kate ate a big plate of it, which pleased him, and they sat at the table in the flat's little sun porch, with its view of the park in the distance, munching apples and a chunk of sharp cheddar while they finished a bottle of Burgundy.

'About Tuesday,' Kate began.

'Yes,' he said brightly, for they were supposed to have lunch – they always did on Tuesdays when she was in town. 'Where do you want to go? The Avenue? Green's?'

'I can't do it,' she said. 'Carlisle wants me to meet a new client. Sorry.'

'No problem,' he said more breezily than he felt.

*

Two days later he was in the menswear department of Dunhill's on Jermyn Street, where he would not have gone of his own accord except that at Christmas Kate had given him a shirt which he had at last got round to exchanging. It was of gorgeous Pima cotton, beautifully made, but it was yellow. Rather than hurt Kate's feelings or impugn her taste, he simply said it didn't fit – even though a 16 neck was his size – and he would tell her that they'd run out of the soft lemon version of the shirt she'd given him and he'd had to make do with another colour.

He stood waiting to effect the exchange, looking out at the street in an aimless time-passing fashion when suddenly familiarity intruded. The loping, rangy walk of the woman in the Burberry raincoat across the street – it looked just like Kate, and when the figure turned to watch and wait for the traffic thundering down the narrow lane of Duke Street, he saw it *was* Kate.

The woman in the queue ahead of him was finished, and the position open. Instinctively he moved forward and put the shirt down, not wanting to lose his place, and, smiling at the woman behind the counter, said, 'Excuse me one sec,' and rushed to the window, where he located Kate further up the street, then watched as she entered the side entrance of the Cavendish Hotel.

Which seemed fortunate, as this way he would find her, either in the bar or lounge on the ground floor, and he relaxed slightly, moving back to the counter where the woman stood looking at him curiously, and he began to explain about the shirt.

He came out with a sky blue version a few minutes later, thinking he would look in on Kate in case her meeting hadn't started, though if she were with a client he would make himself scarce. He reached the corner and waited, as the traffic of black cabs thundered down from Piccadilly. Duke Street, St James's ran sharply downhill, and not for the first time he realised there were slopes in this city; as a veteran of San Francisco, he usually thought of London as prairie flat. At last the light changed and he started to cross diagonally towards the hotel when he saw another familiar figure walking opposite, headed exactly as Kate had been up Jermyn Street. And bristling at the sight of Conrad Benedict, he

221

waited, having no wish to encounter him, but then saw that Benedict also entered the Jermyn Street entrance of the hotel.

He wanted to believe in coincidence, that Conrad Benedict had gone through the same door but for completely different reasons – a drink with a fellow money man, or lunch with a chum, or even with a client in from the Middle East, staying in the hotel.

And God knows, in a world of certain real conspiracies Renoir sought to keep fabricated ones out of consideration, and allow the possible serendipities of life their chance. Although in his military intelligence days it had been different; what odds in thinking a master sergeant, strolling along the Embarcadero on a weekday afternoon, might have run into a major supplier of Oakland's cocaine habit purely by chance? And even, later, in the world of high tech, if three people from a rival software company suspected of black market dumping happened on a Saturday morning to get on the tourist boat to Alcatraz along with one major black market player, was there any point even imagining they had found each other there by chance?

No.

But that was an earlier life.

He kept his suspicions to himself, and managed by the weekend to decide that he was being oversensitive, even stupid. Then the following week Kate cancelled their lunch again. 'Actually,' she said, 'Tuesdays are going to be difficult for a while. Carlisle has a series of client presentations he's set up. Tuesdays are best for him. It shouldn't last long.' She smiled, her infectious grin. 'I couldn't really say they were reserved, now could I?'

'Of course not,' he said.

'That won't do you any good.' This was Ricky, on a health kick, pointing at Renoir's steak and chips, seemingly the safest bet on the clubhouse menu, and although the meat was tough it was flavourful, the chips hot and surprisingly good. Ricky's own plate held a salad of lettuce and grated carrot and sliced hard-boiled egg. But what *was* salad cream, the enormous dollop of yellow goop Ricky now applied to his plate? Renoir felt unable to ask him or the two other cabbies sitting at the table in the Ealing clubhouse in case they thought, to use their favourite expression, he was 'taking the piss'.

It was the third consecutive Tuesday of not having lunch with Kate, and for a change Renoir did go and play golf. He needed a formal alternative to sitting home and biting his nails as he wondered where Kate was, or, worse, worried that she was again in the Cavendish Hotel having entirely unprofessional discussions with Conrad Benedict.

The week before he had rung her office at lunch-time and was told she was out at a meeting. Not *in* a meeting; out at a meeting. That night he asked her, casually as she leafed through the *Evening Standard*, how her day had been. 'Okay,' she said, after a pause. 'The meetings we're having with this new potential client are going pretty well. I think we'll get work out of them.'

'Do you go see them or do they come to you?'

She turned another page. 'I go— What am I saying? They're Indonesian so we can't very easily go to them. Not for one day at any rate,' she said with a light laugh. 'No, they come to us.'

Jealousy was an unprecedented emotion for Renoir. He never understood how people became consumed by the straying of another person; God knows, he'd witnessed it enough, but always without any true empathy. So it took him some time to diagnose the small emotional cancer that was gnawing at him from within – and by the third week metastasising at a rapid rate. *I've got to do something*, he decided. But what? He was in a city without contacts or friends, and the one person he was close to was now the one person he didn't trust.

He needed disambiguation, not an unfamiliar desire for him, but one which had always taken place in his professional rather than personal life. Then he had people, tools, resources and corporate clout to solve the miseries that came his way. Now he had only himself, and his inner resources seemed feeble. *I am in a state*, he declared out loud to the mirror, one morning when shaving, for he could not seem to divert himself from the fearful jealousy that was preoccupying him: he couldn't read or listen to music or watch television without seeing the image of Kate entering the Cavendish Hotel, followed by Conrad Benedict. He struggled to restrain his imagination – the request for a room, the giggly trip up in the lift, the walk down the corridor to the room . . . *Stop! stop!* he told himself. Then the sequence would start again, like an unfinished movie run in a loop.

Of all things, it was golf which rescued him, though in an entirely unexpected way.

It was in the army that he'd learned to play the game. Stationed in the Presidio for over five years, he had the benefit of a world-famous eighteen-hole course, cut out of the pine and eucalyptus growth, which he could play for free virtually whenever he wanted to. His handicap became respectable – twelve when he played often; sixteen when he didn't – and it became his chief hobby. One year he played sixty-five rounds, three of them in an official but undercover capacity with a navy ensign, based on Treasure Island, who was suspected of stealing radar equipment and selling it to private boat owners down in San Diego.

What he liked, curiously for a game invariably played with other people, was the time it gave him for solitary thinking, something guaranteed by playing with strangers. He was the antithesis of the retired brigadier, who came to lunch at Belfield and, divulging a passion for golf, declared, 'I love the game for the people.' Renoir loved the game *despite* the people.

Though when he first came to England, Renoir's golfing life ground to a halt. Nobody in Kate's family played, and it didn't seem any friends of the family did, either. Pukka golf might suit him, Renoir thought wryly, thinking of access to Sunningdale, or the Berkshire (nearby), or even St Andrews, but it seemed Kate's kind didn't play the game. They didn't play any games, preferring their recreation closer to nature and raw – hunting, shooting, fishing. Country pursuits, in other words, rather than the comparatively constrained practice of a game.

So he didn't play, and might never have again had he not fallen into conversation with a taxi driver one afternoon, stuck in traffic on Wigmore Street. The driver exhaled loudly, then announced, 'On the whole I'd rather be playing golf.'

And by the time he'd got out, Renoir had learned that you could play golf in England without belonging to a club or wearing a tie. He'd shown up at Ealing golf club the following week, rented clubs and been put in a four ball which included two taxi drivers, one of whom, Ricky, was now sitting across the table from him.

Ricky was telling a story as he picked at his salad. He was under forty, blond as a German, with an athlete's build but hopeless at golf – except on the greens, where he displayed a snooker champion's delicacy of touch. He was saying, 'This geezer picks me up on Oxford Street and says, "Follow that cab." I said, "That won't be hard to do," because we were stuck in traffic – you don't move much on Oxford Street,' he added for Renoir's benefit. 'Eventually the cab in front turns off and I follow him to the Wallace Collection. A lady gets out of the other cab and my fare says, "Wait here for me," and hands me fifty quid. I sit tight and then I notice the other driver's also waiting. And after about ten minutes, his lady comes out, jumps in and off they scoot. Thirty seconds later my bloke runs out, hops in the cab all breathless, and says, "quick, after them."

'So I manage to catch up and follow them down to the river. This time they go to the old Tate, and the same thing happens all over again – she gets out and goes in; he follows; she leaves; so does he. Next stop is Tate Modern, and there it's such a long wait that I decide to hell with it, and go and break the ice with the other driver. It turns out he's spotted me, though he hasn't said anything to the lady, and we're standing there having a good laugh about these two prats, when he says, "Christ!" and I look up and she's coming out. I run back and get in my cab and sure enough my bloke comes along as well. "Follow that cab," he says, as if he hasn't said it once before.

'This went on for most of the afternoon. And then suddenly, at the V&A, the lady gets out of the cab, only this time her driver pulls out and goes away. And my fare never comes out – I must

225

have waited half an hour. Fortunately, he'd topped me up with another pony, so I made out all right. The thing is, I still would like to know what they were up to.' He looked at Renoir. 'That's the frustration of this business. You get to see something that's secret, like, and then *bang*, off the fare goes and you never find out what happens next. It's like reading a story you never get to finish.'

The other cabbie nodded. And it was then Renoir suddenly had an inspiration. 'If you're waiting for somebody, do you ever get moved on? I mean, by the police or a traffic warden.'

Ricky shook his head. 'Very rarely. Only if there's a security problem – you know, like an embassy or something to do with the royals. The wardens tend to leave you alone – although you get the odd tosser.'

'So suppose I wanted to hire you to sit in, say, Berkeley Square for twenty minutes. Would that be a problem?'

'It wouldn't be a problem if you hired me for the whole bleeding day. I once spent most of the morning waiting for a bloke in the Saatchi building – it was on account, back when I had them. Piece of cake.'

'Ricky, I think I've got a job for you.'

He was rusty, and felt slightly ridiculous, practising a craft that belonged to younger men – boys really – and to fiction and the world of movies. He had never liked surveillance, since it had always seemed a preposterous activity for a grown-up. So not surprisingly he was having re-entry problems, not least a sense of his own foolishness. But he knew now that this arrival of jealousy in his life was not just unprecedented, but would not go away until he learned the truth about Kate. And there was comfort in readopting the detached pose of his former professional mode.

He did a recce first, and spotted a sandwich bar, Italian with a zinc counter, which had a perfect vantage point of the entrance to Conrad Benedict's office building. Renoir knew he was doing this on the cheap: he should have had a minimum of three people to do the job – a spotter, tail and back-up.

But none of this was available to Renoir now, none of the complicated 'tradecraft' espoused by writers of spy novels and peddlers of surveillance seminars. He would just have to do the best he could, though he would rather lose his target than be spotted – how could he explain to Kate that he had been following Conrad Benedict?

He walked past the sandwich bar, then turned and went through the park and over to St James's Square, where he sat upstairs in the London Library for two hours, reading the *Times* and the *Atlantic Monthly* and the *New Yorker*. At noon, he retraced his morning route and twenty minutes later was standing at the window of the sandwich bar with a large espresso and a tuna baguette (lettuce, hold the tomato) which at the rate he was nibbling would take him an hour to consume. A steady queue of local office workers filled the shop, waiting for their sandwiches to be made, but he had a clear view up the street. If Benedict came out and came his way he would move further into the shop, turn his back to the door and drop his plans. But fifteen minutes later, when he saw the now familiar broad shoulders come out and walk the other way, Renoir drained his coffee and left the sandwich bar.

He kept two hundred yards behind the man, and when Benedict turned left towards St James's Park he waited some time, just in case Benedict slowed for some reason before entering the park. But he didn't, and Renoir could see him clearly. Renoir waited thirty seconds and made a call on his mobile. When he heard a voice on the other end he said, 'Where are you?'

'Duke Street, St James's,' said Ricky, easily enlisted when Renoir guaranteed twice his usual take for the two hours or so he expected to need his services. It had been crucial to cover both sides of the surveillance equation. 'Right outside the hotel. I almost lost her waiting on Piccadilly, but when I turned the corner I saw her going in.'

'Okay,' said Renoir. 'This guy's just gone into the park. He's wearing an overcoat – dark blue, expensive. Black shoes, and a dark suit underneath. He's about six foot, maybe a touch over, heavy-set, short dark hair and a moustache. Nice-looking guy – sharp-featured, confident. I'd think he'll be with you in ten minutes.'

By now Benedict was halfway across the park, crossing the bridge over the small lake. Renoir moved quickly to narrow the gap. As expected, Benedict left the park by St James's Palace and turned left at the westernmost end of Pall Mall. Renoir came up very quickly, half running, but when he reached Pall Mall he crossed over, moving straight for Hardy's window, where he looked with intense interest at the fly rod display. There was no sign of Benedict, which meant he had moved up St James's. Crossing that street to be on its west side, Renoir spotted him well up the street, walking quickly. But instead of walking up as far as Jermyn Street, where he would turn right for the Cavendish Hotel, Benedict stopped lower down, climbed the steps and entered Boodle's.

His club? It was Alastair Scruton's as well. Roddy was a member too. Jesus, thought Renoir, the inbreeding of the English. Roddy in particular was keen on clubs, and he liked to expound on their hierarchy: 'Top drawer is Whites and the Turf, followed by Boodle's and Brooks's. Then down to the Athenaeum, Travellers, further down the Reform, and finally, for no hopers, the Oxford and Cambridge Club.' *Who cares?* Renoir had thought then. Having spent so much of his life in involuntary association with other men – school, the army, corporate life – he couldn't understand the urge to seek out such organised company. Besides, he was recognising not only the limits of his ability to assimilate into English life, but English society's lack of interest in absorbing him.

But the nuances of clubland were forgotten as he was swept by the relief he felt that Benedict was not in the Cavendish Hotel. He waited several minutes to make sure Benedict did not reemerge and that it had been a coincidence after all, his initial sighting of Kate and him entering the same hotel. After all, there was nothing unusual about her being in a hotel. Clients from out of town usually stayed in Mayfair, and if the meetings were not in the small offices of the consultancy (which were on one cramped floor of a townhouse on the west side of Berkeley Square) then they were often held in the suite of the client.

He moved slowly down St James's, turning occasionally to check the entrance of Boodle's, until he reached Pall Mall, and his mobile rang. Ricky – such was Renoir's relief that he had forgotten about him. 'The lady came out of the hotel a minute ago, looking at her watch. I thought she was about to give up. But then your punter showed up.'

'*What?*'

'Yeah. Bloke in a dark overcoat, looks cashmere to me, walking up Duke Street. Six foot, just what you said.'

'Moustache?' he asked. *Please say no.*

'Couldn't say for sure. I didn't really see his face.'

His heart sank. 'What happened then?'

'They went back in the hotel.'

It didn't make sense. Unless . . . dark overcoats were not exactly unusual. So was she meeting someone else?

Ricky asked, 'Do you want me to wait for them to come out?'

How long would it take? Renoir thought bitterly. Did they have a drink first while the man unloosened his tie and Kate kicked her shoes off. 'No,' he said, 'I'll see you Thursday. Can we settle up then?'

'Take your time,' said Ricky. 'You might want to use me again.'

Which turned out to be the case. That evening Kate and he sat and had their usual drink before dinner. She seemed nervous, though in fairness – no, *not* fairness, Renoir thought bitterly – she admitted as much, and said why. She had been asked some time before to give the annual lecture funded by the Big Three oil companies in the ballroom of – he saw the irony without pleasure – a West End hotel. The audience would include most major figures from the industry. It was confirmation of Kate's standing that she had been asked, but any sense of pride seemed outweighed by her performance anxiety. She never, to his knowledge, enjoyed public speaking, and this occasion seemed especially daunting. Now she said as much.

'Is it because there are so many people in the audience?'

She nodded. 'That, and what I'm talking about.'

'Which is?'

'Technology and exploration.'

'Is drilling much different from the way it used to be?'

'No, no,' she said impatiently. 'It's the new ways of *finding* it, not extracting it. You should know.'

He did: his old company sold about fifty per cent of the software packages the producers use to find the stuff. 'What's your thesis?'

'That's the problem. I want to warn people about the increasing dependence on technology when they make their reserves estimates. Expert systems in particular. There's an increasingly grey line between proven reserves and suspected ones. You can guess which way the trend is.'

'And they're counting expert system projections as proven?'

'More and more.'

'If it's true why is that a problem for you?'

'Because they're not going to like what they hear.' As she explained, her anxiety seemed to recede. There was always something intensely attractive about the way she became so engaged in her work. 'I'm going to tell them that some of their so-called reserves are just that – so-called. Implicitly I'm accusing them of inflating them. But the industry wants the world to think there's plenty of oil left.'

'Do you name names?'

She hesitated, then said, 'I don't have to. Everybody does it – there's no point singling out any one company.'

'Will it have much impact?'

'It may do. Not because it's me' – she smiled knowingly – 'but because of the venue. And the audience. They'll all be there.'

'You always get nervous speaking in public, and yet you always do it well,' he began.

'I know, and I know what you're going to tell me: "Focus on

what you are saying, not how you're saying it."' She sounded weary rather than tolerant. '"And try and be yourself". What an old-fashioned expression.'

'But a good one.' *God I sound pompous*, he thought. But what could he offer other than platitudinous encouragement? What did he know about oil reserves? Thanks to Ticky, he knew plenty about expert systems, but that wasn't really the issue at stake here.

She sighed. Renoir said, 'What's the matter? Go on, I'm listening.' He waited, fully aware it might not be oil she wanted to discuss. *Is she going to tell me now?*

'The problem with you, Jack,' she said, 'is you always help people who need it, but you never need help yourself.'

'What?' he asked with astonishment. 'You help me all the time. Look how I live.'

She shook her head, almost as if they had had this conversation before. It made him feel she was arguing with an *idea* of him. 'That's not help. I know you – if you were on your own, even if you had all the money in the world you'd still live very simply.'

He waved a hand dismissively. 'Maybe, but what about Burdick's Field? I wouldn't have a place for eight thousand apple trees if it weren't for you.'

'And no Roddy either.' She laughed but it was not happy. 'Or my mother for that matter.'

'I like your mother just fine. You know that.'

She started shaking her head again. 'You know what she said about you, after that weekend when you went down and I was away?'

Kate waited until reluctantly he rose to the bait. 'What?'

'She said you were very *helpful*.'

And Renoir didn't know what to make of this conversation. Everybody needed help; Renoir was no exception. Did he really never make that clear to Kate? There was a resignation to her voice that suggested a dissatisfaction he had not heard before. *With me*, he thought, trying not to think too directly of what she was doing about it. But he needed to know. *Ask her*, he suddenly thought, struggling to emerge from a growing cocoon of secrecy. But how could he? Ask her what? 'Are you having an affair with Conrad Benedict?' Just like that, out of the blue after this bland conversation about her speech the following month. How could he say anything without explaining he had seen her at the hotel – not just once, but twice.

It was raining this time, so Renoir wore a light raincoat. In the coat's deep inner pocket he'd brought along two telescoped umbrellas – one anonymously black, the other a girly number with yellow dots on a blue background. His other inner pocket contained a Red Sox baseball cap, with its bill folded and tucked in, and an acrylic hood taken from a rain slicker which he could wear with its loose bottom tucked into his raincoat. He wouldn't get anywhere near Benedict, but he wanted to ensure that he remained unrecognised even at a distance. The point was not to go unnoticed, for the more you tried to look 'average' the more you stuck out, but rather to be noted as a different person each time.

Weather aside, the surveillance proved virtually identical. Benedict came out of his building ten minutes later, and moved perhaps that little bit faster across St James's Park. Kate showed up early, according to Ricky, who said he was parked inside the hotel's drop-off on Duke Street, St James's, having squared the doorman by saying he had an account fare inside. He rang again five minutes later to say that Kate was now waiting impatiently outside the hotel, just as Renoir, standing two hundred yards away, saw Benedict climb the short steps into Boodle's.

So who was Kate meeting? Renoir moved up St James's, careful not to look into the restaurant windows, since he supposed that in this square mile of Mayfair a high percentage of Kate's acquaintance probably had lunch from time to time. He kept his eyes on the front steps of Boodle's but there was no sign of Benedict, so before he reached the club he turned right onto Ryder Street, and walked along the small, enchanting street of Victorian fronts, home of art dealers in everything from French still lifes to Chinese porcelain. He played the idle tourist stopping to inspect an oil landscape of the American West, while across the street, at the back of Christie's, a porter and a young woman in twinset and pearls stood next to each other, smoking cigarettes without exchanging a word.

Renoir planned to turn right when he reached Duke Street, and started to reach for the raincoat hood, so that even were Kate still outside the hotel she wouldn't spot him so far down the street. He was absorbed in this image of Kate, not a hundred yards away, waiting with unconcealed impatience for what he was now starting to feel must be a lover. And so it was very lucky that he happened to see the man just ten feet ahead of him on the pavement, so close that he hadn't noticed him, thus proving the Sherlock Holmes maxim that the best place to hide is under the nose of the person looking for you. The man wore a dark blue overcoat, its collar pulled up around his neck against the drizzle, and had unmistakably wide shoulders.

Renoir suddenly stopped and stared at an enormous French still life of two roses in a green vase, which was propped against an easel in the dealer's window. He held his breath and resisted the temptation to turn and walk away, since if Benedict happened to look back it was precisely that sudden movement he might notice. All Renoir could do was stare at the painting, trying to ape the look of a prospective purchaser, while waiting for the man just on the edge of his peripheral vision to turn the corner.

Which Benedict only sort of did, cutting diagonally across and onto Ryder Street, striding quickly, his shoes clacking audibly since there was no traffic in this little backwater stretch, and when the noise faded and nothing flickered across his lateral vision, Renoir exhaled and turned and carefully followed. Catching up just in time to see Benedict turn left up Duke Street, though Renoir didn't dare follow any further. Sure enough, not half a minute later Ricky rang to say yes, the same bloke was back, and again he'd gone into the hotel with Kate.

And retracing his steps he saw where he had gone wrong. There, in the small plaza which seemed more Manhattan than Mayfair, he saw a sign for Boodle's Chambers, just across from – another irony – the Economist building, where Kate had once worked. So the mystery was solved. Benedict hadn't appeared out of thin air; he had simply entered his club and then left by the back door. An oversight on Renoir's part which pure luck had exposed; he'd been pretty unprofessional, he dully noted, almost past caring, his attention being swamped really by heartsickness and the knowledge that Kate was spending her lunch hour with Conrad Benedict somewhere in the Cavendish Hotel.

'How is the speech going?'

Kate looked at Renoir blankly, then nodded. 'It's fine, thanks. Just fine.'

'Honestly, Kate,' he started to say, piqued by her abstracted air, but then had enough presence of mind to realise he had to get a hold of himself. *Minimise, minimise.* He had certainly done that successfully in the past. Why couldn't he do it now? He did his best to focus on Kate, if only to divert himself from his own swarming feelings.

He was of course used to watching people hide secrets, expert at detecting the telltale indicators of that most stressful activity – living a lie. But Kate was good, really good at acting perfectly natural. Which meant showing *some* stress (like the natural tension of having to give a major speech), since if there hadn't been any sign of stress, that would have been suspicious.

What he was discovering was that *he* wasn't very good at this lie business. Of course, he was keeping an ongoing secret of his own, the fact that he knew about her secret. Yet he seemed surprisingly bad at it. *If I can keep a secret thirty years*, he thought, *why is a few weeks so hard?* He needed to escalate things, uncover absolute proof of her affair, for anything was better than living with the certainty of betrayal without the certainty of proof. Until he had that, he did not want her to know he had spied on her. In the remote possibility of an innocent explanation, he would be damaging their relationship, possibly enough to destroy it.

234

Who was he kidding? If his suspicions were true, the relationship was finished anyway. What was he going to do then? Retreat to San Francisco? Maybe he should go now, cut his losses and return with his tail between his legs and horns on his head. Back to the security side of the software industry. Or if that weren't possible, a move into the dreaded security industry itself, with its veneer of 'consultants' and 'experts', these inflated titles signally failing to disguise the grubby truth of lowlifes watching over even greater lowlifes.

Yet he wouldn't do this yet. It was not these retrograde prospects that bothered him. It was the thought of life without Kate.

He could not specify the way she had changed him. It wasn't the outward circumstances of his life – the flat, the Gatehouse, his mid-life career shift; those changes were transparent. It was inside him where she had opened up a new world. He found that talking with Kate, or even being with her in silence, made the world come alive for him. Anything and everything somehow engaged him when he was with her: from oil futures to the varieties of apples that had yellow skin, from the homogeneity of English television taste – during one year, gardening programmes were all the rage, the next DIY, the following one food – to the calibre of surfing in Cornwall versus California.

But actually, it was his emotions that had really exploded into life because of Kate. Before her, Renoir had been simple, formal, shut down; with her he felt reborn, as if revisiting an emotional Arcadia. Perhaps it was the Valley Orchard of boyhood. That hadn't lasted, he reminded himself, and he had spent thirty years protecting himself from being so vulnerable again.

By Wednesday it was so bad that he took himself off to Belfield, claiming he needed to do more work on the new plantings and get the house ready for their first stay there the coming weekend. If Kate was surprised, she hid it, and they agreed she would come down Friday night. And he did work in the Old Orchard, clearing the growing grass and weeds carefully around the individual trees, restaking those which had been pushed out of true by the wind, laying out his Israeli system of perforated hose as a trial for the new trees which he now thought he would never plant.

Yet the running battle in his mind continued. Did he really want to throw all this away? Did he need to end the one relationship that mattered to him – the only one, in fact, at least since he was ten years old – because of a lousy rendezvous in a not-so-cheap hotel? It had happened to other men before, and God knows countless women, without triggering the end of what in his case was effectively a marriage. Could he not see past his present pain, his bruised pride, to a healed future with Kate? Did he really want to up stakes and head back to a home that wasn't really home any more because of a slip by the women he loved?

He might have calmed down in the serenity of the countryside, away from any opportunity to torture himself with new evidence, had he not remembered the metal box he had brought over from the Hall. He hauled it out from under their bed. It was about two feet long, perhaps eighteen inches wide, and shallow, capable of containing the thickness of a full file or an average novel but not much else. The lock was old-fashioned, and not easily picked. Renoir toyed with the idea of jimmying it with a chisel, but that would be madness. One look and Kate would see what he'd been up to. But it proved a simple matter to unscrew the hinges of the lid, and lift the entire top off.

Inside he found: two birth certificates, for Kate and Emily, an envelope with cuttings of baby hair, a photograph of Kate's father, and a folded piece of stationery. It was a letter, handwritten, dated fifteen months before, and as he read it he realised who the writer was.

Dear Kate
  I don't know what to say. When this man showed up I couldn't help but think 'this won't last' and now you tell me it's not only going to last but you act as if I never meant anything to you. Though I don't really believe that. You claim

this man is the first person you've ever really totally loved but you told me once you thought love was just infatuation with a fancy name. So don't you think this version of it is going to wear off?

Who is he anyway? Someone with a jumped-up surname from a different country with different tastes and different everything. I asked about him and everybody said he was pleasant enough in a nondescript sort of way. But what does that mean? You can't live with someone because they're 'pleasant'. Please think about what I'm saying. There's nothing I can do right now about my situation, but there's every chance of its changing in the future at some point. Don't close the door on me. I really wouldn't if I were you.

   C.

Renoir didn't know if the letter enraged or hurt him more. He tried to take comfort from the fact that Benedict sounded spurned; he told himself that just because Benedict was in love with Kate, it didn't mean this was reciprocated. Even if, say for old time's sake, she had made a slip. But that was the problem. One mistake, one slip – sure; but *slips*? Week after week, snatched lunch-time hours, as she let another man do . . . as she . . . He stopped, unwilling to torture himself further.

And it wasn't just pride. Her infidelity changed things. However they rebuilt, their house would always have an exposed beam, a suspect foundation.

On Friday night Kate missed the train for Newbury, so he collected her at Didcot instead, driving through the Harwell fruit country down across the A34 and along the grim access road that ran towards the looming towers, which stood like vast bleached beakers in the flat plate of the Thames Valley. As he slowed down near the station, waiting for the emerging traffic and for the arriving commuters to cross the road to their parked cars, he saw Kate standing outside. She looked smart in her belted white raincoat, carrying her briefcase in one hand and an overnight bag in the other, as she looked around for him. Before any other feeling got in the way, he felt a sudden, melting warmth, as if his body were bathed in love. Then a male commuter, wearing a dark suit, walked past her to meet his own ride, and the spell was fractured.

She was all animation in the car, chatting away as the sun set ahead of them and he turned into the folds of the Downs for home. At the Gatehouse he cooked omelettes on the new stove, while Kate opened a bottle of Sancerre and was on her second glass before they sat down.

Later, lying in their vast new bed, he looked out down the slope of Burdick's Field and marvelled at Kate's energy, as she stayed up reading and drinking Ovaltine while he pretended to be asleep, trying not to think about Benedict's words.

Saturday was difficult. They spent the day outside, working on the property. Kate was busy planting for their first summer, adding to the earlier flowers and shrubs she'd placed in a large circular bed on the field side of the house. It was too early for the wildflowers in the meadow there, but already in the bed anemones were in bloom, their round red orbs dotted with black poppy-like seeds, and hyacinths, white and purple, interspersed by brunnera, little blue flowers which Kate said everyone confused with forget-me-nots. She had planted tulips as well, in regular clumps of six, scarlet and purple-black, and a stray dissonant patch of yellow – 'a mistake', said Kate, which wouldn't make the garden's second year, since there was a more tasteful yellow in a light forsythia bush. At the edge of the house, Renoir had planted both a cherry and an almond tree, but neither was yet in bloom – he had a bet with Kate that the cherry would have pink flowers rather than white.

Renoir worked in the Old Orchard on the trees he hadn't pruned earlier in winter. The previous year he had focused on reducing tree heights, since these trees had gone unpruned for over a decade, their leaders useless and the high branches fruit-free. Now he concentrated on taking out large internal branches so the light could work through into interior fruit, since light was as valuable for fruit as water. He cut dead wood and the larger weak-angled branches with a pruning saw, headed back the one- and two-year-old growth with his new lopping shears, and clipped water spouts and young shoots with a pair of double-handed clippers.

He tended to underprune and was insufficiently ruthless about cutting the lower branches (the process known as 'lifting'), which slowed the overall growth of the trees. Yet he remained amazed at how much even such old trees could grow in a year, and with the retained new shoots he either headed them back or tied them down to horizontal (to encourage sideways growth) with a roll of yellow nylon netting. He was careful with the ladder – no one would hear him shout if he fell – but liked standing aloft, leaning against the centre trunk of the older, bigger trees, gazing out over the orchard, the trees in neat lines like fattened soldiers.

Finished now, he unlocked a small hut at one end of the orchard and put his tools on its wooden floor. There had been vandalism the year before, most of it insignificant – initials carved on a few of the trees, trash left around a half-assed attempt at a camp fire – but the kids had broken into the hut, prising its padlock off and throwing the cushions from the bench stored inside onto the floor, presumably to use as a rough mattress for youthful coupling. Renoir had put a stronger lock on, and was happy to see it hadn't been messed with. He couldn't get worked up about essentially innocent trespass through the woods and the fruit trees, but he didn't want to encourage the use of the hut as a local centre of fornication. *Why am I deluding myself?* He suddenly thought. *None of this is going to be my problem.*

They went for lunch at the Hall, where they ate with Beatrice and Roddy, who was in high spirits, lyrically describing his plans for redeveloping the rest of the estate. Over coffee he talked about advertising the shooting – during the past season it had been done by word of mouth – by taking out a classified display in *The Field*. 'Who knows?' he said, putting a sugar in his mug, 'We might even get a sheikh or two. One of your oil tycoons, Kate.'

'Why on earth would they want to shoot here?' demanded Kate, unusually snappy. 'They want grand places, where they can shoot six hundred birds.'

Roddy seemed unperturbed and tapped his nose significantly. 'Blue blood, that's why. They're all terrific snobs, these Arabs. They like the real thing.' He looked at Renoir sceptically.

'Don't worry, Roddy,' said Renoir. 'The days they're shooting here I'll stay inside.'

Which made even Roddy laugh, though Kate was unamused. When Roddy started to talk again, she cut in sharply, 'Oh do shut up.' Her mother raised her eyes in disapproval, and Roddy started to bristle, then seemed to change his mind and smiled serenely, as if deciding not to inflame the child still further.

Normally, lunch at Belfield would have made Renoir grateful to be in his own house at last, but he was dreading nightfall, since on Saturday night Kate and he almost always made love. Reading, he would throw a leg over hers, an arm would caress a shoulder, books would get tossed aside, a light turned off, a top lifted, and the casual but accelerating process would begin.

This night she was reading Harlen Coben; he had started Anne Tyler, but put it down. When she eventually switched off her light and nestled under the covers he didn't move. 'You awake?' she whispered, and he didn't reply. A hand came over and rested on his shoulder, but still he wouldn't let himself stir. He didn't trust himself to make love to her. He could perform all right, since he could subdue resentment with testosterone, but there would be ambivalence and aggression in the act, rather than the assertiveness of undiluted love.

She sighed audibly, then turned on her back away from him, and within minutes was snoring ever so lightly, while he lay there tense and sad at once, until sadness took over, then sleep.

He had not had the dream since moving to England. And what

was odd about its reappearance now was that it came encased in a self-conscious shell that told him he was dreaming while he did so. He was watching the boy in the dream instead of *being* the boy, which had the effect of distancing him, the dreamer, without lessening its horror. In the dream, the man in the Stetson had already shot Will, and Will lay by the pond in the background of the dream's frame, which gave a screen-like constancy to the picture, as if Renoir were viewing a movie. In the foreground, Jack the boy was digging in a hole, as a woman above him was saying, *Don't stop, don't stop.* Suddenly she commanded, so sternly that the spade he held quivered, *Don't tell anyone. You hear? No one.*

He woke wondering at first where he was, startled into consciousness by an intrusion of light. He blinked and saw Kate sitting up in bed beside him, staring at him, with the bedside lamp turned on. 'What's going on?' he asked.

'I think you should ask yourself that question,' said Kate, and her voice was cold. '"Don't tell anyone." You said it three times, and you've said it before. What's the big secret?' He shook his head, and she looked at him wearily. 'I've never pried, Renoir, and I won't start now, but I wish you'd talk to me. Or if not to me, then to someone.'

'Sure. I'll see a shrink in the morning,' he said sarcastically, then he sighed. 'Listen, it was just a nightmare. Why don't you turn off the light? You need the sleep.'

She didn't reply and looking up he found her gaze steady on him, unappeased. 'Come on,' he urged, 'let's go back to sleep.'

And after she seemed to have made some unexpressed decision, she reached over and turned off the lamp. They settled, side by side on their backs, and he lay there trying to sleep, hoping to write off the dream. Then out of the dark Kate's voice came like an unsettling edict, judgmental and true. 'I can't *make* you tell me, Jack. You have to want to tell me.' He pretended he was asleep.

They drove back Sunday after spending the day apart – he worked in the Old Orchard again, and she went through more of her things at Belfield. Again that night in bed, she made advances; this time he did not pretend to be asleep, but pleaded a stiff back from his outdoor work, a manifestly bad excuse since he was playing golf in London the next morning.

'Okay,' said Kate after this excuse. 'But we better talk about this.'

'Talk about what? My bad back?'

'Something's bothering you, I can tell. You've been acting very oddly. If you don't want to sleep with me, you can say so. Though how we'll ever have children this way is beyond me. I can't make them myself.'

Children? He couldn't believe his ears. He wanted to know, if he weren't keen on helping right now, whether she'd chosen Conrad Benedict as her back-up supplier. He wanted to say this, and he almost did, such was his sense of breaking point. But by then Kate had turned off the light, ostentatiously hunkered down for sleep and turned her back resolutely against him.

And the next morning he was glad he hadn't said a word, as he stood at the fifth hole of Ealing golf club.

'I figured you for a spook right away. I *knew* it.' Ricky looked a little ashamed of this confessional rush, which came on the fairway, where they waited for a four ball to clear the green ahead of them. 'I knew you weren't just a sponger.'

'Thanks, Ricky,' Renoir said a little dryly. Was this what the other golfers had made of him? Well, he thought, remembering the snickers of the garage attendants in Notting Hill, they were not alone.

'Though I did think at first that this lady you had me track was just the usual up-to-no-good in the lunch hour and "have we got time for another before I get back to the office?".'

'Yes, Ricky,' said Renoir dutifully. He wasn't really interested in the cabbie's opinion of what he had been watching, but there was no point being rude. He just didn't want Ricky to figure out

242

that it was Renoir's girlfriend he was following; this was a humil-
iation he wished to be spared, feeling he had enough other ones
already.

'It just goes to show what a sly horse you are.'

'What do you mean?' Renoir's reaction now was sincere.

'She's working for you, isn't she?'

'What?' Renoir seemed unable to learn the politer 'excuse me?'
of the English.

'I mean, there wasn't any hanky-panky going on at all. This
was business, pure and simple. I went into the hotel to buy a
Standard, thinking "they'll be upstairs going at it or my name's
Jim Davidson" and what do I see in the bar but the lady and the
gent sitting at a table, papers spread between them, having a right
argy-bargy. And that's when he mentioned your name, not very
politely either. She says, "Leave him out of it. He knows nothing
about it."

'Nothing about what?' Renoir asked, then realised it was an
asinine question. How would Ricky possibly know? But Renoir
didn't care, even when Ricky looked at him dolefully, because
Renoir was happy to look stupid, happy to *be* stupid, if that meant
that what Ricky was saying was true. Yes, Kate had gone to the
Cavendish Hotel and, yes, she had gone to meet a man. But
contrary to all his suspicions, it now looked as if she had gone
there to *talk* with Conrad Benedict. He was almost embarrassed
by the relief he felt – but only almost.

And later that night, after they had made love, Kate whispered
into his ear, 'That was a quick recovery.'

'What?' he said drowsily, an arm draped lazily on her naked
thigh.

'Your back,' she said. 'That hurt so much last night.' She
squeezed his shoulder gently. 'Or were you gritting your teeth just
now?'

'I shut my eyes and think of California.'

So he was freed from the virus of jealousy, though it was replaced
by equally obsessive curiosity. For if they were only talking, what

were they talking *about*? Business, he tried to tell himself, just normal business. *Think of how many men she talks to each week*. How did the jingle go? *Fat men, skinny men, men who climb on rocks; smart men, stupid men, even men with chicken pox*. Thought of like this – one more business meeting in a swanky hotel – it wasn't a problem to Renoir. Nothing to worry about.

But then why had she lied about it?

His curiosity increased after a boozy lunch with Alastair. They met at a restaurant where they had met before, a large and noisy place, which seemed to Renoir virtually predestined to be located on St James's. 'Why didn't he take you to his club?' Kate demanded when he and Alastair had gone there the year before for the first of a series of friendly lunches.

He shrugged. 'Maybe he was worried I wouldn't behave.'

But Renoir hadn't felt snubbed. He was a fish out of water, and he recognised that his anomalous status – not husband, not public schoolboy, not even Englishman – was more uncomfortable for others than it was for himself. If Alastair found it easier, on the whole, to meet him on the neutral ground of a restaurant, that was fine with Renoir. Especially now that Renoir knew that Alastair's club was the same handsome building of yellow brick and white stucco which Conrad Benedict had entered on successive Tuesdays.

He found Alastair waiting in a large armchair of blue dyed leather by the restaurant's zinc bar. He was dressed for work, wearing a suit which even Renoir's untutored eye could see was tailor-made, though like all of Alastair's clothes, it managed to look beautifully cut and yet wonderfully *soft*. In his blazer, Renoir felt both stiff and under-dressed.

In some ways, Alastair represented the kind of Englishman Renoir was coming to distrust. He had a confidence that he carried like a birthright, and a first-rate education: like his four brothers, Alastair was an Etonian ('The fees!' Kate once exclaimed. 'Think of the fees!'), and had read Modern Languages at Oxford. Yet the conventionalism of his credentials masked an eccentric intelligence, which itself was disguised by a languid friendliness which made Alastair appealing to women and unthreatening to men. His manners were excellent but not excessive, his urbanity gentle rather than slick. And any resentment his slightly patrician air might have stirred in people (probably a lot these days) melted in the face of his simple niceness.

They were led to a table in the back of the vast pastel room, which had Art Deco scallops of chrome on its walls, like a designer's small-scale homage to the Bilbao Museum. Before he'd even settled in his chair, Alastair ordered a bottle of Pinot Grigio.

As usual they talked about the Palmer family, in the conspiratorial fashion of (almost) brothers-in-law. As they'd got to know each other, Alastair had grown more forthright, as he was today about the shrinking finances of Belfield. 'It's getting worse, not better,' he declared. 'Roddy spends all his time scheming how to get out of debt, and Beatrice goes on pretending that there isn't a problem.'

'How bad is it?'

'The estate loses money, of course. But that wouldn't matter so much if Roddy had anything to speak of coming in. Kate helps – I'm sure I'm not telling you anything new there – and that's keeping things afloat. But Roddy's managed to get himself into all kinds of debt.'

'Do you know how much he owes?'

Alastair paused and looked at his starter of *insalata tricolore*. 'I think you'd find hundreds of thousands of pounds were the order of the day.'

'Holy smokes,' said Renoir appreciatively. 'No wonder he wants to build houses at Belfield.'

'I know,' said Alastair, 'though it's not going to happen, not in our lifetimes anyway. It's all Green Belt, the woods have preservation orders, most of the rest is some kind of special conservation area, and Beatrice wouldn't tolerate it for a moment anyway. It's one of those assets which bleed you dry, because it's only realisable as a whole. You either find enough money to keep it up, or you sell the whole thing. There's no option in between.'

'Well,' said Renoir, 'he's getting some money from Kate for the Gatehouse.' From what Alastair said, he wished all the more that the contracts had been signed. What was taking so long?

Alastair smiled wryly. 'Hate to say it, but it's a mere holding action, as far as Roddy's concerned. The debts are that bad.'

A little unnerved by this, Renoir shifted the conversation onto less disturbing ground: the standard English topic of conversation in spring – the destination of Alastair's forthcoming summer holidays.

'*La France*,' said Alastair, his eyes misty from the wine. 'Three magical weeks which I prefer to think of as three months. What about you?'

'We promised to take Emily to San Francisco. Show her old haunts and all that. But I don't know – we're only just in the Gatehouse, and there's still a lot to do.'

'Your new neighbour was saying much the same thing the other night.'

'Who's that?'

'Benedict. I saw him at some city dinner at the Guildhall and all he did was complain about how much work there was left to do at Burdick's.'

'Kate said Burdick had let things run down a bit. From what I gather, he was never one for the high life,' conceded Renoir.

'Not in the domestic sense at any rate,' said Alastair with a laugh. 'A wood fire, bottle of whisky and large game pie, and the man was happy. Benedict's something different altogether.'

'Do you know him well?'

'Well enough,' said Alastair, and there was a rueful note in his voice. 'In fact, I was his stockbroker for a while. Not a long while, I have to say.'

'What happened? Did you fall out?' Renoir loved the expression, with its associations, to him at least, of friendships collapsing like deck chairs, or Guardsmen fainting in line on parade on the Queen's birthday.

'Not at all. We are the closest of . . . distant acquaintances now. He explained to me that he preferred to move his assets around – not just in different holdings, but handled by different people as well. I thought this was a bit rum, considering he's a personal banker. How would he feel if his clients did the same thing to him?'

'How many clients does a personal banker handle?'

'It depends. I wouldn't think ever more than a dozen. And if the client's big enough – a Getty, say, or a Rothschild – then it may pay to be full time for the one.'

'Is that how Benedict operated?'

Alastair sipped his wine, then held the glass and looked at it as he spoke. 'No, he had lots of clients, though he lost most of them when he got into trouble for trading personally in shares he was recommending.'

'Is that illegal?'

'Illegal? No, not at all. It's just not done. Conflict of interest, I suppose – in any case, clients don't like it much. Lots of his didn't, at any rate. But he made an absolute killing for himself by shorting some high-tech shares. And he did it again with some dotcom companies. Perfect timing both times.'

'Ah,' said Renoir, trying not to sound too interested. You could never tell with the English: they would say the most indiscreet thing about someone, then look askance if you asked them to elucidate. 'Is that usually a rational kind of thing, or sixth sense?'

'Usually luck. In Benedict's case, however, people wondered a bit – he had got very chummy with some pretty ropey CEOs. He wasn't so close to them after he'd made his killing, which made people wonder even more. If you're going to trade on the basis of inside information you might at least have the courtesy to be discreet about it. Not Benedict – he's an arrogant sod. So there were Chinese whispers for a while, even a little gossip that the Fraud Squad might take a look. But it died away; it almost always does except in the most blatant cases.'

'So that's how he made his money. Burdick's Farm couldn't have been cheap.'

'I know,' said Alastair, looking amused. 'I hate to think what Helena paid for it.'

'I thought you said Benedict made a killing on options.'

'That was long gone – he likes to live high on the hog. That's where a rich wife comes in.'

'She seemed rather nice.'

Alastair lifted an eyebrow. 'I feel sorry for her myself.'

'Really? Why's that?'

'She's foreign, a little wacky – weren't you next to her at dinner? – and not particularly attractive. Given such credentials, it couldn't possibly have been her money that attracted him, now could it?'

'Ah,' said Renoir, thinking if he persisted with the 'ahs' he could pass for an Englishman in as little as fifty years.

'She's said to be the jealous type, and with good reason – Benedict's never been faithful to a flea.' And suddenly Alastair stopped, and as the damning sentence hung in the air Renoir saw that he was embarrassed, which puzzled him until he realised it was because of Kate. Presumably Benedict had run around on her, too, those many years ago.

Renoir didn't like parties; at most of them he felt like a teenage girl playing wallflower. This wasn't helped in London by the tendency of Kate's circle of friends to talk among themselves. They raised a barrier against entry which apparently could be eroded only by time – a recurrent face, if sufficiently recurrent, was gradually accepted. They weren't shy, they weren't reserved; they were simply comfortable only with people they already knew. By now, Renoir had graduated to nodding status.

It was a drinks do on Kensington Park Road, held in the vast ground floor of a house owned by a barrister whose wife had been friends at Cambridge with Kate. It was exactly like all the other drinks parties he had gone to with Kate, responding puppet-like to the stiff white cards which said *At Home*. Then they discovered that neither liked going. They were only here tonight because it was Kate's friend's birthday.

Now one of the waitresses, in black skirt and white blouse, refilled his wine glass as he struggled to look interested while the two women next to him talked about their children at Marlborough. Spying Alastair across the room, he made his excuses and edged his way across to him. He was speaking with a tall man whom he introduced as a fellow broker and, inevitably, from 'School'.

'Ah,' said Renoir with by now almost professional competence.

Alastair said, 'Jonathan was a broker, but he's poacher turned gamekeeper now. He's one of the regulators who keep us traders in order.' He turned to his friend. 'Jack used to work in Silicon Valley. He's an old hand with the SEC.'

The man called Jonathan looked curious, so Renoir explained. 'I used to have a bit to do with them over insider trading.'

'Ah,' said Jonathan with an appraising look. 'There's not much we can teach you over here.' He paused briefly to spear a smoked oyster with a toothpick. 'You're much stricter than we are here.' Looking reflective, he added, 'Though we are getting tougher.'

'Is it a constant problem?' asked Renoir, not sure what would be politic to ask. 'Or does it come and go?'

Jonathan laughed. 'Insider trading isn't seasonal, if that's what you're asking. It picked up a lot after the financial reforms of the seventies, paradoxically perhaps, but I wouldn't say it's increasing particularly now.'

Alastair asked, 'Are certain industries worse than others?'

Jonathan looked thoughtful. 'Lots in high tech, partly because the ups and downs are so dramatic. If you don't cash in when a share's riding high, it might be worthless two weeks later. With a utilities share, probably the most you'd see is a fall of five per cent in its value when results are bad. With a dotcom listing it might be three hundred per cent.'

'So it's mainly high tech over here then?' asked Renoir, remembering what Alastair had told him about Benedict's dodgy dealings in dotcom shares.

'Disproportionate amount there, certainly. But you get it in all sorts of business. Manufacturing companies, media, pharmaceut-icals.'

'Oil?' asked Renoir.

'Sure. Insider trading is sector-blind, as it were.'

'Jack lives with Sarah's sister, Kate. She's in oil.'

'Kate Palmer?' Jonathan's face lit up. 'Is she here?' Scanning the room, he spotted her. 'Excuse me a minute. I must say hello to her. She helped me with a case and I never thanked her.'

And he walked over and started talking animatedly to Kate. Renoir started to ask Alastair more about his friend when they were interrupted by a woman kissing Alastair on the cheek. Seeing Renoir, she shook hands and said with a giggle, 'The apple farmer, yes?'

It was Helena Benedict. 'Ah, look at my husband,' she mused aloud, and both Alastair and Renoir followed her gaze towards the far end of the room. Benedict was there, drink in hand, looking debonair in a dark suit and yellow tie, speaking with obvious flirtatiousness to a blonde woman in pearls.

'It's charming, is it not,' declared Helena, 'how Conrad remains friends with all his exes? He's always talking to them.'

Alastair gave a little hollow laugh. 'Better than non-speaks, surely,' he said.

'Of course,' said Helena. 'You English are so gentlemanly. Though I wonder why he hasn't said hello to *all* his girlfriends here tonight.' She said this so pointedly that Renoir again followed her eyes and found he was looking straight at Kate. She was still talking to Jonathan, but seemed slightly distracted. Her glance kept moving over towards Renoir, but she didn't ever catch his eye. Then he realised: *She's looking at Helena.*

'Give him time, Helena,' said Alastair, trying to keep things light. 'He'll get round to them all. We English always do. It wouldn't be polite not to.'

'Well,' Helena began, but before he heard what she had to say, Renoir felt a smart tap on his shoulder, and turning round found Kate.

'Darling,' she said, 'hurry up or we'll be late.'

Late for what? he almost said, but then remembered it was the pretence they had long before cooked up to get away when a party went flat, or either was trapped by a bore.

He looked at her and nodded slowly. 'Okay,' he said and turned back to say goodbye to Alastair and Helena. Over his shoulder Kate said, 'Hello, Helena, we must rush. Bye, Alastair.'

And as he followed her, he heard Helena say, 'Come see us some time, Kate. I'd love to show you what we're doing to the house.' Which Kate pretended not to hear.

At supper, in the local *trattoria* off High Street Kensington, Kate didn't mention the party, talking instead about her plans for the Gatehouse. 'Once this wretched speech is out of the way, I'll really get cracking.'

'I'm sure I can do a lot of it if you just tell me what you want.'

'Renoir, I am not letting you pick material for the bathroom curtains.'

'Why not? I think a military motif would look terrific. Or the stars and stripes. But seriously, I'd feel a lot more comfortable if you'd signed the contracts with your brother. Wouldn't you?' Renoir asked.

'Yes,' she said, smiling, as if affectionately tolerating his nagging.

'It worries me, you know. What if something happened to Roddy?'

She shrugged. 'We'd buy it from his son and heir.'

'He's seven years old.'

'Yes,' she said cheerfully, 'but Alastair is the executor, so I think it would work out, don't you?' When he didn't reply, she reached over and put her hand on his. 'It will be okay,' she said.

He gave a nod as vague as her reassurance, so he was startled when she said with new certainty, 'We should close some time after the tenth. That's what the lawyers tell me.'

The bill came and he picked it up. 'I'll get this one.'

'Why?' she asked.

'I'm flush.'

251

'I know,' she said, 'you still haven't ordered the trees. You're going to have to plant in autumn now, aren't you?'

'Yes. Have you been reading up or something?'

'Burdick told me when I asked him about starting to farm.'

'When was that?'

'After I'd met you. I was thinking ahead even then.'

'Oh,' he said, feeling only half relaxed, 'so you had it all planned. Me, the apple farm, the Gatehouse.'

'Don't make it sound so clinical. I was in love.'

Was? he wanted to ask. Instead he said, growing intense despite himself, 'Listen, if it would help speed things up with Roddy, I do have some money, you know.'

For a moment it looked like she wanted to tell him something, something important which she probably thought would surprise him. But she gave a light false laugh instead. 'No,' she said, 'dinner will do.'

Afterwards they walked along the High Street and as they passed Barker's, Kate took his arm. 'I saw that witch Helena chatting you up,' she teased. 'Don't you go having any ideas.'

'That man at the party,' he began.

'Which one?'

'Jonathan. The friend of Alastair's. He—'

'They were at Eton together.'

'He said he knew you.'

'Of course. I've met him through Alastair and, you know, the whole bunch,' which seemed a fair depiction of her circle of acquaintances in London.

He nodded. 'The thing is, he said he knew you from work. You helped him with a case he investigated.'

He looked sideways but couldn't see Kate's face. She said in a low voice, 'Well, I doubt it was very much help.'

'Tell me about it,' he said, trying to sound casual.

'There's not much to tell. In the newsletter we changed the rating of a Scottish exploration company, quite dramatically – from good to poor. He thought somebody at the company might have got wind of this early, because there was a lot of trading activity just before the newsletter went out – shorting the shares. When the price fell after our rating drop, somebody cleaned up.'

'Somebody inside?'

'Apparently.'

'When was this?'

'Oh, it must have been three or four years ago. Why?' she asked a little sharply.

'When we first met in Cupertino, you seemed very naive about this sort of thing. You acted like you were surprised people got up to this kind of shenanigans.'

'Did I?' she said vaguely, then gently laughed. 'Renoir,' she said, 'you were enjoying yourself so much telling me about it that I reckoned you were trying to impress me. I hoped you were at any rate. And I didn't want to spoil it by stealing your thunder, now did I?' They were under a street lamp in Kensington Square, and he saw her give him such a loving smile – entirely authentic, no tells there – that he was a little ashamed of his questioning. But only a little.

The question remained, what was Kate up to? Renoir recognised his own prejudiced feelings, but from Alastair's account it was clear Benedict cut so many corners that he was virtually an outright crook. He couldn't touch anything without leaving greasy fingerprints behind, and Renoir was worried that he had drawn Kate into something illegal. He needed to find out what was going on. For Kate's sake, he told himself.

There had been a recent phone bill and he examined it minutely, finding repeated calls to one number he didn't recognise. He dialled 141 and the number and got a taped message from Conrad Benedict. But that didn't really tell him anything.

Neither did the few pieces of correspondence he managed to unearth, after a thorough examination of Kate's desk, in the small room in the flat she used as an office. Several letters and cards from ancient relatives and a godfather; it seemed only members of an older generation conducted correspondence any more.

Midway through a desk drawer, he almost jumped when the phone rang, worried that somehow it was Benedict returning his call.

'Hi, Renoir!' It was Emily, sounding happy.

'Hi, Ems,' he said. 'I'm afraid your mom's not home yet.'

'That's okay, I can talk to you.' And she did for several minutes, alternating between a minute description of her school day and the arrangement for collecting her for her exeat that weekend. She grew especially excited when he told her that her bedroom at the Gatehouse was ready.

'Oh, Renoir,' she said, just before ringing off, 'Mummy hasn't mentioned the time I snuck off to come and see you. Was she very cross about it?'

'No,' he said, 'because I didn't tell her you had. I just said there'd been a mix-up which meant I ended up taking you back to school.'

'Thank you, Renoir.'

'There's one condition, okay?'

'What is it?'

'That you'll never do it again. Promise?'

'Done deal,' she said, an expression Kate complained Emily had learned from Renoir.

Resuming his search, he found a card from Kate's mother, written shortly after his weekend there alone.

Darling

Glad you're back and hope you enjoyed the trip. We had a successful shoot on Saturday and jolly dinner party that night. Jack filled in for you – though there's nothing like the real thing! He was so helpful – he put all those boxes with your father's papers in the cellar for me since I'd forgotten to ask Stacey.

Will we see you the weekend after next? I gather from Hal the workmen are almost finished. You must be so excited.

All sorts of love,
Mama

And that was it. He had already sensed that if he were going to get anywhere it would have to be a real hub of information, and that sat on the small hard disk on Kate's laptop. But access there was nigh impossible. He used an ageing PC for any work of his own, and there was never any reason for him to use Kate's machine. It was her chief work tool and, by unspoken agreement, off limits to anyone else – even Emily had to play hearts on Renoir's plodding computer.

Then he got a small break. Kate was working at home late one afternoon, sitting at the small French bureau she used as a desk, when he stuck his head around the door and asked if she'd like a drink.

'Too early,' she said, looking at her watch, then suddenly gave a small howl. 'I didn't know it was so late.' She stood up and grabbed her coat. 'I've got to catch the last post. Back in a minute.'

'I'll go,' he offered but she shook her head. For which he was grateful twenty seconds later when the door slammed and he was alone, looking at the listing of emails on her screen.

There were three from Carlisle (who was very demanding), there was a press release from Shell, several queries from a researcher they employed on a freelance basis, a bunch of the usual MSN announcements and an Amazon offer or two. Nothing unusual or of obvious import. He clicked back and saw Kate had 384 messages on her machine. And he had about five minutes before she returned.

He managed to keep his wits about him and opening the inbox clicked on the FROM column, which after a seemingly endless second or two listed the messages in alphabetical order. He scrolled through looking for 'Benedict', but to his intense disappointment found nothing. About to give up, he noticed that at the bottom of the screen under the 'C's there were half a dozen emails listed as CONRAD. He looked at their dates and saw the first was from early December. He opened one from January and read:

One o'clock. Same time, same place, unless you want to risk Boodle's and dress as a man.

The next one was five days later:

Tuesday's best for me so let me be piper. One o'clock. I may be five minutes late.

So far, just confirmation of their weekly meets. He skipped the next two and opened one from the end of February, which said:

Are you sure Acer's the 10th? It has to be exact. A day off and we're well and truly cooked. You make sure.

He was trying to digest when he heard a noise in the stairwell corridor and panicked momentarily, relaxing only when he heard a neighbour's heavy tread continue down the hall. He was running out of time. And then he realised he was missing half the dialogue. Switching to the Sent messages he clicked on the TO column and drummed his fingers impatiently on the bureau's top while the laptop alphabetised. There were roughly the same number of messages sent to Benedict as she had received, and he opened the first one, from December.

One o'clock at the Cavendish Hotel then. If we must. And I guess we must.

That was not the voice of an adulteress, though the 'I guess we must' sounded more collusive than he would have liked. He moved forward to February and picked the second message there, which was a reply to Benedict's querying the date:

Yes, it's the 10th. Script follows tomorrow.

And he was about to open the email sent the following day – what was this 'script' she referred to? – when he heard voices in the stairwell. *Shit* – he had forgotten how little time he had. Clicking desperately, he returned to the home page, then moved swiftly out of the room. He heard the key in the lock and knew he would never get back to the living room in time; Kate would see him coming down the hall. He took two steps into the bathroom and closed the door behind him. When he heard Kate coming towards her office he flushed the lavatory, then ran water in the basin and washed his hands. Drying them, he went out and found her sitting before the laptop. He said with false concern, 'Did you make the post?'

256

'Yes,' she said. 'And I ran into Lady E on the stairs. You didn't tell me she'd met Emily.'

'I forgot.'

'She seems to have had quite a conversation with her. Knew all about her school and Belfield, and heaven knows what else.' She looked at Renoir accusingly. 'It sounds as though they spent a lot of time together.'

'I don't think so,' he said. 'Lady E just doesn't see many young people.'

Kate nodded. 'I think she's lonely. Do you know what she said to me? "Everybody thinks I'm dead."'

'Why don't you stop working?' he said, pointing at Kate's computer. 'Let's have an early drink tonight.' And when she agreed he led the way into the living room, thinking what contrast lay between her cheerful communicativeness with him and the tense semaphores of the email exchanges he had just read.

What had he learned from his hasty inspection? That she and Benedict had met several times at one o'clock at the Cavendish Hotel (which he had already known); that something was happening on the 10th, presumably the 10th May. What could that be and why did it sound familiar? Kate said she'd close with Roddy for the Gatehouse some time after the 10th, but that hardly seemed relevant. Whatever else was supposed to happen, Kate obviously thought the date was important (and from his '*we're well and truly cooked*' Benedict did as well).

It was highly improbable he would get another chance at Kate's emails. But if he couldn't get at the problem through Kate what could he do? He wondered about this as he thought fleetingly of how he had followed Benedict, then realised the answer was staring him in the face. *The other side of the equation.* But Benedict wasn't going to open his soul to Renoir or do anything to make his job easier.

What could he find out without being detected? Not a lot, it seemed. Sure, he could buy Benedict's credit rating for a hundred and fifty bucks online, but it wasn't going to tell him very much. As Renoir discovered after moving from the army into the private sector, even rich people could have terrible credit ratings, because even rich people – sometimes especially rich people – didn't like to pay their bills on time. Conversely, people who were broke but careful could look positively A-1.

How then to begin, here in London without the usual fallbacks of his trade – such as people, including private investigators to check references and background stories, or technical resources, some supplied by the Defense Department, which could tell him everything from an applicant's high school grades to the amount of time an employee spent playing solitaire on the company's PC the day before. There seemed only one person he could turn to, and he did it reluctantly.

There was eight hours time difference, but knowing Ticky he called at three thirty in the afternoon his time, certain she would be there. She left her house in Berkeley every morning at six to beat the traffic, arriving at the office forty-five minutes later, when she would first have a run, then shower in the company's solitary stall, microwave a big bowl of porridge, make a pot of herbal tea and start the first of what were usually eleven hours in front of a terminal. Classic Silicon Valley. When he phoned, she answered right away.

'How's Kate?' she asked.

'Fine,' he said but then came to the point. 'Ticky, I need some help.'

'Have you got tax problems or something?'

'It's more high-tech assistance I want.'

'What for?'

'I can't tell you what I'm looking for. Not because it's secret but because I don't know for sure myself. But it's a bad guy, I can promise you that.'

There was a long pause that Renoir ended. 'I need *your* help,' he said again. 'Kate knows nothing about this, and I really need to keep it that way.' He thought, *Ticky, we go back a long way, we worked a lot together.*

She seemed to be thinking along similar lines. '"Auld Lang Syne" and all that, right?' She paused. 'What sort of help do you want?'

'I need to get into somebody's network,' he said, and explained the problem, leaving Kate out of it.

When he finished he waited silently while Ticky considered it. 'All right,' she said at last. 'Have you got a clean machine?'

'I'll buy one today.'

'Set up a Hotmail account then. Make the address that full name you're always laughing at.'

Full name? And then Renoir laughed. *Ticonderoga.* 'The one that's close to home?'

'Precisely. And send me the details of the guy's corporate site – just its web address for starters.'

'I'll do it right away. Do you think you can get in?'

She ignored him and went on, 'I have an intern from MIT who started last week, and I've been scratching my head what to do with him. Maybe he can help. Officially, I don't need to know about it. You'll have an email in the morning your time, provided you send me the info I need. Okay?'

'Okay,' said Renoir.

'Love to Kate,' she said, but then added, 'well, not this time I guess. Bye.'

Renoir was grateful she had said this. She seemed to trust him, but he could tell she was uneasy about acting behind Kate's back. But it would be worth it if she managed to get him into Benedict's network.

She couldn't. The email came later than expected on the following afternoon and read: *Firewalls everywhere and the sharpest password security I have seen this year. I am confident we could get in, but assume from the tone of your voice yesterday that the three-month time frame this would require won't be satisfactory. Can I suggest you take the personal route? Algorithms enclosed.*

He wasn't surprised by her message, reading it on the new laptop he'd bought that afternoon on Tottenham Court Road, going for a high-end machine since he figured he might need all the processing power he could get. If it were any sector other than

259

banking it might be worth her continuing to try and get in, since even very big corporations were sometimes vulnerable – thanks to poor security, or just less of it than they should have. But not in banking, where clients were obsessively security conscious. If there were even a whiff of anybody outside getting into a bank's system, clients would head elsewhere fast. Especially personal clients.

Kate would be home soon, but he ran the attachment of algo- rithmically generated emails, addressed to 1,250 email addresses that were based on the simple combination of two words: Conrad Benedict. He sent these to all the standard providers, including Hotmail, AOL, Virgin, BT and others. He left it to run overnight and came back in the morning after Kate went to work to find he had a winner. He emailed Ticky: *Got it – conrad.benedict@aol.com. Rocket science.*

And virtually by return, after a brief conversation on the phone which found her up and about in Berkeley at three in the morning, Ticky sent him an electronic birthday card attached to an email. 'You've got a choice,' she'd explained. 'You can put something in there that will watch his every move – it takes a snapshot of the screen every few seconds so it captures keystrokes. The problem with that is you're more likely to get caught; the longer you hang around the more likely some security program will alert him that you're there. The alternative is to go in and out. It will grab what- ever you want – documents, email, whatever you specify – and then send them to you, though not all at once, unless he's online for a long time. The advantage is it's not easily detectable and once it's done it comes out of the machine along with all the other material, so there's no evidence you've ever been there. The disad- vantage is you can only do it once. You can't very well send him a second birthday card.'

He thought for a moment and decided. 'One-shot deal sounds best. I don't want him to get suspicious, much less know someone's got inside his machine.'

And so now he was sending a birthday card, from his new PC, and from the equally new Hotmail account of one Linda

Dove. The message was simple: *Conrad, happy (belated) birthday greeting. Next year I'll be on time. xxx L.* Renoir used only an initial, but made it personal (though not louche) so that Benedict would scratch his head and think 'who the hell is this?'. And, crucially, open the attachment, which was a simple Flash animation. It showed a girl in a riding outfit astride a hunter, which jerkily jumped a fence before it came to another, where it baulked. The rider was thrown forward, did a somersault over the jump and landed neatly on her feet. A banner ran across the screen: *I'd jump over anything for you. Happy Birthday!!*

And while Benedict tried to puzzle out just who Linda Dove was and whether he had been drunk when he'd met her, a software application would go to work immediately, sending out copies of the entire email correspondence held on Benedict's computer at whatever rate the connection allowed. If he wasn't logged on very long, then it would pick up where it stopped on Benedict's next visit to the Internet.

Renoir specified that Benedict's emails should be sent first, then Word documents. Nothing else; if he included graphics, the size of the files would take forever to transport. Similarly, he avoided spreadsheets, since he assumed that a personal banker would have about a million of them on his machine. Renoir was in any case looking for the words which triggered a movement in numbers, not the numbers themselves.

He didn't know why he was surprised, since he could not have said what he was expecting, but it turned out there were 2,237 emails in Benedict's Inbox, 1,565 in his Sent box, and 212 deleted. The Junk box was empty, and there were no separate folders. A large, unmitigated mess, in other words, at least for Renoir's purposes. Daunted, he looked to see what else had come in from Benedict's PC, and his heart sank. There were over twenty folders holding Word documents; opening the first two at random, he found that each held over a hundred separate documents. Infuriatingly, both the folders and documents seemed to be labelled in a system that might have been Chinese for all the sense it made to Renoir, with a prefatory capital letter, a lower case one, then a number which ranged on the screens he looked at from 0001 to 1127.

What was he supposed to do? Sift through several thousand emails, addressed to people he had never heard of? The Word documents seemed equally impenetrable. He would have to look through six hundred documents, many of them over 100k in length – it was hundreds of thousands, no *millions*, of words. Even the labelling of them by letter seemed to have no mnemonic value. He looked under 'P', hoping (or dreading; he wasn't sure) that 'Palmer' would show up, but found instead an excerpt from a casebook on natural gas regulations, and a speech given by a New York financier named Platt on the origins of the derivatives market.

He continued to feel entirely at sea until he looked at the email he'd had from Ticky just that morning, with an attachment called simply TOOLS. Her penultimate paragraph said, *If, as usual, you don't know what you're looking for, these bits and pieces may help.*

The tools were listed as forms of search: Keyword or Proximity Search; Free Search (all text), Search By: Email, PDF, Documents. Then Sorting By: Date Received, Dates in Documents, By Recipient (alphabetical), By Sender (alphabetical), and – here it said FUZZY Search – by Dominant Topic.

Maybe this would help. He began, again, with 'Palmer', and was delighted to get back thirty-seven entries. But they proved a farrago of uninformative citations: reference in the trade press to Kate and Seymour Carlisle. There was nothing remarkable in this mix of PDF and Word documents and text files. Until he opened a document with the formidable label ESAf17134.

At first there seemed nothing unusual about it – it was an address about oil exploration. Yet it seemed familiar, and as he scanned through it he recognised the speech that was giving Kate so much trouble. What was Benedict doing with it? He went through this copy page by page, and came to a highlighted section on expert systems, where Kate argued that companies needed to

revaluate how they used them for oil finds. Why was this highlighted, presumably by Kate? He scrolled slowly to the end of the
document, but could see no obvious changes, until he found a
simple dated message at the end:

09/03
Are you happy now? K

This was a few days after she had shown the same speech to
Renoir, her partner. Did she prefer the input of her ex-boyfriend?
He looked through the other documents again, but found no clues
there – and nothing with any message for Benedict.

He scanned the subset of emails, looking at senders' names, and
found his interest piqued by 'Kiki Reisberg', an exotic note among
an otherwise innocuous roster of Anglo-Saxon surnames. Opening
it he read the following:

Mr B,
Sorry the suite at KGH is booked, but never mind –
we'll have more than enough room. And this time I'll
bring the baby oil.
Yours anticipatingly,
Kiki R

So Benedict did enjoy sessions in hotel rooms, only with someone
rejoicing in the name of Kiki Reisberg, who sounded suspiciously
like a high class call girl. *Poor Helena*, thought Renoir, *she must
have baulked at baby oil.*

Where else should he look? Browsing, he would be awash in
an ocean of words. He thought of what he knew about the man.
Surprisingly little. He'd checked *Who's Who* but Benedict had yet
to make it there; *Debrett's* and *Burke's Peerage*, consulted in the
London Library, had proved equally barren. Anyway, what good
would it do him if he knew what school Benedict had attended,
his place of birth, his mother's maiden name? Sweet FA, as the
English liked to say.

Was it possible that Benedict and Kate were up to something perfectly legitimate, some consultancy perhaps, which she was providing? But then why had she lied? Just to spare his feelings, in case Renoir was jealous? No, there was too much subterfuge for anything legitimate. Which left scams, much as Renoir was reluctant to admit it. And from what Alastair had said, Benedict was no beginner in that arena.

Then he remembered the elliptical reference in Benedict's email. Acer, as in Acer Oil, a client of the Carlisle Consultancy. He ran a search, starting with documents, and found two links right away – one in particular to an article in *Business Week* which he reluctantly paid to read. From it he learned that Acer was a mid-sized independent, which specialised in regions which were borderline, in terms of their potential; so much so that the big companies didn't expend drilling resources on what was seen as marginal. Natural gas off Scandinavian shores, unexplored parts of Azerbaijan, once-worked pockets off Indonesia that Acer thought worth working all over again. Nothing remarkable there, but one paragraph near the end of the article caught his attention right away:

Acer's edge is in its exploration of expert systems technology to make oil and gas finds which the more conventional techniques of its rivals cannot unearth. Despite scepticism voiced by these more traditional practitioners, Acer has been consistently successful in locating significant natural gas and oil deposits in areas thought to be of negligible value by its competitors. **SHARE WATCH: BUY.**

Renoir went and found a newspaper and checked the shares page. There was Acer all right, trading nicely at 373p. But wait a minute. He checked the *Business Week* piece again – it had appeared six months before – and discovered the shares had then been trading at only two pounds. The stock was riding high.

And then he understood. It was Acer, it must be, and Benedict would be shorting the shares. Someone – *someone?* thought Renoir bitterly – would have tipped him off, someone who knew the company's reliance on expert systems was excessive, its 'proven reserves' more fiction than fact. He could imagine the market's reaction to X million barrels of oil moving from proven to . . . probable? More like *problematic*.

And any conceivable doubt that he had found what he was looking for was removed when he ran a check through Google, which gave him the most recent mentions of Acer in the press. Preliminary news of the company's half-year results, he read, were positive, though as usual the company counselled shareholders to wait for the official results due on May 10.

The following Friday. And the same day, May 10, when Kate was due to give the speech she had sent in draft form to Benedict. Why? Not that it mattered; the importance of the date had nothing to do with the speech. The real significance, as he looked again at Acer Oil's press release, was that on the same day the company would announce its official results. And Renoir would have happily bet every one of his last remaining dollars that, to an unsuspecting world, these would seem catastrophic. But not, it seemed, to Conrad Benedict. He would make a fortune selling Acer short. Why in the name of God was Kate going to help him do this?

And then it was blossom time. They picked up Emily from school in High Wycombe, then stopped at the pub in the village for supper. When they reached the Gatehouse it was dark. Not having seen the finished house, Emily raced upstairs to inspect her room, a large corner one decorated with blue and pink wallpaper she had picked. She had been allowed a make-up table, though not, blessedly, allowed make-up, since Kate loathed the precocity of so many pre-adolescent girls.

'Do you like it?' he asked as she toured the room, opening the closet door, pulling open and shut the drawers of her dresser, even looking under the bed in her excitement.

Emily opened the window. She cupped her chin in both hands and propped her elbows on the windowsill as she stared out at the black starless night above Burdick's Field. 'Oh, Renoir,' she said, almost breathless in her satisfaction, 'it's perfect.'

In the morning he let Kate sleep and made Emily a big breakfast. 'American style,' she called it – cereal followed by pancakes with maple syrup. She chatted away while he drank his coffee and ate some toast. 'Renoir, did you have cereal when you were a boy?'

'Sure,' he said. 'Why are you asking me that?'

'Because you never have it now.'

'I guess I had too much of it then,' thinking for the first time in over a year of the last apartment he had lived in with his mother, of the high shelf which he had stood on a kitchen chair to reach. And the boxes of cereal he had brought down so many times for himself, annoyed his mother wasn't there to do it for him, worried about where she might be.

They worked outside, and he cut the grass around the Gatehouse with a new tractor mower they had bought in spring, letting Emily do the flat square between the flower beds and the start of the meadow. At tea she and Kate went over to see Beatrice, but then they all spent a quiet night in, eating mussels cooked in white wine and garlic with a long baguette and a bottle of Chablis for Renoir and Kate, watching the terrible Saturday night programmes on the TV that they had put into his office, along with a sofa and two armchairs, to let the room double as a snug. Kate went upstairs before him, and when the late-night movie had finished, Renoir found her sound asleep.

He was wakened early by Emily. 'What's up?' he asked drowsily.

'Rise and shine,' she half shouted, while Kate groaned and disappeared under the duvet. 'Let's go to the White Horse.' He let himself be cajoled, and got up and got dressed. He drank some coffee, depositing a cup of tea, milky with lots of sugar, on the bedside table for Kate, then drove out with Emily into the trafficless morning along the Downs. They got out at the higher of the two car parks, and climbed to the very back of the earth fortifications which Emily loved; she ran up and down the sides of the grass moat. The wind picked up and he wished he had brought a kite. As they walked towards the downward slope of the vast hill, and the Bronze Age horse carved out of the chalk, the Thames Valley opened ahead of them, an asymmetrical checkerboard of cultivated fields, interspersed only with the odd clump of copse and the man-made intrusions of Swindon sprawling to the west, and Didcot with its towers to the east. Yet even the landscape was largely man-made, the land deforested and moulded according to the changing agricultural practices of millennia. Ironically, it was California, the newer land of swimming pools and plastic, that held more untouched wilderness, from the desert of the southeast corner to the redwoods stretching up the state's north Pacific coast to Oregon.

A solitary visitor walked by with a black Labrador, and in the distance another early riser, with two small children, was playing out an immense red kite high up into the wind-swirled sky.

'So how's school, Ems?' he asked dutifully as they stood on the ridge and caught their breath.

She sighed, and he regretted asking, though she didn't actually answer. 'We are going to California this summer, aren't we, Renoir?'

He hesitated. 'I'm not sure. You'd better ask your mother.'

'Oh, Renoir, *please*. You promised.'

'I know I did, but the problem is, Emily, there's so much to do here. I've got to ready the field for the apple plantings, and the Gatehouse still needs work.' He was taken aback by the extent of the disappointment on her face. 'We will go, Emily, I promise. But it may have to be later in the year. Christmas,' he offered, trying to placate her. 'Or Easter,' he said. 'California will still be there. It's not going any place.'

'But don't you think it's time to head home?' she asked, in an odd singsong voice.

He stared at her, picturing the copperplate swirl of the writing, the garish colour of the Golden Gate Bridge on its picture side. 'What did you say?'

'Nothing,' she said, looking away.

'Was it *you* who sent me that postcard?'

He must have sounded angry. 'It was only meant to be a joke, Renoir. I got one of the teachers to do the writing. I explained you were taking me there this summer. Don't get cross,' she pleaded.

'I'm not cross,' he said. And he wasn't, simply relieved to discover that his paranoid imaginings of an anonymous enemy were so utterly misguided. He laughed, but saw that Emily was frowning. So he stopped and faced her, putting a hand lightly on her shoulder. 'Why do you want to go to California so much?' She lowered her eyes, not demurely but to avoid his gaze. 'Come on, Emily, spit it out. What's this really about?'

When she shrugged he took his hand away. 'I don't know,' she said with a nervous, teenaged giggle. 'I just thought it would be nice. For all of us. And maybe you and Mummy . . .'

'Yes?' he said, unable to keep a slightly insistent note out of his tone.

'Well, you know, that maybe you and Mummy,' she repeated and faltered again.

He said nothing, to avoid pre-empting her. At last she blurted out, 'That maybe you and Mummy would get married.'

'What?' he said, and he laughed nervously, which made her laugh back at him in relief that she had at last come clean. 'Why do you want us to get married?' he asked. 'People can love each other just as much without it.'

'I know that,' she said confidently, 'but I bet it helps.'

Sunday he drove Emily back to school since Kate had work to do. The two of them had been snappish with each other much of the weekend, and he wondered if he was witnessing the prelude to the wars of adolescence he heard so much about from parents. Kate could be firm with Emily, which was no bad thing in Renoir's view since although she was sweet tempered and very loving, Emily was also accustomed to getting what she wanted, including her own way. This weekend, however, Kate seemed oddly picky about trivial things, and as if to reciprocate Emily did her considerable best to wind up her mother.

The girl was quiet in the car, and when they arrived she said goodbye almost perfunctorily. 'Hey,' he said. 'What's the matter?' since usually he got a big hug goodbye, while he gave a promise of something to look forward to – the expedition to California, a theatre date in London, even just a trip to the White Horse. That way, if she were even half as miserable at school as he feared, she would have something to hold onto and get her through the worst patches. Tonight, however, she resisted his efforts at cheering her up.

'Nothing's wrong,' she said with a blank face that said he was no longer inside the loop.

Christ, he thought, *she's edging me out*. And then to his shame, he wondered, *Has she got a secret too?*

When he heard the shot he was in the kitchen, stuffing two small poussins with bread and fruit, enjoying the ample counter space of the butcher's block Kate had insisted on. It came from close by – a shotgun. There were two more shots, even closer, too close for comfort, especially at night. Poachers? Perhaps. Poachers who probably didn't know the Gatehouse now was occupied.

Kate was upstairs napping, and he didn't want to disturb her. He grabbed his Barbour from the laundry room and a long metal flashlight, and stepped outside. He waited for a moment outside the back door, as his eyes tried to adjust to the dark of a moonless night. The wind was up and the air was nippy – there had to be a chance of a frost. He felt unprotected, having the American desire for a weapon. But Kate didn't want a gun in the house, and he didn't have a shotgun licence anyway.

There was another shot, which came from the direction of the Old Orchard. He took the path through the small copse which divided the ageing apple trees from the Gatehouse, turning on his torch to see his way. Shouting was pointless: the wind was too loud, alternately whistling and moaning.

On the edge of the orchard he stood quietly, with his flashlight pointed down. He could make out the rows of trees in the large clearing against the backdrop of woods leading to Treefall Down.

At the end of one row he thought he saw the light of another torch, but when he stepped forward to get a clear view it was no longer there.

He felt exposed again. If these were poachers how would they take his sudden presence? Put another way, was he more likely to get shot intentionally, with his flashlight on, or accidentally, with it off? He didn't fancy getting shot in either way, but felt that, having come out, he could not just slink back to the house. Sensing his own growing apprehension made him determined to ignore it.

With his flashlight off, he walked the perimeter of the orchard but saw no one and no lights. Finishing his circuit, he started back towards the Gatehouse, and just before entering the copse he saw two figures ahead, turned sideways to him, one holding a torch and the other a raised gun. *Boom.* There was a loud guffaw. He turned on his own flashlight and walked quickly towards them. As he drew near, he saw it was Hal the keeper and young Stacey.

'What are you doing?' he asked.

Stacey's face was hard to see in the dark, but Hal moved up and stood close to Renoir. 'We're after rabbits here. Shooting's done now.' Hal had been a sergeant in the Guards for twelve years, seen duty in several continents of the globe, and spoke perfectly clear English – except with Renoir, when he insisted on affecting a West Country twang, with the 'ers' and 'ars' of a Somerset cider drinker.

'I know that, Hal. But you're close to the house. Too close. I'd rather you didn't shoot small game up here.'

'Small game? Is that what you call it?' He laughed, not pleasantly. 'Vermin's the word here, though I will stick one in the pot once in a while.'

Stick it up your ass if you want to, Renoir thought, but he kept his temper. 'I don't care what you do with them; I just don't want you shooting them right outside our door.'

'Mr Roddy wanted us to do this.'

'Well, *I* don't.' He saw this wasn't going to get him anywhere, and perhaps that was Hal's point. 'Neither does Kate.'

270

Hal smiled broadly. 'Perhaps you'd ask her to have a word with her brother then. You see, it's her brother what gives us our instructions.'

How Renoir wished he'd said 'and pays our wages', so he could have had the satisfaction of pointing out that, actually, Roddy usually didn't. But he left it alone and walked down the path, suppressing his annoyance when he heard Hal give out a large derisive laugh behind him.

As he neared the Gatehouse he saw that someone was coming out the back door, a male figure framed by the light of the laundry room through the open door. It was Roddy, and as the door closed his silhouetted figure disappeared into the dark.

'Roddy,' he called out, rushing forward, and he saw him at the corner of the house.

'Yes, Renoir?' It was more imperious than questioning.

'Are you looking for Kate? She's in the bedroom upstairs.'

'I found her,' he said cheerfully, and started to move off.

Renoir called out, 'Hal's been shooting rabbits with Stacey in the Old Orchard.'

'Splendid!'

Renoir ignored this. 'I'd rather he did it in daylight. Or not at all. It was awful close.'

Roddy turned. 'Oh no,' he said, with a friendly air that was entirely unconvincing. 'You're much better off having a go in the dark. You can shine the little brutes that way. And, besides, it's one of the perks of the keeper's job.' His voice softened unctuously. 'Old as the hills. Mustn't interfere with that. I'm afraid it's another of our little traditions you'll have to put up with.' And this time he moved off into the dark before Renoir could reply.

Renoir took his time, hanging up his Barbour, turning off the lights in the tack room and kitchen. When he came into the hall the door to the sitting room was open and he saw a light on in his study at the far end of the house. When he walked through he found Kate, sitting in the room's one armchair. A song was playing on the CD player they'd originally bought for Emily, and he recognised Aretha at once.

He started to smile, until he looked at Kate's face and saw tears on both cheeks.

'You okay?' he said quietly, and she nodded.

'Did Roddy upset you?'

She shrugged.

'Is there a problem?' he asked gently.

She roused herself enough to give a little snort. 'With my brother there's always a problem. And the problem's always the same.'

'Money.'

She nodded. 'What else? I wouldn't mind so much if he'd just come clean about it. But it's always "next week the deal's going through". I honestly think he believes his own . . . crap. Until it's too late and then he expects me to bail him out. At whatever cost . . . to me.'

She wiped her cheeks dry with her hand. 'But you see, the alternative doesn't leave me any choice, and he knows it. I mean, he is my brother, and then I think about Belfield, and how my father worked so hard to keep it, and my mother, who seems to think nothing will ever change simply because she doesn't want it to change.'

He came over and kneeled down by the chair. With one hand he stroked Kate's hair. 'I wish you'd let me help. I don't have to plant the trees this autumn, or buy the machinery.'

She shook her head, in a kind but weary way he didn't like. 'Renoir, you are so many things I admire, but one of them is *not* rich.' She smiled knowingly. 'Besides, I want you to plant the trees; I want you to start farming. It's sweet of you, but there really isn't any point.'

'It's that much money?' he asked.

'And then some,' she said, with only half a laugh. She seemed to pull herself together. 'You've caught me at a weak moment. Don't worry, nothing's changed. We'll be fine, I promise. The deal will still go through, probably the week after next. It's all in hand.'

'That's what worries me.' She shrugged again, and he said, 'I wish you'd tell me the whole story.'

272

To his surprise, he could feel the muscles in Kate's neck tauten. 'I haven't lied to you,' she said tartly.

'Just not told me some things,' he said gently.

'Look who's talking,' she said bitterly. 'What am I supposed to have lied about?'

'Tuesdays,' he said, and she looked at him in puzzlement. 'You're not seeing Indonesian oil men. Not at lunch-time anyway,' he added, against his better judgement. If Kate could be so forthcoming at last, perhaps in a limited way he could let her know what he knew.

But it was a mistake, he saw at once, for colour was rising in Kate's cheeks like the gauge of a warmed thermometer. 'Who am I supposed to be seeing instead?'

He sighed and stood up. He turned to face Kate and found her staring at him defiantly. 'Conrad Benedict,' he said, deciding not to say where.

Her eyes widened into disbelieving moons, and for a split second he wondered whether he had been wrong, somehow got the whole thing horribly askew. But that was ridiculous, he just as quickly realised; he wasn't living in a counterfactual world.

'You think I'm sleeping with Conrad Benedict?' She said this coolly, which Renoir found more disconcerting than outrage.

'I did for a while,' he admitted. 'But I know you're not.'

'You *know* I'm not. How do you *know* that? What does that mean? Has someone said something to you?' He shook his head. 'Well then, how do you know? Have you been following me?'

'No,' he said which, he told himself, was strictly speaking true. Ricky had been following her. 'Anyway, it's your turn to explain. How can I help you if you won't let me know what you're up to?'

'I don't want you to help me. You can't help me. Trying to help me is going to make things worse, so don't touch it. Unless you already have.' She was looking at him with a mix of suspicion and growing anger. 'What have you done?'

'I haven't done anything,' he said, unwilling to return her gaze.

'Oh yes you have.' She sat up in the chair, thinking hard. 'Have you been *spying* on me?' she demanded. 'You have, haven't you? Oh, Christ, just what have you found out?'

At a loss, he told the truth: 'I think there is a scam being planned. It has to do with an oil company; I even think I know which one. It's probably some kind of insider trading, though I don't know how it's going to be done. But Benedict's used information about company results before, so I assume he'll think of something.'

'*Oh, Christ,*' she said in a rising wail. 'You have been spying on me. With all your little gadgets and gizmos, no doubt. There's probably a hidden camera in my handbag, and a microphone in Seymour's office, and God knows what else from your pathetic little bag of tricks.'

He knew it was only vanity making him cross, and he thought, *If I say anything it will only make things worse. We are near to saying the unforgivable.*

She got up from the chair and he could see she was enraged. 'Kate,' he started to say, and put a hand out to touch her.

'Don't,' she said sharply, and walked out of the room. She didn't bother to slam the door. He heard her stalk across the sprung oak floor of the sitting room but stayed where he was. He thought he could hear Kate moving upstairs. Through the window outside he could see the tall protective alders on the far edge of the field moving in the wind, swaying like shaggy maypoles. He was confident Kate would come back downstairs once her anger had subsided.

He heard more bass-like rumbles from above and wondered whether he should go to her. Explain that he hadn't been spying – well, he had been, but make her understand he had only done it for *her* sake. And he'd been right; she was heading for serious trouble. So why wouldn't she let him help?

He listened to Aretha until the CD finished, then decided not to wait any more, and walked through the ground floor and climbed the stairs. There was only one light on, in their bedroom down the hall, and when he got to the doorway he saw to his surprise that Kate wasn't there.

She had gone, after all, he realised, and through the window he saw a car's rear lights moving down the track along the south side of Burdick's Field. Had she taken the car, too? He would have to take the train back to London, he thought, until he saw a light on the roof of the car and realised it was one of the local taxis.

And he felt panicked by her departure, since she had never walked out on him before – not even out of a room when they were having a rare argument. And on the bed there was a note, scribbled on a piece of her London stationery, thick blue sheets from Smythson. *I've gone back to London. Please don't follow me there tonight. Or tomorrow night either. In fact, please don't follow me any more at all.*

He began to realise how much he had underestimated her fury at discovering his intrusions. He had expected denial, perhaps even anger, but he had been sure Kate's astonishment at his discoveries would eventually be followed by relief.

Though he hadn't seen it, they were walking on ice, the two of them, and Kate seemed to think she was out too far to be rescued by him. The ice was cracking, sure enough, and he realised he had better find out just what was at the bottom of this mess if he expected to keep Kate. D-Day was the 10th, which gave him just five days to discover what she was playing at, and to stop it. Otherwise, he felt certain he would only be able to watch as Kate went through the ice alone.

The Yellow Shirt

He WENT UP and then down, several times, like a ride on a seesaw, and he started to feel sick and disoriented, even more than he felt scared. He had to get free of this iron grip holding the back of his shirt, a grip which held him with the certainty of a mechanical arm. And the next time that his feet touched the ground, and the arm paused momentarily before beginning its inevitable lift into the air, he turned and tried to bite the arm – which was human after all – just above the wrist. He couldn't reach it with his mouth, however, and he was in any case too slow, and suddenly the other arm came sweeping out of nowhere and BANG! the very end of it, which he realised was a flattened hand, exploded against his cheek, making a sharp crack in the air like a rifle shot.

He was motionless now, standing there, the pain cascading through his cheek up and into the entire side of his head, and the voice above the arm barked out, 'That's it, you little bastard,' and as both arms came down and seized him by his shoulders he felt his fear return and override the swelling pain in his head, and he wanted to cry out when suddenly there was another crack in the air, only flatter this time, and away from him. As he waited for a new pain to commence, the arms grabbing his shoulders released their fierce grip, and he watched as a large sod-sized piece flew out of where the scalp of the man in the yellow shirt should have been, and blood spurted up, and as the figure before him collapsed to its knees the boy stepped back, instinctively, but watched as the man's eyes struggled to focus on him – the boy – then the eyes rolled as the man's knees no longer gave support and he fell flat on his face into the dust.

And the boy saw the gun first, watched as it emerged from the wooded trail he had himself run along just minutes – no seconds, actually – before. Watched it dully since something had given way inside him; his capacity to fear had lapsed in the face of so much violence. When Maris came out holding the deer rifle with both hands, he felt no elation, but only mild curiosity, as if thinking, though he was not really thinking at this point, that it was interesting to find her there.

'Stand over here,' she told him as she came into the clearing, and for the briefest second he thought that she proposed to shoot him, too. 'Go on,' she said and she kneeled down by the bloody figure in the dust, and he reckoned she was shielding him, so he did as he was told and looked away, though when she exclaimed lightly, he turned back and saw that she had turned over the dead man – for he was clearly dead – having laid down her rifle. 'Jesus H. Christ,' she said more loudly, and looked over at him. 'He was going to kill you with his bare hands, I guess,' she said, in a detached and purely observational tone.

She stood up and put her forehead in one hand while she held the rifle with the other. 'Jesus H. Christ,' she said again, stating each word distinctly. 'What are we going to do?' She looked at the boy, not as if she thought he had an answer to this, but as if contemplating him as part of the problem.

'Why H.?' he asked for no reason he could understand.

'What?'

'Why "H."? You keep saying "Jesus *H*. Christ". Why "H."?'

She looked at him dully. Then as if she had decided something she said, 'Holy. H. is for holy.'

He nodded as if this should have been obvious to him. Then she said, 'We have a problem.' She took another deep breath. 'Leastways I do.'

'What's that, Maris?'

'I have shot this man because I thought he was about to kill you.' She was speaking formally, as if testifying in court. 'I bet you thought he was too.' The boy nodded. 'But you see the thing is,' she went on, 'he didn't have a weapon on him. And I will have a problem with the police if they come out here. He didn't have a weapon, but I shot him anyway. They'll argue that I didn't have to do that. But they didn't see Will the way I did or what this man was about to do to you. Or the other man he killed.'

What? He looked at Maris and spoke for the first time. 'Other man?'

She looked at him, at first disinterestedly, then, as something showed in his face, with growing recognition. 'There's another dead man back there,' she said slowly. 'Did you see him?'

He nodded but wouldn't look at her. 'Well,' she said, about to continue, but then she stopped, and he felt her eyes on him. And then she said, 'Oh,' with a small gasp. 'Was it you . . .' and before she could finish the sentence he nodded again, keeping his eyes locked downwards.

He started to cry and she came right over to him and hugged him. She let him sob for some time, then stepped back, though she kept her hands on his shoulders. 'Listen,' she said, 'I have to go back to the barn and get something. I'm going to be a while. But don't worry: I will come back. Promise. If you hear the tractor you'll know it's me. Okay?' And he nodded. 'I want you to stay right here. Don't touch anything. Sit over there' – she pointed to a clump of azalea bushes; they were flowerless at that time of year, but a dark green. 'Just keep your eyes closed. Maybe you can sleep a little. I don't suppose you got much last night.'

'Can't I come with you?' He knew he really didn't want to stay alone for two seconds just then.

'No,' she said. 'You've seen enough.'

And he started to bite his lip in order to be strong, but then something gave way: he could not face the solitude again, not knowing if terror would again erupt into his life, not sure if the violence was worse than the fear of violence. 'Please, Maris, don't leave me here. Let me come with you. Please.'

She eyed him thoughtfully, and he felt that she was listening to him, which was not usually her way once she had made a decision. That much had changed in their new and extraordinary circumstances. 'All right,' she said. 'I guess you've already seen the worst of it. But you're going to have to help me.'

And they walked back through the woods until they came to the rocky sandy slope and Maris scooted down it first, with the rifle in a sling over her shoulder, and the boy followed, feeling the sand slide into his sneakers, and they walked past the pond on the house side, and the boy didn't even look across its still expanse of water towards the greenhouse where his uncle lay dead, and they entered the edge of the woods where he had hidden in such fright, cutting across until they reached the path that took them to the barn.

'When will the police get here?'

She inhaled deeply. 'They won't be getting here.'

'Why not?'

She looked at him. 'What good are the police going to do? They're too late to help your uncle, now aren't they?'

He nodded his head in agreement, though after a moment he found objections forming in his head, inchoate strings of thought he struggled to put into words. 'But,' he began to say.

'I've thought it all out,' said Maris, talking through the boy. 'If we call the police, they'd find three dead men lying here, and guess what? We killed two of them. I could go to jail, and I don't know what they'd want to do with you – maybe put you in some juvenile offenders' place.'

He felt entirely confused. 'But they killed Will. And they would have killed me.'

'I know that. You know that. But what would the police think?'

'So what are we going to do?'

'Bury them.' She mistook the look on his face for revulsion. 'I can do it alone if you like.'

'No,' he said sharply. 'It's just . . .' and he paused.

She looked at him calmly and said, 'I'm not going to bury Will with them, if that's what you're thinking.'

And, almost crazily, he felt relief, really for the first time, and about something which had nothing to do with the real danger he had faced, and the real horror of what he had witnessed. 'But won't people wonder what happened to them?'

She shook her head. 'I doubt it. I checked their wallets and they were both from Portland. Probably small-time dealers there. Frankly, I doubt anybody up there knew where they were going – and if they did, I can't believe they'll want to investigate the issue. That's in the nature of the business. Believe me, no one's going to come looking for *them*.'

This seemed unanswerable, and Maris didn't wait for him to think of more questions. 'Now,' she said. 'Can you drive the tractor if you have to?'

'I think so,' he said, trying furiously to remember the few lessons he had had from Will.

'Good, because I want you to bring it out of the barn and around to the house end of the pond – the house end, okay? It's got the flatbed on the back, so take it slow.'

He was concentrating on her instructions, finding it easy to immerse himself in the detail. 'Should I unhook the flatbed?'

'No. We're going to need it.'

He managed to start the tractor all right and back it slowly out of the barn, then drove it jerkily between the house and Maris's vegetable garden until he saw her at the near end of the pond. He stopped just short of some rolled-up tarpaulin at her feet, and he was glad that he had, since as he got down out of the cab he saw there was a body rolled up in the tarp.

Maris said, 'I'm not going to pretend this will be easy. When it gets too much just shut your eyes, okay?' He nodded, and following her lead reached down with both arms for one end of the canvas tarp. 'Ready?' she asked, gripping her end. '*One, Two, Three*,' and together they lifted the heavy roll and Maris swung round until she was closest to the flatbed, and in a tandem shuffle they moved to it, the boy scuffing his feet to stay in synch with Maris, and as she swung her end up and onto the deck of the flatbed he lost his grip and his end – which was the legs – started to slip down towards the grass, and he fumbled desperately to regain his grip and halt the downwards sliding weight and then Maris's hands were next to his on the rough canvas, and they both gave a great heave and the whole dreadful human sausage was on the flatbed with a thud.

They stood there, out of breath from their exertion, until Maris said, 'I thought we'd lost him for a minute,' and she gave a short, bark-like laugh which conveyed more pain than humour.

'Sorry,' said the boy, and Maris put a hand on his shoulder.

This time she drove the tractor, and he stood behind her as he had always done with Will. To his surprise she drove around the house and then down the track towards the mountain road. She drove fast, bouncing them about, and at one point he looked behind at the rolled-up tarp, but it had barely moved. They passed Truebridge's shack, and to his astonishment Maris kept going, and pulled out onto the hard-packed sand of the mountain road.

She turned her face sideways and he strained to hear her words as she explained, half shouting above the engine noise. 'We've got to get the other one, and this won't make it through the woods. If a car comes by, just wave.'

But no car came by; there was rarely any car at all on this high road, since anyone going around the mountain would take the quicker, paved road at its base. They drove for what to the boy seemed an endless, infinite time, but was probably no more than sixty seconds, to a point several hundred yards down from the entrance to the farm, near to where the boy had been about to emerge from the woods when he had been grabbed by the man in the yellow shirt.

And suddenly Maris swung the tractor left, off the road, and she cried out 'Hang on tight!' and he thought she must have gone mad. But then he saw they had turned onto the fire road cut out of the woods, slightly overgrown, unused, but with the outline of a rough track discernible. Brush had overgrown it, but there were no trees, which with the tractor was all that mattered. And they moved bumpily through the high ferns and grass, but hit no solid obstruction, and suddenly Maris braked hard and they stopped, with the flatbed shuddering to a stop behind them,

When they found the body of the man in the yellow shirt he was on his side, crumpled up like a vast seahorse beached on a shore. There was no tarpaulin this time. Maris picked the corpse up under his shoulders, and waited impatiently until the boy grabbed each of the boots. He looked away – he did not want to see the dead man's face. He was heavy, heavier than the man in the Stetson, and they had further to walk to the flatbed. When they got to the tractor he had to rest, and told Maris so.

'Okay,' she said reluctantly, but when they put the man down on the grass she didn't let go of his shoulders. The boy looked away again while he caught his breath and waited for the ache in his arms to disappear. 'Ready?' asked Maris, and he nodded and grabbed the boots again. Without saying a word, they both seemed to know what to do, and swinging the body once, twice, then three times landed it onto the flatbed. Backing away, the boy discovered that his hands were wet, and looking at them saw that they were streaked with mocha-coloured stains. Then he realised it was blood. He felt his gorge rising and bit down hard on his lip to keep from being sick.

He got up behind Maris on the tractor again, and instead of turning around, Maris drove further down the fire road, into the woods where he had run just an hour before. She stopped after several hundred yards, seemingly in the middle of nowhere, for here the fire road was largely overgrown with ferns, and saplings were starting to move in from either side of the track.

Maris got down without speaking and walked off to one side of the fire road. The boy followed her, a little anxiously, and within twenty yards they came to the edge of the swamp. Maris stopped and nodded to herself, not even acknowledging that the boy was with her, and then she turned and walked back to the flatbed, where he now noticed beside the two bodies a large coil of half-inch rope and a double cinder block.

They unloaded and carried each body right down to the edge of the swamp, which was such back-breaking labour that carrying the cinder block after that seemed child's play. At the edge of the swamp, with the bodies lying next to the cinder block, she said, 'Take a breather, Jack.' He was glad to, and sat down on the ground and watched as Maris set to work.

First she unrolled the tarp, and the boy dully regarded the man in the Stetson as she unfolded the canvas flat around him. Pulling roughly on the legs of the man in the yellow shirt, she started to pull him onto the tarp as well, but his trouser belt caught on its edge, pulling the corner up in a hump. She struggled vainly to smooth the canvas, and finally snapped, 'Come and help.' The boy got up, and kneeling down held the canvas corner until she had pulled the corpse onto it without ruckling the end. Then she drew the two long tarpaulin sides over both bodies; there was overlap to spare.

She pointed wordlessly at the flatbed, and he went and retrieved the rope. Together they managed to ease it under the tarp at one end and wrapped it all the way around, and then three times repeated the process sideways along the length of the package, then drew the remaining length of rope back along the top under the loops. It was like stringing a rolled roast, which the boy had seen Maris do before. When Maris tied the rope firmly at one end, they were left with a sealed package of canvas and a length of rope attached to it. This she took, and poked the free end through the opening of the cinder block, drawing it all the way through, then wrapping it twice around the block before tying it tightly in a series of overhand knots.

'Take that end,' Maris said, and he grabbed the far end of the tarp. He could feel the legs of a dead man through the canvas. There was no way they could lift the canvas now, with two dead men inside, so Maris turned sideways, and motioned him to imitate her. 'One, two, three,' she called, and though they couldn't lift the canvas they managed to slide it clear of the brush on the edge of the swamp and into the water. Maris got on both knees and reaching out pushed the near end of the tarp a few feet further out into the swamp until it was in deeper water, where it sank immediately.

He felt immense relief at the disappearance of the two bodies until Maris stood up again and announced, 'They'll resurface when the gas inside them bubbles up.' Before he could ask what they could do about this, she walked over to the cinder block, which was still attached by the rope to the sunken tarp. The rope was taut now, and the boy hazily deduced that this meant the bodies could not be that far down – the cinder block had not been moved anywhere when the bodies had submerged.

Together they slowly lugged the cinder block over to the swamp, taking care not to trip over the loose rope connecting it to the canvas at the bottom of the swamp. Maris counted *one, two, three* yet again and this time, with a final exhausted heave, they threw the cinder block out just far enough to reach the deeper water, where it joined the rolled-up tarp in what Maris must be hoping would prove an eternal grave.

By now the boy felt incapable of being surprised, and when Maris managed to turn around the tractor in a clearing and pulled back onto the mountain road he thought it entirely natural. Again, they passed no one.

Back at the farm they stopped outside the barn, where Maris collected two shovels, then drove around the house and the pond, to the front of the greenhouse where Will's body lay in the afternoon sun. Not more than thirty feet away lay Ellie, the silky gold of her flank stained the colour of prunes from the shotgun blast.

'Poor bitch,' said Maris, and enough city remained in the boy that he was startled by the word, until he realised she meant Ellie. Maris stabbed her shovel in the earth and crouching down scooped the dog into her arms, then walked down to the pond and lay her on the reeds on its bank.

Here the earth was moist and soft, and when the boy joined her they found the digging easy and soon had carved out a small grave. As Maris gently put the dog's body into it, the boy kneeled down and quickly plucked out two worms, then tried not to look at the dog as Maris gently covered her with dirt. He thought, *Goodbye, Ellie,* and started to cry.

Will was harder in every respect. The boy was still upset and Maris didn't let him help, wrestling Will's body onto the flatbed herself. He didn't understand how she found the strength, but wouldn't look until Will's corpse lay flat on the wooden slats. They got onto the tractor and drove back around the pond, but this time Maris veered off down the path through the copse. She drove fast now, staring straight ahead of her, and he hung on for dear life until they emerged into afternoon sun with the Valley Orchard before them.

She cut the engine and sighed. She propped her elbows on the steering wheel and stared out at the vista of rows and rows of trees before them. For the first time the boy noticed the dirt streaked on both her arms, and how the back of her head was slick with sweat. She pointed out across the orchard. 'Your uncle loved this place. It's what drew him here to begin with. I figure if he wanted to be buried anywhere, it would be here. What do you think, Jacko?'

And he didn't know how to answer, for all he could think of was how he had been dazzled by his first view from this very position, standing on the tractor behind Uncle Will, relieved to move out of the dark of the small one-acre wood, but stunned by what emerged before his eyes.

'Jack?' asked Maris, and he came to.

'Yes,' he said simply, like a grown-up.

It seemed they dug for hours, though truth be told Maris did the lion's share of the work, and the boy mainly helped collect the dirt she emptied out onto the dry packed ground. He was aware that he was talking a lot. In the heat they sweated like pigs. After a while, Maris even took her shirt off and worked in her bra. He found himself looking at her entranced, in an embryonic pre-adolescent way he would not have even six months before, and she caught him at it, saying brusquely, 'Keep your eyes to yourself.' He pretended not to have heard her but didn't glance her way after that.

Until, suddenly, she stopped, and stepping out of the hole she said, 'It's a shallow grave, but that's just the way it's got to be. I'm too tired to dig any more.' She looked at the boy. 'Will would understand.'

'Sure he would, Maris.'

This time he helped her, holding tight onto the heels of the work boots Will had always worn. He kept his eyes focused on them intently; he hadn't once looked at Will's face, not once inspected the carnage of his chest wounds. The grave wasn't long enough as it turned out, but he let Maris come to his end and bend the legs, and looked away as she began to shovel dirt over the body from the pile of it he had collected.

Finished, Maris smoothed the dirt along the top of the grave then stood and looked at her work. 'Come here, Jack,' and he went and stood next to her. 'Your uncle wasn't religious – your gram and he never saw eye to eye on that, especially after Vietnam. So I think it would be hypocritical – I mean phoney – if we said a prayer. But I want to say something, okay?' And as they stood together and looked down at the grave, she started to speak. 'I loved Will and he loved me. You loved him and he loved you. Goodbye, Will.' She nudged Jack and he said, 'Goodbye, Will,' though by then he would have said anything Maris asked him to say.

They returned the tractor to the barn and went into the house. Inside Maris said, 'Now you go upstairs and take the big army bag of Will's from our bedroom. I want you to put some clothes in there. Think about what you need: socks, underwear, pants and shirts, got that? And your favourite books. Don't forget your toothbrush.'

And when he came downstairs with the bag, he found Maris at the table in the big room, and she motioned him to sit down. She put a blue plate on the table in front of him, and he saw it was a ham sandwich. He looked up at her questioningly, for he definitely wasn't hungry.

'You've got to eat something,' she said. 'Try and get it down. We've got ourselves a drive.'

This alarmed him. 'Where are we going?'

She looked at him calmly. 'To your grandmother's of course.' He must have shown his panic at the idea, for she said, 'You can't stay here, Jacko. You can see that, honey.'

And he supposed he could, if Maris said so, though he realised he had taken comfort during the last two hours from the idea that if he had lost Will, somehow he and Maris could stay on the farm. He asked, 'But what are you going to say?'

'Say to whom?' she asked back mildly.

'About us,' and then he realised one of 'us' was dead. 'What are you going to tell people happened to me and Will.'

'Oh that part's simple. I'm going to say Will got fed up. Everybody thought what he was doing was crazy anyhow, you can't make money in this part of Sonoma growing apples. I'll say we split up and he moved north to try his luck somewhere else. This is my cousin's land – it's not as though Will owned it; I can sort out the rent he owed. As for you, I'll tell people the truth. You went back to live with your grandmother.'

And he could not dispute the logic of this.

He felt they drove through the night, though of course they could not have, for the trip could not have been much more than two hours. At first, Maris turned on the radio, but she soon snapped it off. As they drove south along Route 101, Jack turned to look at her from time to time, and saw her in full profile: that long strong nose, and the stub chin, and ever so slightly prominent upper lip, pressed out by her two big front teeth. She had her hands in a severe old-fashioned ten and two o'clock grip on the wheel, and she stared straight ahead through the windscreen, as if to look anywhere else would somehow derail their journey.

Gram was up way past her bedtime waiting for them. She made a great show over Jack, which was unlike her, and showed him into the guest bedroom where again she'd cleared the boxes and made up the bed. At her insistence he had a bath, covering himself with a towel as she came in when he'd finished, then put on clean pyjamas which Maris must have packed, and got into the bed. When Gram came in to say goodnight he asked for Maris, quite insistently.

She came in and kneeled by the edge of the bed. Neither spoke for a long time.

'We've had a long day, you and me,' she said at last. 'It's time you got some sleep.'

'What about you? Where are you going to sleep?'

'Oh, I'll be all right,' she said. 'Don't you worry about me.'

'Is Gram going to put you on the sofa?'

'I imagine so,' she said, and he thought for a moment she had something caught in her throat. Then she put her hand on his forehead and stroked his hair. He liked this, though it made it hard to keep his eyes closed, and when he opened them he found her staring at him.

'What's wrong, Maris?' he asked, though even at that age he knew it was a stupid question. 'What's right?' would be more like it, after what had happened to them both.

'Your hair's wet, Jacko. You can't go to bed like that.' She got up, and after a minute she returned with a hand towel which she worked between the back of his head and the pillow. 'I'll spare you tonight,' she said and he smiled, since she usually ignored his howls and rubbed hard until his hair was dry.

'Listen, Jacko,' she said, stroking his forehead and hair again. 'When you wake up in the morning, I won't be here. There's a lot to do back at the farm, and I've got to go do it.'

'Let me come with you, Maris.'

'No, you've got to stay here with Gram. Besides, you've got to go to school you know. You may be Einstein, but even Einstein finished the fifth grade.'

'Why do I have to go to school down here? Why can't I come live with you, Maris?'

She stopped stroking his head and for a moment he worried that he had angered her.

'Did you tell Gram, Maris? I mean about Will.'

'She knows he's dead.' She hesitated a second. 'She knows what happened. And she knows it's a secret between you and me. Okay, Jacko? Just between you and me.'

'So I shouldn't talk to Gram about it?'

'No. She knows enough, and she told me she doesn't want to know anything more. Okay?' She waited until he had nodded. 'It's a secret, remember? Between you and me. Everything will be fine if you don't tell anyone. I promise. No matter what happens – to me or to Gram or to anyone, you will be just fine if you don't break the secret.'

'What's going to happen to you?' He felt agitated despite his fatigue.

'Nothing's going to happen to me.'

'When will I see you again?'

She was stroking his hair slowly now, long slow strokes. 'Oh, I don't know yet. You just be patient. And if things get tricky for a little while, just try and remember what a good time we all had. Promise me you'll remember that.'

He didn't hear from Maris again.

At first he told himself she was busy, clearing out the house he guessed, and probably building a bonfire with the contents of the greenhouse's secret room. Maybe, too, she was selling things off – like the tractor, or Uncle Will's truck.

But when two weeks passed, this rationalisation failed to contain his concern. He wasn't worried about Maris – no, now he was worried about himself, about the impact not hearing from her was having on him.

He said nothing to Gram, not sure what Maris would have told her, and Gram in any case did not encourage either questions or confidences. But he waited until Sunday when Gram had gone to church and Miss Lily, who was meant to look after him, was in the bathroom, and he dialled the farm's number with great care. And to his astonishment it said the number was disconnected. *I suppose she's closed it all down*, he told himself, and when Miss Lily turned on the TV to watch the gospel music he called information. And when he tried Maris's own house in town the phone rang, and rang and rang.

He managed to try four more times in the next ten days, but no one answered. And only by saving quarters and using a pay phone – the one near the principal's office in his school – was he able to call his old school. He panicked when Mrs McReady answered the phone in the school office, but he put a Kleenex against the speaking part of the instrument and though Mrs McReady sounded suspicious she didn't say anything and answered his request to speak to Maris by saying that Miss Thompson –

funny, he thought, he knew that was her last name but had hardly ever heard it said before – was away on sick leave, indefinitely. And he managed not even a thank you but hung up right away, and now he felt bereft and frightened in a new kind of mix. With his mother it had been bereft or, when she had hit him, fear, but never both at once. And he thought, trying to say it aloud to himself in as grown-up a way as possible, *You're on your own, Jack*.

Which was not a disaster but not really a success – he didn't like the school there, and he didn't like living with his grand-mother. She had rules and routines where his life heretofore had few or none: she limited his television watching, she cooked pota-toes with every single meal except breakfast, and she grumbled not so privately that he was there. For she wasn't really prepared to raise another child, least of all an energetic little boy.

She was strict with Jack and never particularly loving, and as time passed and his hope of going back to Sonoma and Maris became just that – hope rather than an expectation, and then in time a fantasy – he learned to swallow his resentment and just get on with his life. Which meant that despite pretty good grades and a surprisingly high set of Board scores, he was happy to forsake the local college prospects which were all he (well, Gram really) could afford, and instead enlisted in the army when he was only seventeen. Not to flee drugs or the ghetto or the cycle of deprivation half of his fellow recruits seemed to be escaping from, but to strike out on his own for the first time in almost seven years, and – he felt guilty about this but not immensely so – to get away from the trimmed-down version of life he'd had with Gram. To get away from the grim and daily truth that life in the Sunset wasn't life in Sonoma, that the people he loved best were absent – one taken from him, one inexplicably and heartbreak-ingly gone away.

And did his heart ever heal? *Anneal* was perhaps the more appropriate word, for by the time Jack Renoir had grown up his heart had hardened over.

*

There had been an old apple tree in the Back Orchard, a Gravenstein which his uncle Will had been determined to save. Apparently, each year more of it had died and each year he had cut off more of the dead wood, until by the time Jack arrived on the scene there wasn't much tree left – and Maris pointed out that Will was killing the tree in order to keep it alive.

And on each stump where once a bough had been, Uncle Will had painted over the gaping wound, with a black tar concoction that sealed the wound tighter than the tightest applied bandage, and kept out parasites and infection in the air and just about anything else which might hurt it on the inside.

And what Jack Renoir came to resemble was no less than this tree, cut down to size to stay healthy, and sealed off virtually hermetically from the external world. No one got in – not Gram, not his best friends, not all the girls he slept with, not Jenny the antiques dealer, the longest relationship of his adult life. And he was increasingly aware of this as he became first more man than boy, then a mature man, nearing forty.

But of course he had long before made the decision that he could live without emotional engagement if it meant there was no *drama* in his life – since for twenty-four hours on a mountainside in Sonoma County at the age of ten he had experienced enough drama, in his view at any rate, for an entire lifetime. And he supposed the price he paid was the absence in his life of anyone who mattered to him more than safety did; the absence, not to put too fine a point on it, of love. Because love involved a risk; love was not safe. Love was dangerous.

And though this was not the first time he had had these thoughts, they seemed particularly apt that morning, when, having driven out to the Palo Alto office, which despite the presence of Ticky and Prolog Alley's inhabitants he didn't really like, he found himself waiting around, growing increasingly irritated. He had been told by Eckerly, the personnel head, who was away on his golfing holiday, that he had to stand in for him that day with a VIP visitor, and Renoir wondered where in the hell was this person he was supposed to show around, and what was their name? He looked at the printout he had of the email from Peterson's secretary and saw the name was Palmer. Katherine Palmer. *Where is she?* he thought, as he looked at his watch, which had stopped the day before but was now moving again.

The Dead Man's Hat

FIVE DAYS.

At Kate's end he didn't know where to look. He had checked out the flat thoroughly, and there was no chance of getting on her machine again. Here at the Gatehouse, they had barely moved in; he couldn't see what he would find that might suggest how Kate and Benedict were planning to operate. The answer to his questions had to lie with Benedict, and with any luck on Benedict's PC. For that, Renoir at least knew the help he needed.

'Tell me again why I can't mention this to Kate.' It was Ticky and he had reached her at home, in what was late afternoon California time. 'I was just about to go out for a run,' she said. 'You're lucky to catch me.' He pictured her in the kitchen of her little house east and above Berkeley, standing in the kitchen while she spoke, looking out over the deck towards the peak of Tamalpais north of her. If you walked out into the steep street, you could see all of Berkeley and the Bay stretching below you.

'I told you. She thinks I'm out of the business for good.'

'So did I.'

There was no point arguing about it. 'Ticky, you've got to trust me on this one. If Kate finds out, I can't begin to tell you how bad it would be. I'd rather stop digging than take a chance on her finding out.'

Ticky ignored this. '*Unless*,' she said, almost wistfully, 'this is something Kate herself is involved in.'

He held his breath, unwilling to say anything. 'Okay,' she said quietly. 'You've answered my question. Then I'd better keep helping you, don't you think?'

'Please,' he said with relief. He moved into the problem before she could change her mind. 'I'm not finding what I need.'

'Maybe that's because it isn't there.'

'I know, but I have to go on the assumption that there's something on his PC that will help. I'm looking at his home machine after all; where he thinks he's safe.'

'All right, but it's still impossible unless you narrow it down. You've got to give me some idea of what you're looking for.' She took a deep audible breath. 'Come on, Renoir, your turn to trust *me*.'

He hesitated but he knew Ticky was right. 'It's a scam,' he finally declared. 'To do with shares.'

'Our old friend Insider Trading?'

'I'm almost certain.'

'Do you know the shares he's dealing in?'

'Yep.'

'Well that's a start. Do you know how he's doing it?'

'No, and I need to, because that way I might be able to stop it. He must be doing the trade through somebody else, because he's got a bit of a record in this field himself, and because it wouldn't be that hard to trace this guy back to . . . the information he shouldn't have.' He groaned slightly. He'd now gone through all the documents and emails mentioning Kate – or sent to her, or received from her – but nothing there helped him figure out just how the dealing was done. He explained this to Ticky. 'So my only hope is that there's a name in there somewhere which will lead me to the trader. But I won't recognise the name. It won't mean anything to me.'

'In context it might.'

'Meaning?'

'Meaning, let's try and extract proper names. If we can isolate them then it might just be manageable to view the context in which they occur, then decide if that tells us anything.'

Tells *us*, thought Renoir – this was a good sign. 'But, Ticky,' he said, 'there're so many emails and documents on his PC that there must be millions of words. Sorting all those isn't going to help.'

'You'd be surprised.' Ticky's voice was calm, yet somehow also hopeful. 'Word frequency throws out a really sharp curve. Let's run a sort and you'll see what I mean.'

300

'The thing people don't realise,' Ticky explained, 'is that for every million words that get written, an astonishingly high percentage are the same words over and over again. An average person may know thirty thousand words in the sense of knowing what they mean, but they actually *use* about eight thousand of them, tops. Articles, conjunctions, connectives – "and", "the" and "of" probably account for at least fifty per cent of the occurrences if you take a large enough sample. And the one hundred most common words account for over seventy-five per cent.'

'That still leaves an awful lot of other words.'

'Sure. But we'll run them against a lexicon and throw all the matches out. That should leave only proper names.'

'How long is it going to take to do this?'

There was a snort from Ticky's end. 'I said I'd help you, didn't I? Let me send you a utility so you can get started.'

'But, Ticky, what if this guy's name is also a common noun. What if he's called "Jimmy Blacksmith" or "Malcolm White"?'

'In that case you're done for. The only way to handle that would be to go through the entire word list and disambiguate every occurrence. That would take you six months, I figure, so you just have to hope that's not the case.'

And as he went to bed in the earliest hours of Monday morning, the professional part of him was optimistic; his personal feelings he was trying to ignore. If Kate were in trouble (and he had no doubt she was), what if he couldn't help get her out of it?

Twelve hours later, after a bad pizza in Wantage, two walks around the Old Orchard and an awful lot of daytime television, the program Ticky had emailed him at last finished its processing. It came back with 434 isolated proper names, reduced to the 83 which were addressed in an email or letter from Benedict, or which came from them *to* Benedict.

In mid-afternoon, he left a message on the answering machine at the flat: 'Hi, it's me. I think maybe it's better if I stay down here this week, give us time for things to calm down. I need to think before we talk, and maybe you feel the same way. I hope we could meet up here at the weekend.' He paused. 'I love you,' he said, feeling awkward declaring this to a machine. 'Take care.'

The utility had listed the names with their immediate context, and he spent the evening looking through them, eliminating anything that seemed completely conventional – *Dear Mr Peterson, I am happy that you have received the dividend from Flanner Agricultural Holdings at long last, and am sorry for the mix-up about your new address.* Etc., etc.

By the time he drove into London Tuesday morning, late enough to be confident Kate would have left the flat to go to work, he had reduced the list to nine names which might, through a stretch of his imagination, suggest some sort of business relationship that wasn't above board.

He left the car on a meter in Queen's Gate, then went up and retrieved a digital video camera from the hall closet of the flat. Kate had also been living off pizza, he noted sadly, looking at the empty carton on the kitchen table, and a half-drunk bottle of Burgundy. In their bedroom a paperback thriller sat pages down on the bed, which was unmade. He packed an old navy bag with clothes for three nights, took care to leave no sign of his having been there, and waited until the stairwell was empty before leaving the building.

He was gone two days. Five of the nine names were in London; he would deal with them later and get the travelling out of the way first.

He started with the most remote, Charles Linklater, Summer Copse Cottage, Ludlow, Shropshire. The instigating email was from Benedict to his secretary. Among a list of terse instructions, one said, *C present to Charles Linklater,* followed by the address.

He arrived in mid-afternoon, only to find he'd made a long trip for nothing. Charles Linklater, he discovered from the Mrs Linklater who opened the door and proved unusually forthcoming, was nine years old and Benedict's godson. The senior Mr Linklater now lived in London, she informed Renoir through pursed lips, where he could be found shacked up with the next Mrs Linklater to be.

The next stop was Oxford, and he drove south in the late afternoon, stopping on the outskirts of town and booking into a Travel Lodge. He was tempted to go into the city to look around, but in working mode he avoided distractions, however pleasant. So he ate a terrible dinner in a motorway restaurant next door, watched two movies on Sky in his room and slept badly, waking repeatedly as lorries changed gears and pulled in for petrol. In the morning he waited until Arthur Kennedy would have gone to work, then rang his house in Summertown (he could almost walk there, he noted from his local map), where his wife answered the phone. 'Is Mr Kennedy in?' he asked, making no effort to sound less American.

'No, he's in college.'

'College?' He was not expecting this.

'Who's calling?'

'I'm with Redwill Vacation Homes. We're offering special discounts on luxury timeshare villas in Orlando Florida. I'd be real happy to send you further information and arrange for a free ten-minute video to be sent to you which highlights—'

Mrs Kennedy interrupted. 'No thank you. I thought you were one of his students. And we already have a holiday home, so thank you very much.'

'But let me just tell you a little more—'

'Goodbye,' she and hung up the phone.

The email prised out of Benedict's inbox hadn't given any indication of Kennedy's vocation. *Dear Arthur (if I may), Would three o'clock at Boodle's (my club) in St James's Street suit? That should give us enough time to go through the numbers.*

It took him most of the rest of the morning to locate the college where Mr Kennedy taught. He had already Googled the name and got 53,000 hits, which was the practical equivalent of getting none, but after several frustrating phone calls succeeded only in teaching him that Oxford University didn't seem to have a central telephone number or a faculty directory, he suddenly thought to try Google again, and with a refined search of Arthur Kennedy + Oxford narrowed it down to 493 results. Twenty minutes slog later he was confident he'd found his man; Arthur Kennedy, former fellow and tutor of Modern Languages at Christ Church, author of a biography of Cervantes, two editions of *El Cid*, and editor of *Romance Language Quarterly*.

And Renoir got luckier still. For if Arthur Kennedy was past retirement age, then he almost certainly would have taught a certain undergraduate twenty years before, a competent speaker of French and Spanish, the stockbroker and brother-in-law of Kate Palmer, Alastair Scruton. Further proof to Renoir that a certain kind of England was inhabited by ten thousand people who all knew each other.

Yes, Alastair remembered him. 'Terrible old fart even then,' he said on the phone, sounding relaxed after lunch. 'He must be positively ancient now. How did you say you met him?'

'With an old friend from the States,' said Renoir, who had his story prepared. 'He teaches Spanish Lit at Berkeley. We had coffee in Kennedy's rooms.'

'I'm surprised Kennedy's still got them. Isn't he retired?'

'I don't know. But he remembered you fondly.'

'That must be the onset of senility. We didn't get on at all.'

'He seemed to know a lot about the City.'

'What?' Alastair was incredulous. 'I don't believe it. He was the epitome of an academic when I knew him. Lived in a scummy little house in North Oxford – bicycled to college, dressed like a librarian. You sure you have the right man?'

'I think so. He seemed to know your friend Benedict as well.'

'My friend? Ah, you're being facetious, Renoir. I think you're in danger of losing your Americanness. How on earth does he know Benedict?' He thought for a second. 'I know. It must be through Benedict's wife. She's very keen on Spanish stuff.'

'I thought she was Turkish.'

'An interest and a nationality are not mutually exclusive. I take back my suggestion that you are no longer quite so American.'

'Thank you Alastair,' said Renoir, in as dry an English manner as he could manage, thinking that there was no point being lucky if your luck was about the wrong man.

*

He dreaded the prospect of a second night in the Travelodge, but wanted to stay clear of the Gatehouse in case Kate rang, and the London flat was out of the question. He didn't seem to be getting anywhere, but he wasn't sure if he expected to. Once engaged on the hunt, with its minor discoveries, minor setbacks, strokes of luck and complete dead ends, you sometimes forgot all about the chances of actually finding what you were looking for.

He slept badly again, and woke in the middle of the night. Had he been dreaming about the farm again? He wasn't sure, but he wished that Kate were there, although, as he recognised, it was not so much the physical separation that bothered him as the fact that she was not there in his head to call upon. *Better get used to it*, he thought, feeling so uncertain of her that he was already hedging his emotional bets. He was heading back to where he had spent most of his adult life. On his own.

Would she have levelled with him if he had been different with her? What had she said? *I can't* make *you tell me, Jack. You have to want to tell me.*

Why couldn't he? He tried it out and saw at once it was . . . impossible.

I saw my uncle murdered.

Terrible, I'm sure, said the voice of the solitary Renoir (the black-and-white one now again in charge), but doesn't trauma diminish over time?

I was certain I was going to be murdered too. Then I was saved when my uncle's girlfriend shot the man holding me. Killed him with one shot. I had his blood on me.

It sounds like many hostage situations. At least she didn't miss.

And I killed a man myself.

Africa is full of children who've killed people. You'll get over it. You *have* got over it. Pull yourself together.

Yes, that was right – *minimise* he told himself. Far better than talk, or talk therapy. That wouldn't work. Why dismantle a life-long strategy – *minimise minimise* – that had done its job?

He remembered meeting a marine named Makinson, who'd

survived the Lebanon barracks bombing. Describing the explosion, the unbelievable carnage, his eyes had started to glaze, and it had been obvious that the memory was with Makinson as if he had been blown up only the day before. Three years of seeing shrinks and Makinson hadn't been helped *at all*.

To Renoir, someone like Makinson was living proof that people are hard-wired – not blank plates on which a big pile of slop had fallen, waiting there to be cleaned up by a short course of intensive psychotherapy. Renoir thought Makinson was still a mess because he hadn't learned he had to clean it up by himself.

Renoir had. Renoir coped, Renoir managed. On a basis of telling no one anything about it at all. Only here, in England, had he allowed himself to recall even the sweet side of that time. He'd actually told Emily about the apple-loaded life of Will and Maris and Ellie the dog. But never a hint of the rest. Certainly not to Emily and never even to Kate. Not to anyone. *Maris*, he thought, as he finally began to fall asleep, *I never told a single soul*.

In the morning he drove in the warming sun to Brighton, late enough for the motorways to be uncrowded. Further east, the town of Deal would be next, after this visit doubtless proved another dud.

Parking in Brighton was a nightmare. He had a map off the Internet, but discovered that in the middle of Brighton all the car parks were full. He finally left the car in a supermarket lot on the town's outskirts and walked in the general direction of the sea.

He found the Grand Hotel easily enough, and, resisting the temptation to stop and eat lunch, forged ahead, into a nearby quarter with narrow streets. This was The Lanes, and he wound his way through its sinuous Bohemian turns until he came to a slightly wider street, the one he wanted. It was lined by small Victorian terraced houses on either side, which had somehow survived the 1960s urban renewal that seemed to have ruined the historical interior of virtually any British town of size. Most of the houses had been recently gentrified, newly painted in seaside pastels by their occupants.

Number 27, the one he was looking for, was in poorer condition, with the white of the windowsills yellowing, and a front door that was battleship grey. He hadn't known what to expect. The evidence this time had been a letter, apparently typed personally by Benedict, which was in itself suspicious. *Dear Mr Urowski, I am delighted that you are interested, and if we could meet next Thursday I feel confident we can iron out any remaining details. Shall we say 11 a.m. in the lobby of the Grand Hotel? Yours sincerely, Conrad Benedict.*

The bell worked and Renoir could see a figure come along the hallway inside, magnified by the warble of the door's glass pane. He was surprised when a young man opened the door. Dressed in a brown sports jacket but no tie, he looked like a club doorman, out of type in this neighbourhood of web designers, for he was powerfully built. He hadn't shaved, and looked distinctly unfriendly.

'Hello,' said Renoir brightly. Behind the man someone was moving around at the back of the house.

'Hello to you too. What do you want?'

'My name is Renoir and I'm looking for Richard Urowski. Is that you?'

'No,' the man said impatiently. 'You're looking for my father. He died two months ago. What do want with him anyway? Are you *selling* something?'

'No, no. Nothing like that.' Renoir struggled to explain, half tempted to quit right there, make his apologies and leave. What a waste this day had turned out to be. But at least if Richard Urowski were dead he wouldn't have to concoct anything – for this call, he had come up with a special deal on vacation cruises, with a brochure to show that he'd found in the *Sunday Times*. 'I wanted to talk to him. I thought maybe he could clear up something for me. It's not important. I'm sorry to have bothered you.'

The younger Urowski was starting to shut the door in Renoir's face when a voice came from the hallway right behind him, where a very old woman was standing, looking distinctly doddery on her pins. Her voice was thin and reedy, though Renoir did not catch what she said.

'It's nothing, Mum,' said the son. 'Just someone looking for Dad.'

She came up behind her son, a small woman wearing an apron. She had a rich head of grey curls, and wore glasses thick as goggles. 'Oh, you're not the same man,' she said once she had peered at Renoir.

'No,' he said.

'Did the other man send you?' she asked. There was agitation in her voice, which despite her Polish name was perfectly English – the voice of a seaside boarding house landlady, perhaps.

'No one sent me,' he said.

'Then what—' the son began to demand, but the mother interrupted.

'Hush,' she said firmly, putting a hand on the elbow of her son, who towered above her. She lifted her chin to address Renoir. 'Did my husband do something wrong?'

'No, I don't believe he did. That's not why I'm here.'

'Did the other man do something wrong?'

Renoir hesitated, then said, 'I think he probably did.'

'I *knew* it!' the woman said. 'Terry,' she commanded as she turned and began to shuffle towards the kitchen. 'Take the gentleman's coat while I put the kettle on.'

Settled in the kitchen, with Terry looming from the doorway and Mrs Urowski sitting across the Formica table from him, her hands clasped and elbows propped on top of a biscuit tin, Renoir wondered how to proceed. Fortunately Mrs Urowski required no prompting.

'You have to understand it was a thousand pounds. In cash. And after that, one hundred and fifty pounds every month, in cash also. Three fifty pound notes in an envelope. They came like clockwork every month. It made a difference, you know, especially once my husband was in hospital.'

'I'm sure it did,' said Renoir sympathetically. The money – how much, how often, how it arrived – was obviously the key component in Mrs Urowski's memory of it all. 'But what I don't quite understand is what your husband had to do in return.'

'*Do?*' She seemed greatly surprised by the question. 'There wasn't anything he had to do. Once he'd signed the papers, I mean.'

'Were there a lot of them?' asked Renoir, trying to feel his way.

'Just the one. Opening the account.' She sipped her tea, which had far less milk added than Renoir's. 'Actually, there may have been a few other ones.'

'Did your husband know what he was signing?'

'Certainly. Though he was happy to play dumb. He told me later he'd written it down. Just in case.'

'In case?'

'In case there was any funny business. Richard said, "Margaret, should there be any kind of trouble I need to protect our interests."' She paused and smiled a little self-consciously about her husband's description of their assets.

'But there wasn't any trouble, was there?'

'No, and to be honest we would have forgotten all about it. Except that every month the envelope arrived. I can't pretend I didn't notice that. Who wouldn't? Though once my husband died the money stopped.'

'It did?'

'Yes. Immediately he passed away. You might have thought they'd wait a month. If only' – she seemed to be searching for words – 'from *respect*. But no, that was that.'

Renoir asked her, 'Did you ever happen to see what he wrote down?'

She looked at him again with mild disbelief. 'See?' she said. 'I have it upstairs.'

And later, having written down the details of her late husband's note onto a sheet of his own pocket diary, as he thanked her for the tea he realised that there was still a missing aspect of the equation, which was going to gnaw at him if he could not lay it to rest now. So he asked, 'Did your husband know the man who came to see him?'

She shook her head, to Renoir's disappointment.

'Did you ever see the man?'

'No,' she said emphatically.

'I see,' he said, wanting to proceed carefully but determined to find out. 'When I got here you said something like "You're not the same man." But if you hadn't ever seen the man how did you know it wasn't me?'

She looked at him as if his idiocy had at last been irretrievably confirmed. 'It couldn't have been you. Richard said he had a moustache. A thick, bristly one – like a shaving brush he said.'

He nodded, then asked, 'Was there any connection between this man and your husband before he came here that you knew about?'

Again she shook her head, and he searched for a way to keep the conversation alive. 'Have you always lived in Brighton, Mrs Urowski?' They were standing in the hall, Terry having gone sulkily upstairs.

'Goodness no,' she said with a modest laugh, as if he had complimented her on her beauty. 'I'm a Londoner. As was my husband.'

'Oh, you retired here then?' And the old lady nodded. 'From London?' She nodded again. 'What did your husband do in London?'

Now she puffed herself up proudly. 'He was in the legal business.'
'Really?'

'Absolutely. He was a solicitor's clerk for over forty years. Nowadays they'd call him something grander. But a clerk meant something then.'

'Did you work too, Mrs Urowski, or were you busy with your children?'

'No, I worked,' she said. 'Thirty-seven years I did. I was a cleaner. When I retired the people at Tallmadge said I was indispensable.'

'Where was the building you worked?'

'In Victoria,' said the old lady proudly. 'Just off Victoria Street.'

A bell went off in Renoir's head, and grew louder. 'Near the Underground? I mean, St James's?'

'That's it,' she said, pleasantly surprised. 'We were almost next door to it. A lovely modern building.'

310

Renoir said goodbye as cheerfully as he could, but as he drove out of Brighton his mood was grim. He was confident now, in the strict sense of knowing what was supposed to happen, and because of that confident of keeping it from happening. What had the old woman said? 'The signature didn't mean anything once my husband was gone.' On the contrary, thought Renoir, that was precisely when the signature came into its own. He remembered the woman from marketing who had made over half a million dollars from inside information; as he had told Kate at their very first lunch, she had disappeared into thin air, only to be picked up on another charge months later by the FBI. What was it Ticky had called her dummy trading account scam? He remembered now. He had found the Dead Man's Hat.

Once again he bought a cappuccino at the Italian sandwich shop and kept a keen eye out on the street. This time there was no need to disguise his watching presence, and when he saw the man he left his now lukewarm coffee and moved fast, catching up to the target on the pavement almost twenty yards short of the office block.

The man was wearing a summer suit of khaki-coloured cotton, and when Renoir tapped him on the back of the shoulder he could feel this muscles bunch through the thin fabric. 'Hi there,' Renoir declared, easing alongside.

Benedict's head swivelled sideways, and as he recognised Renoir his stride slowed and then stopped. 'Ah,' he said, 'it's Jack, isn't it?'

'That's right, Conrad.'

They faced each other, but neither man offered to shake hands. As a slight awkwardness grew, Renoir said, 'Have you got a minute?'

'I'm sorry?' Benedict replied, but his surprise seemed too deep and too polished to be natural. He might never in a month of Sundays have expected this encounter, but, equally, he couldn't possibly put it down to coincidence.

'I said, could we have a word please?'

'What, right now?' Benedict looked around them as if perplexed.

'Sure,' said Renoir affably. '*Carpe diem* and all that.'

'Look, Jack,' Benedict said as he moved closer, speaking with a suddenly confidential tone. 'I'd love to have a chat but I've got a client waiting upstairs.' He pointed vaguely towards his office. 'Business before pleasure and all that. Give my love to—'

Renoir's voice was deliberately flat, expressionless. 'I'd never been to Brighton before. It lived up to its billing.'

Benedict looked to be fighting an internal alarm that was ringing loudly. He fell back on the standard ploy of vigorous expostulation – which Renoir had variously encountered in every form known to man. '*Listen*,' and there was nothing chummy in Benedict's voice now. 'Lovely to see you and all that, and any friend of lovely Kate is a friend of mine. Etcetera, etcetera. But I really *must go*.'

'And you'll never guess who I ran into in Brighton. Not in a million years.' He had Benedict's attention now. 'Go on, Conrad. Make a guess.'

'Haven't a clue. And to be honest, haven't got time to come up with one either.' He made to walk away.

'The Merry Widow of course. Frail, but sharp as a tack. None other than *Madame Urowski*,' he finished, half shouting the name since Benedict actually had begun to walk away.

Benedict stopped, like a predictable puppet, and turned back to Renoir, though he made a show of looking at his watch. 'Perhaps there's time after all. Why don't you come up?'

Renoir shook his head. 'Let's keep this outside. Come into the park,' and from his voice it was clear this wasn't a suggestion.

They walked in silence into St James's Park. As they neared the bridge over the duck pond Renoir led the way to a bench, empty but surrounded by pigeons. He sat down first and after a slight hesitation Benedict joined him, saying, 'A little knowledge is a dangerous thing.' His voice had regained its bass certainty.

'Possibly. I know what I know; the question is, is it enough?'

'Enough for what?'

'Don't you want to know why I was in Brighton?'

Benedict said with ironic dutifulness, 'So why were you in Brighton?'

'I was looking for Richard Urowski. Do you want to know why I was looking for him?'

Benedict leaned back against the bench and crossed his arms. 'I imagine you're going to tell me in any case.'

'I wanted to find him to understand what his connection was with you. You see, I knew there was a connection' – he paused – 'but for the life of me I couldn't see how it fit into the other thing I knew about you.'

'What was that?'

'That you had inside information on an oil company's results. And the only reason for getting that was to make a killing on the share price. But how were you going to do it? It's really pretty hard to get away with it.'

'I would have said it's impossible for it to go undetected,' Benedict said firmly. He gave a little grin. 'And of course entirely illegal.'

'Unless,' said Renoir, 'you were to do it through someone who was a stranger – with no connection to you that could be traced.' Renoir leaned forward and looked ahead at the nearest pigeon. In the distance, approaching the bridge, was a tall blonde woman in Kelly green shorts. He said, 'Here's how it works. A man, let's call him the Benefactor, shows up at the house, or maybe even it was the hospital bed, of Richard Urowski, who is ill, terminally ill with cancer; only months to live. The Benefactor makes Mr Urowski an unusual offer, really an irresistible one. One thousand pounds in cash, with more to come, every month, also in cash. In return all he has to do is sign a bit of paper.

'That opens a trading account in his name. It's an online account, which the Benefactor takes control of – literally, in this case, since he runs the account from his own laptop. There's nothing for Mr Urowski to worry about – he hasn't got a clue what's happening in his account, and the statements of it get sent to a PO box where the Benefactor collects them.'

Benedict protested at once. 'But why wouldn't they trace any funny business directly to this man Urowski? And then he'd finger this Benefactor chap of yours.'

'Who said there was any funny business?' demanded Renoir, and for the first time he could see Benedict squirm ever so slightly. 'I didn't say anything about any funny business. Because in fact there *hasn't been* any funny business. Not yet. Oh, the Urowski account has done a little trading – maybe even quite a lot of trading. But it would all be above board, and you'd move money from time to time out of the account.' The 'you' seemed to startle Benedict, uncertain whether it was American for 'one' or was directed personally.

'What for?' Benedict asked.

'To rehearse things for when the real money arrived. You wouldn't send it to Switzerland, which behaves itself now despite the stereotype, but somewhere new, which hasn't signed any of the international treaties. The Seychelles, maybe, or even Uzbekistan. An account there, from which the money doubtless gets shifted again, and again. So that even if an investigating agency could get the name of that first bank account holder – and that would be a dummy shell company – they'd never be able to trace it all the way through the other accounts. Not with different banks involved and doubtless some other dodgy countries. But that has nothing to do with Richard Urowski's trading account, which as I say is at the coal face of the activity. It has been moving along nicely, getting ready for the Big Kill.'

Benedict snorted derisively. 'The Big Kill. This sounds like a film you're describing.'

'It would make a good movie,' Renoir conceded. 'But let's stick to the real story. Now as long as Mr Urowski's alive everything works above board – I mean, the trading that goes on is unexceptional. Maybe it makes a little money; maybe it loses some; but in either case it's trivial.' Renoir stared at Benedict, who was looking impressively impassive again. It seemed clear he wasn't going to say anything, so Renoir continued. 'But then Mr Urowski dies, as predicted by the doctors. Whatever his estate consists of soon gets wound up – bank account, building society, membership of the local bowls club. Etcetera. And in the normal run of things, you'd expect his online trading account to wind down pretty pronto too. But it doesn't.'

Renoir looked out across the park, where the blonde woman had crossed the bridge. His audience of one was proving hard to read. Usually by now fear, or contempt, or puzzlement, or even genuine outraged innocence would have emerged. But not this confident-seeming silence.

'Why not?' Renoir asked rhetorically, trying not to over egg the performance. Benedict managed to look supremely uninterested in the question. 'Because,' said Renoir slowly, 'nobody has ever told the brokerage house that Richard Urowski is dead. As far as they know, he is still alive – and still trading. But *then*, out of the blue, he's going to make an absolutely massive trade – at least compared to the chickenfeed stuff he's used to. Acer Oil. Options which you plan to exercise tomorrow, the same day the Acer share price tumbles by almost forty per cent of its value. What a killing!

'Such a killing in fact that maybe more than one eyebrow will get raised, and pretty damn quickly. "Who is Richard Urowski?" somebody will ask, "and where did he come by his remarkably gifted sense of timing"? A few more eyebrows will get raised, and they'll decide to have a little chat with Richard Urowski before turning him over to the Fraud Squad. Only they can't, can they? Because Richard Urowski met his maker some time ago.

'And when they try to trace the paper trail, they find it's stone cold. The money's gone God knows where – offshore banking is alien stuff to an American halfwit like me – and there's more chance of bringing Richard Urowski back from the dead than there is of finding who's perpetrated the scam.'

Benedict spoke up. 'Or of actually doing anything about whoever might do such a thing. It sounds like it would be awfully difficult to prove.'

'Oh, I don't know about that,' said Renoir, trying to sound casual. 'They might hit lucky and find a link through Mr Urowski, dead though he is. After all, even widowed cleaning ladies talk.

And you'd be surprised what they remember. Facial characteris-
tics. Moustaches. That kind of thing.'

'But she never saw—' Benedict began to protest, then stopped
short. He smiled wryly at Renoir. 'Nice try. But that's not a lot
to go on, you have to admit. Take that to the Fraud Squad and
they'll laugh in your face.'

'If that's all I had I'm sure they would. But ask yourself this,
how did I find Richard Urowski? Or, more pertinently, how did
I link him to you? Excuse me, I mean the Benefactor.'

Benedict shrugged but looked more uneasy now. He clenched
his jaw as if literally ruminating then shook his head decisively.
'Let's drop this Benefactor crap. Even if you had more, I can't see
you using it – that is, if such a trade were to happen. Which, I
think we both understand, it hasn't. Because it wouldn't just be
me you'd be landing in it, now would it? I am assuming you're
not out to get Kate a prison sentence.'

The woman in shorts had stopped on the bridge and seemed
to be looking in their direction, even looking at Renoir. *Don't
flatter yourself*, he thought. 'No,' said Renoir quietly. 'I'm not.
But I want it to stop and that's why I came to see you. I'm not
going to do anything about this, unless you exercise those options.
If they get exercised I will know right away, believe me.'

Benedict said, 'Why not just leave it alone? What's it to you
anyway, Jack?'

'Kate is what it is to me. You of all people must understand
that. And it's Kate who gave you the tip. That's never going to
change.'

When Benedict didn't argue, Renoir asked, 'How was Roddy
going to explain his windfall anyway? Presumably he's got to pay
off his debts in this country. Having money in some offshore
account isn't going to help unless he brings the money in again.'

Benedict looked at him knowingly. 'Let's just say one of his
Latvian deals would come through. We might know he's a hopeless businessman, but the Revenue doesn't. But you tell me, who
is supposed to swallow the price of the options?'

'You are. I can't believe they cost very much; I'm sure Helena will be happy to pick up the tab. It will seem a mere bagatelle to her.'

Benedict started to say something, then stopped. Renoir went on. 'I don't know how you got Kate to help you, and I don't want to know.' He was pleased to see Benedict's surprise. 'But I don't want her involved in any way – no more requests for info, no meetings, nothing. The only woman you're going to meet in a hotel is Kiki Reisberg.'

Benedict spoke up, provoked. 'You couldn't resist that, now could you, Renoir? You seem to know everything about me. What is your problem?'

'In your case it's purely professional interest,' he said, knowing this was untrue. 'But do what I say, Benedict, or I will blow you sky high, even if that means Kate gets blown up too.' This wasn't true either, but he looked directly at Benedict as he said it, speaking without menace, and reducing the natural intonation of his voice.

Oddly enough, Benedict looked relieved. 'I've no intention of going any further. It's not my call anyway, Jack.' He shrugged as if hoping to persuade Renoir of his sincerity. 'Honestly. I'm out of it. My debt's been paid.'

'What debt?'

Benedict looked at him with amusement. 'You amaze me, Renoir, you really do.' He waved a dismissive hand. 'It was just a figure of speech. You wouldn't understand.'

'Of course not. You're a gentleman, Benedict, and I'm not,' he said sarcastically. 'Forgive me for forgetting.'

Benedict looked at him, and Renoir found him hard to read. 'Are we finished now?' asked Benedict, with a small smile. He looked around them. 'Believe it or not, I really do have someone waiting for me in the office.'

Renoir nodded and the two men stood up together. To his surprise, Benedict offered his hand. 'Some day I'd like to know how you got to me,' said Benedict as he shook firmly. 'It wasn't Kate. She doesn't have any idea who Urowski is. Or was.' And without waiting for a word from Renoir, he walked quickly along the path towards the gates.

Renoir sat and looked across the park at the small bridge, where the blonde woman in shorts had turned and started walking towards him. She was attractive, he noted absent-mindedly, then noted he had noted it. Funny that, for over two years he had not even looked at another woman, not in that way – that hound-like sniffing inspection that had marked his bachelor years. Was he going to have to start all that again? 'Dates' in his fifth decade?

It was sticky warm all afternoon in the flat, which wasn't air-conditioned. He sat in the sitting room with the windows open, and listened to CDs and read old copies of the *New Yorker*, watched *Countdown* on TV, and allowed himself only one large highball from a duty free bottle of Old Grand-Dad which Kate had brought back for him from a trip. It wasn't really hot, not by the standards of Sonoma, but somehow it seemed debilitating.

He moved to the rocking chair with his drink, and ten minutes later when the front door opened he sat still. He heard her in the hallway, putting down the post and hanging her coat up in the closet. A moment later she was in the room.

'Hello,' she said, without intonation. 'I thought you might be here.'

'Why's that?'

'I had a call from Conrad Benedict. I gather you paid him a visit.'

'I did. We had an interesting conversation.'

'He said you did all the talking.'

'Well, I needed to get his attention.'

'You did that all right,' she said, and he could see she was angry.

'Have a drink,' he said, raising his own.

She looked at him for a moment, bemused. 'Why not?' she said, and went into the kitchen, where he heard glasses clink and an ice tray being emptied. She came out with a glass of tonic and poured a large slug of gin from the drinks tray. Then she went to her usual place on the sofa, but sat there, rather than lying down as she usually did at the end of the day. She raised her glass. 'Here's to you, Renoir, and a brilliant piece of detective work. The one thing I asked you not to do you've gone and done. Are you happy now?'

'No.'

'Why not? You seem to have covered the territory brilliantly.'

'In for a penny . . .' he said.

'Did you enjoy it?'

He thought about this. Peculiarly, perhaps, there *had* been something comforting about his spying. It let him control the jealousy which had been driving him to despair. After that, he saw now, his professional instincts took over and he simply couldn't stop. The old Renoir had returned with a vengeance. If he didn't feel completely sullied by what he'd done – going through her letters, her emails, her belongings – it was only because there had been something to find. Though did that justify his snooping? He didn't know.

'Well anyway,' Kate said when he hadn't replied, 'congratulations. You seem to know it all.'

'No, I don't,' he said, looking out the window. The leaves on the lime were almost full and blocked the view of the park. 'I know what, and I know who, but I still don't know why.'

Kate laughed harshly. 'Conrad said you threatened him. He thinks you believe he's been blackmailing me. He was very offended by that.'

'I guess I *wished* he was blackmailing you. I was still hoping that this was all his idea. That would make it all a lot easier to understand.'

She seemed suddenly subdued by this. He looked at her with curiosity. 'When did it all start?' he asked.

She inhaled slowly before speaking, and when she started to talk she did so slowly and deliberately. 'Towards the end of last year, Roddy came to see me. It must have been two or three weeks before Christmas. We'd agreed the price for the Gatehouse and land, and I thought he was coming to tell me when we would exchange. But no, he said he'd had second thoughts; he wanted more money for the properties. A lot more money.'

'How much more?'

'Over £800,000. I said it was ridiculous. We were almost paying market price already, and if he went to open sale he wouldn't get much more than what we agreed, and who knows what sort of people he'd get to live on the estate. Plus, my mother would never stand for it. As you know,' she said wryly, 'my mother's views carry a lot of weight with my brother.

'Then Roddy came clean. He said he'd got himself in trouble, some company in Latvia he'd put a lot of money into had gone belly up. If he couldn't raise the money to pay what he owed in the next few months, he'd have no choice but to sell Belfield.'

'So you decided to help him?'

'I didn't see any real choice. I know you feel differently about things, but Belfield has always been my home. My only home. I thought it would kill my mother if the place were sold. Roddy would be left high and dry – I know, I know, it's not as if he's been thriving anyway.' She stopped momentarily, then added, 'And then there was us.'

At this, he waved a hand dismissively; he didn't want to hear it. 'What did the speech have to do with it? Why did Benedict have a copy of your speech?' And, asking this, he realised she was due to give it the very next day.

'Nothing, really, except that originally I thought I'd stick my neck out and actually name names. You know, when I talked about companies using expert systems to inflate their stated reserves.'

'And Acer was top of the list?'

She nodded. 'Yes. But I've changed it, made the criticism more general so there's no link between it and the trades in Acer shares we've been planning for tomorrow. It seemed too big a coincidence to go unnoticed. It was Conrad who pointed that out.' She added caustically, 'My speech is positively anodyne now.'

So now he knew why Benedict had the bowdlerised speech on his computer; Kate was reassuring him that she wasn't taking any unnecessary risks. What had she written – *will this do?* Something like that. On discovering it, the email had sounded to Renoir like that of a schoolgirl trying to please a favoured teacher. But it wasn't like that. Benedict hadn't been Kate's Svengali. Accomplice yes, lapdog possibly, but not demonic master.

'What did you need Benedict for anyway?' he asked, unable to keep the jealousy out of his voice.

'I needed somebody to help with the trading. I couldn't go to you, now could I?' she said bitterly. 'Good old upright Renoir, Mr Morality. I knew what you'd say, "Well, it's a hard thing, but I guess Belfield has to go."'

'Probably.'

'But also,' and her voice softened, 'I thought we'd be happy there. I thought we could make a go of it in the Gatehouse.'

'All right,' he said curtly, 'so I was out of the help equation. But why Benedict and not someone else?'

'He knows all about this sort of thing; I think he was born trading dodgy. If anyone could figure out a way to do it, it would be Conrad. And I suppose he felt he owed me one.'

'Owed you one?' he asked but Kate merely shrugged. 'So,' said Renoir, 'you used the Dead Man's Hat. That's what Ticky called it.'

She nodded. 'You said it was foolproof. If that woman hadn't run away to Florida and tried to write a bogus cheque, you said she'd never have been caught.'

'How did you find Mr Urowski?'

'Who?' She seemed genuinely puzzled. 'I've never heard of him.'

For all his distrust, he believed her. Benedict had told him the truth: Kate knew nothing of the incriminating details. It was almost chivalrous of the man, Renoir had to admit. He asked, 'What was in it for him? You?'

'I wasn't sleeping with him, if that's what you think. Not in the years before I met you, and no, not since.'

He believed her, but could not keep himself from saying with heavy sarcasm, 'He must love you very much.'

Kate ignored his tone. 'Benedict doesn't really love anybody.' She hesitated. 'He's one of those people who want whatever they can't have. He'd love to have seen you off, I'm sure, but believe me, as soon as you'd gone away his interest would evaporate. He had his chance with me years ago, and he didn't take it.'

'You've been better off without him. Though I've never understood why you married Angus.'

She looked again at her glass, then spoke quietly with her head down. 'Maybe I needed a husband.'

He looked at her, trying to read her expression, slowly picking apart her words. She wouldn't return his gaze, still staring at her drink. 'You needed a husband,' he said slowly, then waited as the full sense of this sunk in. 'Were you pregnant?'

'Something like that,' she said, lifting her face up and throwing her hair back, almost defiantly.

'But not by Angus,' he half asked, half announced.

She nodded.

'So who was the father? Or weren't you sure?'

'Thanks a lot, Renoir,' she said softly. 'Yes, I knew who the father was.'

'Benedict.'

'Yes. And yes, he did know, though, actually, he didn't want to know.' She spoke in a low voice, wistfully, almost a whisper.

He didn't say a word and she went on. 'I didn't know what to do. I was determined to have the baby; it's not something I can explain. But I knew I didn't want to raise a child alone. Maybe that was cowardly, but at the time I thought my child should have a father. I knew how much that mattered.'

'And Benedict wouldn't act the part.'

She shook her head. She seemed close to tears. 'He did offer to pay for the abortion.'

'Jesus.' He paused as this sunk in. 'So you latched onto Angus. Did he know the baby wasn't his? Or did you trick him into it?'

'Try and give me some credit, Renoir. I would never do that, whatever you think. Of course I told Angus.'

'Were you ever going to tell me?'

'Yes, I was, but I was waiting. It's only been a year and a half since you moved over here; I didn't even know if you liked it. Actually, I still don't. It may sound strange, Renoir, but I fell so much in love with you that I couldn't actually believe you felt the same. It's seemed like a dream half the time; I kept thinking the dream would end and you'd scarper back to California. You know, "London was fun but it just wasn't me." There was also Emily; I didn't know what knowing might do to your relationship with her.'

'I love Emily,' he said without hesitation.

She nodded. 'I know that now, but I wasn't sure before. She needs a father, yet Angus isn't much of one. But I didn't know if you wanted that. I still don't. I mean, if you'd shown the slightest interest in marrying me, I'd have told you straight away.'

'I didn't think you cared about that,' he said, discomfited. 'I didn't want it to look like I was after your money. I know what people think.'

'Oh, fuck "people". You can't build a life on what "people" think. People will *always* think that about you, to our dying days. But I know you're not like that' – and she gave the barest hint of a smile – 'though sometimes I think it would all have been easier if you were. Only I don't seem to have enough money, after all. Which is why I've got into this mess. Though if you really loved me, why couldn't you leave it alone?'

'I thought our only hope was my *not* leaving it alone. How could we have lived with such a secret between us?'

'You of all people can't talk that way about secrets.'

He paused, feeling uncertain, for he knew she was right. Finally he said, 'I went along with something once because I had to. I couldn't do it again.'

'No one was asking you to.' Kate put her glass down on the coffee table. 'Well, now you know it all. You don't have to spy any more; there's nothing left to find out.'

'If you do this,' Renoir argued, 'it won't be the end. It never is. What makes you think that if you bail Roddy out now, he won't do it again? He's not going to change.'

'I'll just have to take that chance.'

They sat silently for a while. Outside the rush hour traffic noise was picking up, and a horn sounded. Kate said, 'Before I do anything, I'm going to tell Roddy you know.'

'No you're not,' said Renoir. 'I am. I'll go down tonight and

323

talk with him. If tomorrow's D-Day, it's not as if it can wait.'

She didn't say anything. He got up from his chair. 'I better get going, Kate. I'll take the car if you have no objection.' She nodded dully. 'I've got to go by the Gatehouse anyway and get . . .' And he paused, searching for indeterminate words. 'Some things,' he said at last.

His words hung between them in a kind of no-man's-land neither dared to explore. Did Kate think 'get some things' was code for collecting his stuff before he left for good? He couldn't tell, because he wasn't sure himself.

She looked up at him, too upset for tears. 'Oh, Renoir,' she said, her voice cracking slightly. 'Has it really come to this?'

'I don't know,' he said evenly, and left the flat.

He got to Belfield at the far end of dusk. Again, Beatrice was in the kitchen, seated in front of the small television watching a CSI show. She seemed a little embarrassed when Renoir came in, and turned it off.

'Hello, Jack,' she said. 'What a surprise? Is Kate with you?'

He shook his head. 'I'm on my way to the Gatehouse. I was hoping to have a word with Roddy? Is he in?'

'No, actually. He went out with his gun about half an hour ago. He said there's a fox in Burdick's Field that's been bothering the pheasants. I'm sure he won't be very long. Would you like some coffee, or a drink?'

'No thanks. When he comes in would you ask him to give me a ring at the Gatehouse? Tonight if at all possible. I'll be up late.'

'Of course. Will we see you tomorrow?'

'If you don't mind, I'll have to play it by ear. I'll ring you.'

'All right,' she said, looking slightly puzzled. She must have sensed that something was amiss.

He found Roddy sitting above the irrigation pond near the top of Burdick's Field. Approaching him quietly from behind, Renoir felt a peculiar sense of déjà vu, and realised it was triggered by the memory of his Uncle Will sitting on the rough diving board by the frog pond, smoking a Winston, its tip glowing in the dark.

Then Roddy moved and the vision dissolved.

'Don't shoot me, Roddy. I'm not a fox.'

'Then don't sneak up on me like that.' Roddy stood up with his shotgun.

'I need to talk to you. Let's go into the house.'

At the Gatehouse the back door was unlocked. Inside a light was on in the corridor between the mud room and the kitchen. Renoir walked through and turned on the kitchen lights. To his surprise he saw a bottle of Famous Grouse and a used glass on the table in the centre of the room.

'Who's been in here?' he asked as Roddy followed him into the room. 'Was it you?'

Roddy nodded and put his gun on the table, then poured himself another drink.

'Do help yourself,' said Renoir sarcastically. 'How the hell did you get in?'

'I've got a key of course. Didn't you know that? Kate left one at the Hall for emergencies.'

'You might have asked. If I'd come in alone I'd have thought someone had broken in. I might have called the police. I like visitors to my house to be invited.'

'Let's be honest, old boy, it's not really *your* house, now is it? Technically, you don't own any of this – who, therefore, has the better right to be here? I'm the brother of your girlfriend; I own the estate, not you. Should the police arrive, I would claim a completely understandable confusion.'

'But what were you doing here?'

'Waiting for you of course. There was a fox in the field, and I expected you in the house.' He took a drink of straight whisky, and said sharply, 'Two different kinds of vermin.'

Renoir ignored this. 'Roddy, I know all about Acer Oil.' He couldn't tell if Roddy was surprised by this, for his expression didn't change. 'It's madness, Roddy. You will all get caught. If I can discover the scam, so can other people. It wasn't exactly rocket science discovering how it's supposed to work.'

'Nonsense. It's entirely foolproof, or at least it was until you poked your nose in.'

'You'll end up losing a lot more than Belfield.'

Roddy went to the sink and added water to his glass, though this struck Renoir as closing the stable door after the horse had bolted. 'Look,' said Roddy, and his voice was softer now. 'Be reasonable. Why don't you come in with us? I'll cut you in myself from my share – Kate never has to know.'

Renoir just looked at him.

'Then do it *for* Kate,' said Roddy. 'She's utterly besotted with you, Renoir; I admit it, even if I can't understand it. Now perhaps you don't feel the same,' he said more dryly, 'but that needn't matter. You'll make her very happy, while you enjoy a prosperous way of life doing whatever you want. Apples, raspberries, you can try bananas for all I care.'

Renoir still said nothing, and Roddy seemed to mistake his silence for active consideration of his offer. 'Name your price, Jack. I'm sure we can come to some agreement.'

Renoir shook his head. 'Can't you see how offensive that is to me?'

Roddy lowered his voice. 'And can't you see how close you've come to destroying everything?' He put his glass down on the table between them, then reached for the gun. Renoir tried to grab the barrel end but Roddy was too quick, and swung the gun off the table. He took two steps back towards the sink, holding the shotgun with its barrels down.

Renoir felt his adrenalin surge but tried to stay calm. 'So it was you who shot at me after the horn went that day?'

'What?' said Roddy, incredulously.

Renoir believed him. So it must have been Hal, after all, trying to land Renoir in it. And scare him. 'Did Kate tell you I was coming down?'

'She did.' He laughed thinly. 'I think she was concerned how I would react to your interference.' His voice was crisp again, and hostile. 'She was right to be concerned,' he announced, and Renoir kept his eyes on the barrels of the shotgun. Agitated memories suddenly crowded in, and he felt momentarily panicked by what he saw in his mind's eye: the screen door to the porch gave way and the man in the Stetson took two steps forward, and the barrels of that gun slowly lifted, and the boy grabbed the knife on the table in panic.

But there was no knife on this table. Renoir shook off the mesmerising fear that was beginning to envelop him and stepped quickly around the table, reaching out with his hand to push the shotgun barrels towards the floor. Roddy tried to lift the gun, and this time Renoir grabbed the stock with both hands. They wrestled briefly for control of the gun, and Roddy was surprisingly strong. But then instead of pulling at the shotgun to wrest it away, Renoir pushed it, and Roddy slid backwards as if the floor were greased. Keeping the pressure on, Renoir propelled him without hesitation straight into the larder, where Renoir suddenly let go of the gun. As Roddy fell back heavily against the shelves, dropping the shotgun, Renoir swung the heavy door shut and turned the oversized key in the lock.

He stood listening at the door for a moment. 'Roddy?'

'WHAT?' came a muffled roar through the thick door, and Renoir was relieved that he sounded enraged rather than hurt. 'Let me out of here,' the voice commanded. Then, more pleadingly: 'I wasn't going to hurt you.'

'Oh? What were you trying to do?'

There was a long pause. 'I was going to put you in here until tomorrow afternoon. After the trade went through. I didn't want you persuading Kate not to go through with it.'

'Great minds think alike, I guess. But you'll be safe as houses, and God knows, you've got plenty to eat and drink – I think there's even another bottle of whisky in the wine rack. I'll make sure someone comes and lets you out.'

'When?' Roddy shouted.

Renoir paused. 'In due course,' he said, using an English phrase he loathed for its bogus precision.

Kate answered the phone in the flat on the first ring.

'It's me,' said Renoir. 'I'm at the Gatehouse. Along with your brother, though sadly he can't come to the phone right now.'

'What have you done to him? Did you hurt him?'

'No. I resisted the temptation. Even though he seemed more than willing to try and hurt me.'

'Are you all right?'

'I'm fine. Just fine. And so is your brother – I put him in the larder. You always said it would make a good gaol. This way you'll know where to find him.'

'What do you mean?'

'I'm leaving it to you to let him out. I'm not going to risk opening the door; he's got his shotgun with him. As for Acer Oil, don't worry about me. I'm not interested any more in getting in the way. It's up to you now.'

'What does that mean?' She sounded almost childlike, bewildered, and scared. For a brief moment he wanted her there with him so he could take her in his arms and comfort her.

Instead he steeled himself. 'Just what I said. The decision's all yours. I'm out of it.'

'But where will you be?'

He hesitated. 'Far away,' he said at last, and the words came back to him, sung so lightly as he lay on the back seat of his uncle's car, trying to choke back his tears:

> *Far away but gentle now,*
> *Let me show you how to love.*

'Far away,' he said again, abstractedly, though he knew exactly where he was going next.

Sonoma Farewell

WHERE THE BUS had once set him down so long ago, fresh from San Francisco, there was now a restaurant, which looked fashionable, with a solid mahogany bar and light oak floor. Across the square there was a bookstore and a fancy coffee shop next to it, and at the corner a small boutique hotel. Surprisingly the square seemed bigger than his memories of it.

From the address he expected her to be out of town, since it was the road that wound east, through a ravine, a stone's throw above the Russian River. But she was in a white clapboard house just a few blocks from the square, on one of the lots of the town's old original grid.

He parked now across the street and waited, taking out the letter he'd received that morning.

Dear Renoir

I was very cross to hear you have gone alone without me but Mummy says there is a reason and that either you or she will explain to me when I am older. How much older, Renoir? If you say sixteen I will be really cross. Thirteen seems fair to me since it is over a year away and you have to admit that is a long time at my age.

I hope you will bring me back some apple butter. And photos please, especially of the places you promised to take me. Why is it called the Russian River by the way?

Now, just to fill you in. Mummy and I went to the White Horse first thing on Sunday morning and all is unchanged there I can report – Surprise! And Belfield should be sold by autumn. Everyone is sad about it, but Mummy says it was time to move on anyway. She never said that before. We'll live in London for a while but Mummy is looking for a place

331

in the country – If, well you can guess what the If is, Renoir. You are the If.

And Mummy says that maybe next year I could weekly board. Could you put up with seeing me every weekend? I hope so.

Oh and Granna had a cold but is better now. And Uncle Roddy is moving to France and Granna may go with him. Mummy says we can visit him during school holidays and I can get to know my cousin there, though she also says we are not going there for a while.

I hope you are 100 per cent A-okay as you would say and the aeroplane ride was a good one. Will you see Will after all these years and why are you staying in a hotel? Will you take his picture for me please? And send him my best wishes. Is that okay?

Mummy will not say when you are coming back, Renoir, and she seems sad. Most of the time actually. I asked her if she missed you and she got cross. Though then she said do fish swim? I miss you anyway, Renoir, and you know this fish can swim.

xxx

Ems

He'd flown out of London telling himself he didn't care what Kate decided to do, yet reading Emily's letter he realised there was no point hiding behind a front of indifference. Her news did not exactly make him happy, but the regret he felt at the prospect of Belfield's sale was rapidly overtaken by his relief that Kate had not gone through with her plan. Contrary to all his fears and expectations, Kate had done the right thing. How often he had misjudged her in their time together. Part of him wanted to tell her this, although he doubted that she would believe him – unless this doubt was just another instance of his misjudging her.

He had in any case unfinished business of his own. Sure enough, within a few minutes she came out onto the front porch, sweeping it with a broom, then watering the flower pots with a shiny aluminium watering can. He watched her for a while, then drew on some sense of resolution and got out of the car. She glanced at him, but only momentarily, then resumed her watering, and it was only as he came up the walk to the house, with neat lawn on either side (though it was yellowed from the California sun), that she gave him her attention.

'You looking for someone?' she asked, and he knew now for sure it was her. There was that same tone, not impolite or aggressive, but blunt.

'Maris,' he said quietly, and he could see her examining his face as he approached, trying to determine if she knew him. 'Maris,' he repeated, 'it's me.'

'What?' she said slowly.

'It's me. Jack.'

She put down the watering can without taking her eyes off him. He was at the porch now but stopped at the bottom of the three steps, waiting and unsure. And then she said, as if acceding to the inevitable, 'I guess you'd better come inside.' And he followed her into the house.

The living room was tidy and simply furnished: an old large television, a sofa with plumped pillows, a recliner and an oak rocking chair.

'Should I be expecting any other visitors?' she said. Her tone was laconic rather than worried.

He shook his head. 'Only me.'

She had him sit down in the rocking chair and asked if he wanted something to drink. 'I've got coffee or tea, or herbal tea. There's some orange juice too if you want it. I haven't got anything stronger.'

'I'm fine thanks,' he said and she sat down on the sofa.

'I don't know what to say,' she said with an awkward laugh. 'It would seem a little peculiar after all these years to ask, "So what have you been up to?" On the other hand, I'd like to know. What *have* you been up to all these years?'

So he told her what he'd done with himself, and what he'd done for a living – this without the usual amusing asides. She looked at him impassively as he recounted his years in the army, then the short stint in security firms, and then his move into HR and security clearance. He left off the years in England, the years with Kate. When he'd finished, she shook her head in wonder. 'I never imagined any of that.'

'Really?' he asked. What did she expect? A lawyer? Or 'my son the doctor' – only it was really 'my dead boyfriend's nephew the doctor'? Was she disappointed that he hadn't flourished in conventional terms? Well, he'd done what he felt he had to do. Whatever that meant.

'I thought you'd work outside,' she said. 'I don't know, farming or become a gardener. Anything outside. I never saw a boy take to the country the way you did. I've seen lots of city kids come up here – their parents decide to move out to the country, especially if they've made a pile in Silicon Valley. They buy some place up in the hills,' she said and paused, and he knew they were both thinking of the farm, 'and all their kids end up doing is sitting inside watching cable TV. You were never like that.'

How did you know? he wanted to say, stunned that she had sensed the lifelong impact that his twelve months in Sonoma had made. She said, 'Did I say something wrong? Sorry – I guess I haven't changed.'

'No, you haven't,' he said and smiled. 'But funny you should think that. Eighteen months ago, I left my job and moved overseas. I was hoping to farm there – apples, you won't be surprised to learn.'

And Maris looked at him for a moment and then she laughed out loud, her two front teeth moving slightly in front of her mouth with the same ungainly awkwardness he remembered.

He waited for a moment. 'I kept your secret, Maris. I mean *our* secret.'

She nodded slowly and looked away. She was only twenty years older than he was, but from his viewpoint he was still ten years old and Maris – look at her! – Maris must have now been over sixty. On the phone the school had said she'd retired.

She gave him a look of sour appraisal. 'So why have you come to see me? To tell me that?'

'I thought it was about time,' he said, forcing a smile. 'I'm sorry, I should have given you warning.'

Maris didn't reply. She sat down suddenly at one end of the sofa and fished a cigarette from the pack on the coffee table. Lighting it, she sucked it in intensely, then blew the smoke out fast in a long burst. 'Do you know how often I've imagined this? You sitting there, talking to me?'

He shook his head. 'I assumed you didn't want to see me.'

'Because you never heard from me?' When he nodded she said, 'It seemed best for us both. Safer too. Let's face it: what good would it have done you to be reminded of what happened by seeing me?'

'You could have kept in touch somehow.'

'I thought it best not to,' she insisted. 'The first couple of years I moved away. Went up near the Oregon border, where my family's from. I taught school in the back of beyond and just tried to get hold of myself.' She looked at him sternly. 'I wouldn't have been much help to anybody then. I knew I'd been wrong.'

'To shoot that man? He killed Will and he would have killed me too.'

'I don't mean that. You were right to do what you did. You told me exactly what happened – I was digging and you couldn't stop talking. If you hadn't killed that man what do you think he was going to do? Kiss you?'

He felt they were talking at cross purposes. She sat there with a challenging look on her face and he didn't say anything. She stood up and walked to the kitchen door. 'I'll fix you something to eat,' she said, and when he started to get up she added, 'Stay put. I won't be a minute.'

He came to the door anyway, and watched her as she filled a bowl from a large crock pot on the stove. 'You still eat chilli?' she asked.

'I do. You still say "Lordy" when you're worried?'

She smiled. 'Only when Albert's not around. He's a believer.'

'Do you have kids?' he asked.

'No. Albert had two little boys already,'

'Good kids?' he asked, feeling a twinge of jealousy. How bizarre to feel this way, he thought.

She chuckled. 'Not exactly kids any more. Jerry, that's the eldest, he'll be thirty-five next week. He works for the gas company. The other one doesn't seem to know what he wants to do – that's Billy, he's three years younger. "Still finding himself", whatever that means. But they're good kids.' She put something in the sink. 'Not as quick as you though.'

'I was quick? You had to tutor me, remember?'

'That wasn't because you were slow. That was to get you going, that's all. There were no flies on you.'

They sat at the dining room table to eat. On the sideboard there was a china figure of the Virgin Mary. She asked, 'So do you have somebody in your life?'

'I thought I did,' he said, tasting the chilli. She still made it spicy. 'Now I'm not so sure.'

'Tell me about it,' she said, with the same easy command that thirty years before had made him want to win her approval.

So he did, describing Kate and the set-up over there, explaining at length what had gone wrong, and what he had found out.

When he finished, Maris pushed her upper lip over her two front teeth and grimaced slightly. She asked, 'Does what she planned to do bother you that much? I mean, the fact she was going to break the law?'

He shook his head at once. 'Not once I learned why she was going to do it. It wasn't for herself. It was for the place, and her mother, and her sad sack brother. And, most of all, though I didn't see it when she told me, I guess it was for me.'

'And are you bothered that this little girl has this man Benedict as a father?'

'A little,' he admitted. 'Though it wasn't as if I ever thought she was my own daughter. Then it would have bothered me a lot more.' He thought for a second. He didn't really mind that Emily had Benedict genes, provided she didn't grow up with Benedict morals.

'So it was the fact she didn't tell you that really got to you?'

'Yes. It was the lies.'

'Lies? I wouldn't call it that. She just didn't tell you the whole truth about herself.'

'Comes to the same thing.'

Maris's eyes widened. 'Maybe you ought to think twice about that. What is there you haven't told her?'

'It's not the same,' he said, reddening.

'You sure of that?'

And he didn't say a word as he sat and thought about this. Then she said, 'So have you got what you wanted?'

'How do you mean?'

She leaned forward from the end of the table, put her hand on his arm. 'Jacko, listen to me.' And as she spoke, her voice lowered to a whisper, gentle and confiding but somehow *honed*. 'You and I got thrown together by accident, when your mom got sick and I was with Will. If you wonder sometimes if I ever really cared for you, the answer is I did.'

She looked at him and he saw that her eyes were wide and wet. 'But honest, Jack, I truly believe I was right to take you back to Gram's. As for the other,' she said slowly, 'I just don't know. Call it shock, call it whatever you want – I made the wrong call. When we drove south that night I kept thinking, "Turn back and head straight to the Sheriff's office in Healdsburg now." But I didn't. Because once we'd buried them, there wasn't any going back. How was I ever going to explain that? I couldn't.'

He spoke up, finding it difficult to ask questions he had wanted to ask for thirty years. 'What did Gram think? I never knew how much she knew.'

'She was horrified, of course, and also horrified I hadn't called the police. She wanted me to. But when I explained *why* Will had been killed – that it was over drugs – she wasn't quite so sure. It's not as if calling the cops would have brought her son back. And there was no one left to punish. His killers had been killed;

if anyone got punished it would be me. I think she was worried about your having to testify. She wanted to spare you that.'

'Did she know I had killed one of the men?'

Maris looked him in the eye. 'Yes. Otherwise I think she would have made me call the police regardless.' She was still staring at him and paused before continuing. 'I know I was wrong to do what I did, but I like to think I did what I did for the right reasons. Otherwise, I couldn't have lived with myself. It wasn't easy anyway. The dreams, Lordy, the dreams I used to have.' She smiled wanly. 'Sometimes I still have one every now and then.'

'Me too,' he said quietly, and they both sat in silence.

'But anyway,' she said at last, ' I guess what I am trying to say is, it's been thirty years. Lots of people only live that long. The farm's not even there any more; it's part of a big vineyard – they bought Truebridge's and the farm and the acres on the far side of the Valley Orchard. You wouldn't recognise the place – the house is long gone and the pond was filled in years ago and they even chopped down the wood where you had your tree house. The farm you knew doesn't exist any more.

'And that's true of everything, Jack, and everybody. Whatever person called Maris you've had in your head all that time just *isn't there* any more.

'So go back to England, Jack. You've gone and built a life for yourself over there – only you don't seem to know it. You should see it through; it sounds like that's something you've never done before. Go find this woman Kate.' She hesitated. 'And tell her everything. Tell her about Will and how he died. Tell her about the men, and how they died, too.' She stopped, and he saw she was close to tears. 'But tell her also about the good times we all had, Jack. Tell her about Ellie and your tree house and the Valley Orchard and learning how to swim and Will's dumb jokes and how I made you do your homework before you could watch TV. Tell her all of that, too.'

She stood up and took away their bowls, as if part of a normal routine. In the doorway to the kitchen she stopped and turned around to look at him, still sitting at the table. 'Jacko, I don't think you should visit back here again. It isn't going to do you any good.' She smiled gently. 'It isn't going to do me any good, either. I'm not being unkind and no, it doesn't mean I didn't love you like a mother once. But it was long ago, and the future, well your future is now and it isn't here.'

And five minutes later he left her house, and when he said goodbye to her he did so almost absent-mindedly. For already he was looking ahead: to the check-in at the airport; the flight which with this new impatience of his would seem interminable; the landing in grey fog at Heathrow; the taxi to Kensington. He could see himself in roughly twenty-four hours as he took the stairs two at a time, past the poet's widow's flat and the burnished bowl of roses, until he was knocking on the door of the flat upstairs – he wouldn't use his key. And readying himself to say, *Kate, I want to tell you about my Uncle Will and his girlfriend, Maris. I lived with them for a while when I was a boy, and then something happened . . .*